THE MIRACLE VALLEY

The Miracle Valley
Ken Mishima

Published by Spines
ISBN: 979-8-89691-093-0

THE MIRACLE VALLEY

KEN MISHIMA

CONTENTS

PROLOGUE

Once upon a time, there existed a rural community nestled in a lush valley known as Kasuga. Encircled by a majestic mountain range, this place acquired the epithet "Land of Myths." Though the village possessed an idyllic and picturesque charm reminiscent of a landscape painting — quaint houses with thatched roofs, a winding river, and rice paddies — the region was notorious for its frigid winters and sticky summers. The unforgiving climate inevitably molded locals into a perseverant and taciturn bunch, much like those found in any countryside. They staunchly resisted the winds of change that sought to govern their lives, remaining steadfastly devoted to their ancient traditions and customs. Among these traditions was a collection of folk songs titled *The Ballads of Kasuga*. These ballads, unlike those sung elsewhere, were not imbued with sentimental or romantic themes. They conveyed a motif more directly related to the way of living in the village.

———————* ———————* ———————* ———————*

"Grandpa? How come we can't go into Mt. Toki?" Shin, a local

Kasuga boy, asked as he chewed on a knotweed stalk, his chest smeared with its juice. Next to him sat Chiyo, his younger sister, playing with her shabby dolls. They had been keeping an eye on their grandfather, Yujin, all morning while he rehabilitated his fractured ankle at home.

Yujin sat up in his futon. "Did you ask your mother or father about it?"

"Yeah, I did, twice," replied Shin, still gnawing on the stringy plant. "But they didn't tell me anything about it."

"Ahh..." Yujin leaned forward. "Let me guess. Instead, they said you're too young to know, right?" Shin dropped his midday snack on the floor and nodded, pouting. Chiyo continued talking to her dolls. Yujin adjusted his posture. "You two are Kasuga children and deserve to know about it no matter how old you are." Shin mimicked his grandfather's posture and pulled Chiyo's sleeve. Yujin smiled and began, "Mt. Sakuri, more commonly known as Mt. Toki, harbors a sense of wickedness. A forbidden territory. So, parents tend to...." As he went on, Chiyo leaned against her brother, her shoulders tensing.

Shin clutched his kimono. "You still remember the songs, Grandpa?" he asked, his voice barely audible.

"'*Do not leave little ones alone in the house after dusk, a malevolent soul creeps in, whispering a lullaby of hell, alluring and tricking them, stealing their innocence, and making them disappear from this life.*'" Yujin sang softly, with his eyes closed.

Chiyo gripped Shin's hand, cowering. He patted her thigh and asked, "And what happened to the man and woman?"

"'*Heedless man and wife return from a fatal escapade, him with crimson slashes on the neck, her with a demonic smile.*'" Finishing the verse, Yujin shrugged theatrically. "Maybe she sliced his throat. But who knows?"

"No, it was the *oni*!" Shin shrieked. "Right, Grandpa? Tell me more about him."

"Ahh, the *oni*. Hmm, should I?" Yujin squinted.

"Please!"

"Alright. He's lived on the summit of Mt. Toki for centuries. He is huge, vicious, and cunning. He has two sharp horns, fangs, and a rugged body with bloody-red skin. And he possesses supernatural powers, harming the village and transforming himself into anything. People believe he eats humans —"

Suddenly, Chiyo burst into tears. "No! Mommy!"

Yujin opened his arms, guilt swelling up. "Oh, I'm so sorry, Chiyo. It's Grandpa's fault. Come here, you poor thing." Chiyo jumped into his chest. "There, there..."

The door slid open, and their parents walked in. The mother immediately took Chiyo in her arms. "What happened to her?" She eyed Yujin suspiciously. He scratched his head and grimaced. "Oh, you did not..." she said, shaking her head.

"Mom, Grandpa's story was so scary!" Shin said innocently.

"Hey, listen kids. Grandpa's right," the father interjected. "Mt. Toki isn't safe, even for adults. The oni may eat you the moment you go in there." His tone conveyed theatrical exaggeration. Chiyo clung harder to her mother.

"Seiji!" Sumi, his wife, spat.

Seiji shrugged. "But, Chiyo, don't you worry. You're a good girl, and the oni doesn't harm well-behaved children like you. You see? The ballads are also meant to remind you to behave." He paused, acknowledging Chiyo's little nod, and continued, "Your mom and I didn't teach you the songs because of those shocking parts. They scare children so easily and take away the idea hidden behind them." Now, the children listened keenly to their father, though Chiyo continued to sniffle.

"But, the story is true? And the oni...?" Shin asked, his voice quivering.

"Oh, YES, Shin! That's why you kids have to stay away from Mt. Toki. Very dangerous, even for strong grownups like me." Seiji stroked his beard dramatically. Sumi shook her head again. "What?" he mouthed.

With a faint smile, Yujin lay back again on the futon, content with how his son had navigated the conversation.

——————— * ——————— * ——————— * ——————— *

I know their mockery. An oni? A man-eater?

He thought as he envisioned his reflection — ashen as snow on Mt. Toki, wrinkled like well-worn washi, yet gentle like Bosatsu — that floated on the water in a stone bowl. He caressed his face as if to make sure it was still there. It felt almost like searching for something unknown. He could not even remember the last time he had examined himself. His skin had further hardened, and his wrinkles had multiplied. *Fifty years? Or, perhaps ninety years would be more accurate.*

It was not that he did not want to do so, but he did not need to. His appearance held no interest. Nor did he care how others perceived him. *Refuting superstitions would be nearly impossible anyway, especially among simple and vulnerable people.*

He closed his eyes, reminiscing about the days when he was as young as the villagers in the valley, when he shamelessly thought highly of himself yet held a shameless grudge inside him, and when his hubris screamed for the insignia of a spiritual master, all alone on Mt. Toki, for centuries. Time had, however, become his ally, mentor, and his spiritual regimen, humbling and molding him into a wiser self.

After what felt like an eternity, he became what people despised and avoided, a devil incarnate concocted in their minds, not because they knew him, but because they did not. *If they decide I'm a monster, let them. It's better that way, so they'll forever stay away from me, my secret, and of my mountain.*

He opened his eyes, but what was in front of him was what he could not behold. And yet, he did not need to because it was only the same gray horizon of nothingness that loomed in front of him. Though nearly blind, he could sense and feel everything.

It was telepathy, enabling him to detect and even communicate with his surroundings.

And then, a familiar hush whispered in his ears, soothing and caressing him. Like a gentle breeze, stillness allowed him to be who he was. He indulged himself for a while as he *saw* everything vividly. Contentment washed over him.

His tranquility, however, was short-lived. What sounded like a man's faint cry pierced a nearby marsh, invading his sacred territory. He moaned as he had exactly one hundred years ago and shut his eyes melancholically.

Once again, darkness swallowed him.

Part One

A MYTH, 1220

1

AN INNOCENT LEGEND

— *'The path is a point of no return. Have the strongest faith to enter...'* —

The Sacred Path, as marked on a tattered map, bore no resemblance to anything holy — if anything, it appeared ominous. The terrain stretched at a sharp angle and unevenly, covered in slimy moss and strewn with rocks. Two glistening centipedes entwined on the damp moss, their crimson legs writhing as their long bodies heaved. The thick fog shrouded the path, obscuring any visibility from ten meters above. Even the lower regions offered little hope, with a treacherous gradient that threatened both humans and wildlife. Centuries-old majestic cedars lined, their soaring heights of over 30 meters casting eerie shadows — as if to keep all living creatures on the ground dormant. The overgrown vegetation miraculously spared from an ongoing drought and the lack of sufficient air circulation, created oppressive dampness. Rather than the pleasant fragrance of a forest, the entire area emitted the putrid stench of a decaying swamp. Although it was a mid-summer afternoon, an unrelenting chill permeated the air, while sporadic gusts from above draped the surroundings in a foreboding veil.

For the entire morning, two Kasuga locals, Teishi and Yorogi, and a little boy, Tsurugi, had been treading along a winding game trail. The trio donned identical attire: dark brown hemp shirts with patches on both elbows, matching ankle-length pants, and well-worn warajis with loosened straps. Each of them bore what appeared to be a thick thread affixed to their backs. The men, approximately of the same age, in their late twenties, exuded a demeanor lacking in warmth and cheer. In stark contrast, Tsurugi, who had just turned six, radiated innocence, experiencing the happiest day of his young life. It marked his first excursion far from the village, and his mother had assured him it would be an extraordinary experience. "Dad, Mom was right!" he shrieked, his little eyes darting all around the area. Teishi, observing his son's beaming smile beside him, dropped his head. "Yes, she was..." He held back a sob, his face etched with guilt and pain.

"Hey, Teishi, I doubt the validity of the map, to be honest. The pathway can't be like this," said Yorogi, not truly expecting a response from his companion. The trio stood at the start of the Sacred Path. Yorogi glanced at Teishi, whose mind seemed to drift in a somber abyss, but remained silent. "But, as far as I can see, this looks like the only route," muttered Yorogi to himself. He looked up the rocky slope, drew a resolute sigh, and began ascending without another word, cautiously placing one foot in front of the other. The father and the son followed suit.

After another two hours of dangerous trekking, they finally managed to arrive at a relatively cleared area. Within a 15-meter radius, there were no trees, rocks, moss, and animal excrement in sight. Tall trees standing around the clearing formed a natural canopy, creating a perfect refuge. Teishi, whose mind had drifted aimlessly since the beginning of the journey, had now dumped their decision-making on Yorogi. The new team leader, Yorogi, called it a day and decided to take shelter there for the night. Although the sun had yet to set, the map indicated they still had another three kilometers to cover before reaching their final destination. Furthermore, the impending Rite had specific requirements that needed to be met, including the timing, which would be indicated at the site sometime during the day.

—'Were these requirements not met, then.....'—

As Yorogi cleared the area to make their shelter, he said, "You remember the details about tomorrow we discussed at the Guild meeting a month ago? I still don't —" He paused to glance at Teishi, who was staring at Yorogi, his eyes blank. *I'm so sorry, Teishi...*

Yorogi and Teishi woke up at dawn and decided to let the boy sleep for as long as possible. The woods were about to come alive with the cheerful chirping of birds and the distant sounds of four-legged creatures. Yorogi ventured deeper into the area to find a stream while Teishi sat on a fallen tree, lost in these thoughts, dreading the impending moment that would be the worst in his life. Stroking his unshaven chin, the father reminisced about his son's short life, from the day he was born to the summers they spent fishing together. Overwhelmed by a fleeting glimpse of joy, a warm tear trickled down his cheek, painfully aware that he would never feel the same again.

Yorogi interrupted Teishi's emotional turmoil, returning with three bamboo canteens brimming with spring water and a handful of *kukonomi*—goji berries. Before Teishi asked, Yorogi began, "I'm sure these are the Antidote mentioned in the scroll. Found them in the bush right over there, just as the document says. Never seen anything like them before," fiddling with the fruits in his palm, he continued, "your boy won't feel any pain and suffering after he eats these. He's supposed to fall asleep and lose all his senses. Well, that's the only comfort we could provide him. I'm so sorry, Teishi." Yorogi placed a gentle hand on his friend's slumped shoulder.

Teishi vacantly gazed up to observe what was in his friend's hand but made no effort to stand up. "That's it, huh? As simple as that? My little boy's going to leave this life in a few hours. He is going to heaven. What has he done wrong? He's only six, an innocent child. I don't understand...I just don't...." The rest of his words trailed off as they changed to suppressed sobs that seemed impossible to contain.

Suddenly, the boy woke up from his leafy bed and stood next to his father. "Daddy, how come you're crying? Does your tummy hurt?" He looked genuinely worried, touching his father's abdomen.

Unable to find the words, Teishi simply held his boy tightly in his arms, more tears filling up his swelled eyes. He eventually broke off the embrace and took out a small parcel made of a bamboo leaf from his pouch. "Let's eat breakfast, yeah?" Teishi said as he handed the boy one of the rice balls wrapped in the leaf. The father stroked his son's cheek tenderly, knowing it would be their last meal together.

Meanwhile, Yorogi kept his distance from them, giving Teishi the final moment of fatherhood.

After a two-hour trek to the summit, the long-awaited moment time had finally come. The trio meandered through a series of marshes and arrived at the fog-covered Pond. At the edge of the water stood a roughly carved stake.

Yorigi took out a piece of paper. His handwriting on it read clinically.

— 'Two days after the second full moon of the eighth month, when sunlight falls upon the engraved symbol of the sun in the middle of the stake, the Rite must commence. If the timing is right, the Chosen Boy will

enter the Pond while asleep. He will have consumed at least five berries prior to the Rite.'—

Teishi got down on his knees and held his son one last time, fighting back the tears. "Hey, Tsurugi, here are your special berries. You're gonna enjoy them. They're so sweet."

The boy beamed at his farther and stuffed them all into his tiny mouth. "Wow, Daddy, it's so sweet. Thank you!" he shrieked, munching on them with delight. Yorogi intently watched the boy eating, but Teishi stepped away from his son, for he could not take it any more, fixing his gaze on the gentle ripples on the water.

When Teishi staggered back, his son was lying in Yorogi's arms. "He's just as beautiful..." mumbled Yorogi in tears. Teishi fell on his knees, with his hands over his face, and sobbed uncontrollably.

The next moment, just as described in the document, the entranced boy, with his eyes wide open, suddenly stood up as the sun illuminated the carved symbol on the stake. He began to walk slowly yet steadily, into the mystical water. Yorogi and Teishi, as if struck by a profound realization, stood in silent awe while watching the boy descend deeper and deeper into the dark abyss. Before long, the Pond swallowed his small head.

The Chosen Boy Tsurugi became a legend at last.

2

THE GUARDIAN OF MT. TOKI

A wise man knelt before a weathered wooden stake that stood by the water, meticulously restoring its worn surface. The stake bore a greenish hue, covered in lichen patinas. He diligently cleaned the engraving on the center. Although the sun hung high in the sky, a gentle breeze brushed against his cheeks and neck, offering momentary respite. Every once in a while, he tended to the sign-post and ensured its functionality — an age-old responsibility he had shouldered for centuries, safeguarding the Pond.

But, this day would prove historical significance, for it marked the day of the Rite. He had dreaded this day to come for a hundred years, though he had anticipated it would. The wind picked up fast, conjuring immense emerald swells as the reeds surrounding the water swayed in sync.

"Oh wow! Daddy, Mr. Yorogi, look!..." a child's voice shrieked, piercing the air for a split second before being cut off by a gust of wind.

"Finally...," murmured the old man to himself when three sets of footsteps tramping through marshes gradually approached the Pond. As if in response, a faint veil of fog loomed, draping a white blanket over the water. The temperature instantly dropped as the dense fog enshrouded the perimeter. Despite the early afternoon, gloominess crept in across the area, the dramatic stage for the final act.

By the time the trio arrived at the Pond, he had been long gone.

The old man had spotted the group of three at the Sacred Path a day earlier and observed their progress. One of the two men piggybacked a little boy while climbing up the rocky hill, with the other cautiously trailing behind. The two men panted and groaned with each step. Though they were both young and strong, the journey only grew more arduous. Their faces contorted with both emotional and physical strain, while the boy showed no sign of distress or fear, giggling and rocking himself on his father's back. The sun continued to beat them, and climbing up the slippery, rugged terrain had become a dangerous endeavor. Had the old man stood watching them struggle from the sidelines, they would not have noticed. He, in fact, was nowhere near the path the trio was on as he visualized them from the confines of his humble dwelling.

Over the course of practice, he had honed and exercised this unusual ability, the third eye. Since the dawn of his spiritual life in Mt. Toki, a group of three villagers — always two men and a boy — had climbed up the path every hundred years. Each time he observed their journeys from his cave, he could not help but reflect on life's cruelty, particularly toward the innocent children. "And yet, no matter what lies ahead and how harshly it treats you, you can't alter your fate. And you must not. You live with it until you breathe your last," he had murmured.

Now, within his concealed cave directly across the Pond, the guardian of Mt. Toki bore witness to the fateful ritual. He sat cross-legged with his hands placed on his lower abdomen while his eyelids were tightly shut. Clad in all white, with long white hair, he resembled a mummified corpse in a coffin, his skin callous and wrinkled. As the Chosen Boy swallowed the berries, he began to intone a mantra. A moment later, he watched the boy's head disappear below the water. "May his innocent soul rest in eternal peace..." His mournful words mingled with the anguished cries of the grieving father, resonating through the hushed chamber.

Gradually, the cacophony of devastation subsided. Then, layers of ominous clouds loomed out of thin air across the striking blue sky. Thunder rumbled ominously, and for the first time in two years, he saw bolts of lightning dance across the sky.

Part Two

A SUMMER TRAGEDY, 1321

3

THE CHRONICLE OF THE RITE

'Do Not reopen'
'Do Not rediscuss'
'Do Not recall'

Amid the unbearable heat, ten people crammed into a half-dilapidated house. They all keenly fixed their eyes on a middle-aged woman lying on the wooden floor as they held their breaths with trepidation, oblivious to beads of sweat on their foreheads. Yone, a midwife, checked her friend's pulse on the wrist and let out a faint sigh. The ailing woman lay unconscious, her shallow breaths a testament to her worsening condition. Her pale face bore deep lines, evidence of a hard life, her skin weathered by decades of sun exposure. Yone gently lifted the woman's head just enough to allow her to drink some water, but it only dribbled down her cheeks. Tetsu, the ailing woman's son, whose expression conveyed mental agony, leaned forward. "Mother?" he cried with a suppressed voice. Then, Yone gave him a resigned gaze and shook her head. As if on cue, all her family members and relatives dropped their heads.

The door slid open, and a little girl's face tentatively poked in. With an innocent expression, she observed the mood in the house before stepping inside. "Is Grandma okay, Daddy?" she asked, her voice slightly trembling with concern. Tetsu approached his daughter and knelt down, his arms enveloping her. Unable to bring himself to answer his daughter's question, he quickly stepped outside and closed the door behind him. His wet cheeks glistened in the sunlight.

It was another suffocating September day in Kasuga. The dry air remained oppressive, and winds, even if they blew at all, only brought misery to the arid land. The irritatingly blue sky hung higher than ever, and the merciless sun not only scorched everything below but also toyed with all life. Mother Nature's abandonment had cursed the village with a 10-month draught. With the valley's main water source, the River Hasu, on the brink of drying up, Kasuga farmers had little choice but to abandon their fields. A sense of doom had eventually engulfed in the entire village.

Kayo, Tetsu's mother, became the first resident who had succumbed to the draught. Though she was barely in her mid-fifties, her strength had begun to diminish as soon as the family's food supply hit the bottom. Their twice-a-day meals had quickly turned into a once-a-day luxury, and with their meager savings long gone, they became destitute. Since then, the family had relied solely on foraging and charity from their neighbors.

One day, a few months into their misery, the bedridden Kayo had had Tetsu and his wife, Midori, by her side and told them a folklore involving an unspeakable act: destitute families in isolated communities endured an ultimatum, sending their elders, particularly those with terminal illnesses, to a remote mountain and leaving them behind. Nature and their fate would take care of the rest. Although this solution ultimately aimed at reducing the family burden, it would leave an enduring wound on the surviving members. Despite being unsubstantiated, this *ubasute* legend had persisted generation after generation, a testament to the harsh feudal life.

Listening to the horrified narrative, Tetsu raised his voice to stop Kayo while Midori simply put her hands on her ears. Even before his mother had finished, he shook his head, denying her impending plea. After a while, the three of them had born an excruciating silence, their eyes reddening with tears.

Now, recalling that emotional conversation, Tetsu felt relieved that he had not even considered Kayo's implied suggestion. And though in a deep void, he could at least find some solace in having nursed her until she breathed her last. The sun punished his incapability, failing him as a provider for his family. Glaring back at the merciless sky, he roared, "Take me next time if you dare! Take me!" He wiped the tears, his clenched fist numb, and went back into the house.

Her tragedy simply heralded an avalanche of nightmares set to corrode the entire village, until...

————— * ————— * ————— * ————— *

A small repository stood within the precincts of Kasuga Shrine. From a distance, it resembled more of a shed than anything else. The weathered exterior walls and front door bore many cracks and holes, discolored and stained with age-old mildew. The interior, too, endured the similar fate: a musty odor permeated in every corner; countless ancient scrolls and documents were haphazardly scattered upon what were once functional shelves. Although the building screamed for care, the locals affectionately referred to this humble shed as the Nishiya — the west wing — which had served as 'a den of sages' for worshippers for centuries. Although small in size, its wisdom had withstood the test of time, and both young and old pupils alike admired and respected it for what it taught. In the past, parents used to bring their children there — similar to modern-day school — whenever they had a spare moment, allowing them to connect with sage proverbs and knowledge. The people of Kasuga Village never took this privilege for granted, since they recognized that their neighboring communities did not have such luxury. In its own way, the village had long enjoyed relative prosperity compared to its uneducated neighbors.

However, everything had changed when a band of rogue samurais ruthlessly invaded and seized control of the region. They committed all kinds of sins — pillaging businesses, vandalizing buildings, and assaulting female residents including young girls — and devoured whatever the community had while they remained for months. A government order eventually compelled the armed outlaws to retreat, but the damage had already been done. All the benefits the village had once enjoyed, including the precious wisdom of the Nishiya, turned into nothing but sorrowful tales for future generations.

Nearly sixty years had passed, and the Nishiya still stood in a dilapidated state.

Sweating profusely in the suffocating Nishiya, an old man groaned to himself, "It must be in right here, I know for sure!" Jintoku, the eldest in Kasuga Village, coughed a few times and continued to rummage through piles of the paper and parcels. Dusts flew up in all directions of the semi-dark room every time he picked up artifacts and documents and dumped them on the floor. His bald head glistened with a mixture of sweat and dark particles. He wiped his forehead with the back of his smeared hand and groaned louder. He snatched a bamboo canteen from a shelf, only to find it empty, and then flung it on the dusty floor. A curse echoed through the room. Panting and wheezing, he paused to catch his breath, hands on knees. With a loud moan, he grudgingly resumed the search.

Unlike his physicality, Jintoku's profanity-ridden language and slightly blunt mannerism remained intact. With his tiny head wrapped in a hemp *tenugui* and his sleeves rolled up, he looked more like a *miyadaiku* than a seasoned mentor. As he flipped one dust-covered scroll after another, his voice and tone grew louder, allowing anyone outside the building to hear the commotion inside. "Agh...crap! What A Mess!"

A younger man stuck his head through the door and did a double take upon seeing the dust-covered figure. "Good afternoon, Sir Jintoku? Is that you?" he called out cautiously, expecting the elderly man to notice him. "Are you alright, sir? Would you mind telling me what you're doing here?" He tentatively approached the old mentor, making sure not to knock down the heaps of documents on the floor. Immediately, he felt the urge to sneeze as a cloud of dust from the scrolls got into his nostrils.

"Ohhh, Heijiro, what perfect timing!" exclaimed Jintoku as he glanced at the newcomer between the stacks of papers.

Heijiro scratched his head. "Umm... what exactly are you doing, sir? Looking for some— "

Jintoku pulled the makeshift mask down to his chin and took a deep breath. "Such a pain in the ass! That's what I'm dealing with here. I never knew the inside was this dusty. And there're way too many documents!" He spread out his arms. "Help me out here, will you?"

"Yes, yes, of course, sir," replied Heijiro as he eyed the scattered scrolls. "So, what're we looking for? A particular document, I assume? How can I tell it apart from others? Is there an inscription on it?" He had already began to rummage through a cache of dusty ancient documents.

"It's a scroll, I believe. My grandfather once told me it must be here. He said when I was a little boy that it should have knots on both ends of the rolled paper. Very unique for a peasant document. And the color should be *uguisu* green, he said. And it has an inscription on the cover."

"An inscription?"

"Yes. 'Chronicle of the Rite' or something like that. But it's probably hard to read because of the damn dust!"

Trying to stifle a laugh, Heijiro maintained a straight face. "Well, Sir, now you have another pair of eyes and hands. I'm more than happy to help and you can count on me. By the way, Sir, have you been here long?"

"I've totally lost track of time. But I came here right after I heard the Big Bell, and it's getting dark now, which means we're gonna be fucked really soon. Say, you have a lantern with you by any chance?" Jintoku smiled sarcastically and added, "I don't think so. So, yeah, we have to call it a day soon."

Suddenly, Heijiro gasped. "I think I found it, sir! It's got two knots, very intricate, and it's green!" he shouted. "It says...yes, 'Chronicle of the Rite.' This looks really old and fragile, though." He carefully handed it to Jintoku, who then took it with his both hands. "Sir, I've never seen anything like this elaborate before. How old do you think it is?"

"No idea. Your guess's as good as mine. But, it must be around one hundred fifty years old, at least." As he fondled the scroll, Jintoku began to recount the story his grandfather had told him.

"My grandfather, Utaji, said he had heard the details about this scroll from his own grandfather. It contained instructions on how to handle a deadly famine just like the one we're suffering now, and a prescription for the disaster. But Utaji had never seen it himself, because such an evil famine only occurred once every hundred years or so. And after each use of the information, the document must've been hidden from the public or simply went missing. So, by the time the next famine hit the village, no one knew for sure about the existence of the document. It became nothing more than a damn ancient myth. After all, no human can live for a hundred years!"

Fascinated by the narrative, Heijiro had some questions on his mind. "I got an overall picture, sir. But what I don't get is, how come the scroll had to be kept secret from the villagers for centuries? I mean, couldn't they appoint a trusted guardian and have him and his offsprings look after it? That way, when another famine came, they wouldn't have had to panic, right? Whatever the wisdom scripted on the scroll, it contains the information we can rely on for generations to come. So, why such secrecy? Why not bother to share it?"

"Yes, I understand your point, Heijiro. But hey, even I had completely forgotten all about it until yesterday. So, I've got no answers to your curiosity." The old man shrugged.

With his eyes glistered, Heijiro leaned forward. "Yes, you do, sir," he said, "you have the answers right in your hand. And there is only one way to find out." He swallowed hard. "So...now? Sir?" He almost touched the document.

The old mentor stepped back from the younger companion and said, "I'm sorry, Heijiro, but I'm afraid I can't allow that." He shook his head firmly. "This document may hold a key to the survival of the village. I'll hand this to the Guild. And you must not tell anyone about the discovery. Not even to your wife. Did I make myself clear?"

Heijiro drew in a breath. "Yes, sir."

4

THE KARUBES

A sense of uselessness plagued Amuro, a 9-year-old Kasuga local. He slumped on a fallen tree, his head down, his eyes filled with disappointment. He spat contemptuously, thick saliva containing fragments of brown leaves hanging from the side of his mouth.

Since the early morning, the woods had turned against Amuro. Thickets scratched his face and limbs; hard surfaces of the ground reddened his fingers; and dead branches fell on his head, all exact replicates of the previous day. Except today's version carried an added layer of desperation. Time idled on, just as his earlier eagerness for success had waned. Now, it had all come to an abrupt halt.

Amuro had yet to find anything precious he could bring home regardless. All the edible things that had survived the drought were now virtually gone. As far as the eye could see, only barren land stretched out before him. He bent down and grabbed the dry, lifeless dirt, cursing his luck and the uncontrollable circumstances he found himself in. Thirsty, he walked toward the familiar boulder near the creek, only to discover that the spring water once oozing out of a crevice in the rock had dried up.

Amuro swore as he looked up and shielded his eyes from the relentless sun with his hand.

In normal years, the woods would thrive with edible plants, mushrooms, and various fruit trees during the summertime. However, no one would bother to go there to forage as they had their own systematic agriculture, blessed with an everlasting water source — the River Hasu that flowed through the middle of the village. The hardworking Kasuga peasants had benefitted from their fertile land for generations, which yielded healthy crops and vegetables throughout the year. They had never even had a single bad season as far as they remembered, let alone a bad year, until some 18 months ago.

The initial sign of the drought had seemed insignificant. The villagers paid no attention to the streak of dry sunny days. Some even said it helped the healthy growth of their crops. But, as soon as one farmer had expressed concern about the noticeably low water level of the river at the Guild meeting, everything began to unravel like an avalanche. Crops withered, and green vegetables wilted. Some livestock animals even scummed to heat exhaustion. Then, rice paddies dried up. So did the River Hasu, eventually. When they finally acknowledged the existence of a famine, the entire village went under. Panic reigned, turning to each other and stealing from neighbors becoming more common than having a once-a-day meager meal. Before long, foraging proved a reliable lifeline, though ironic for a celebrated agricultural village.

While adults resorted to hunting and fishing, which proved daunting and unpredictable, children had to pitch in and help their parents by venturing into the woods. Most of the older children, capable of manual labor, dedicated themselves to this task. Getting food — or more like scavenging — required diligence as the resources became more and more limited. And they often engaged in fistfights for their precious booty. They painfully realized that they and their families endured a threat to life, facing imminent starvation. The famine had turned foraging into a battle for survival.

As he wiped his muddy, sweaty face with an equally dirty tenugui, Amuro decided to search the area one last time. While dragging his hunched body, he nearly fell. The westering sun nauseated him, sucking up his patience and spirit. Days like this left him feeling helpless, particularly because, in the end, his earlier determination to succeed gave way to despair. *Just another miserable day in the woods*, he thought. As soon as he began to inspect the grounds, a familiar voice vigorously called out his name from behind. Before turning to face the caller, he asked, "Hey, Kento, any luck?"

"No...I'm so sad, Amuro. Nothing, three days in a row. My dad'll be disappointed. What about you?" replied Kento, a neighbor's boy who Amuro felt more like a little brother than a friend. Kento had neurological conditions — he might be diagnosed with autism today — from a young age, and Amuro always looked out for him. As Kento struggled to socialize with other children, Amuro acted like a trusted cohort. And Amuro adored his younger friend and cherished their fellowship.

Holding up both hands, Amuro grimaced. "That makes two of us! Foraging sucks! Where have all the berries, beans, and mushrooms gone? I swear I saw them on the other side of the thicket yesterday. And they've all gone today. Must've been taken by kids from the village over there." He pointed to the east, indicating the direction. "Anyway, it's getting really dark. We should wrap it up and head home."

On their way back home, the pair stopped dead upon spotting a lone wild bore roaming around the dried remains of a puddle. The sturdy animal oinked while sniffing at something on the ground and then began to plow the earth with its strong tusks. Captivated, Amuro could not help but compare the bore's vitality to that of his mentally-battered fellow villagers. His heart pulsated with the heavy, blunt thuds, and he envied its animal instincts. He longed for the creature.

All of a sudden, as if snapping out of his deep thoughts, Amuro elbowed Kent, who had frozen over the rare sight of an aggressive animal. "Hey, look how that bastard digs! Must be food there. We've got to scare him away. And we dig! You with me, Kento? Food!"

Scared, Kento said, "B-but... isn't it dangerous? He's huge! What if he attacks us? I don't wanna get hurt."

"Don't worry about it. I'll protect you. Nothing bad will happen, I promise. Besides, you're my lucky charm. Remember the barking dog we fought last year? We didn't get bitten because of you!" Amuro put his firm hand on his friend's trembling shoulder and winked. Kento smiled weakly in return.

After they retreated into the nearest bush, Amuro grabbed a large rock and gestured for Kento to get down. Amuro swung his arm twice as practice and with a deep exhalation threw the rock as hard as possible at the unsuspecting bore. Then, he quickly crouched in the bush. The rock missed the mark, but it startled the bore to dash in the opposite direction from the bush. The pair stood up slowly and watched as the animal disappeared into a thicket in the distance. Amuro and Kento smirked at each other triumphantly, and approached the spot.

Amuro had already spotted something sticking out from the soil. "Yes, I knew it! I knew it!" A partially milky lily bulb, as big as an adult's fist, had some deep scratches on one side, but it made his mouth water all the same. Not wanting to damage it further, Amuro carefully dug deep into the soil and gently cupped around the precious sphere.

He felt a jealous glance as he put the bulb in his worn-out satchel. "Here, Kento, you should have it. I couldn't have pulled this off without you. So, it's yours." With a straight face, he handed it to his friend.

"Why Amuro? It was your idea...so this is yours. I won't

take anything that belongs to you," Kento replied, slightly confused.

"Umm... then how about giving it to your mom and sister? I heard they've lost some weight. This bulb's really good for them. Yeah?" Amuro feigned nonchalance.

After contemplating for a while, Kento nodded. "Okay, I'm gonna give this to my mom and sister! And I won't eat it... because...because you can't either!"

Amuro and Kento, standing side by side, heard the toll of the shrine bell as they walked home. Dusk slowly crept over the sky, causing the tow figures to fade away into the early summer twilight.

——————— * ——————— * ——————— * ——————— *

Despite the early morning, the long and steep stone steps leading up to Kasuga Shrine emanated a scorching heat. The sizzling heat of summer. On both sides of the staircase, dead trees stood alined, their bare branches offering no respite from the raging sun. The callous, lifeless slope painted the despair of the brown world.

A lone gray grasshopper, unaware of the scorching air, hopped busily around the steps. Hundreds of them would have invaded the area if it were a normal year. Its faint swishes punctuated the deathly silence as no other sounds, not even a single blow of wind, contributed to the stillness. With its hunt for food in vain, the insect eventually abandoned the stairs. Sooner or later, it would probably flee the village altogether. And quite possibly, all the surviving wildlife might follow suit. They, unlike humans, instinctively knew when to desert the sinking ship.

At the top landing, about 50 meters high, an early worshipper turned and bowed to a young woman standing on the bottom landing. She returned the favor, with a deeper bow, and pushed her daughter's head down gently to show how to bow properly. The mother, Katsue, smiled at her child and patted another on the back. The baby boy slumbered away in a cocoon of linen furoshiki. "Okay, now, we're going up." Katsue took her child's hand.

"Mommy, this is so high up. I'm tired and hungry," the little girl, Yuri, whimpered, sucking on what looked like some kind of stalk.

Yuri had been whining about the heat and her persistent hunger since they left the house. Katsue and her family had gone three days without a substantial meal, although they had preserved some crops.

"I know, Yuri. But tomorrow is porridge day. Our four-day rule, remember?" The mother grimaced. "I know you're hungry. And I'm so sorry Mommy can't feed you today. But, please, let's finish up what we came here for. Okay? You're such a good girl, Yuri." Katsue tried to cheer her daughter up and gently wiped the girl's sweaty cheeks with a cloth.

Yuri nodded, her gaze fixing on the long stairs.

The mother and daughter began to climb, their backs beaten by the sun.

Kasuga Shrine had witnessed countless unexpected events throughout the centuries: deadly conflicts with hostile outsiders, fatal diseases, and natural disasters. Unlike the neighboring shrine in Inaki Village, no one had ever desecrated or burnt down this sacred place. The people in Kasuga had somehow managed to preserve the sanctity of the shrine for generations, respecting and trusting the divine inspiration it bestowed upon them.

Katsue and Yuri stood silently side by side in front of the main sanctuary. With no one else in sight, the absolute stillness created an ominous air rather than solemnity. Even usually unrelenting cicadas seemed to hold their breath here. So did the baby boy, who cooed in his mother's arms. The mother handed the infant to her daughter, whose face instantly lit up with sisterly affection.

A wooden offertory box in front of them made Katsue feel ashamed as she had nothing to offer. She just hung her head with guilt. But, she proceeded to ring the divine bell, say a prayer in her heart all the same, and then stepped aside.

"Yuri, say your prayer. You remember how to do it, right?" said Katsue as she took the baby back into her arms.

Yuri nodded and mimicked clumsily what her mother had done.

"What did you pray for?" asked Katsue.

"I promised to be a VERY good girl and prayed for lots of white rice!" Yuri giggled.

"You bargained with your god, didn't you? What a smart, mischievous girl!" Katsue chuckled.

"I think I did! And what did you pray for, Mommy?"

Katsue caressed Yuri's skinny cheek. "Mommy prayed for your health and your brothers' health. And for this." She gently stroked her stomach. "Your new sister or brother."

There was no such thing as family planning in a rural community. Or, within any other society, for that matter. Married couples had to have children as a society valued fecundity as a blessing. The more offspring they produced, the better, particularly boys who would become much-needed manpower for their families.

However, Katsue and her husband, Gensuke, had tried to avoid conceiving for a year or so given the unprecedented circumstances they were facing. They deemed it wise to avoid it. "No, not in this calamity. What if you had a miscarriage or stillbirth? Or, what if you died?" Gensuke had reminded Katsue, as much for himself as for her, of the potential outcomes.

And yet, she stood in front of the shrine, wishing for a healthy birth and receiving a full blessing from her family.

"A baby? Oh, Mommy, I want a baby sister! I have two brothers already. Please, Mommy...a girl!" Yuri tugged at her mother's sleeve and giggled.

Katsue felt warmth as she looked at her little girl's innocent excitement. But at the same time, she could not shake her doubts about whether the new life growing inside her would make it out.

"Let's go home, Mommy!" chirped Yuri. "I wanna talk to Amuro about this!" Yuri pressed her ear against her mother's stomach, forgetting about the heat and her hunger.

——————— * ——————— * ——————— * ——————— *

The leaves rustled somewhere in the woods, then all fell quiet again.

"Hey, Gen, did you hear that?" whispered a man, pulling his friend's sleeve.

"Hear what?" Gensuke glanced around, brows knit.

"There was something behind us. I heard it. Something passed by," insisted Heijiro, keeping his voice low.

Gensuke shook his head. "No, I don't think so, Jiro. How about you, sir?"

Shodai signed, removing the lid of his bamboo canteen. He poured a bit of water onto his palm, dabbing his mouth and neck. "Didn't hear a thing."

The three Kasuga locals crouched on a narrow animal trail, sweat beading down their dirt-matted faces as the afternoon sun broke through the canopy. Gensuke and Heijiro carried bundles on their backs, while Shodai tightly clutched a bow, four arrows strapped at his side. Just as they straightened, a louder rustle came from their left.

Heijiro's head whipped toward the sound. "There it is again! You both heard it this time."

"Yeah, that was a wind, Heijiro. Just the wind," said Shodai, shrugging.

"Sir, I believe it was an animal. Could be a pheasant, an

owl, or even a wild boar. Why don't we—" Heijiro stepped toward the thicket.

Gensuke grabbed him back. "Jiro, forget it. We don't have much time left."

Shodai nodded. "Gensuke's right. We've been out here since dawn, and this isn't our land. If the Inaki folks find us roaming around, they won't hesitate to retaliate."

"But —"

Gensuke squeezed his friend's shoulder. "Just let it go, Jiro."

Heijiro remorsefully glanced back at the thicket.

Mt. Yashiro loomed ahead, its slopes veiled in haze. To the Kasuga men, it was Hunter's Hill — a lifeline and a risk. Gensuke glanced up at the peak as they trudged on. "Two, no more," he murmured, repeating the rule under his breath.

Shodai heard him and nodded. "In and out by noon. Same as always. No one's been caught yet, and we're not breaking the streak now."

Heijiro trudged behind them, his gaze darting toward every rustle. "Still feels wrong, though," he muttered. "The Inaki folks wouldn't forgive us if they knew."

"That's why we're careful," said Gensuke. "Keep to the rules, and we'll be back soon. With or without game."

"That's right." Shodai patted Gensuke on the shoulder.

However, Gensuke suddenly became wary. "Sir, do you think the famine killed off all the animals? Or, the Inaki folks have caught them all? Because our snares caught nothing." He looked out over the ocean and added, "I don't mean to nag you, but we'll have to fix our boats up as soon as possible and go out to sea. That would make more sense." He clicked his tongue.

"Yes, I know, Gensuke. We all know that. And I have four men working on the boats at this moment. But in the meantime, this is what we have to do, whether we like it or not. We've got no other option. So, let's not lose our patience,"

Shodai reasoned, putting a firm hand on Gensuke's broad shoulder.

"No, I won't. I'm sorry, sir. It was just a moment of weakness. I felt useless, not bringing anything back to the village, and to my family while my son is out in the woods following my directions." Gensuke confessed, his tone remorseful.

Heijiro fidgeted with a dead twig, shaking his head. "Me too, Gensuke. My boy goes out to the woods almost every day. And your boy Amuro always looks after him out there." He patted his friend's back and nodded to him. "We've got responsibilities for them, and for the village. Now that so many of us are suffering serious weight loss from a lack of nutrients. My wife and daughter included."

"That's right. And you two are among the precious few who are young and have managed to stay healthy. I'm counting on you both. The whole village is counting on you. So, stay strong for us." The headman of the Guild encouraged his younger companies, assuming a fatherly role as both of their own fathers had already passed away.

Gensuke and Heijiro grabbed each other's shoulder and shook it.

Yet, Heijiro, his expression growing somber, dropped his head. "But, Sir, what'd you think is gonna happen to us if..." He paused and stared at his smudged hand vacantly. "If... this situation doesn't —"

"Heijiro, there are no ifs, son. We've come this far since the beginning of our toughest battles. Along the way, though, we've lost many dear people. And contemplating the darkest possibilities right this second is so disgraceful to those who fell in the fight. Imagine how much they would've wanted to keep fighting to stay alive. It's not the time to think. It's not the time for thoughts. It's still a time for action and focus."

"And to hope?" asked Heijiro.

"I don't like to *hope*. We need to make this work no matter what. To prevail." said Shodai firmly. "And Gensuke, you too. Please, concentrate on what we can do in this moment."

Gensuke wished he could share that same optimism, but he simply nodded.

As they kept trudging on, Shodai, leading the group, suddenly froze and stretched an arm sideways. The others halted. He turned, pressing a finder to his lips, and mouthed, "A fawn!"

Ahead, a young deer stood on the trail, its slender legs trembling lightly. It tilted its head from side to side, ears twitching, oblivious to the men watching from the shadows. No mother in sight. Sunlight filtered though the canopy, glinting off its sleek coat. Perfectly still, perfectly exposed.

Shodai wasted no time. With a practiced ease, he unhooked a bow from his waist, his fingers already fitting the arrow to the string. His movements were swift and precise, every step of the hunt ingrained in his muscles as he was the descendant of a *matagi* clan. He drew back the string, the wood creaking softly as the tension grew. His gaze fixed on the fawn's delicate neck. The sunlight gleamed off the arrowhead. For a breathless moment, the forest seemed to hold its breath with him.

The release was clean, and the arrow sliced though the still air. But, the dazzling light caught his eyes — just enough to skew his aim. A muted thwack broke the silence as the arrow struck the fawn's flank. The creature crumpled silently, its body hitting the earth with a faint, pitiful thud.

The three men dashed toward the fallen animal, only to find the violently convulsing body with its eyes opened. Blood kept seeping from the wound, the arrow bobbing with each weakening breath the fawn took. The once velvety amber coat now became matted and wet.

"Oh, no. Poor thing...," murmured Shodai, his voice heavy with grief, gazing down at the spasming fawn. Then, with a pained expression, he pulled out the arrow and without hesitation stuck it into the creature's neck.

Gensuke and Heijiro involuntarily gasped at the sight.

The tiny body twitched for a little longer, its vacant eyes staring back at its cold-blooded killers. Eventually, it stopped moving, laying in the puddle of blood.

"This is more humane," said Shodai. His younger companions reluctantly nodded.

Despite the successful hunt, the sight of the execution in front of them left the two young fathers stunned. Their thoughts unavoidably overlapped the fawn's fate with the potential peril that awaited their own children in the near future. They became quiet.

Sensing their distress, Shodai merely gestured for them to pick up the small lifeless body without another word.

———————— * ———————— * ———————— * ———————— *

Gensuke's ancestors had long embraced the power of unity, both within and outside the home, for generations. They firmly believed that working collectively yielded far better results than individual efforts alone. Gensuke still remembered his father's pet phrase: "Working with those you trust and working for them. Respect will find you, not the other way around."

As the patriarch of the blacksmith family, each and every male breadwinner before Gensuke built a well-organized clan that would only grew stronger through the generations. Eventually, the manor lord bestowed the surname Karube upon the family, acknowledging their influence and economic status in the community. Since then, the family had become more actively involved in the societal affairs.

Despite having the rare privilege within the village, the Karubes remained humble, honest, and selfless. At the onset of the drought, Gensuke generously had donated a significant sum of money to aid those in desperate need. Moreover, under the authority of the family matron, Ine, a series of intense financial negotiations took place both with the lord and neighboring villages unscathed by the drought. The Karubes' benevolent actions garnered them high regard within the farming community. The people held them in great esteem in good times and bad. Had it not been for the Karube family the entire village might already have met its fate.

"Hi, Mrs. Karube, it's Jintoku. I apologize for not being able to visit you in a while," said Jintoku as he leaned toward the laying woman. "And I heard that you've missed my profanity. Well, I'm here now. Should I give you an update on the village? Maybe some gossip?" His usually raspy voice switched into an age-old love song. Ine, bedridden since the onset of the famine, fondled his weathered face.

Ever since Jintoku's wife passed away suddenly a decade earlier, Ine had become one of his dear companies who he looked forward to visiting for endearing conversations. While his witty banter with male friends reminded him of his age, Ine's presence alone made him an 18-year-old lad again.

Despite being blind, Ine's face immediately lit up. "Oh, Sir Jintoku. How wonderful of you to come to see me. And I'm so sorry for not visiting you lately. Amuro's been busy these days venturing into the woods and hills, so he barely has time to take me outside. My strength feels like ancient history."

"Well, that makes two of us. I'm struggling to climb up and down the stairs to the shine. My damn knees! I need some shoulders to lean on!" Jintoku burst into laughter for a moment before speaking in a hushed tone. "So, how are you holding up? The circumstances have been beyond imaginable for everyone, but especially for the elders. Have you been able to eat regularly? I heard that your son and grandson are doing their absolute best to bring back food."

Suddenly, Ine's eyes welled up with tears, and she fought to hold herself together. "I'm incredibly grateful to have such a wonderful family. That's more than enough for me. I may be old, but I'm still sagacious. And I know my time may come at any moment," said Ine, and wiping off her tears, she calmly continued, "I've lived a great life, and I'd rather be reunited with my late husband in heaven than burden my family and the village. I have no regrets, and rather feel euphoric." She smiled weakly.

Jintoku could not help but feel the utmost respect for this dignified woman, who exuded both humility and strength. He resonated with every word she said, and it tugged at his heart. He held her hand tightly with both of his, and they exchanged heartfelt smiles. He held onto her hand a little longer than what would be considered a mere friendly gesture.

He hoped that within her, her inner soul could see his smiles.

While the elderly pair was sharing a quiet moment, the sliding door suddenly burst open, and Amuro rushed into the house. He panted heavily but grinned broadly, triumphantly holding up a couple of pears in his hands. "Look Grandma, what I've got!" he exclaimed, thrusting his hands forward. "I snuck into the Inaki territory and snatched these last two. I can't believe my luck!" His youthful energy radiated, with beads of sweat glistening on his forehead and neck. "I'm sorry it took me so long, but these are for you, Grandma. They've got to be the sweetest pears!"

Nearly in tears, Ine held the ripe fruits tenderly in both hands. "Aww, Amuro. Thank you so very much, my sweet, sweet boy..."

Three days later, Ine passed away quietly and painlessly while the rest of the family was fulfilling their responsibilities away from home. She smiled peacefully, drawing her last breath.

Next to her futon, she left Amuro a pear and a note.

'Amuro, this is for you as you deserve it.

The time has come to say goodbye to you. But, this is hardly the saddest moment, at least not for me, because I had the most fulfilling life one could ever ask for.

One of my happiest days was when you came to my world. No amount of words can fully convey the gratitude I feel to my god for the joy you've brought me. And thank you, my dearest boy, for letting me be your obliging grandmother.

Before long, you'll become a strong, compassionate young man. I can picture you working hard and helping others. You'd make me proud more than ever. So, promise yourself that you'll survive this calamity we're facing now. I'll forever think of you. And we'll meet again sometime... your Grandma.'

—————— * —————— * —————— * —————— *

The next day, almost the entire village, one family after another, visited the Karube family for Ine's vigil. Though no one had anything to offer the Karubes, they all wanted to pay their respect to the wise woman one last time. All the attendees and the bereaved family spent the night sobbing and reminiscing about Ine's memories, except for Amuro. In fact, he had not shed a tear since his grandmother's passing. Instead, he had remained by her side throughout the night, silently talking to her in his mind. But his parents were too devastated to notice.

"I really like him. He's a nice, kind boy. Always looking out for Kento, even when he's not in trouble with other kids," said Tami, Kento's mother, as she and Heijiro, her husband, walked back to their house.

Heijiro's mind was racing. "What did you say?" he asked his wife.

"Amuro is a good, kind boy, is what I said. You asked me how I felt about him a just moment ago."

"Right...I'm sorry, Tami. I was thinking about what we saw at Gensuke's. It's still on my mind."

"I know, Jiro. It's just heart-wrenching to see people we care about going through such a loss. And Ine-san was a beloved and fine woman. People will remember her for the rest of their lives."

"Yeah, for sure. But...didn't you notice nothing about the boy? I found his behavior a bit cold or distant considering the circumstances," said Heijiro as he stroked his chin, with his eyebrow arched. "He didn't cry even for a second. Just staring at his grandmother with a stone face. How was that even possible? I know they're a very close family."

"Well, probably he's still in shock, you know? She passed away so suddenly. I wouldn't judge anyone for reacting differently when things like that happen," said Tami in a definitive tone.

"Oh, I don't blame that poor boy. I'm just saying his behavior struck me as strange back there, that's all." Heijiro shrugged unduly and continued, "Actually, it's not just today. His mannerism also has thrown me off before. Like, A LOT. It's like he knows everything about anything, but tries not to show it. He's abnormally bright for his age, I sense, and that creeps me out. Haven't you noticed that?"

Tami threw her husband a side-eye. "No. Not me. Like I said, he's a sweet, well-behaved boy. Don't give me weird ideas about him, please."

"But —"

"Uh-uh. No 'but'"

He shrugged again.

The following day, while Gensuke and Tami were arguing over whether they would eat barley porridge or wild vegetable soup, Kento burst into the house. With a wide smile on his face, he triumphantly swung a half-torn parcel leaking water.

"Look what I've got, Mom?" Kento's grin stretched even

wider as he waved the parcel over his head. "It's oysters! Lots of them!" His kimono carried the unmistakable smell of shellfish, water dripping from the hem.

Both his parents opened their mouths, staring at their son but remaining speechless. Tami eventually recovered from her momentary shock. "Where...how did you get those? I know you can't swim, Kento. Don't you dare tell me you stole them from someone!"

"No, Mom. Amuro gave these to me!" gushed Kento.

"He What?" Heijiro's eyes almost popped out. "Why?"

"He said, 'Give them to your mom and sister. Good for ver... *vertigo*.' I don't know what vertigo means, but that's what he told me. Isn't he so nice?"

This time, Tami was so utterly aghast. "How...how did he ever know? I mean, why on earth??"

"What did I tell you about that boy yesterday, Tami?" Heijiro gave her a side-y-eye.

Kento smiled at his parents.

5

THE GUILD TORN

Situated to the east of the Nishiya, with the primary sanctuary in between, this modest assembly hall bore the name the Higashiya. It boasted an altar and a low shelf adorned with intricate moldings that, even after the occupation lasting more than three months by rogue samurais half a century ago, still stood as a testament to the community's pride. Up until the famine, parents often brought their children to the Higashiya to teach ancient wisdom and proverbs. The Higashiya also served as the designated headquarters for the Guild, the municipal committee of Kasuga.

The Kasuga Guild consisted of 13 local men, with the headman at the helm, and each man, excluding the headman, representing an assigned lot. The 12 members deliberated and voted on every community matter regardless of its significance, with the headman's decisive ballot in case of a tie. The Guild always operated in a civil and just manner but had the secretive ambiance of a fraternity, as the lord of the manor had yet to sanction such an institution.

"All right, folks, is everybody present? Anyone missing?

Well, I see all the familiar faces," said Shodai, the headman of the Guild. After counting his 12 members seated cross-legged on the floor, he addressed the members at the altar. "Ok, now, pay attention, please. The reason I've convened this meeting is that we may have a solution for our nightmare within our grasp." He paused, waiting for all eyes to focus on what he held aloft. "This scroll 'The Chronicle of the Rite' discovered by Sir Jintoku in the Nishiya, likely contains detailed inscriptions that could guide us to avert the worst. His late grandfather once advised that we should open this only at the Guild meeting. Whatever is inscribed within represents our only hope, the last hope." With that, a hushed silence settled over the auditorium for a moment, followed by an eruption of excited murmurs.

One of the older members eventually spoke up aloud, "Well then, let's take a look at it already! We can't bear to endure suspense like this, Shodai."

The headman quietly stepped down from the altar and handed the scroll to Jintoku, who nodded as a gesture of acknowledgement. "Why don't we have him read it aloud for us all? I believe he should do the honors as the rightful owner. Would you all agree?" Shodai scanned the members, confirming the consent of the Guild. All the heads moved up and down in unison.

Ensuring everyone's agreement, Jintoku untied the knots on the scroll, unrolled it, and started to recite the ancient text. "'*First, under no circumstances, do not reveal the existence of this document until....*'" As he continued, his face twisted in horror, his voice trembling.

The initial shock of the detailed description of the Rite ceremony, following its horrifying revelation, left everyone speechless. However, when the realization of whether they had to contemplate such an atrocity hit them to the core, they started yelling and swearing at each other. The more intense the discussions became, the more desperately the Guild members went around in circles. No one came up with alternatives that were both sensible and humane. The tension inside the Higashiya spiraled out of control.

"As we did months ago, why don't we just buy more provision from neighboring regions? It seems more practical and sane than looting them," Kyubei, a cunning merchant, proposed.

"What?? Are you out of your fucking mind?? Have you even recognized our current financials? We ain't no money! And you're the reason we went broke so quickly, asshole!" Heijiro fired up, pointing a trembling finger at Kyubei.

Turning furious, the merchant approached Heijiro. "Hey, shut it, you fool! 'We ain't no money!' Yeah, sure, what a pity! But think for a moment! We've still got plenty of children to trade." He paused, enjoying Heijiro's expression. "I heard a region two mountains over is in desperate need of kids. Seems like the strange disease has been spreading there, causing women to have miscarriages and stillbirths." He sneered and added, "You've got two of your own, Heijiro. Why don't you —"

Before Heijiro could react, Gensuke and another member stepped in to pull them apart. The meeting turned into total chaos, with jeers and curses echoing in the otherwise silent auditorium. Everyone pointed an angry finger at someone next to them, shouting and calling names. More physical confrontations broke out sporadically, as if their despair and pain, accumulating over the years, had waited to erupt until this moment.

Jintoku felt responsible for all the madness unfolding in front of him, regretting ever having discovered the Chronicle in the first place. *What good have I brought here?* He could not take it any longer and banged his cane on the floor once, twice...until all twelve pairs of wide eyes fixed on him. "Damn it, everyone! Stop fighting, please!" He was crying. "What can we achieve with this ugliness? We all understand the gravity of what we're contemplating. I can't even bring myself to say the word out loud. But resorting to violence... for what? I know we're better than this.

We got to be better for *this* boy." Some of the members covered their faces with their hands.

The rest of the men dropped their heads, some nervously clearing their throats and others fidgeting with their fingers, all avoiding eye contact. Shodai eventually pounded the altar with his fist to break the silence. "Come on, folks. Sir Jintoku is right. We've got to stop behaving like this. And I don't wanna hear any more cursing. I understand it's difficult for everyone to stay civil and constructive, but we have to. So...does anyone have a better solution? Anybody?"

All members exchanged tentative glances and shook their heads in despondence.

A young member exclaimed, "Let's read it again! There may be some advice or clue hidden between the lines!" He picked up the scroll from the altar and showed it to his fellow members.

"Renji, we've read it more than three times. Every word. There are no hidden messages there. Each sentence has brutally clear and simple information," Gensuke responded in a resigned tone, his vacant gaze turning to Shodai.

With his eyes wide open, suddenly, Kyubei snatched the Chronicle from Renji. "Wait, wait... So, this Rite was performed at least four times in the past, according to the description. The 519, 820, 1,022, and... 1,220 marks that we can read. Might've happened more, but the record could've been lost. Or, it was done when no one could write," he said, running his index finger along the text. "Anyway...yup, right here. About how to select the boy. In 519, he was determined by voting by fathers who had eligible sons. But in 820, Chosen Boy was selected by drawing lots among the fathers. And...the same in 1022."

"Yeah, so? That won't change the fact that we still have to *choose* one kid from the village. Can you imagine? We, the Guild, have to give up one innocent child for the sake of the rest. And that's what we're discussing right here, in case you've forgotten."

Heijiro challenged Kyubei, his piercing eyes meeting the merchant's.

"I merely pointed out a potential message. And you threw a tantrum —"

An elderly member snapped, "Enough! Both of you! Haven't you heard what the headman just told us? One more word, and we will throw you out!"

The Guild went silent once again.

The headman grew solemn as he reread what Kyubei had pointed out. It clearly indicated that they had changed the selection system. He understood that 'voting a boy' must have become too much for the past Guild. *We, too, can change it for this one*, he reflected.

He made up his mind. "This marks the single most crucial moment of our lives. No one wants to repeat what our ancestors did. No parents should outlive their children. But the decision will have to be made no matter how cruel it is. Right this moment." Shodai took a deep breath, holding himself together as he set up India ink and a brush. "Now, please, come up here, draw one line on your stick if you're in favor, and drop it in the box. Those who are against, draw two lines."

One by one, each man went behind the altar and cast his vote.

After the last member cast his vote, Heijiro showed mixed emotions of desperation and resignation. "Sir Headmaster, how can we be so sure if the Rite will work and save the village? I mean, because nobody's ever seen it through, right? And *if* it didn't work, then we would make ourselves nothing but monsters, no? Sir?"

"Heijiro, we're never certain if it worked every single time. But what I'm so sure of is each entry was documented *after* the Rite, which proves it did work out, if not every single time. And without the Rite, we'll meet our fate anyway. Many of our beloved neighbors have already perished. With that, sadly, I have to admit defeat to the famine. But, I simply can't surrender to a senseless annihilation of our village. I just can't. Can you?" Shodai's calm, resolved tone left no room for doubt.

The result indicated 9 yeas to 3 nays. Whether it rendered any consolation or more misery, most of the Guild members cared little, for they painfully understood that someone would have to die. And it was only a matter of *how many*. However, for Gensuke and Heijiro, it meant their sons' lives, Amuro and Kento, who both happened to meet the age criterion. The rest of the Guild could hardly extend any comfort and merely stood by while the devastated fathers sobbed with their hands on each other's shoulders.

Shodai approached their side and gently began to explain what would happen next. After listening to the headman for a while, both men nodded with blank stares. Then, he summoned the rest of the members and repeated what he had just told the other two and then reminded them not to discuss the matter outside the Guild.

As he dismissed the meeting and called it a night, Shodai quietly said to Gensuke and Heijiro, "I'd like you to bring your boys to the next meeting."

———————— * ———————— * ———————— * ———————— *

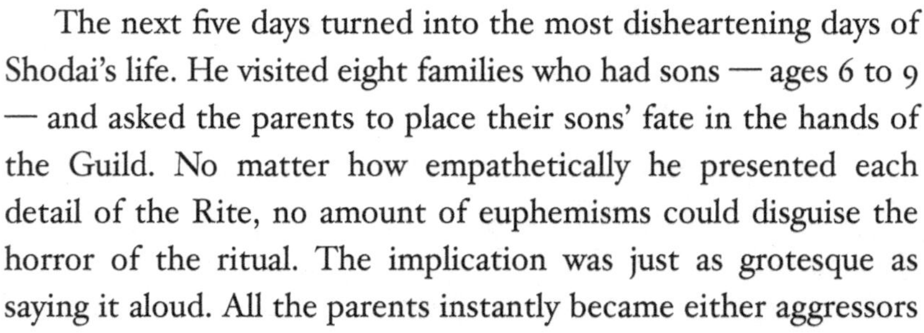

The next five days turned into the most disheartening days of Shodai's life. He visited eight families who had sons — ages 6 to 9 — and asked the parents to place their sons' fate in the hands of the Guild. No matter how empathetically he presented each detail of the Rite, no amount of euphemisms could disguise the horror of the ritual. The implication was just as grotesque as saying it aloud. All the parents instantly became either aggressors or wrecks upon hearing the potential death sentence for their sons. Whereas the mothers simply collapsed and wailed, the fathers cursed the headman, spat at him, grabbed him by the neck, and then fell on the floor. While watching their agony, Shodai sat still, tears wetting his cheeks. In the end, resigning themselves to the fate, they agreed to bring their sons to the Guild.

"We'll never forget your loyalty," said Shodai to the parents, listening to their cries of anguish, and left. *This will haunt me for the rest of my life.*

6

THE CHOSEN BORN

"So, Kyubei-san, Sir Shodai got the families to agree to the Rite, right? I can only imagine what those fathers are going through right now," sputtered Renji, his cheeks reddening with excitement. "Especially Narihei and Roshin. They both have three sons, all between 6 to 9 years old!"

"Keep your voice down!" hissed Kyubei, nervously glancing outside, "all the village can hear you!" He smacked Renji's head. "Don't you remember the clause that says 'the youngest one must be a candidate if there is more than one eligible boy in the household'? You should be glad you've only got girls."

The two Guild members skulked in the Nishiya, alone, almost suffocating in the dusty air, yet they played a game of hide-and-seek.

Renji looked slightly guilty. "Yes, Kyubei-san, I should. And so should you. You've got no children. I really feel sorry for all the fathers who have those young boys. I'd go insane...."

"Well....what can we do about it, huh? said Kyubei, shrugging. "At least, those fathers won't have to vote or draw lots. Their kids will do it. The headman asked me to bring a set of writing materials. And he's gonna put a mark on one stick at the tip with the ink. Anyway, all this hassle will aim to keep the fathers out of it to minimize their agony. But who knows?"

"Right. Hope what we'll have to do is worth the price we pay. You know? But, all the same, I just wish there were different ways to save the village instead of sacrificing an innocent boy..."

Amuro, who happened to have come searching for a food source, froze under a vent on a wall of the Nishiya, his instinct telling him not to make a sound. He shook violently, leaning against the wall, his breathing becoming shallowly. *This can't be true...can't be true...*

The chirps of crickets echoed through the shrine as dusk approached. Checking to see his two accidental informers had gone, he jolted up and started heading back home, his expression hard with resolve. *I'll never let this happen to anyone.*

—————— * —————— * —————— * —————— *

Three days later, 20 men and 10 boys jammed into the Higashiya. Beads of sweat glistened on their foreheads as the blistering heat penetrated inside through every crack on the walls. While the adults either just stood or roamed vacantly around the floor, even avoiding polite pleasantries, every single child had a blast together with other boys, except Amuro. He meticulously scrutinized the space for the first time as the Guild banned children from loitering inside the Higashiya. His acute eyes quickly caught sight of a thick wooden cylinder and a scroll on the altar, where headman Shodai stood still guarding them. Amuro also noticed that Kyubei and Renji whispered to each other once again and discreetly observed the boys. The laughter of the boys grew louder as time went by. Shodai and Jintoku exchanged words in a manner that emphasized the utmost secrecy of the gathering.

Shodai cleared his throat theatrically. All the men instantly eyed him warily, while the boys kept giggling and shrieking. "Alright, quiet down, boys," he announced. "Your fathers have brought you here, because you all behave well even in these difficult days. We've heard good things about you. And for your good behavior, we're gonna play a special game today. Then, guess what? One of you will win a prize." He scanned the room, observing the eager children with their wide eyes, and felt sick. He had to make a fool of himself, pushing down his own discomfort. "The winning boy and his father will go on an adventure to Mt.Toki and bring back some very special berries. It's a two-day journey filled with fun experiences. But, Mt.Toki is very dangerous for a young child without the guidance of an adult man, as you all know. So, the boy'll need his father's help up there." He almost choked up, lamenting their innocent excitement. "Ultimately, we hope this adventure will help him become a strong young man who can support his family." He beamed at each boy, killing his sympathies. "Who among you wants to win the game, go to Mt. Toki, and become a strong, responsible boy?"

Amuro sensed the pain and remorse in the headman's voice. While the other children enthusiastically responded in unison, "I DO! I DO!" he saw the torment in their fathers' faces, and in Heijiro and Gensuke's. Heijiro approached Gensuke and whispered something to him. But Gensuke just put a hand on his friend's chest, shaking his head, and stepped away from him. Amuro felt a profound sense of guilt. *I shouldn't've listened to the secret...* He covered his ears, but the cacophony of the boys' cheerfulness and the mourning fathers' despair deafened him.

"Now, boys, you come up here right next to me. One at a time. And pull one stick out of this box." Shodai instructed, pointing at the cylinder and lowering his voice, making sure the children gathered closely. "Each stick has a piece of paper wrapped around its tip, but you can't peel it off until all the boys have had their turns. No cheating. And the winning stick has a black mark at the tip. Got it? Then, let's get started!"

All the boys rushed toward the altar. Amuro scurried past the swarm of children and stopped in front of the headman, who looked somewhat surprised by the boy's determined look. Without waiting for any instructions, Amuro extended his hand and took one stick from the cylinder. He, then, hastily headed to a corner of the room that he had scouted earlier. At this secluded space, he picked up a brush from an inkwell on a small table. His heart raced, his hand violently shaking. Glancing back to make sure everyone's attention, including his father's, remained focused on the game, he brushed his stick's tip.

The timing was perfect. When Amuro returned to his group, he saw the last boy draw his lot. He wrapped the paper back on his stick and stood next to his father, who remained oblivious to his son's actions. Gensuke's tense gaze fixed on the stick that held his son's fate.

Shodai called out, "Ok, boys, peel the paper off and hold up your stick for me. Who won?"

To Amuro's horror, Kento's triumphant voice echoed through the Higashiya. "I won! I won!"

In the next moment, Heijiro sank to his knees, his shoulders heaving violently. Gensuke hurriedly pulled his friend up and led him out of sight, while the other fathers breathed a sigh of relief, embracing their respective sons. Heijiro dropped to all fours, tears welling up out of his eyes as he stifled his violent sobs, while the clueless Kento dashed to Amuro, exulting and waving his winning stick over his head. Gensuke looked away from the father and son.

The next moment, out of the blue, Amuro shouted at the top of his lungs over the whining boys, "I got it too!"

The Higashiya fell silent in shock, all eyes fixed on him all at once, as if they had heard him wrong. Shodai dropped the cylinder. A blank clunk momentarily pierced the room, but no one paid slightest attention to the rolling wooden tube on the floor. He shot a baffled stare at Kyubei, who seemed equally shocked and mouthed, "No, I didn't!" The headman took the two sticks from Kento and Amuro and examined them. They were identical, each having an inked mark at the tip.

The entire room's attention shifted to Shodai, who became lost in thought as he kept staring at the two marked sticks. Amuro stepped toward him. "Sir, can't Kento and I go together? Please? We both won. It's more fun with a friend, no?" he pled, faking an innocent tone. "Or, are there any reasons only one boy can go?" He pouted.

Weighing Amuro's innocent plea and dreading the prospect of a redo, Shodai sighed resignedly. "Okay, Amuro, why not? I guess the two of you can go together. You and Kento. But let me just discuss this new plan with us adults, first. Alright?"

"But, Sir Shodai — " Gensuke and Heijiro tried protesting almost simultaneously.

Shodai raised his hand to interrupt them, saying, "You two, not now, not now. I know you've got a lot to say and ask, as do all of us. I know that." He looked over all the confused men and gave them a reassuring nod. "Folks, are you all still with me? Supporting this change of plan? I do hope so, and I'd like you all to bear with me. That's what the Guild is about — unity."

All the Guild members nodded back in agreement, but Gensuke and Heijiro still looked desperate.

Shortly after that, As the children descended the shrine's long staircase to head home, Amuro told Kento, "Aren't you excited? We can have an adventure together! In Mt. Toki!"

"I am, Amuro! You and me! I can't wait!"

Seeing Kento excited for the wrong reason made Amuro feel a little guilty. "Oh shoot...Kento, I forgot to ask Sir Shodai one another thing. Have to go back there. Okay? See you in a couple days!" With that, he sprinted back to the shrine before his friend could say his goodbyes. *I won't allow anything to happen to you, Kento.*

"With all due respect, Sir, you made a grave mistake by promising to let the two of them go together! How could you make such a paramount decision without the Guild's consent? I won't give up my boy, just because you let your tongue slip!" Gensuke blurted out, his saliva flying everywhere, just as Amuro returned outside to the Higashiya.

"I won't either, Sir Headman!" exclaimed Heijiro. "Someone must've rigged the game, which means there may be a traitor among us. We must cancel it altogether. And we must redo the procedure." He and Gensuke nodded to each other.

One of the other fathers rose to his feet, anger etched across his face. "To hell with it, Jiro! We're not gonna do that again, ever! I won't allow my son to do that again. And I don't give a damn about a traitor!"

"Me, either!" shouted Narihei. "And this man must've attempted to sabotage the procedure altogether. Well, he failed, 'cause we're done here. One of those two sticks stands valid. I'm so sorry, Gensuke and Heijiro, but we won't ever reconsider." He confidently glanced around the room. The rest of the men nodded in agreement.

Amuro was still panting as he listened to the heated argument.

"Even if we found who rigged it," said Shodai, with a sympathetic shake of his head, "he wouldn't be able to tell which stick he marked. All we know is that either Amuro or Kento is the Chosen Boy." He paused, checking the two fathers, who stared back at him in disbelief. "I can't choose between them. The Guild can't. It'd bring an unforgivable sin if we did it. I'm so deeply sorry, both of you, but the outcome must stand regardless. Amuro and Kento both go — "

"No, he won't. But I will. Alone. I'm the Chosen Boy," Amuro suddenly declared. All the men stared at him as he stood on the threshold of the dimly-lit Higashiya. He looked almost celestial, bathed in the fading sunlight from behind, exuding a divine aura that compelled everyone into submission.

As the piercing eyes of the Chosen Boy met his, Gensuke realized he had already lost his son.

7

THE MIDSUMMER MIRAGE

The Terminal at the foot of Mt. Toki stood shrouded in quiet, its clearing dappled with sunlight filtering though ancient trees. The villagers called it the realm of the dead — a place of both reverence and fear. They kept their distance, wary of the spirits said to wander its slopes as the folklore claimed that death tainted the living. But for Amuro, this place felt like home.

He knelt by his grandmother Ine's resting place, tracing her name on the wooden marker with his fingertips. He suddenly felt closer to her here than ever in her lifetime. The mountain, feared by so many, was, for him, a sanctuary and a bond between the living and the dead. Dying on Mt. Toki felt fitting. To rest where she rested would be no coincidence but a certainty.

Amuro gazed up at the peak and whispered, "I'll meet you soon, Grandma."

———— * ———— * ———— * ———— *

Katsue awoke with a start, her breath ragged and her nightclothes damped with sweat. The nightmare lingered, vivid and cruel: Amuro screamed for her help as he plunged from a cliff. She pressed a trembling hand to her chest, her mind racing. *This is what I've feared the most, she thought.*

Her son had always been different. Even as a toddler, Amuro had a stillness that unnerved her. While other children broke dishes and ran wild, he would sit quietly observing the world with an intensity far beyond his years. By six, he had brokered peace between his mischievous friends and older Inaki boys, which left adults scratching tier heads. His cleverness amused most, but to Katsue, it was like peering into a storm she could not control. The more she loved him, the more unreachable he seemed.

She remembered catching him in small acts of mischief, only for him to disarm her with a cunning smile and a cleaver excuse. By eight, he had begun pointing out contradictions in adults' conversations, his sharpness earning equal parts admiration and unease. To Katsue, he was not just precocious; he was a child touched by forces she could not comprehend.

And now, that otherworldliness had taken him beyond her reach. In their final conversation, as she pleaded with him to reconsider, Amuro had simply smiled, his expression both kind and enigmatic. "I know that you already know you can't stop me," he had said, making her aghast.

Katsue's hands clenched the fabric of her blanket. She had known this moment would come, but the knowing did not ease her pain. She had no choice but to let him go.

That afternoon, she endured hours in the midst of a parched rice field, yet again. The relentless sun bore down upon the already arid fields, hills and woods, stretching far beyond the boundaries of the Inaki territories. She returned to this place repeatedly, despite knowing the futility of her actions. Every morning, she went to a communal will, but the next moment she found herself in the brown rice field. The repentant morning sojourn served her as a form of psychological asceticism. She needed to remind herself why her boy had to choose the martyrdom. *Why? Is that all for this?* Katsue spat onto the land that had once provided abundance but now lay barren. She understood that all the blame fell on the drought, yet unable to vent her frustrations in any other way, she pounded the ground and stomped on it until she felt numb.

"Katsue, please, come out of there! It's no good for a pregnant woman to stand in this scorching heat. Please!" Tami called out from the edge of the dried out rice paddy. She waved a tattered paper umbrella over her head. As soon as she ventured onto the hardened paddy, Katsue sank to her knees. "Oh, no, Katsue. That's why I told you. Are you okay?" asked Tami as she unfolded the umbrella over Katsue.

As Katsue sobbed, she struck the ground with her fist. "I don't understand, Tami. Why Amuro? How did this happen? All he said to me was 'It's my calling.' I know the Guild's involvement in his action, but Gensuke never told me about the details. I've heard about Inaki people sending their sons away as collateral for loans, so I mentioned it to him. But he insisted it has nothing to do with child trades. Normally, I don't fuss with the Guild's discussions. I understand my place and accept what men expect from women. But it's my son's life. And still, I'm not allowed to know why, and I can't say no? I feel so useless and left out."

Tami nodded empathetically, gently stroking her friend's back. "I can't imagine what you're going through. I asked Heijiro about it, too. But he only said, 'You're better off not knowing the specifics, for your own sake.' He was really upset when he came back from the Higashiya that day. I've never seen him like that before." Tami shook her head resignedly, then she showed her friend a reassuring smile. "But right now, you need to stay strong and take care of yourself for your baby. Your family would be devastated if you had a miscarriage." She helped Katsue to her feet.

The two women slowly retreated from the scorching sun and made their way back to their respective homes.

—————— * —————— * —————— * —————— *

"My dad t-told me we're going the d-day after tomorrow!" exclaimed Kento with stuttering excitement, speaking fast. "My mom is making r-rice balls for me, Amuro! Can you believe it? Rice! I haven't eaten rice for a long time." Each boy swung a long twig vigorously, exploring the bushes as usual to find something to bring home.

Amuro forced a smile as he shared in his friend's innocent joy. "That's so great, Kento! My mother also promised me some rice to take along. We're so lucky to have this adventure together. And after that, we'll become even closer, like real brothers. Hey, promise me we'll never forget each other and stay friends even when we get old."

"Of course, Amuro! We'll be friends forever! Why would you ask something like that?"

"Oh, I don't know. I guess I'm just too excited to think straight. By the way, I'm gonna have another sibling soon, and I'm hoping for a brother."

Kento's eyes sparkled, and he stopped halfway down a parched stream. "Really? Wow.... I'm so jealous. I've always wanted to have brothers!"

"Well, then, can you become his best friend, like we are? He'll need a really good friend by his side. And I know you'll make a perfect friend. What do you think?" Amuro gripped Kento's shoulders and shook them strongly.

Kento beamed back at Amuro. "Yeah, of course, I will! And I'm sure my sister and yours will become best friends, too. Our families will be close forever!"

As Amuro nodded his head with a smile, his eyes unexpectedly welled up. He quickly hugged Kento, his face on the slim shoulder, and remained in the embrace until regaining his composure. *I'm sorry for leaving you, Kento. But you'll be fine. Stay strong and survive this mess...*

They did not find anything good by the end of the day, but Kento's spirited voice continued all the way home.

——————— * ——————— * ——————— * ——————— *

The Karubes' home saw unusual bustled for the first time in months as all the family members worked together. Gensuke and Amuro repaired their *warajis* and *sugegasas* for the journey, while Katsue and Yuri cooked rice and prepared food for the journey. The little girl giggled as she shaped rice balls, unaware of the fateful day ahead for her family. She licked her fingers covered with steamed rice. "Oh, it's so yummy! We haven't had rice for weeks! All thanks to Amuro!"

Katsue's hand slipped, and her chopsticks clattered on the table. She turned away, pressing her hand to her mouth.

"What's wrong, Mommy?" Yuri put her bowl down.

Gensuke gently stroked Yuri's cheek, a weak smile twitching at the corners of his mouth.

"Hey, Yuri. She's just really happy," said Amuro, pulling her chin toward him and away from their parents. "Sometimes grown-ups cry when they're happy."

"But if she's happy, shouldn't she smile?" Yuri tilted her head.

Amuro shrugged. "It's what adults do when they're really emotional. Right, Mother?" Katsue nodded with her back to them. "But we kids don't." He winked at his sister.

Yuri giggled.

After their frugal feast, Amuro stepped outside with Gensuke. They stood together in silence, staring at the brown barren fields stretching to the horizon under the first light. Dilapidated houses dotted the hillsides like graves. Abandoned livestock sheds loomed along the dried-up creeks. Amuro clenched his fists, feeling the weight of it all. The Rite was his calling, a sacrifice he embraced without regret. *I'd do it a thousand times over if it could bring this village back to life.*

As the cicadas started their familiar chorus, Shodai, dressed similarly to Gensuke and Amuro, approached. "It's gonna be another hot day," mumbled the headman awkwardly, glancing up at the rising sun. "I just stopped by Heijiro's to make sure his son is unaware of our plan."

Amuro nodded sharply. "So, Kento still believes the mountain trek is tomorrow, right, sir? And he has no idea what we're up to right this moment, does he?"

"No, he doesn't, son," replied Shodai in a gentle tone, shifting his gaze away from Amuro's steady eyes.

"Thank you, sir. The last thing I want is him following me to the mountain," said Amuro, his voice deep and mature.

Fidgeting beside his son, Gensuke placed a trembling hand on Shodai's shoulder. "Sir, I...I should let my wife know..." His voice broke as he pulled Amuro close, his eyes brimming with tears.

Shodai nodded solemnly. "Yes, please do, Gensuke. We'd better get going now before the whole village wakes up."

Just as Gensuke opened the sliding door, Amuro's firm hand grabbed his shoulder. "Father, you're not coming," he said, pulling Gensuke away. "Sir Headman and I will go alone. I don't want you to see my last moments. And I need you here to look after Mother and Yuri. Especially Mother. She needs you more than ever."

Gensuke and Shodai fell silent, staring at the boy they no longer recognized. Turning back inside, Amuro met Katsue's gaze and gave her a solemn nod. Her lips parted, a soft cry escaping. Yuki did not see him juggling her beanbags.

"Goodbye, Mother." With that, Amuro closed the door softly.

Katsue collapsed to the floor.

Outside, Gensuke and Amuro stood face to face. Amuro's eyes lingered on the line deepening on his father's face, and he choked. For a moment, memories of piggyback rides and kite-flying flooded back.

"Son, oh...I'm so sorry...I couldn't..." whispered Gensuke, his voice cracking.

"I know, Father. But I have no regrets or fears now. You've done the best any father could, and there's nothing more you can do for me. Let me do this for you, for Mother, for the village." Then, Amuro turned and stood next to Shodai, who turned his face away from them.

"Amuro..." gasped Gensuke.

"Goodbye, Father." Amuro turned around and set off toward Mt. Toki.

Gensuke stood still, watching as two hazy figures gradually evaporated into the midsummer mirage.

8

TO HEAVEN

Amuro regained his consciousness as if waking up from a long sleep. Instantly, he touched his limbs and checked his pulse on the neck, his mind clear as ever.

Only a short while ago, Amuro had said goodbye to Shodai, who suddenly became hesitant to give him red berries until he insisted. Even then, Shodai had tried to talk Amuro around to changing his mind, admitting that he had, after all, not been chosen and accepting his sacrifice violated the faith of god. However, Shodai's self-righteousness only aggravated Amuro. He snatched the berries from the headman's hand and swallowed them in one gulp, leaving him shocked. They tasted surprisingly sweet. No wonder they fool a little boy, he thought.

Amuro did not remember what happened after that. Just as stated in the Chronicle, he had lost consciousness immediately after taking the berries. Otherwise, he would have had to suffer through all the wails Shodai expressed while entering the foggy Pond. Also, the icy water would have mercilessly attacked all his senses.

I'm sure I'm dead. Am I? Now, he watched rare fish like

catfish crawl through the mud on the floor of the Pond. The slimy mud suddenly rose to his knees. He struggled to free himself but to no avail. Despite hardly no light reaching there, the water looked clean to his eyes, so he instinctively felt his way through it. He immediately realized he stood inside some kind of bag or soft case, transparent and thin, his body dry as a summer scarecrow. And for some strange reason, the thing that swallowed him inside moved along with him as he traversed under the water. A cloud of muddy sand roiled up as he moved, but it instantly vanished as if being blown by a wind, so his sight remained intact.

The bottom of the Pond seemed boundless. Amuro assumed that he had covered quite a large portion of the area, and yet no end had yet to appear. Worse, every spot he reached looked exactly the same as the one before. He had lost his bearings under the water. How could that even happen? The flat floor had no objects laying and plants growing on it. And the Pond, he remembered, was surprisingly small. He could have gotten out of the water by now. It became apparent that he had circled around, though he kept walking in a straight line. All the while, he could only see his own silhouette reflected vaguely on the film of his translucent barrier.

Then, it finally happened. With a ray of rainbow-colored lights, a figure reminiscent of a human emerged in front of him. Tall and white, it had no definite features to claim its identity. The lights beamed so intensely that Amuro could not keep his eyes open for more than a few seconds at a time. Between his blinks, he watched the figure getting close to the barrier. His heart raced. The white object kept coming at him until they faced each other within a few steps. Now, he could faintly see its delicate eyes and mouth, and the figure struck him as a woman. She seemed to be smiling at him and moved both her arms up and down smoothly in the way a bird did. He had no clue what the gesture meant and how to react or whether or not she expected him to react. Her motion became faster as she looked at him intently. The rainbow lights flickered blighter, responding to her choreography. The elegance she and the lights together brought out mesmerized him, and he completely lost track of time.

Amuro's daydream came to an end when the colorful illumination suddenly dimmed down to a single white beam. With one last flash, the light penetrates the thin barrier. At the same time, she embraced Amuro with her long, soft arms. He found himself in a cocoon of gentleness. She then jumped up from the bottom of the Pond, and before he knew it, they flew up in the air. He looked down in sheer shock as he ascended higher and higher into the blue sky. The valley gradually dwindled and eventually became a dark dot.

Just as Amuro found his bearings, the white deity landed softly on a large mass of clouds. They had reached the region of void vastnesses with no end in sight. After releasing Amuro, who experienced vertigo because of the high altitude, she opened her arms and beamed at him. "Welcome home, Child," she said as if singing.

When he regained his composure and got up, she had vanished into thin air of heaven.

Part Three

RESURRECTION,1326. FALL

9

A CONVERSATION WITH GRANDMA

The serene cocoon of warmth.
No more pain, no more deaths.
A euphoric province that man dreamt of.

Amuro walked, or more like glided, between two colonnades shrouded in dense vapor. The sun stayed so unusually large and close he could have touched it if he had wanted to. He breathed in the thin damp air deeply. It somehow smelled similar to the morning dew he had so loved when he was a little boy. Was he dreaming or hallucinating, or feeling homesick, maybe?

The promenade seemed to stretch endlessly, obscured by the white gas. And yet, he continued along the mysterious path as usual.

Then, he froze, his eyes glued to a column in front of him. He tentatively touched its tip and instantly recoiled with a gasp. One of his family's neighbors who had perished during the famine stared at him blankly. "How did I not notice this before?" he murmured incredulously. He now recognized all the familiar figures standing there motionless. But no one paid any attention to him. Nor did they even recognize him, completely consumed by self-love, their smiles unwavering. "Creepy..." he whispered unconsciously.

All of a sudden, a bamboo gazebo materialized in front of him, seemingly out of thin air. He grinned. Inside, Ine, Amuro's late grandmother, sat cross-legged on a purple *zabuton*. She blinked just as weakly as he had last seen her do and gestured for him to sit, pointing to an empty *zabuton* opposite her own as she smiled coyly. Her blindness posed no hindrance whatsoever in this heavenly realm. Their eyes met, but neither opened their mouths. The white vapor completely concealed her torso and limbs, her floating face posing like a *kokeshi* doll.

"Grandma, you do know how to make an entrance," chuckled Amuro. Ine shrugged with a humble smile. "By the way, what are they doing back there? Just standing like ghosts. Well, technically we're all ghosts, so to speak. But, how come they're not like you and me?" he asked, peering in the direction he had just come from.

"Never mind them. They have found solace at last, free from hunger and destitution. Some denizens of this afterlife may seem paralyzed, but they're content in that state," Ine replied, her nod carrying an air of wisdom.

"Good for them, good for them. Anyway, Grandma, let's keep it short this time. I've got to study. Soon," said Amuro.

Nearly five years had passed since the Rite, and he would have reached 15 years old if he were still alive. Reuniting with his grandmother in the afterlife had given Amuro pure joy. But, engaging in banal conversations again and again wore him out lately.

"Oh, don't be such a know-it-all, my dear," said Ine and giggled with coltish grace. "Humor your beloved old lady with your wit. So, what'd you like to discuss today?"

"Really, Grandma? It's your turn to come up with a topic." Amuro rolled his eyes.

She just kept smiling at him, fully aware that he would give in, anyway. "We have all the time we want, in case you've forgotten."

"Yeah, sure. How about the *Nintoku* tumulus? No one knows for sure if he actually lay buried there."

"Ahh, that's too easy, my dear. You know the truth, and so do I." She made a face. "Besides, it's a taboo subject," whispered Ine.

Amuro winced, pacing on the heavenly cloud. As he gazed down at the land he used to belong to, he let out a sigh. "Well, sooner or later, they all have to face the reality they hesitate to admit. It's not just about that enormous tumulus. It's everything about their lives."

"Uh-huh. Alright, young sage. Tell me then, what's troubling you? I've noticed since you returned to me that something or some things are bothering you."

Pondering deeply, he ceased his pacing. "Well..."

"'Well'? Go on."

"Well, Grandma...do you think I did good for the village? Don't get me wrong, though, I felt happy for them, and would do that again. But, I've read that every little thing and everyone has their own fates, and altering them brings some evils. In that principle, I've sinned, right?"

"Hmm, I think you have, for a noble cause, though. You saved many lives, including those of your family and a little friend of yours."

"Would you have done the same? Knowing the potential consequences?" Amuro's eagerness flashed in his eyes.

"I could have, but wouldn't have done it, because everyone has the capacity to accept their own future, regardless of what it may hold. I'd have let things be."

"So, you believe you died five years ago because it was your fate? Dying of malnutrition triggered by the famine? Is that it?"

"Correct."

"Then again, do you think I've disrupted everyone's fate?" His thoughts delved deeper.

Ine became pensive as well, staring hard at her grandson. "What if you were destined to make choices for yourself and those of others? Everybody has their own destiny, and yours must shape it in your own way. And I don't think there's anything wrong with that. That's a spiritual gift when used wisely."

"Actually, I can see things, good and bad, that are about to happen to the people I care about. I don't know why, but I can. I don't want to see them suffer. And I know I can save them." His eyes simmered with intense zeal.

"Ahh, I see. Now, this is getting complicated. You can't save them all or intervene every time they're in trouble. And remember, you've done it once already."

"Yes, Grandma, I'm aware of that. But, I just can't sit here and observe them from high above."

"I understand, my dear. But, you've already fulfilled your fate. Restoring it would come at a cost. To balance your gift." Ine had a feeling about it, which worried her.

"Such as....?" He leaned forward.

"I'm not sure... but falling into hell might be one possibility. Whatever that entails, your tranquil circumstances here will change, I'm afraid. And you can't see that far ahead, even with your gift. So, think carefully."

Silence engulfed them. Down below, a cluster of clouds was mirrored in the Pond's glistening surface.

"Anyway, enough of my premature solicitude. What's the next subject?" asked Ine.

But, Amuro contemplated all the possible outcomes while his gaze followed the enormous white cotton floating on the glistering mirror of the water.

Ine beamed her grandson as she nodded. “I adore a moment like this, my Amuro,” she murmured to herself.

10

SHINZAN THE SENNIN

Tick. Tick. Tick.

The crisp clacks reverberated rhythmically through the damp air. Shinzan, a white-haired *sennin*, looked up at a gray sky as he trod steadily along the Sacred Path, his walking cane moving in sync with his heartbeats. He inhaled deeply. Over the centuries, he had morphed into a frail, skeletal carcass, a testament to his lifelong asceticism. And yet, despite his longevity, his strides remained as vigorous as those of any 25-year-old sinewy peasant, his bare feet remarkably nimble.

Shinzan lived alone on Mt.Toki and guarded the natural order, his mere existence phenomenal. For centuries, the people of the valley remained unaware of his presence, so close yet so distant. Living in complete isolation, he dedicated his immortal life to spirituality and its inherent wisdom and power. A daily pilgrimage along the Sacred Path served as one aspect of his quest. According to his philosophy, all manifestations of the natural world ultimately mirrored the deeds of mortals. And he staunchly believed that attempting to alter or manipulate them would yield little merit, if not bring about retribution.

As Shinzan returned to his cave, his thoughts lingered on the Chosen Boy from five years ago. Since that fateful Rite, the young martyr's nirvana-like composure had taken hold of him. The contrasting composure of the boy and his senior company at the Pond particularly struck Shinzan. The boy spoke like a seasoned mentor, admonishing, "Sir, you have to let me go", whereas his guardian fell on his knees and sobbed. The boy showed not only a profound understanding of his actions but also a sense of orchestrated calmness, which unnerved the sennin. The seemingly tranquil performance had grotesquely transfixed Shinzan. He could not help but ponder the brevity of the boy's life and the motivations behind his dire decision that would alter the fate of the village.

The following day found Shinzan trekking wearily through marshlands. The darkness had fallen, but he, just like a nocturnal animal, needed no external light source, his third eye guiding him away from danger. He arrived at the Pond, usually serene from dusk till dawn. Reeds lined the water, gently swaying in unison, and its rippling surface shifted from placid to tempestuous, reflecting the capricious nature of fate. Though the tarn had claimed many young lives, it exceeded neither horror nor despair, maintaining its bucolic allure. However, its legend endured as long as the natural world dictated human existence. Fate always reigned supreme. A scholar and a guardian of nature, Shinzan adhered steadfastly to its principles and upheld them.

"Until that boy showed up," murmured Shinzan to himself. "And audaciously carved his own destiny to save others. How could such a thing be possible? All my life, I've examined and witnessed fate surpassing mortal control..."

His gaze caught something amidst the dancing shadows on the water's surface.

Much to his astonishment, a soft childlike voice emanated

from under the water, or so he believed. "What? What did you say?" Shinzan called out, scanning his surroundings. "Are you who I think you are?" The silence had no answer to his desperation.

On his way to a waterfall where he cleansed his body and spirit, Shinzan gazed up at the sky."Please, guide me through my spiritual discipline,"he pleaded with his supreme deity. "I still have a long journey ahead..."

After Shinzan left the Pond, a *toki*, the Japanese crested ibis, emerged from the dense fog above the water. The bird tilted its red-skinned head from side to side before emitting a series of dry staccato sounds, as if making a conversation. Eventually, it took flight, disappearing into the nearby marsh.

Serenity descended upon the Pond once again.

11

A WHITE ANGEL FROM THE SKY

A gentle rustle in the lush leaves barely disturbed the tranquil stillness.

The next moment, in the blink of an eye, a majestic white bird took flight from the summit of Mt.Toki, gracefully soaring high into the sky. No clouds dared to mar the beauty of this late-summer morning. The white bird left a captivating afterimage as it brushed the endless blue sky.

With astonishing precision, the bird glided effortlessly, flapping its wings just once every three seconds. It moved with effortless grace, adjusting its position with the fluidity of a skilled dancer, ascending and descending, and gliding back and forth. An observer from below would have marveled at the elegance of its aerial choreography on this grand stage.

Then, the white bird altered its course, its fine black beak turning as if signaling its next move. It traced a sweeping parabola in the sky, soaring up and down. Throughout this graceful performance, its vigilant eyes meticulously scrutinized the landscapes below.

The vast expanse of verdant valleys stretched into eternity, glorifying divine life. Farming villages punctured them, with laborers toiling in the fields. A warm, gentle breeze carried the ripe scent of vegetation, suffusing the air with life. The land itself thrived like never before, with gardens and rice paddies poised for bountiful harvests. The River Hasu carried more water than ever. To the north, the Sea of Japan extended far and wide. On boats, fishermen threw and hauled their net, exchanging words and pats on the shoulder. On a cliff along the beach, a gang of little boys armed with slingshots in their hands zigzagged across the grass field, laughing as they took aim at each other.

Only five years ago, the valley had endured an unfathomable famine that persisted for well over a year. Many precious lives had perished, and hopes and prayers shriveled as the disaster-ravaged both the land and the community's livelihood. A will to live had nearly deserted the tormented villagers until the young savior miraculously came along and ended their suffering. Soon after the miracle, the Guild had organized a memorial ceremony to commemorate the boy's heroic action. However, his parents had insisted on not having his name mentioned in any way. So, the people in the village had collectively chosen to put the tragedy behind them, avoiding its discussion as if it had never happened.

Strong winds almost threatened to carry the bird away, but it skillfully navigated through the air. The diligent avian remained focused on the land below, refusing to change its course.

After a while, moisture in the air transformed the azure sky into a canopy of swiftly gathering clouds. As a light drizzle began to fall, the bird adjusted its course and descended back into the mountain, whirring through the wind.

With a haunting cry, it bid its farewell and immediately disappeared into the lush forest canopy.

———————— * ———————— * ———————— * ———————— *

The rhythmic movements of the sea surface reflected the calmness of Wakasa Bay, which lay north of the Kasuga Valley. Yet, the water had already turned chilly for early fall, cold enough to make people think twice about taking a dive. White froth on its surface slowly dissipated, one bubble at a time, as gentle waves carried them away.

Suddenly, the wind ceased, creating a complete calm in the surface. Then, with a desperate gasp for air, a girl around twelve years old surfaced from the dark depths below. Her arms reached out for an elusive hope, her legs kicking against the abyss of horror. She fought and struggled, her eyes darling around her immediate surroundings and then to the horizon beyond. *Please, someone! Anyone! Help!* She pleaded inside, her chest throbbing with pain. "I'm going to die!" she cried. "No, I don't want to die!!" The ocean showed her no mercy, continuing to pulling her deeper. Her limbs nearly lost sensation as the water was nearly frigid, and her heart slowed dangerously. She stopped fighting.

Then, a deafening splash exploded next to her, with jets of water shooting into the air. The violent disturbance created a tsunami-like waves that gradually turned into concentric ripples. Just before it all happened, the girl might have caught a glimpse of what appeared to be a large white mass diving into the water a few meters away, a fleeting image reflecting her desperate struggle and panic. She slowly lost consciousness as the dark water swallowed her numbed body.

Yuri continued sinking and sinking. But, her thoughts somehow reached her dead brother. *Oh, Amuro*...She felt ready to reunite with him. The next moment, she felt a powerful force tugging at her sleeve. The incredibly strong grip thrust her upward. Her submerged, lifeless body began to rise as the tenacious force grew even stronger. She suddenly opened her eyes and tried to breathe in, only to fill her nostrils with cold liquid. She swallowed salty water, her lungs screaming for oxygen. She swallowed more until she saw a glimmer of light above. The enigmatic savior yanked her up one last time.

With a deep, animal-like gasp, Yuri burst out of the water and inhaled deeply. She gasped for more air and coughed, her body trembling violently. The ocean returned to its eerie silence, except for a lone seagull poking at the water. As her shivers subsided, Yuri regained her composure and looked around to locate what or who had rescued her. At the same time, she continued treading water to stay afloat. The seagull fixed its small, inquisitive eyes on the strange, frantic figure floating not so far away. Their gazes met, and she wondered, "Didn't I see a white bird hit the water right before I went under? Was that YOU?"

"Why did you get into the ocean if you can't swim?" A young male's voice came from behind Yuri.

She turned her head and gasped. A teenage boy's gentle eyes instantly melted her insecurity. She tried to say something, but no words came out of her salty mouth. They simply stared at each other while keeping themselves afloat.

"Alright," the boy finally said, "I see you can tread water just fine, which means you can swim after all. Right? Let's make our way back to the shore. Our legs are getting tired now." Without a second thought, he began a smooth crawl toward the rugged coastline, not glancing back to check if the girl could keep up.

Though still in shock, Yuri followed him closely behind. At the desolate shore, a sheer cliff that soared on the edge of the beach prevented casual access to the ocean. Had Yuri screamed louder while drowning, nobody would have heard her cries. After a while of lying on the sandy beach, she examined the boy's face more closely. They both continued to pant from their swim. Despite the sunlight, their wet, glistening bodies, now covered with sand, began to feel the chill.

"It's you who saved me, right? Who are you?" she asked, breaking the silence.

"I'm Ryu," replied the boy.

"Thank you, Ryu. I'm Yuri." She instantly liked him and enjoyed his company, though she could not know why. "It's a brave thing to do, really."

"I'm just glad you're okay, Yuri." Ryu's tone sounded crisp but had some intimacy in it.

"So, how did you end up in the ocean? From WHERE? You weren't there when I was struggling."

Then came an awkward silence.

"You were sinking. What happened to you?" He quickly changed his question to hers.

"Both of my legs suddenly cramped up. Couldn't move them," responded Yuri swiftly. "Your turn. You haven't answered my question, Ryu." She pressed on again.

"I was...down below you, diving...for oysters or whatever. And saw you struggling, so I helped you." Ryu managed to put the clumsy words together.

Yuri pursed her lips. "I didn't see you under the water when *I* was diving for oysters, though. By the way, which village are you from? You must live near here, right?"

"Uh, yeah. My family's just relocated to Inaki. My father works as a seasonal hand, so we have to move where he can get a job."

"Oh yeah? I have a distant cousin over there. She's around your age, so I'm gonna ask her to be friendly with you next time I see her." Yuri's nose twitched mischievously.

Feeling desperate, Ryu got to his feet. "A distant cousin... huh. Sounds interesting. Anyway, I've got to go now."

Yuri widened her eyes. "Wow...you're so tall! How old are you?"

"Fifteen...I think. I'm not quite sure what year I was born," Ryu stuttered.

"Hmm...funny because you speak like someone much older. Just like my big brother. Well, my dead brother, who would've been fifteen by now. I'm almost thirteen, by the way."

"Well, Yuri the Thirteen, I really have to go. Bye for now. Pleased to meet you again." With that, before Yuri's further interrogation taunted him, Ryu sprinted toward the cliff.

"I'll find out who you really are, Ryu. Soon!" yelled Yuri, her eyes following his back.

On the top of the cliff, where the magnificent panorama of Wakasa Bay stretched out before him, Ryu watched Yuri making her way toward Kasuga Village. Her gait was exactly of young girls — inconsistent and impatient — yet her demeanor exuded precociousness. He wondered whether encountering her again and delving deeper into their acquaintance would bring any good for both of them. *Best to let this encounter be a mere coincidence.*

Ryu gazed out at the tranquil ocean, the salty breeze carrying a familiar sense of calm that he had before the drought. Below, small mounds dotted the waters. A flock of seagulls gathered on one, their cries mingling with the soft rhythm of the waves. The mineral-rich ocean had been a lifeline during the famine years ago, and its bounty had become the staple of the Kasuga village. Ryu's thoughts lingered on Yuri. *Could she be one of the divers?*

He headed for the nearest thicket. Before disappearing into its shade, he glanced back to make sure no one followed him.

Before long, with a graceful glide, a toki jumped out of the underbrush. Its wings flapped elegantly in the air, almost resembling an angel's, as the bird increased its velocity and gained altitude.

And then, it vanished.

12

POETIC AND CRUEL

The toki reappeared above Mt.Toki, a mountain named after the bird. The top quarter of the mountain stayed nestled in the dense ghostly fog. The once dark green, triangular- shaped mass had transformed into a black pedestal of unmeasurable proportions. Ominous clouds shrouded the sun, stretching all the way to the coast and beyond. The white bird stopped flapping its wings, momentarily entranced by the entirely murky skyline. After battling strong winds, it lost a sense of direction and strayed off course. The toki soon glided like a kite with its string severed, having no control over its bearings. Its incredible speed had now diminished, and an agonizing sound escaped its throat. After hovering around for a few more seconds, it suddenly dove into the thick veil of mist. A moment later, a large splash echoed through the dim forest.

The Pond was still rippling when a man in white emerged from the water. He panted and shivered heavily, his pale face twitching as he embraced his drenched body. With the reminder of his stamina, he dragged his wet body out of the icy-cold water and leaned against the wooden stake, his shoulders heaving laboriously as he breathed in and out. His lungs ached, and he kept exhaling visible breath, even in the mist. He had never felt this fatigued.

The gray sky had turned into a dark backdrop. Rain began to fall, and the roar of thunder from afar shuttered the silence of the forest.

Move your limbs! Shinzan's inner voice urged as he dragged himself onto the muddy ground. Even a single step required immense effort. The slimy mud continued to toy with him as if testing his limits. The further he proceed, the more he struggled. His jaw clenched desperately and instantly sent excruciating pain through his toothless gums. He took several short breaks to cover half the perimeter of the Pond, making his way back to his cave.

The circular cave, about 5 meters in diameter, did not have much: a small alter and an elevated sleeping bunk constructed from a stone wall. Because of the mild, stable temperature throughout the year, Shinzan rarely needed to make a fire in winter nor put a water tub on the earthen floor in summer. If not being outside overseeing the orderliness of the mountain and performing spiritual ablutions and asceticism, he spent most of the day in this humble cell focusing on his discipline.

And yet, despite being back in the familiar cocoon of stillness, Shinzan had hard time fighting off his inner turmoil — the churning remorse for assisting Amuro in tampering with Yuri's fate. Now that the sacred line he himself drew had slipped from his grasp, and he lost his role as an observer of the natural world. Worse, the fact that he had become an accomplice to the young boy's audacity shook him violently, even long after the initial chill he suffered at the Pond had gone. *Why did I have to be persuaded by a 15-year-old, after all?*

"*Because I needed your help.*" Amuro's voice resonated in Shinzan's head. "*To have myself temporarily reincarnated.*"

That's wrong, utterly wrong! Shinzan began to pace back and forth on the well-stamped floor, a nervous trot-like walk. The voice he heard brimmed with confidence, an irritatingly stark contrast to the whirlwind of his emotions. *Look at what I've just done. So much for my centuries-long discipline!* He shook his head like a mad man, his feet stomping harder and harder.

"*I know you're not supposed to do what I ask,*" continued Amuro's voice, "*but, if you desire to understand more about the world, I'm a part of it, and you need to examine it, whether willingly or not.*"

Shinzan put his trembling hands over his ears and said aloud, "Stop, please stop! I don't want you in my head!" His involuntary howl momentarily broke the serenity of the cave.

"*I only exist in your mind, and you can easily shut me out. But you haven't, unintentionally or willingly. Because, deep down, you need to understand why I came back and what my destiny entails. You're simply hesitant to admit it.*"

Shinzan's mouth opened wide, his cheeks twitching with defeat. The astute young spirit somehow penetrated the defensive mind of the wise man. *How could someone so young possibly possess such cognitive prowess to orchestrate an audacious plot and outsmart a sennin?*

——————— * ——————— * ——————— * ——————— *

"*I have a favor to ask, sir.*"

Amuro's spirit had initially contacted Shinzan about a month earlier, when he had been meditating under a waterfall. He stuck his head out of the water, a dubious expression in his face, unable to decide wether the voice had come from a nearby bush or his imagination. Then, the voice called out again, "*Can you hear me?*" in his head. He gasped in awe.

With his ascetic practice already forgotten, he impetuously waded out of the plunge basin and frantically scouted around the area, his hands clutching at empty air. *Where're you hiding, boy?* He eventually slowed down. *Oh, no! It's finally happened after all these years?* While Shinzan had always believed in the existence of apparitions and had even seen some wandering around the Pond and the Sacred Path, none had ever reached out to him before. Nor had he managed to communicate with them. "H-how did you find me!?" he shouted involuntarily, still turning his head around.

"*From the beginning. I knew you were watching me go into the water that day five years ago,*" answered the dead boy's spirit, his tone exuding confidence and youthful vulnerability at the same time.

Shinzan went speechless.

Then, the departed Amuro began to lay out audacious stratagems.

As Shinzan became drawn to the calm voice resonating in his head, he could not help but feel a shiver run down his spine. "*This is all wrong and beyond formidable, and then, so poetic. How can a single individual foresee and concoct anything like this? And he is only an adolescent!*" The sennin's frail body trembled compulsively, his head spinning with nausea. He collapsed to the ground, struggling to catch his breath.

"*Sir, are you alright? Please, stay strong for me.*"

Shinzan only dropped his head in defeat.

———————— * ———————— * ———————— * ———————— *

Shinzan now sat down cross-legged in his serene cave and reflected on his encounter with Amuro's sister, Yuri, in the ocean. The vivid scenes revisited the back of his eyelids as his mind replayed the mischievous conversations.

"*Thank you, Sir Shinzan, for saving my sister's life. It was a daring thing to pull off,*" Amuro's voice stated matter-of-factly to the sennin. "*That was exactly what I would have done myself.*"

"You told me to save her. But it was you who did it. I merely let you have my 15-year-old body. And you didn't even mention that *I* had to dive into the water from such a height!" Still irritated, Shinzan jolted up, uncharacteristically struggling to contain his composure. "We need to establish rules: no physical activities and, more importantly, no emotional attachments."

"*But…all this was deeply personal. That's the reason I wanted to come back and help. So executing the plans while ignoring that part is almost impossible.*"

"No, it has to be done objectively and anonymously. Namely, do not reveal your true identity. It would bring chaos to the whole village if you ever did. Not just in your family. So stay out of their personal matters. I insist. Never become emotionally involved with anyone."

"*Who'd believe me if I told them who I am, anyway? And what exactly do you mean by not emotionally?*"

Shinzan wondered whether Amuro was playing a fool or toying with him. And then, he realized he was conversing with a 15-year-old boy who had no experience with romances. All of a sudden, he felt sorry for the boy who had died before experiencing feelings for someone beyond his family.

"What I mean is, stay away from your sister. It's for your own good and hers as well. Especially hers," sighed the sennin resignedly. "Did I make myself clear, Son?"

There was a long pause, and Shinzan thought Amuro in his head had gone.

"*I'm not quite sure what you're getting at, Sir, but staying away from her is what I intend to do, anyway.*" The voice finally came back. "*Seeing my preadolescent sister after a five-year absence would be too sentimental to handle.*"

"She may harbor different — " Shinzan stopped himself, Yuri's earnest gaze popping up in his head. He grunted. *He'll figure it out himself, their youthful poetry and cruelty. I'm already too much involved with his larger-than-life ambition.*

"*What did you try to tell me, Sir?*"

"Life"

"*Hmm... anyway,* we *need to go over details of my next visits to the village, so we'll be on the same page. Please bear with me....*"

While Amuro's monologue continued rhythmically, Shinzan's mind wandered to a different space, somewhere far removed from the moment they were sharing.

13

THE SAGACIOUS DAUGHTER AND THE GRIEVING MOTHER

A month had passed since Yuri's dramatic encounter with the mysterious Ryu out in the ocean. The boy's convenient presence in that particular moment continued to nag her. She found his careful choice of words rehearsed rather than spontaneous, as if he had foreseen their meeting and what she would ask. *But how could that be possible? I have so much to ask. I need to see him again.* She went back to the beach many times and, out of desperation, even got into the cold water. Katsue caught her daughter wet and shivering more than once. Yuri simply doubted that Ryu had dived under the water the whole time.

"It's really annoying. I still can't wrap my mind around the whole thing, Mom," said Yuri as she absentmindedly folded the laundry. "Ugh...nothing makes sense."

Katsue sat opposite Yuri in their family room, mending tears in her children's clothing. She stifled a chuckle, pretending to focus on her needlework, and cast a furtive glance at her daughter. "Well...this is much better than listening to a silly dream of becoming an ama," she mumbled with her head down.

"Mom, how's your demanding sewing going?" Yuri's furrowed bow conveyed as much frustration as her sarcastic tone did. "I'm talking to you about that boy. Don't you think how surreal it was? The way he emerged? Almost like out of thin air. Air, air...wait, the air! Could he have fallen from the sky? Is that what happened? Yeah...that splash explains it! But, HOW??" A tiny sash fell from her hands, joining a pile of miscellaneous clothes.

Katsue stole a peek at her daughter with affection again. Each time Yuri talked about the incident, she became overly animated, which made her even quirkier, albeit a bit coquettish for a 13-year-old girl. Word had it that quite a few boys her age showed keen interest in her. Katsue, as a mother, saw this as advantage for her daughter to stay ahead of other Kasuga girls in the potential bride pool. *In four years, one of those boys will ask for Gensuke's permission to marry Yuri. He may be from other village. Maybe? Will she make a good wife to her husband? And in five years, she'll become a mother. How many children?*

"Mother! You're not even listening, are you?" said Yuri aloud, bringing Katsue back from the daydream.

"Oh, Yuri, of course I am. I just didn't want to interrupt your tale. You're such a good storyteller. I'm really enjoying it."

"'My tale'? 'Enjoying'? So, you think I'm making all this up? The incident and the boy?" Yuri looked both defiant and incredulous.

Katsue smiled exaggeratedly. "I know how good you are with words. But, a boy falling from the sky is just too good to be true. A brilliant tale, though." Instantly, Yuri's lips closed tightly. "Well...perhaps he did stay underwater from the beginning, just as he told you. You'd be amazed at how long some people can hold their breath."

"So, you ARE saying I made everything up. I get it, it's fine, Mom. Even *I* can't believe what happened." Yuri gave her mother a side-eye and shrugged.

A sense of happiness filled Katsue, yet at the same time, a tinge of sadness pinched her as she watched her quickly maturing daughter. *Hope she won't scare the boys off with her wit and sagacity.*

"Oh, and Mom, there's one another thing about Ryu. For some reason, he reminded me a lot of Amuro. Funny because they don't look alike at all."

———————— * ———————— * ———————— * ———————— *

"No! Stop! Where are you going??"

That night — one of those nights — Katsue jolted up from her slumber, her own scream piercing the stillness of midnight. The same dream — the same haunting sequence where Amuro had left the house for the last time that summer five years ago — kept coming back, squeezing her throat.

She wiped her neck with a wet cloth, slightly out of breath. Gensuke, who lay still next to her, did not flinch in the slightest. She took a quick sip of water from a cup on a tray by her side. The room's outlines gradually took shape as her eyes slowly adjusted to the darkness. The aftereffects of the nightmare made her agitated and wide-awake. The insomniac Katsue then slipped out of the futon and tiptoed barefoot out of the house.

Dawn approached with a faint hint of faded blue in the sky. The tranquil sound of the River Hasu drowned out all other noise in the already quiet surroundings. The absolute stillness not only reminded her she was alive but also blamed her for what had happened five years ago. Katsue took a deep breath, and immediately, a sharp sensation prickled her lungs as the cold autumn air pierced them like a needle, causing her to shudder violently. Yet, she let it attack her until numbness completely consumed her. Surrendering control strangely calmed her, as if her body, along with her emotional pain, belonged to someone else. Her vacant gaze followed her white breath as it drifted over the pre-sunrise riverscape.

The fateful event from five years ago continued to haunt Katsue as though it had happened only yesterday. In her head, that summer morning five years ago tauntingly replayed as if it had happened only yesterday. Amuro looked just as vigorous as ever, striding with purpose, never once looking back. But all the same, she watched him march on the sandy path and stood still long after he had vanished from her sight, from her humble, conventional universe. She remained standing, staring blankly at the spot where Amuro had been, half-expecting him to reappear. Her baby boy, Kairi, pleaded with his mother to come back inside the house, cooing in his blanket. His sister, Yuri, engrossed in beanbags, sat in the corner. Katsue felt numb, not because she could not move but because she did not want to. She watched her surviving children, from the outside, as they carried on with their normal lives. Out of the corner of her eye, she watched Gensuke hammer a piece of iron, a seemingly futile attempt to divert his mind from what had just happened. Jealousy and anger welled up in Katsue. *How dare you have the luxury of escaping into your work! What about me? Where's my escape or solace? The children? Then, tell me how I'm supposed to look after them. I've already lost one! How dare you neglect me when I need you the most!* Her open mouth trembled, unable to let her emotions out.

Back in the house, the first light gently seeped through the cracks in the front door, promising a sunny day in the valley. Watching Gensuke's chest heave peacefully only deepened Katsue's enduring sorrow and made her feel lonely, although she sat in her own home. On an impulse, she checked on the children, all of whom were sound asleep in the smallest room adjacent to her and her husband's. Kairi, at six years old, and Yoriki and Haruki, both four, occupied much of the space, all lying on their backs and forming a jumbled triangle on the tatamis, whereas

Yuri, who adamantly refused to share the same futon with any of her brothers, lay humbly at the corner.

Before Katsue closed the shoji screen, Yuri raised her head in her mother's direction and rubbed her eyes. "No way...already morning? I barely slept because of... that." Yuri pointed at the innocent geometry of the triangle formed by the three small bodies. "I know there're no more rooms in the house. And I know you gave me twin boys when I asked for a baby sister. But, can I please NOT share this room with them, Mom? Is it okay to share the room with you and Dad? Or, I'd rather sleep by the kamado." She made a face.

A pang of guilt overtook Katsue's lingering sadness. Her daughter was on the cusp of adolescence and needed more female guidance than ever. Motherly guidance. Yet, five years had passed by her pointlessly, and she could not afford to squander another year, month, or day for Yuri. "Of course, Yuri. You can sleep next to me and your father," she assured her daughter. Katsue entered the room and sat beside Yuri. "You're becoming a young lady and want some privacy. It's natural. But for the time being, sharing a room with your father and me would give you some insights into this transitional stage of your life." As she combed Yuri's hair with her fingers, Katsue added, "And hope it's the closest thing to privacy."

Yuri's eyes instantly widened. "Thank you, Mother! Which means, we can talk more about Ryu every night, right?"

14

ANOTHER CONVERSATION WITH GRANDMA

Up in heaven.

Nothing clouded the blue sky, even when a heavy storm battered the valley below. The eternal sunshine gently bathed the atmosphere, rather than scorching it. The air, though thin, remained pure, granting crystal-clear visibility, free from the ambiguities and secrets that often tainted human perspectives. Heaven dwellers indulged in leisurely strolls instead of hauling heavy hoes, in frivolous conversations instead of backstabbing each other, and in books instead of worrying about how to make ends meet.

Ine and Amuro perched on a soft cloud. Nearly three months had gone by since their last serious conversation when Amuro had ventured deep in the ocean. Now, her pupils dilated like a hawk sizing up its prey, reading the grandson's mind. After letting the suspense sufficiently to unsettle Amuro, she finally broke the tension with a calm and inquisitive voice. "So, the sennin. Tell me about him."

"What??" said Amuro, his forehead furrowing. His expression grew tightened as he frowned."Why? I thought you wanted to know how I handled my first mission since you encouraged me to help Yuri." Ine nodded in agreement. "The water was bitterly cold, and she would've drowned if I hadn't dived."

She nonchalantly shrugged her shoulders. "Well, that's why you wanted to be there for your sister, didn't you? To save her. I knew you would manage. Compared to what you're going to do for the years to come, it was a relatively straightforward mission, I suppose. Not that I didn't care, though." Ine widened her eyes. "So?"

"What 'so,' Grandma?"

"The one and only 400-year-old sennin, of course!"

"How do you know he's that old?" Amuro was taken aback.

"I have many sources," Ine smirked slightly.

"Like what?"

"You'll see." She chuckled playfully.

"Agh... Grandma!" Amuro shot her side-eye with his hands up and then leaned forward. "You've met him before, haven't you? You've known him long before I rejoined you here. So, how come you insist on asking about him?"

Ine nibbled her bottom lip for a while. "Yes, I *saw* him, and he saw me for sure, at the Terminal just as I was about to ascend here. But, we didn't exchange any words. He's not supposed to initiate such actions, and we, as spirits, lack the ability to communicate with anyone or anything outside of ourselves." She paused, pointing at Amuro. "But, you? You're different. You're something else, Amuro. You possess the special power that connects you with the world beyond heaven, for whatever that's worth." Her playful tone shifted to that of a more serious monologue.

Amuro went on to recount his deep encounter with Shinzan and shared his impressions of the wise man. Ine listened intently with her eyes closed throughout.

"Grandma? Are you okay? Something wrong?" asked Amuro, noticing Ine had not even budged.

When she opened her eyes, her previous jovial expression had vanished. "Are you fond of him?"

"What kind of question is that??" spat Amuro involuntarily.

"Well....how's the question so confusing to you? It's simple. Did you like him or not? Or did you have any other feelings? I need to know, Amuro."

Her unexpected persistence rattled him. "Why do I have to answer that, Grandma? What's going on with you? There must be some reason behind your insistence. What is it?"

Ine sighed heavily and nodded. "Alright, dear, I'll tell you what it is. But before that, no matter how absurd it sounds, can you just answer my question first?"

Replicating her sigh, Amuro finally gave in. "Sure. I've no idea why it's so important to you, but... sure." He paused, collecting his thoughts. "Here is what I thought about him. Even though we had just met, he felt strangely familiar to me. I can't explain why or what it is, but I sort of knew how he would react. Like I had known him for a long time. Does that make any sense to you? So anyway, yeah, I definitely felt some connection between him and myself. It's not that I like him or not, though."

A profound silence draped the gazebo where the grandmother and grandson sat. Ine's chin cradled in her hands as she stared downward, while Amuro's eyes fixated on her, attempting to read her mind. The clouds that enveloped them began to thin out. Absolute blackness would soon claim heaven.

"Hey Grandma, you've been awfully quiet. And you're scaring me a bit. What's bothering you? Did I disappoint you? Or, wasn't my answer what you expected?" Amuro frowned, shifting nervously in his seat. The temperature had considerably dropped. "Grandma, let's go back to the sleeping quarter before the sun gets completely behind us."

Ine finally broke her silence and replied, "It was, my boy, it was."

"What is *it*?"

"Your answer. It was what I half expected. And half dreaded. You simply confirmed my finding."

Amuro scratched his head. "I... don't understand, Grandma. You've lost me. Umm...your *finding*? What is it? Where did you come across it? And how on earth does it have anything to do with me?"

"I'm not so sure if revealing the information I stumbled upon will do any good to you," said Ine, stone-faced, as if she read something. "And even if some things might be best left buried..." All of a sudden, she stood up and got out of the gazebo.

Amuro followed suit, still wearing an expression of utter confusion. "Are you not gonna tell me what it is that you found?"

"Shall we, my boy?" Without making eye contact, she started walking.

"Grandma! Please?"

"There's an astounding connection between you and the sennin. It's truly surreal. It could be wrong, I could be wrong." She continued on the cloud-covered path with her gaze fixed ahead.

"How?? How can I have any connection to him? Obviously, I never met him when I was alive. You must've been misled, most likely." Amuro slowed his pace to match Ine's. "By the way, where are we heading? The sleeping quarters are in the opposite direction."

"To the Archive," said Ine, nearly panting.

"The what??"

"The Archive. That's where the truth lies."

"Like the Nishiya?"

"You could say that, but imagine bigger." She picked up her speed. "And we'd better hurry before it turns completely black."

Amuro crouched in front of his grandmother. "A piggy-back, Grandma. This should be much faster. I've no idea what the Archive is, but show me the way."

Ine's bashful smile glimmered in the dimming light.

15

THREE REVELATIONS

Ine tapped Amuro on the shoulder and said, "We're here."

"Huh? I don't see any—" Then, Amuro gasped, almost dropping Ine. "What the.... H-how??" In front of them, the Archive glowed brilliantly amidst the clouds, its presence commanding the very heart of heaven like an ethereal beacon. Its golden facade soared into the dark sky. The double doors was adorned with intricate woodwork, with a keyhole neatly hidden between the panels. "How on earth did I not notice this before?" he murmured, gazing up.

Ine shook a long iron key triumphantly as she chuckled and pushed it in the keyhole. Despite its sheer size, the doors, however, opened with the ease of paper. "Elder-friendly, I assume," said Ine and carefully tucked the ancient key back into her sleeve.

Once inside, Amuro gasped even louder as a myriad of candles lining the walls instantly illuminated the vast rectangular room. The line of sconces arranged horizontally on the walls, extended beyond his eyes followed. Walls and ceilings consisted of crystals of every conceivable hue — ruby, purple, amber, turquoise, and teal. A cornucopia of sparkling colors he had never imagined danced in the air, casting a mosaic of light on the clear quartz floor. Granite shelves lined the lengthwise walls, their milky-white surfaces filled with an array of artifacts and documents. A rotunda protruding from the ceiling emitted a soothing melody as a faint female voice sang a mantra stenciled inside the amber dome. Amuro's neck started to ache from gazing up for a long time, and his mouth remained agape.

"So much for our frugal peasant life, wouldn't you say?" said Ine, reading Amuro's thoughts. "This is one of the many reasons the afterlife isn't so bad. We, as lay people or peasants, were raised to be austere throughout our whole lives. From birth until our deathbeds. And yet, deep down, we all yarned for a comfortable living. And *this*, Amuro, is it. All of us here have endured enough suffering. Why not embrace a brighter existence? And by the way, there are no social hierarchies in heaven, as you already know.

Amuro tried to take it all in, mumbling, "But... how is all this possible? I mean..." He spread his arms. "Who built THIS??"

"Who cares? We're in heaven, Amuro. Anything goes. Any way we desire."

As he wandered among the shelves, touching and scanning artifacts, documents, and books — priceless treasures of history — his thoughts flitted between his memories of rural life and the people he had left behind. A twinge of guilt prickled him. *They're not allowed to have this kind of life*.

"Oh, dear, don't feel sorry for what's been done. You've earned this. Their time will come sooner or later. All of them," she said to herself rather than to Amuro, "besides, you freed them from their suffering. And the village is now thriving like never before."

"I never knew this euphoric life was waiting for me..., " whispered Amuro.

"Of course, you didn't. None of us did. But, here you are.

So, indulge yourself. You deserve it more than anyone else after what you've done for the village."

Amuro paused his exploration on the vast floors and gazed unconvincingly at his grandmother. "Okay... I guess. But, how did I NOT know about the existence of this grand structure until now? I've walked past this area so many times before."

"Because you don't have access to the Archive," explained Ine, taking the key out again. "You'll receive the same one when you turn fifteen, and only then will you be able to see the facade."

"But, I AM fifteen!" protested Amuro.

"But not quite, I guess," Ine shrugged.

After scanning his surroundings one more time, Amuro cleared his throat dramatically. "Well, Grandma, are you gonna tell me about the connection I have with Sir Shinzan? Or, do I have to find that out by myself from, maybe, these piles of documents?"

Ine beamed at him. Then, without a word, she signaled for him to follow her. As they ventured deeper into the Archive, Amuro noticed a tantalizing aroma of pine, but he could not locate where it came from. The flames of the candles seemed to intensify as they proceeded further, and so did the captivating scent and the colors that surround them.

At the far end of the corner opposite the entrance, a sizable podium — similar to a modern reception desk — emerged as if out of thin air. Behind the podium stood a tiny elderly lady, Ine's contemporary in age. She had remained invisible until Ine and Amuro leaned over the table. The hem of her one-piece garment rustled on the floor like fallen leaves. Her eyes opened and glistened in the illumination. "Evening! How can I help you, Ine?" Her unexpectedly loud voice echoed through the entire Archive for a good five seconds. "You've got to speak up, otherwise I won't hear you!" The curator's authoritative tone, despite her small stature, straightened Amuro.

Ine struggled to stifle a chuckle while Amuro stayed rigid

like a scarecrow. "GOOD EVENING, Tsugumi!" said Ine loudly, "Lovely to see you again! I brought my grandson Amuro. Anyway, could you please, point me in the direction of the document that I read last time?"

"The WHAAAT??"

"The DOCUMENT you helped me find?" Ine nearly screamed.

"AHH," groaned Tsugumi, and extended her index finger toward the third shelf from where they stood. "THEREEE!"

"Thank you, Tsugumi!"

Ine and Amuro trotted back to the shelf that had a paper tag hanging from the top drawer: Myths and Legends. Each drawer had different items neatly placed: documents and scrolls, what looked like roughly woven straw figures, human-shaped clay figurines, and rusty iron blades no larger than a man's middle finger. Ine carefully selected an amber-colored scroll from the second drawer at the bottom. The title, in barely legible text, read *The Wise Man*. She handed it to him with a sense of reverence. "Take as much time as you need and read carefully." Then, Ine walked back toward the entrance, opened the door, and disappeared into the darkness.

After the door closed, Tsugumi, the curator, gave Amuro a cryptic smile. He simply cocked his head courteously and turned his attention to the scroll. At the base of the shelve stood a pair of cylinder-shaped granite stumps. Amuro fetched one of the embroidered zabutons from a nearby corner and placed it on the stone pedestal closer to him. He sat on it.

After examining the fading texts on the scroll, he tentatively unrolled it and began to immerse himself in the bizarre history of the sennin.

Page after page, the ancient document unfurled the tapestry of Shinzan's life. A Kasuga local, purported to be born between 710 to 720, he emerged as an orphan, the origins of his birth veiled in mystery. From the outset, he stood as a misfit in the tight-knit community. Growing up under the guardianship of his distant uncle with six other children, his early years proved a crucible of survival, a landscape marked by incessant bullying and neglect.

One summer, the 13-year-old Shinzan surprised other children by spotting flying game birds — pheasants, geese, and ducks — from far distance. His weather predictions, whether rain, snow, or storm, also resonated with uncanny precisions. A lone savior against a plague, he singlehandedly purified the wells when he was fifteen, eradicating the menacing specter of death that loomed over the village. However, as his formidable abilities continued, fear cast its shadow over admiration. The Guild requested spiritual and physical examinations on him. When they proved futile, his family finally kicked him out, and his neighbors simply shunned him.

By the time he turned seventeen, Shinzan found himself an outcast, abandoned by the entire village that once bore witness to his miracles. When they found a makeshift alter at the foot of Mt. Toki, his uncle reported him to the regional government. One dawn, as the authorities marched into the valley, young Shinzan, carrying what a villager later dismissed as 'a bag of junk,' snuck out of the only home he had known. With no predetermined destination, he traversed the winding banks of the River Hasu, swam its currents when necessary, scaled mountains, and eventually settled in a land where the shadows of Kasuga did not follow him.

The details of Shinzan's subsequent existence became obscure, veiled in the shroud of rumor. Whispers spoke of a mysterious companionship with a young woman, an outcast just like him. Then, at the age of 25, he returned to the valley, specifically to Mt. Toki. Local accounts revealed his sporadic visits to the village for provisions, but after a year, he vanished from his birthplace. Rumors persisted that years later a local man who had accompanied a Chosen Boy glimpsed a mysterious old man in all white in the mountain.

Meanwhile, Shinzan delved into the arcane study, mastering alchemy and astrology over three and a half centuries and purportedly achieved the status of a sennin, with his paramount commitment to safeguard the natural order as it was.

As Amuro immersed himself in the unfolding narrative, an impressive genealogy caught his eye. Instantly, a cascade of names, some generations missing due to negligent research or lost records, continued on page after page. The chart showcased Shinzan's progeny, children identified and unidentified in name and gender. Then, Amuro froze as his eyes fixated on the last known descendant's name:

AMURO, male, 1195

Amuro gasped, with his hand over his mouth. The scroll fell on the floor.

"AHH, you found it!" shouted the curator of the Archive, rising from a granite stump by the podium. She picked up a stone bowl as large as her head from the opposite corner and handed it to Amuro. "HERE! This will calm you." Inside the bowl were burnt pine needles diffusing a therapeutic fragrance. Amuro, still processing the shocking discovery, shot her a vacant stare. "And go back to your grandmother. She'll take care of the rest."

By the time he eventually collected himself and thanked her, the curator had already disappeared behind the podium.

——————— * ——————— * ——————— * ——————— *

Heaven's sleeping quarters sprawled across four locations —

the east, west, south, and north wings — each conversing at a grand botanical park in the heart of the cross. The denizens of heaven could stake their claim in any wing, their choice a reflection of personal preference. However, the north wing was the least favorite, shrouded in the superstition that the north symbolized death. Despite their ethereal existence, the heavenly dwellers persisted in detaching themselves from reminders of mortality. Also, many residents felt the north wing a bit colder than the others, as well. For these reasons, the south wing, the farthest from the grim north, stood as the most crowded of all four, though a select few escaped the crowd for the solace of quiet.

Ine's abode, a modest four-and-a-half-tatami room, lay within the north wing. Sparse in furnishings, it boasted only a futon and a small low table with an open copy of *"The Tale of Genji"* on it that Ine, a voracious reader, had rented from the Archive. Ine stood gazing out into the abyss of the pitch-dark garden through a small vent on a wall. "You can see colorful flowers during the day," she said cheerfully. Amuro sat with his head down, making no reaction. "Are you sure you're okay, dear?"

Amuro nodded slowly but did not know what to think. He no longer believed in his identity. *Who am I? Where am I from? Why did I not know about it? How come nobody told me before?* The questions reverberated in his head over and over after he had stumbled across the lineage of Shinzan. He shifted his gangly frame and absentmindedly fidget with a corner of Murasaki Shikibu's book. The flips of the pages created impersonal sounds in the silent room. No words had escaped his lips since he left the Archive.

"Quite a shock, wasn't it?" said Ine as lightly as possible, "I know it was, my boy, because I've never suspected he had even had a family. Let alone you as a direct descendant of the spiritual myth. Never."

"A.... What?" His accusing eyes locked on her. "You...umm...

I was actually expecting you'd deny it. But now, sounds like you don't even doubt it. Why, Grandma?"

"Because I wasn't completely convinced until you told me how you thought about him."

"Wait...are you saying you knew all along?"

"Amuro, my dear..."

"Does *he*?" interrupted Amuro, his expression demanding the truth.

"No, he doesn't know anything about the origin of your lineage. I doubt he's even aware he became a father," Ine replied firmly.

"But, you do, right Grandma? That I wasn't born into the Karube? Don't you?"

Ine had never treated her grandson as a mere child, even when he was six or seven. And she was painfully aware this was not the moment for condescension. After letting out a determined sigh, she slowly began to unburden herself of the family secret that had long remained protected.

Everything had begun before baby Amuro changed the course of the Karubes' lives.

When Katsue gave birth to her first baby, the family instantly knew something was seriously wrong, as his tiny lips remained closed. Despite the midwife's efforts, the motionless infant survived for only half a day and passed away quietly without even receiving a name. Blaming herself for the fatal birth defect, Katsue withdrew from life, isolating herself from her husband and mother-in-law and becoming a prisoner of despair. Her grief persisted for months until she found solace in the shared experiences of other mothers who had suffered similar losses. Eight months later, a new life blessed her womb.

Traumatized, Katsue, along with Gensuke and Ine, held her breath during the next 10 months. When the winter of 1195 arrived, the Karubes welcomed their second chance at parenthood with tears of joy upon hearing a baby's vigorous shriek. They named their first son Amuro, and he instantly became the center of their lives, Gensuke the sole provider, worked tirelessly to feed the fledgling family. Katsue regained her strength and supported her husband while nurturing their newborn. And Ine proudly showed off her first grandchild to the village. Everyone appreciated renewed purpose in their lives.

A few months later, Katsue noticed the baby's unusual coughs. As the days passed, the coughs worsened. Before long, baby Amuro suffered a high fever and shortness of breath. A local physician told the family their son had pneumonia and that there was little anyone could do but pray. Despite their pleas, two days later 2-month-old Amuro quietly breathed his last. Gensuke fell on his knees, howling and sobbing for hours. That night, Katsue escaped from the dark, cursed home and dragged her numbed body into the icy River Hasu, turning to death rather than seeking ablution. A neighbor rescued her just in time.

Five days after her grandson's departure, Ine embarked on a pilgrimage to temples, praying for Katsue's well-being. Treacherous mountain routes and unexpected detours constantly slowed her down, but Ine's determination and resilience carried her forward day after day. Then, seven days into her pilgrimage, a spring storm flooded the upper reaches of the River Hasu and destroyed the main route, forcing her to give up her journey. Disheartened, Ine stopped by Kasuga Shrine upon returning to the village. Just as she was about to leave after her worship, the faint coos of an infant from the Higashiya stopped her. Under the *engawa* lay a male infant in a bamboo basket. He smiled, wrapped in a cocoon of a clean cloth, with a piece of paper bearing a short message placed on his torso.

'This baby boy is 5 months old. He is healthy and quiet. May this boy bring you joy...'

On impulse, she picked up the baby and quickly left the shrine with him. On the way home, she visited Jintoku, the eldest of the village, and told him what she had just done. They both agreed to keep the story between him and her family for the baby's sake. The moment Katsue saw the baby, her trembling arms gently cradled him, streams of tears wetting her bony cheeks. Then, she fed the baby boy as if he were her own. "You're home now, my Amuro," she whispered. Gensuke embraced the mother and son, with tears in his eyes.

The poignant incense of burnt pine Amuro had brought from the Archive permeated Ine's small room. Its soothing effect had kicked in, calming the lingering tension, although the shocking revelation set his mind racing. "Wow...another inspiring revelation," murmured Amuro with a simper. "Well, I've learned three things about myself tonight. I was an abandoned child, a replacement, and the last heir of supernatural power. But I have to say it's a little too much to take them all in, though."

"You were never a replacement, Amuro. Not for me. Not for your parents. You were as much a son to them as their late babies. Believe it or not, as far as parental affection goes, you were much more cherished," said Ine firmly.

"Then, how come they gave me the exact same name?" Amuro crossed his arms, pursing his lips.

"That I'm not so sure. I would've done the same, though. And that wasn't a big decision. What was important for all of us, your parents and myself, was, I believe, that we embraced you being the continuation of the love they had nurtured so dearly. A living proof that their first and second son did exist, however short their lives were. Your parents suffered every parent's worst nightmare. Twice. They were beyond devastated, especially your mother. So, don't blame her for not having given you a different name," explained Ine, then shook her head sternly. Amuro's shoulders slumped. "And to protect her and you from the prying eyes of the neighbors, we decided to tell them you were a child of my distant relative who had died at birth. No one else besides Sir

Jintoku knew about the truth. The point is...," she broke off to gaze at her grandson and continued, "your parents went through so, so much."

"And I made myself their third dead son...." Amuro lamented after a long pause. "That's what I did. Why did I do that? I'd never have become a Chosen Boy if I'd known all about this. I could've shown them my filial piety as long as they lived."

"What're you talking about? You saved their lives. If that was not the utmost filial affection, then what is?"

"But, it was never meant to be. I just wanted to believe we'd never fall victim to a so-called fate."

"I know. You told me that before. Still, your selfless action saved many more lives. So so many of them. And for your parents, it proved ultimate love, no matter how painful it was. I can only imagine their sense of loss after you're gone. But, they'll eventually find peace inside, and I know they'll understand your decision someday."

Amuro folded his arms again. "Grandma? Am I meant to be a...savior?"

Ine gently embraced him. "You can be. You want to be?"

Part Four

A SPRING MIRACLE, 1331

16

TWO OLD FRIENDS

The River Hasu turned into a pink carpet with petals fallen from a row of sakura trees lining its banks. The wind, gusty for two days, had whisked away the transient blooms, leaving the river's surface in irregular undulations. Each gentle sway evoked a tranquil reverie. On the other hand, it masked the turmoil that continued to brew beneath the mesmerizing coating of nature as the water gradually gathered momentum. It had been raining intermittently for days, and distant rumblings of thunder, accompanied by flashes of lightning, heralded an uncharacteristically early spring storm. The air felt heavy and damp, imparting a sense of impending danger.

Kento leaned against the bridge fence, watching the springtime spectacle unfolding on the water. The rain drenched him. His fixed gaze induced a momentary vertigo, and he almost collapsed. As he steadied himself, a surge of negative emotions, stirred by recent arguments with his father, washed over him.

He froze.

Water droplets on his chin dripped down with increasing speed as the rain intensified. The steady drumming of rain on the bridge gradually brought Kento back from the deep state of paralysis. But, he still felt hallucinated. For a while, he gazed toward Mt. Toki, where ominous fog veiled the summit, looming frighteningly before him. He instinctively crouched down, dodging the threatening vapor in front of him, and mumbled what sounded like an incantation of some sort. His eyes remained shut tight, his body trembling as he muttered incomprehensible words.

"Hey there, are you alright?" A loud voice came from behind. Kento slowly turned around and saw a young man approaching. The stranger was equally drenched, without a *mino* — a straw cape. "What on earth are you doing here in this downpour? Are you hurt or something?"

"I...ah...uh, nothing. Just tripped in a gap," defensively responded Kento, eyeing the newcomer suspiciously. He remained on his knees.

"You sure? 'Cause I was watching you. And you didn't trip, you fell like you fainted."

"Did I say, 'faint', huh?" retorted Kento. "No. Like I said, I just tripped on a stupid plank. That's it. Don't make up a whole story about me...please." The young man made an exaggerated shrug. Kento rose to his feet, a proud facade masking his embarrassment.

The young newcomer observed Kento from head to toe, giving him a knowing nod. "Alright, my friend, 'tripped' or 'slipped' if you say so. I just wanted to make sure you're okay."

"Don't you dare patronize me like that!" Kento's eyes flashed. "And I'm not your friend. We've never met before. You're not my brother or anything, either. You're only a stranger in the pouring rain. And you look too young to act like a know-it-all anyway. Just leave me alone." With an indignant look, he abruptly turned away as the rain nearly turned into hail.

"Where're my manners? You're right. Let's start over again, okay?" The newcomer hurried after Kento. "I'm Ryu. How do you do?" While trying to get Kento's attention, he pointed at a nearby shed. "Let's go over there."

Kento finally stopped and took shelter under the eaves. "Hi, Ryu...I'm Kento," said Kento guiltily, "I didn't mean to be rude. I've been having a bad day. Actually, for a while now. I just wanted to be alone."

"It's alright, Kento. Bad days happen all the time." Ryu winced at Kento as he held back a wave of nostalgia. "So Kento, would you mind telling me about yourself?"

"I'm a peasant, or supposed to be one, and live in this suffocating village. What about you?"

"What about me, what about me...hmm," said Ryu, pretending to take his time. "I'd like to call myself a jack-of-all-trades. I've been a peasant, a carpenter, a fisherman, and even a blacksmith, an apprentice though. Now, I'm a seasonal worker looking for whatever job I can get."

"Hmm...I see." responded Kento as he squinted at Ryu. "But, you're not from this village, are you? I know all men my age here. And I've never heard of a young fella who fits your description. So, where are you from, Ryu?"

"Oh, I'm sorry, Kento. I live or used to live in a small region two mountains away from here. I'm sure you've never heard of it. After my family and relatives died from a terrible famine and some infectious disease years ago, one by one, I became a loner. And after my father passed away, I had to do anything and everything to feed myself. There're many young men like me back there. Anyway, that sums up who I've become."

"Wow...you've had some tough life, I can only imagine!" exclaimed Kento. "But...I'm sure you could've had any job you wanted back where you lived. How come you left there?"

"Well...Kento, tell you what. That entire region's gotten just too much for me to bear. Wherever I go, whoever I talk to, the memories I don't want to remember haunt me. My parents, my siblings, uncles, aunts, cousins...and my bride-to-be. The people I cared about. It was almost like reliving those tragedies all over again, you know? And I didn't want to become a prisoner of my own past. I wanted to get out of there and explore my future. A better future. I believe I can find it somewhere else. And this village is my first choice." He winced inside, anxious about his overly rehearsed wording.

Kento shook his head. "You lost me, Ryu, I'm afraid. What's got you fooling yourself so ridiculously? What is a future anyway? We only have miseries ahead of us. One after another. Isn't that what happened to your people? How come you don't see it? Now, you're all alone. And you've driven yourself irrational," he rattled on scornfully as he glared at Ryu's confused face."The best thing we can do with our lives is survive one day at a time. Peasants must not pursue a future."

The cacophony of hail and thunder temporarily drowned out the dead silence between Ryu and Kento. As he examined Kento's twisted expression, Ryu could not help but wonder what had changed the once innocent 7-year-old boy he remembered so vividly as if it had been yesterday. Dejection and self-loathing flared in Kento's eyes. With overwhelming compassion surging up, Ryu suddenly ached to hold Kento and assure him that everything would be alright. "You could use a friend, a good friend," he said instead. "That's what you need right now. Looks like I'm gonna stay in this valley for a while, and I'm sure I'll make a great friend." Ryu beamed at Kento with a mischievous look.

Unexpected joy calmed Kento down, and he quickly masked his tears. Looking at Ryu's smile, he found it oddly familiar, but could not place when and where he had seen it.

——————— * ——————— * ——————— * ——————— *

A week had passed since Ryu's unexpected reunion with

Kento for the first time in ten years in the rain storm. The light cascade from the sky continued to drench the village, turning the fields into shallow marshes.

Huddled behind a towering cedar, Ryu stole glimpses of a rare spectacle unfolding in the distance: the venerable *muneage* ceremony, marking the completion of the framework of the new lord's manor. He watched in awe as the intricate framework reached skyward.

"You'd have to be a load to afford such extravaganza," remarked a peasant standing a few meters away from the tree.

"Have you seen this before, Father?" asked his young son, his eyes glued to the esoteric ceremony.

"Uh-uh. This is the first one in more than forty years."

Ryu's stomach nearly clenched as the constructional ritual continued. Amidst the rain-soaked beams high up, he spotted his father, Gensuke, a figure he saw for the first time since that fateful summer morning a decade ago. His muscular shoulders heaved rhythmically under his *happi*, and thick veins bulged out along his hard thighs as he moved. His ever-vigorous presence evoked not nostalgia for Ryu but an odd sense of deja vu. Shinzan's word of warning — *Do not attach yourself to anybody* — struck him, and he nodded in silent acknowledgment.

Both Gensuke and the lord exuded fearlessness as they showered the jubilant spectators below with coins and food. Each toss ignited fresh fervor among the onlookers. With every shift in Gensuke's position and each bellowed command to the crowd, a nervous pang gripped Ryu's senses.

On the opposite end of the beam, Heijiro crouched, dutifully presenting offerings to the lord. His face beamed with pride at every call from the crowd below, even waving cheerfully as he threw provisions. The young lord, successor to his late father's mantle, then exchanged animated words with Heijiro. Exhilarated, Heijiro smiled at Gensuke and said something animatedly. Overjoyed, Heijiro gestured enthusiastically for his son, Kento, in the crowd to join him on the beam. Nearly two hundred pairs of eyes fixed on the boy in unison.

Kento shook his head three times in defiance, his silent protest rippling through the curious crowd. The people around him slowly backed away and whispered to each other, giving him disapproval looks. Steady streams of water kept falling freely from his chin. He heard nothing but his own heavy breathing.

"Boy, don't you dare embarrass me in front of the whole village. You get up here right now and show them I have a SON!" bellowed Heijiro, his fist trembling, glaring at him. Kento shook his head firmly again. "You have no idea how deeply honored I feel to be invited by our lord and to be part of such a rare ceremony, don't you? Huh? You disgraceful lad!" The lord tapped Heijiro on the shoulder, wincing.

The heavy silence settled over the crowd and drowned out their earlier exuberance. All eyes darted between the father and the son. Kento's distorted expression swung from contempt to agony as he glared back at his enraged father. Yet, he remained unmoving.

"I'm warning you, boy! This is your last chance to change your mind. Now, move your ass and get up here, already!" Heijiro's malicious words pierced through the tense atmosphere.

"No, Father, I won't." Kento corrected his posture and crossed his arms on the chest.

"Don't make me come get you, son!"

"To show people how bigoted you really are?"

"That's it. Get the hell out! Go somewhere far away from me. Anywhere but here. I don't wanna see your sissy face tonight!" Heijiro threw a piece of mochi at Kento. It fell short.

Watching the unexpected family feud, Ryu's heart sank. *This explains why he behaved that way the other day...poor Kento.* He wondered how the once endearing bond between the father and the son had soured over the past decade and why Heijiro spat 'sissy.'

The father and son kept glaring at one another in a silent battle, breathing shallowly. Suddenly, Tami stepped forward from the crowd. "Just cut it out! Both of you! I can't..." Her voice cracked, her head dropped, and tears fell down. Kento looked away and then caught sight of Ryu, who still stood behind the tree. Ryu lowered his half-raised arm as their eyes met. Kento revealed the resigned smile of a captive, his glistening eyes brimming with tears. He approached his mother but then stopped, quickly turning away from the stunned onlookers and heading toward the woods, away from the unfair yet inevitable ignominy. Ryu slipped away from the scene, too, and went after Kento.

When Ryu eventually spotted Kento, his tormented friend was climbing up the stone stairs leading to Kasuga Shrine. Even from a distance, the newly-constructed majestic *torii* gate standing at the landing appeared otherworldly in the misty rain. Ryu trailed silently after Kento until he reached the shrine ground.

There, the violent slam of the front door of the Higashiya startles Ryu. As he approached the building with trepidation, he heard another loud noise from inside, followed by a haunting howl. As soon as he opened the door, yet another resounding bang deafened him. The altar and a small wooden shelf lay toppled on the floor. Also, several smaller objects including a writing set and a few paperweights were scattered all over the room. Black ink splattered across a wall indicated the force of the crash.

In the center of the chaos, Kento knelt on the floor with his back to the door while his fists hammered the hard floor. The heavy, rhythmic thuds and his wails penetrated the otherwise silent room.

Ryu tentatively approached Kento. "Hey, Kento. It's

alright. I'm here for you. Just let it out," he said in a brotherly tone.

Kento stopped pounding, but remained motionless, his head bowed. Then, his shoulders began to shake. Ryu sensed his friend's tears before Kento finally turned his head to face him. His sardonic smile twisted his gentle features, his wet cheeks faintly glistening in the dim space. "It's you again, Ryu, my new friend! Why? You just can't leave me alone, can you?" he blurted out. "You so annoyingly remind me of my old friend, who left me friendless ten years ago,"

Ryu knelt down beside Kento. "So, what happened to your friend? Why did he leave you?" He pretended to be ignorant, masking his unease.

"He died. Or, more like killed himself for the greater good! Supposedly. Ha!" Kento's despairing smile widened. "He turned himself into a hero, a fairy tale, and a legend! 'The icon of the village,' now everybody calls him. What a man! Really...how can anyone despise such a man, huh?" His eyes flashed with bitterness. "Can't they!?"

"I...um...don't know. But how come trashing the shrine has anything to do with your friend's death?"

"Oh, yes, it does! Because this damn shrine, this room right here, was the place he and I stood next to each other for the last time! And three days later, boom, he died and left me! He didn't even say goodbye. But, I was told the truth about his death years later. So, imagine my mild surprise. The thing is, I HAD somehow coped with his sudden disappearance until my father told me. He never should've told me! Why the hell did he..." Kento's voice cracked, more tears streaming down his face. "He... he even said he felt prouder of my dead friend Amuro than of his...his own son. And he still does..."

Without a word, Ryu held his friend in his arms.

17

ANOTHER DRAMATIC ENCOUNTER

Yuri had always stood out for her looks among the children her age from an early age. Boys either picked on her or ignored her deliberately, while girls eagerly asked her to play with them. But then, around the time of her first period, her beauty and brilliance truly began to shine. The elders in the village once praised her for her grace and charm, describing her as 'a breath of fresh air in the remote valley.' Almost all the adolescent boys in the village suddenly gravitated toward her magnetic aura, but her sharp intellect and eloquence ended up outwitting theirs. To those boys, she stood simply out of their league, both inside and out.

Yuri's reputation swiftly had spread beyond the valley. One day, a young heir to a distant lordship paid her a visit in the village. Her beauty aside, the poise and agility she possessed won him over in their first meeting. "He likes you, Yuri. A wealthy, handsome heir likes my daughter," said Katsue proudly. For Yuri, his lack of charm posed no issue, nor did his striking looks and wealth distract her. His intelligence compensated for his shortcomings. "No need to worry about affection now. It'll come to you later." Katsue patted Yuri's thigh.

Yuri smiled sarcastically. "I guess affection brings nothing but a trouble, huh."

"Name any wife you know of who married for love. Hmm?" sighed Katsue and gently poked Yuri's forehead. Yuri winced. "That's right, Yuri. Not even our lord's lady didn't. Women are chosen by men. Not the other way around."

"Is that so?" she asked Katsue challengingly. Yuri's heart ached for only one person.

"Oh no, Yuri...you still — "

"I know, Mother. I know..." Yuri's stomach churned. "'Accept female responsibilities, be a wife, be a mother, accept female responsibilities, be a wife...'" she intoned.

On his second visit, the young successor, Seito, formally proposed to Yuri in front of Gensuke and Katsue. Her unsmiling acceptance did not stain his pride. The daunting realization that she could not have Ryu in her life after all pained her, as did her parents' joy.

Two months later, 16-year-old Yuri left home to assume her role as a woman in a foreign land. Her husband, preoccupied by his own affairs, left little time for them to bond as a couple. Their communication was mostly one-sided, with Yuri doing the most of the talking while her husband showed little interest in reciprocating. Also, from the very beginning their physical relationship lacked intimacy as she had anticipated. Then, as if the cold reception from her in-laws and adopted community did not do enough damage, two miscarriages shattered her spirit. After two years of desolation and isolation, she barely managed to crawl out of the house of oppression. As she dragged her numb body across the same mountainous terrain where she had once been carried by servants amidst the blooming sakuras, she felt cursed. Yet, to passersby, she remained a rare sight — a blend of ephemeral blossoms and mesmerizing beauty in the heart of a remote mountain.

———————— * ———————— * ———————— * ———————— *

"Hey, Sis, when are you gonna marry again?" Kairi casually blurted out, with his mouth full of food. Yuri's chopsticks froze midway to her mouth. She trembled, her expression clouding over. He gave her the side-eye while chowing. The twin boys, Yoriki and Haruki, continued to devour their food, with their cheeks dotted with rice, while Gensuke and Katsue exchanged uneasy glances as they put down their utensils.

The light rain intensified, and the roof began to leak immediately, allowing droplets to fall on the dinner table. A deep woof from behind the door jumped Katsue. She let a soaked Akita in. After circling on the doma, the dog vigorously shook off water. Yuri's face was sprayed, but she remained vacant.

"So, Sis, you're going to, aren't you?" Kairi poked Yuri in the arm.

"Shush! Quit it, Kairi," snapped Katsue as she slapped his thigh. "It's none of your business if your sister remarries or not."

"Oh, but it is, Mother. When she does, she'll leave the house once again and give us all more space. So —"

A loud bang jolted everyone. Gensuke's fist lay heavy on the table as he stared down at the unfinished meal before him. "Enough of this. Let's just appreciate our time together. Can we do that?" His tone imparted calmness and patience. He looked around the table with patriarchal authority. Everybody nodded in unison.

Nearly ten days had slipped by since Yuri's unexpected return home. Yet, she remained mostly silent, withholding the reason behind her shattered marriage vows. Throughout the day, she sat by the irori, her gaze vacantly fixed on the dancing flames and the bellowing smoke that rose to the ceiling, never once leaving the house. Despite that, gossip had already permeated the village as it fueled the curiosity of nosy neighbors craving the tantalizing details.

"You don't owe an explanation to those people, Yuri," said Katsue firmly. "But, at least can you tell me and your father what really happened between you and your husband?" Katsue asked gently after dinner. Gensuke sat silently next to his wife, at a loss for words, nervously toying with the ashes in the irori. Yuri's exhaustingly stubborn silence weighed heavily on them both. "Yuri, please," Katsue begged.

Yuri, seated across from her parents, looked them in the eye through the drifting steam from the iron teapot. "Father, Mother. What did you feel the moment you learned your first baby had died?" she asked, her expression bordering on madness. Katsue and Gensuke's faces contorted, their mouths agape. "And how relieved you felt when you realized you might have another chance?" Her words filled them with guilt, cold and accusing. "Their family doctor told me I'll probably not be able to conceive again," Yuri continued, "even though I did miraculously, the chances of the baby surviving would be slim, considering I've already lost two." Yuri trembled, her emotions oscillating between a fragile smile and tears. "So, Mother, I'm glad you could eventually have five children."

"Oh, no....my poor girl..." Katsue's voice trailed off as she broke down, burying her face in her hands. Gensuke, his head bowed, gently wrapped his strong arms around her shoulders, while Yuri watched her parents weep, her expression vacant.

——————— * ——————— * ——————— * ——————— *

Ryu gazed up helplessly. It had kept pouring like a sieve since he returned to the valley. He involuntarily clutched his chest as vivid mental images of furious, muddy streams swallowing the village consumed him. Even with the clear visibility of the imminent catastrophe in his mind, he grew terrified as he could not pinpoint the exact location, his eyes darting across a riverbank and beyond. Three little boys came into sight as they snuck into a dilapidated house by the river. *If it happened now, those children would be swallowed by the debris.* Despite his concern, the rain continued to intensify.

Ryu and Kento leaned against the shed by the River Hasu as they observed the rising water and its enraged current. The mesmerizing sakura petals that had adorned the river's surface just days earlier had now gone, replaced by debris and torn branches being rapidly carried downstream. Ryu continued scanning the surroundings anxiously while listening to Kento half-heartedly.

"....had the usual argument last night. He made it clear this time that he would disown me if I kept '*doing what I've been doing,*' because he doesn't want a '*soft son.*'" Kento's words carried unmasked contempt as he mimicked his father's tone and mannerism. "Soft, really?" he asked rhetorically. "You think drawing is soft? Unmasculine? All the artists I've heard of are men. History proves it. I know it won't pay at all unless you train through an apprenticeship. Unfortunately, I'm a son of a peasant, so I'm supposed be one, too. I'm aware of that, of course. But what if I moved to a strange land where nobody knows who I am? I know what I'm good at, Ryu." He took out a piece of paper from his shabby kimono. An elaborate, india ink landscape sprung into life. "What do you think of..." Ryu's intense gaze fixed on the water, prompting Kento to pause. "I'm sorry? Am I boring you? I guess I am. Our conversations have been always about me since we met."

"What? I'm sorry Kento I was just lost in thought," responded Ryu, finally turning his attention to Kento. "No, you're not boring me, and no, drawing is not unmasculine. It's just that your father doesn't understand your passion."

"Are you defending him? He is such a bigot!"

"Is he? Since when? He wasn't, the last time I talked to —" Ryu stopped himself.

"What're you talking about? Have you met my father before?? You told me you had never been in this village before we met."

"Of course, I haven't met him. Sorry, I'm still preoccupied by the river situation. It's dangerously high now. It's gonna overflow if the rain continues." Ryu's heart beat fast.

"Hmm, ok. Let's hear it. This is your topic."

They began to walk toward the bridge for a better view of the water. Then, they noticed a young woman halfway across. Her umbrella sealed her face. As Ryu and Kento passed her, she lifted her umbrella just enough to acknowledge them.

Surprised, Kento spoke up. "Yuri?? Is that you?"

"Oh, hi, Kento, long time no see," replied Yuri with a look of resignation and sorrow. "Yes, it's me."

"So, it's true after all. I heard you had come back, but... umm, I'm really sorry. I don't know what to say. But I don't wanna pry, Yuri —"

"Then, don't, please," Yuri pled.

"Yes...right. I know exactly how it feels to be the subject of conversations."

An awkward silence crept on the bridge.

"Thanks, Kento," mumbled Yuri and lowered her gaze.

"Oh, by the way, this is my new friend, Ryu," he said in a cheerful tone. "He's an expat but a rare gem."

Yuri's breath instantly caught in her throat. Her heart began to pound violently, while her mouth dried out. The cold, pouring rain stopped around Ryu and Yuri, and nothing hindered her from seeing him clearly. At the same time, everything around Ryu vanished before her eyes, leaving him the only reality. Her breathing became shallow. She flinched at his every little movement, feeling sharp stings in her chest. Yet, she kept staring at him as she tried to enter his head. *Does he remember me at all? If so, what does he see inside of me? He finds a mature woman in me?* Unconsciously, she traced the contours of his face, so asymmetrical and so beautiful. Then, with the same fingers, she fondled her trembling lips, coloring them in his hues and tasting his existence. Streams of water dripping from his chin made her thirsty. When Ryu noticed her hidden eagerness, she reflexively looked away, mortified. His tender smile bound and suffocated her, and she lost all her senses.

"It's you from the coast, five years ago. Wow, you've... grown. I mean, you look so different I didn't recognize you right away." Ryu lied, though he remembered every detail — her mischievous dimples and her defensive frowns. He felt himself losing control, his cheeks blushing in the rain.

"Wait...you two have met before? Fives years ago?" Kento's eyes widened as he pieced together the scene in his mind. "But, again, you told me you've never been here, Ryu. What else are you keeping from me?"

"I've been honest, Kento. I just forgot about the incident, and never realized the coast was part of this village." Ryu winced.

"What incident?" Kento demanded.

"He saved me from drowning in the ocean," interjected Yuri with a wet voice, her words pleading to Ryu's heart. Ryu's heart skipped a beat.

"...Okay. But how come you were in this village, Ryu?" Kento narrowed his eyes.

"Uh...Oh yeah, it was a two-day excursion, I remember now. Right around when my mother passed away. I needed to get away from everything in my village." Ryu made up the story like a pathological liar.

Yuri let out a faint gasp. "Didn't you say at the beach that you were from Inaki?" she asked with keen interest. "I asked my cousin who married into a family there, and she told me she didn't know anyone named Ryu."

Ryu cursed himself inside, feeling cornered. *I should've gotten my story straight before coming back to the village or from the very beginning.* The four inquisitive eyes of Yuri and Kento firmly bore into him as his mind raced. For a moment, he considered telling them the truth, but quickly dismissed the idea. *Who would believe such a story anyway*, he thought. Ryu fidgeted, face down, his hand nervously stroking through his soaked hair. "Well...you know what...umm..." His words trailed off. Kento and Yuri continued to stare at him with a perplexed expression, expecting an explanation.

Then, something snapped under their feet, and the next moment the trio fell into the murky river. The water, deeper than ever, instantly engulfed their vulnerable bodies. They found themselves at the mercy of the relentless current before the shock of the icy plunge even registered. Their bodies helplessly drifted downstream like straw scarecrows in the fury of nature's wrath. Ryu, in a frantic struggle, somehow managed to break the surface. He gasped for air as he fought to regain his bearings amidst the tumultuous flow. Yet, the raging water toyed with him mercilessly, refusing to yield to his desperate attempts at control. Panicked and disoriented, he desperately stretched his arms as fallen leaves, twigs and branches passed him. His head bobbed like a buoy in the stormy ocean, his sight constantly blocked with each bob. Confusion clouded his sight as he grappled with the reality of the situation he was in. All the while, the dark water made him gag, and he fought to spit it out. When he glanced toward the bridge they had stood on moments earlier, he saw only two poles sticking out of the water at either bank. Just then, a large timber, likely a fragment of the destroyed bridge, drifted close, and Ryu clung to it all his might.

Meanwhile, on a distant stretch of riverbank, Kento struggled to haul himself onto solid ground. He lay face down on the sodden meadow and forcibly coughed out the dirty water from his lungs until the violent heaves of his shoulders subsided. He squinted through blurred vision to find Ryu battling the current while clinging desperately to the timber. Kento waved his hand frantically as he shouted. But, the deafening roar of the river drowned out his words. With a shrinking hope, he watched Ryu drifting further and further down the river. Before long, Ryu disappeared from Kento's view.

As Ryu was carried further away from the village by the violent current, his thoughts raced to Yuri's safety. He frantically threw his head right and left, his eyes darting from drifting branches to a timber and over the bank. With the heavy rain subsided, now powerful gusts buffeted him. He struggled to stay afloat on the timber. There was no sigh of Yuri, in the water and on the riverbank. Panic gnawed at him as he remembered the looming waterfall at the river's end with its treacherous cluster of sea stacks below. "Yuri! Yuri!" he bellowed between anguished gasps.

The serene landscapes of the bucolic village had long disappeared, replaced by untamed fields. Suddenly, his eyes caught a black dot bobbing near the cliff's edge: Yuri's head, motionless and unconscious, her body entrapped by a limb sticking out of a large pine tree. To his horror, he noticed that it was slowly breaking away with each blow of the current. Ryu instinctively abandoned his timber and swam with all his might toward the water's edge. Upon reaching the ground, he sprinted toward Yuri, who dangled precariously above the churning water.

Ryu scanned the area and found a fallen branch. He repeatedly shoved it forward to catch her, fighting against the raging current, yet each attempt pushed her away. With a final desperate lunge, he managed to snag her clothes, right before the lifeline limb finally gave way. He gently laid Yuri down on solid ground and checked her pulse. Weak yet stable beats slightly lessened his tension. All the while, she continued shivering, half-conscious. Urging her so stay still and breathe slowly, he cradled her in his arms and gently wiped dirt from her pale forehead as relief flooded through him. "Yuri, are you okay? Just focus on breathing." His voice trembled.

"Umm...I, ahh...," moaned Yuri in a raspy voice.

"Oh, Yuri..." Ryu's heart clenched while he rubbed her wet body.

"Ryu, is that you?" Yuri, with her eyes closed, mumbled weakly.

Her shivering had intensified, her temperature dangerously low to the touch. "Come on, Yuri, hang on," he said gently. The wind had picked up, and the daylight was waning. He swiftly hoisted Yuri on his back and set off toward the home he still remembered.

18

HOMECOMING

The village Ryu had left ten years ago welcomed him with a sense of newness. The well-maintained fields and hills, instead of the stretch of barren land, shone with abundant produce and wild plants, releasing fresh grass smell. The once arid rice paddies silently waited for their time.

On his way to the house of his birth, Ryu passed many familiar faces, feeling strange. They had aged a decade since his departure. But, to him, it felt merely a year or two. "Time," he mused, "must bend differently in the afterlife." Most of them immersed themselves in their daily tasks or propping up their homes against storms and paid little attention to Ryu and Yuri. Yet, some cast disapproving glances at the sight of a well-known girl piggybacked by a complete stranger.

Two women on a narrow footpath by the rice paddies exchanged whispers, their vegetable sacks dangling from their hands. "So, yup, that's Karube's daughter all right. What happened to that girl, coming back home after barely two years?" said one of them, her eyes narrowing.

"Your guess is as good as mine. And who is that young

fella? Wow...is she eloping with him or what?" The other one shook her head.

"Ohh... maybe that's the reason she fled her marriage? That must be it. What a shocker!"

"Well, well, well. Never thought the day would come when the prominent Karube family had to go through shame and disgrace." Both women pursed their lips as they followed the back of the young pair traversing across the field.

Ryu took a shortcut through Kasuga Shrine. As he had anticipated, the sacred place was virtually deserted after the heavy rainfall. Its derelict state saddened him, the doors detached and broken, mildews spreading on the walls. He noticed that the buildings were leaking from multiple spots and could not shake the worry about whether they could endure the forthcoming rainy season.

A long straight path along thick woods that lay by the shrine came into view. A feeling of nausea crept up on him, and his legs went numb. He stopped for a while, watching himself walking on this very path that summer morning ten years ago. Suddenly, Yuri felt heavier on his back, bringing him back to the present.

Upon reaching a sharp turn where a large cedar stood, Ryu arrived back home and his past. The humble facade remained unchanged, whereas other aspects had seen deserving improvements. Gensuke's workshop now boasted an additional shed and a roofed hallway connected to the house, and a long *engawa* had been installed where the south-facing wall once stood. Even a well pump had been installed between the house and the workshop. A small vegetable garden along the *engawa* adorned the modest property as a finishing touch.

When Ryu stood before the sliding door, with Yuri still on his back, a large Akita came pounding toward him from behind the workshop. The dog stopped by his side and sniffed at Yuri's foot, whimpering. "Taro, what is it?" yelled a male voice. Gensuke emerged from his workshop, hammer in hand. "Come back here, boy, Hey, Taro..." Gasping in horror, he dropped the hammer and yelped, "Yu...Yuri! What happened?" He stared at his daughter's wet hair and clothes, and at the stranger carrying her.

"She was washed away in the river...um...sir," answered Ryu, suppressing his strange emotions, neither sentimental nor rueful. "We were on the bridge and it collapsed all of a sudden. Kento was with us, too."

Ignoring Ryu's response, Gensuke caressed Yuri's forehead, his face turning as pale as hers.

"Sir, she needs hot porridge or soup as soon as possible. Do you have it ready? Her temperature is still very low."

"Umm...I think so. My wife is fixing something in the house," responded Gensuke, then fixed a hard stare on Ryu. "Who are you, young man? I've never seen you before."

"I'm Ryu, sir, a friend of Kento's," said Ryu tentatively. "I recently relocated to this valley." He awkwardly looked away, his head down.

"Well, thank you so much, Ryu, for saving my daughter's life," said Gensuke, admiring the young man who had rescued his daughter. He saw Ryu's clothes dripping. "It must've been cold out there. What you did is beyond brave. Come, come inside, please. My wife will want to thank you, too. And fill yourself up something hot." Gensuke placed a firm hand on the young stranger's shoulder.

"Umm...thank you, sir. I'd really appreciate your hospitality, but that won't be necessary. Please, take her inside and feed her. I'd much happier when she fully recovers."

"Oh, don't be silly, young man. We're deeply indebted to you. Please, this is just a fraction of our gratitude. And I won't take no for an answer!" Gensuke beamed at Ryu as he pushed him inside the house, nodding approvingly to himself.

Ryu's eyes darted everywhere as he took in the interior of the house. The irori still occupied the center of the family-cum-living room that also served as the sleeping quarters for Gensuke and Katsue. Separated by a thin shoji screen door from the living room sat a smaller room that had once been Ine's nursing room and was now occupied by three boys. The *doma*, with its earthen floor, appeared slightly smaller than Ryu remembered, yet it boasted a larger cooking area with an additional cauldron atop the fire pit. Despite the familiarity of the details, none of it resonated with him. It was simply someone else's house. And he felt a sense of relief in that realization. *Never be attached to anything and anyone from the past*, he reminded himself.

After a series of heartfelt expressions of gratitude and a hastily prepared porridge, Ryu went over details of the river flood, while Gensuke and Katsue sat silently beside the irori. Yuri slumbered peacefully behind her parents, whereas her three younger brothers, Kairi, Yoriki, and Haruki, engrossed themselves in the reading material Katsue had made for them. Ryu beamed at them with brotherly curiosity.

Ryu shifted on a zabuton and fidgeted with his hands as he kept stealing a glance at his parents. He noticed the changes that time and grief had etched on Katsue's face and the streaks of gray that now mingled with Gensuke's hair and beard. He cleared his throat, toyed with the ashes, and avoided making eye contact by studying the ceiling.

"I never thought you existed. Yuri talked about you all the time and...yes, she's been right for all these years." Katsue said to Ryu, her eyes sparkling with admiration.

"What? I'm sorry, ma'am?" responded Ryu, feigning confusion.

"Five years ago, she told me you two had met at the beach or out in the ocean. Her story was so bizarre I thought she had made it all up." Katsue was still smiling.

"Ahh, I see. Yes, ma'am, she and I did meet at the coast. I happened to be there and saw her struggling in the water. Jumped in and pulled her out. It was nothing heroic or anything like that, really. In fact, I had totally forgotten about it until now." The lie made him feel guilty.

"Oh, so you actually saved her twice, Ryu!" exclaimed Gensuke, "that IS quite something, young man!"

"It was just a coincidence, Sir," Ryu replied instinctively and scratched his forehead.

Ryu's gesture triggered a flood of memories for Katsue. "This might sound insane, but, you very much remind me of our late son Amuro," she paused to glance at her husband and continued, "he would often scratch his forehead, just like you did, when he got nervous. And he would've been around your age if he were still alive. It's just...you know." Her tone became soft as she reminisced.

Ryu winced and looked away, again, awkwardly. *What am I doing here??* He cleared his throat, once again. "Umm... so, speaking of coincidences, sir, I actually saw you the other day during the muneage ceremony. Was the man next to you the new lord?"

"Oh, yes, indeed. There's something quite magnetic about him. And graciously generous as well. In a stark contrast to his late father, if I may be honest. Somehow he's fond of me and my friend Heijiro, who played his part with me on the beam." Gensuke exaggeratedly corrected his posture, his voice becoming boisterous.

"And they're all about the same age," interjected Katsue.

"Right on, Sir. I still remember how harsh the former lord — excuse me, MY lord was. And that majestic framework is going to be the new lord's mansion?"

"That's correct. And it's going to be something beyond anyone's imagination. Just look at the sheer size of it!"

"Yes, indeed, sir," agreed Ryu politely, though in his mind, he pictured the Archive and its opulent architecture.

"But the hillside sits right behind the premises, and that's a small concern we should take account of. It's been always vulnerable, and with all the rain —"

"The hill!" Ryu's shriek made Gensuke and Katsue jump.

In an instant, the atrocious images flooded back into Ryu's mind: villagers screaming and running from an immeasurable surge of wet earth and debris, some swallowed by the mud, others swept away. And he vividly saw the sturdy woodwork of the manor being completely devoured by the relentless force of the mudslide.

"Are you alright, Ryu? You looked like you just saw a ghost." Katsue knitted her brow.

"What about the hill, Ryu?" added Gensuke, equally puzzled.

"Sir, ma'am, I'm terribly sorry, but I've got to go now!" Ryu blurted out. "It's just...Please, forgive my rudeness."

With that, he sprinted out of the house, leaving the married couple speechless in his wake.

19

THE RAINY NIGHT PHENOMENON

Dusk had fallen already. Flocks of bats monopolized the sky, flying freely in the dark. Hardly anyone was outside, the air chilly and laden with moisture. Despite the cold, Ryu was sweating profusely as he ran, his thoughts racing. The horrifying mudslide relentlessly played its terror in his mind. "Can I stop the disaster?" he mumbled unconsciously.

Ryu took a shortcut through the pitch-dark shrine. Near the main sanctuary, two silhouettes moved toward him. As he drew closer, the lanterns the pair held illuminated their faces: a woman and a young girl. He instantly recognized Tami, Kento's mother. "Oh, good evening, Mrs. Tami!" he nearly blurted out. "Umm... this might sound quite strange to you, but... please, stay here overnight and get in the Higashiya."

Tami's mouth hung halfway open, her dilated pupils glittering with the lantern light. "Wha...what're you talking about? How come you know my name? Who the hell are you??"

"I'm sorry, ma'am, but there's no time to introduce myself properly. Please, do not go back to your home. There may be a mudslide coming from the hill behind the manor construction site. It would be catastrophic."

"A what?? I don't understand. You sound insane. Are you all right, young man?"

Ryu let out a heavy sigh. "Look, Mrs. Tami, I quite understand how my story sounds to you. But, please, stay here just in case. I'll fetch your husband and Kento." With that, he dashed off into the pitch black.

"Mother, who is that? Do you know that man?" asked Chisa, Tami's daughter.

"Weirdo. That's what he is," Tami replied, frowning. "And listen, honey. Promise me not to marry a man like that."

Ryu continued to run, his strides steady despite the strain on his legs and lungs. The construction site lay near the village border, while the shrine sat diagonally opposite on the map. As slimy, slippery fields considerably slowed his progress, he cursed between laborious breaths while fighting to push vivid, horrid images of the village being washed away out of his mind. His body begged for rest, his mouth sucked out of saliva. He stopped at a communal well. After a short yet precious break, he resumed his run, racing against time.

Ryu finally came to a halt near Heijiro's home. His fear returned as the village's geography confirmed that the house stood in the path of the impending mudslide. No lights shone inside, no signs of activity. He knocked on the door of a neighbor of Heijiro's. An elderly man opened the door and growled in Ryu's face. "Umm...good evening, sir. I'm so sorry to bother you like this." Ryu paused, putting on an innocent face, and added, "Do you happen to know where your next door might be?" The man growled again and slammed the door with *'No!'* "Sir, you might want to evacuate — " He changed his mind, scanning the residential area, and sprinted toward the lord's construction site.

After racing on an uphill with a grueling effort, Ryu arrived at the construction site. The grand framework of the new manor loomed under the half-veiled moon. The area lay still, completely devoid of human activities. He pressed his palm hard on the glassy ground. Runoff instantly seeped over the back of his hand. He clicked his tongue.

Thunder rumbled over a distant mountain. And a strong gust slammed on cedars lining the rim of the hill. "That's it," Ryu said to himself as he grew more tense. He rushed over to the hill behind the construction site. A narrow path ran between the premises and the foot of the hill. With measured steps, he traversed its width and nodded with confidence, although the tension gripped his mind. Methodically, he inspected each towering cedar encircling the hill, tapping them with a plank to assess their density and sound. When he reached twentieth tree, he stopped his sacred ritual. With premeditated precision, he then gently touched his selected trees and whispered something to each one.

As if on cue, rain began to fall. He shut his eyes.

As if propelled by an immeasurable force of wind, twenty massive cedars soared into the air one after another, reaching heights of about fifty meters. Soon, a massive square frame took shape, outlined against the backdrop of the dim sky. It hovered for a while, each cedar adjusting its angle and position. A series of swishing sounds echoed across the hill as they moved. Then, shifting to a shiplap-like structure with spaces between the laps, the trees shed all their leaves and branches on the ground. A neat, massive floating raft appeared at last, poised in the air to serve its purpose.

Ryu slowly opened his eyes, his dilated pupils flickering from within while his slim body rhythmically swayed like a reed in the wind. With his arms outstretched above his head, he gazed at the formation of the timbers, then began to intone something between a mantra and a magic spell. Heavy raindrops pelted his face as his chant grew louder and increasingly unintelligible.

A bolt of lightning struck the hilltop, followed by another and another. The fourth bolt hit the ground where Ryu stood, but he remained unscathed. His body emitted rays of light, aglow and mystical, encircled by an effulgent sphere. Then, with a piercing shrill, he swung his arms downward. The hovering timbers stopped swaying, and the next moment the bottommost timber dropped horizontally onto the hill's edge. Immediately after that, the one that formed the bottom fell and perfectly landed on top of its predecessor. Another timber followed suit. After the fifth timber landed, the configuration stood like a wall taller than the most houses around the hill.

Ryu repeated his abstruse performances. And before long, another configuration emerged right in front of the first one, doubling the wall. After the second layer, he performed the ritual one more time. When he finally completed his task, he dropped to all fours on the soggy ground, violently shaking. The threefold timber fortress soared almost ten meters high before him.

Slowly, Ryu regained consciousness, though his face had become as pale as Shinzan. He staggered to his feet and banged on the timber walls. Nodding firmly, he leaned against them, with his ear over the coarse bark. A heavy rumble from the other side of the wall made him recoil.

All of a sudden, the rain-soaked slope gave way with such force, like an avalanche. The earth began to roar, the combined sounds of trees being uprooted and heavy soil bellowing. Within seconds, the entire hill collapsed downward while toppling and swallowing everything in its path.

A moment later, the first wave of the raging nature attacked the fortress, wet masses of dirt and clay flying. Ryu instinctively jumped back. The second and third waves came in no time, causing tremors on the ground upon impact. The relentless pounding and the incessant groans of earth seemed to last forever. Bracing himself in the dark, he paced around, his bloodshot eyes glued to the all. Constant bangs made the fortress squeal, but it firmly held its ground.

Eventually, rumbles and vibrations, together with lightning, died down as abruptly as when they had started. The night reclaimed its usual stillness as if nothing had ever happened. Ryu tried to focus on the tranquility. Only the rhythmic sound of rain pervaded his surroundings. He quickly scanned the area, then climbed up the timber walls he had conjured.

The top of the walls overlooked the neighborhood where Ryu had stopped by earlier. Lights from the houses relieved his dread. He spotted several lantern light slowly coming toward the construction site. On the other side of the wall, dirt had accumulated almost as high as the top timber, the matte black horizon merging with the darkness of the night. Every part of the once verdant slope had disappeared, dark soil beneath the grass exposed. The lord's cabin, once perched on the highest point of the hill, had turned into ruins before colliding with the walls. An intense earthy smell permeated the ground zero. Standing on the top of the walls, he began to shake uncontrollably. *Have I done this??*

Soon, Ryu heard voices and footsteps getting closer to him. "Hey, folks, what on earth are we looking at?" said a male voice at the bottom of the walls. Ryu quickly jumped over the top timber and, upon landing on the newly emerging field, dashed toward the River Hasu.

Ryu's mind raced as his premonition replayed in his head. The rain continued to pelt the area. While he traversed through the neighborhood where a potential flood threatened, a jolt of terror grabbed his heart as all the homes stood defenseless. Thunderous sounds of the raging River Hasu came from where the bridge had collapsed in the afternoon, and Ryu increased his pace.

Upon arriving at the vulnerable banks, Ryu gasped. The river surged ominously, its surface nearly level with the banks, leaving him no time to spare. Sizable oak trees stood along the river. He hastily selected forty or so of them and replicated the earlier ritual. The trees flew high above his head, transforming into timbers as they shed their leaves, and lay flat on top of the previous one along the water's edge. Makeshift levees soon came to life atop the banks on the either side, broader platforms as opposed to tall walls like those at the hill.

The next moment, the vicious muddy streams, with deafening roars, charged the levees, yet they found no weak spot. Trapped between the sturdy barriers, the water redirected its course downstream, flowing away from the threatened homes and toward the ocean.

Ryu, as he listened to the menacing sounds the current created as it scraped the riverbed, endure the overwhelming exhaustion he had never felt before and fell on his back on the levee with his eyes closed. A sudden clack immediately brought him back to consciousness. Frightened, he darted a glance at the direction of the sound, but saw nothing but the glow from the houses. Ryu sluggishly got up, scanning the area one more time, and left the riverside.

Hidden behind a lone oak tree standing away from the bank, Kyubei, a Kasuga merchant, trembled in awe with his mouth wide open, his hand grasping a broken twig. He could not think straight. *How?? How could anyone...? What have I just witnessed?* Despite his disbelief, a cunning idea took hold. "I could exploit this witchcraft for my gain. And I'll find out more about this son of a bitch, one way or another," he muttered to himself defiantly as he watched the young wizard walk away from the river.

———————— * ———————— * ———————— * ———————— *

Dawn was slowly breaking over Mt.Toki.

A hint of sunlight appeared across the purple sky for the first time in nearly ten days. The rain storms that had saturated the valley finally passed, leaving the dump air gradually drying up. The lingering fog shrouding the forest had begun to lift as well.

"It's going to be a nice day at last," panted Ryu while climbing up the Sacred Path. Extreme fatigue blurred his eyesight as the two consecutive conjurings had taken their toll on him physically and mentally. He stumbled on a mossy rock and hit his shoulder against a tree. His heavy groan sent a flock of birds flying out of the forest. Summoning all remaining strength, he finally managed to drag himself into his cave.

Once inside, Ryu collapsed face down on the cold floor and closed his eyes for a moment's respite. When he finally sat up, 20-year-old Ryu had transformed back into 4-century-old Shinzan. The sennin breathed in and out shallowly, adjusting to the damage his body had endured, then coughed and groaned theatrically. "Oh, what a memorable act of god it was, wasn't it, boy?" he exclaimed, with his both arms stretched out, his tone laced with unmasked mockery. But, no answer came in his head. "Hello? Am I here alone?"

"I'm here, sir. I'm sorry. Fatigue temporarily shut my mind off." Amuro's voice echoed matter-of-factly in Shinzan's head.

Impatient, Shinzan pressed on. "Yes, I hear you, and I know a thing or two about mental strength myself," he said, as if talking to someone sitting right in front of him. "Oh, by the way, haven't I stressed the importance of minimizing contact with the locals? That the less the better? You spent too much time with that boy and your parents yesterday, which was utterly foolish —"

"We"

"Look, son, I am trying to reason with you, whether you like it or not," said Shinzan and drew a heavy sigh. "You need to be more discreet than you think. If you think you're being cautious, think twice before going into your old home. You almost exposed yourself."

"Yes, I understand. That was a monumentally stupid move."

"What you're doing proves impossible. Earning the locals' trust while minimizing contact with them requires more than a mere miracle. Once you turn into Ryu, I won't be able to assist you in any way. I can't even communicate with you, as you already know. It's all on you."

"Yes, sir, I'm well aware of that."

"And I probably don't need to remind you about this, but, never let anyone see you use your power. Understand? Once that happens, it's all over. Your grand plans will come to nothing."

"Yes, sir, I'm well aware of that as well."

Shinzan crossed his arms and shook his head. "I have no idea what you hope to achieve by being insolent. I don't know where you've picked that up from, either."

"Maybe from you, sir."

"What?"

"Nothing, sir. I just want to feel close to you..."

"What are you getting at, son?"

"Never mind, sir. Please, forgive my insolence. And please, rest well, sir." With that, Amuro's voice evaporated into the air.

Shinzan groaned loudly. *I'd probably never be able to truly understand him.*

20

FOUL SNORT, VILE FACADE

Ever since the mysterious walls and platforms emerged seemingly out of thin air on that rainy night, the whole village had been consumed by absurd hypotheses regarding who had built them and how. With no one stepping forward to claim responsibility for the peculiar structures, the eager locals indulged in wild speculations. Some speculated that the new lord had commissioned the creation. Others believed that some people in Inaki had simply sought to make Kasuga indebted to them. Some of the elders even attributed the phenomenon to their god, suggesting miraculous intervention. In the end, the villagers concluded that their land existed in incomprehensible ways, much like the miracle from ten years ago had proved.

Two months after narrowly escaping the potential disaster, the construction of the new lord's manor completed the architectural innovation. The three-story mansion screamed its opulence louder than the residence of the former ruler. Its pristine white, plastered walls, a stark contrast to the wooden houses of the peasants, gleamed brilliantly in the late spring sun. Accentuated by the *yakisugi* roofs and framed against backdrop of the blue sky, the manor exuded a picturesque aesthetic. The onlookers, including those from neighboring communities, murmured their admiration and confirmed the manor exceeded their wildest imagination.

"So, this is the latest talk of the valley, huh?" said Yuri to Kento, "how delightful to see them find something else to gossip about."

"Right, I get it, Yuri," replied Kento to Yuri's sarcastic remark. "But don't you think it's so impressive? I've never seen a building like this in my life." He gazed up at the grand structure. "No wonder my father raved about this so much."

"But don't forget, Kento. I've lived in more ostentatious estate for two years," Yuri retorted.

Kento stole an empathetic glance at her. "So, anyway, we're here to talk about Ryu, right?"

"Yes, Kento, and I hope you've heard from him?" Yuri asked.

Ever since the river accident, the pair had been meeting regularly to exchange information about Ryu, who had vanished without a trace. They both had grown attached to him, particularly Yuri, whose suppressed feelings had developed into an obsession.

"To be honest, I don't know much about him. He never spoke much about himself, aside from why he came to this village. He didn't even tell me where he lives at the moment. And apparently, no one has seen him for almost two months since the three of us got washed away in the river."

Disappointment clouded Yuri's expression. "We're completely stuck..."

Since her unexpected homecoming, Yuri had become the subject of whispered gossip among the villagers who had somehow learned the true reason behind her sudden return. Wherever she went, she had to deal with a mixture of sympathetic glances and disapproval stares, as if being accused of some unspoken transgression. Then, after years of absence, her reunion with Ryu unfolded as dramatically as their initial encounter. Thoughts of him served as a welcome diversion from the events of the past two years and the prying eyes of nosy neighbors.

"He's a bit secretive, but I'm sure he'll show up again soon," Kento said, with a firm nod. "I don't believe he's gone for good. So, try not to worry too much about him."

"I'll do my best, thanks, Kento," responded Yuri, her voice faltering slightly. "You're so compassionate and insightful. Girls in this village are blind and have no idea what they're missing out on."

"Uh...umm, Yuri, I'm not so sure about that." Kento looked away, scratching his head.

"Oh, yes, Kento. They absolutely are." Yuri mischievously smirked. "Speaking of girls, out of all the boys in this village, you're the only one who's never come on to me. And I wonder you have someone special in mind? I'm just curious."

Now, Kento had visibly blushed, nervously toying with a thin branch he had picked up earlier. *I can't possibly share the real reason with anyone, especially her. How can I tell her I adored her dead brother so much in a completely wicked way?*

"N-not like that, Yuri," stammered Kento, sensing her innocent gaze. "I...I've got other passions to pursue, rather than chasing after girls."

"Your artistic talent, right? Sure, Kento, if you say so." Yuri gave him a friendly chuckle.

"No, I'm telling you the truth, Yuri. I'm so committed to the art of drawing. And that's why I'm seriously considering seeking an apprenticeship in a distant region beyond this valley."

"But...what about your family and your father?" Yuri asked, worried.

"I couldn't care less about my father," Kento spat. "If he wants to disown me over this, then so be it."

"You've certainly grown into a young man, Kento." Yuri's

tone conveyed admiration. "Whatever you decide, I'll support it. Nobody will take your passion away from you."

"Believe it or not, Ryu is the one who inspired me to follow my path. He shared his story of how he had carved out his own path all alone after losing his parents and relatives. And I want to experience that kind of self-reliance, just like him."

"Well, that's another reason for us to find Ryu and get to know him, then," Yuri said. She shielded her eyes from the sun as she pointed at the lumber walls. "I just heard someone caught a glimpse of a stranger standing on top of that thing in the rain. Right after the earth stopped rumbling. Do you think it could've been him?"

"Could be, considering we rarely see strangers in this village. But I don't know, Yuri —"

"Tell me, young lovers, that you two are talking about a lanky young fella, say, around twenty years of age?" interjected a reedy voice.

Startled, Kento and Yuri slowly turned around. An unexpected man greeted them with a forged smile, much like a vile facade that people would want to smack. The pair instantly became repulsive.

"Well... are you or are you not?" demanded the noxious merchant, completely ignoring the defiant expression of the young pair.

"Ah, good afternoon, Sir Kyubei," responded Yuri with exaggerated amiability, emphasizing the word 'Sir.' "What a lovely day today. Isn't it?"

Kento, lowering his head, managed to suppress a snicker.

Unfazed by her derision, Kyubei kept his insincere smiles. "Yes, indeed, young lady, especially after all those storms." His expression gleamed with eagerness. "Anyway, about the young fella. I'll take your non-response as a yes. Are you familiar with his whereabouts? Where to find him? I know you both know him. I heard that you two were hitting it off with him quite well two months ago. Especially you, young lady, riding on his back all the way home." He gave Yuri the side-eye.

Yuri's noses swelled instantly, her face flushing. "Sir, I'm not quite sure what you're insinuating," she countered. "Seems like you've been misinformed."

Kyubei let out a snort. "And what about you, lad?" demanded Kyubei, "tell me you know this individual." His voice dripped with condescension.

"I know of no such individual, sir, I'm afraid," replied Kento calmly, his expression neutral as he shrugged. "However, I'd recommend trying Inaki. I've heard there are lots of lankier young fellas over there." Yuri nodded with agreement.

A flush on Kyubei's face vanished as quickly as it had appeared. He plastered his insincere smile back on his face, feigning ignorance. His gaunt features oozed with deep-seated hubris as he inspected the reactions from Kento and Yuri. Then, without another word, he turned his back to them and slowly sauntered off.

The pair whispered to each other as they stared at Kyubei's back, exchanging puzzled looks.

Before long, however, Kyubei's march came to a halt. Casually scanning his surroundings, he fervently waved to Kento and Yuri. All the eyes around him fixed on him. "Oh, young man. Almost forgot to congratulate you on the MANLY hobby of yours! Your father told me you're quite an abnormal boy, whatever that means! And as for you, miss lady, my sincere condolences to you and your UNBORN babies!" His high-pitched voice echoed across the area.

He remained there, smirking, as the murmurs of the crowd turned into sweet music.

Kyubei returned to his store, Tsubaki-Ya, which sat on the village's busiest street.

His business had been thriving for decades, especially since the famine had miraculously ended. His store stocked a variety of essential items: all kinds of household products, farming, fishing, and hunting tools, and even clothing. The only commodity he did not offer was food. Rumors had always circulated that he had an indirect access to the *bakufu* — a shogun's government —in Kamakura. They somewhat explained why he had become one of the wealthiest merchants in the entire province, despite his predominantly peasant clientele.

The Tsubaki-Ya employees scattered upon hearing their employer hum a cheerful melody as he emerged from the back-room. Kyubei greeted them just as cheerfully, further paralyzing them. Nonchalantly checking the inventory, he chuckled, "I can't get enough of those idiots' torment!" Kento and Yuri's humiliation in public had made him elated. "The young and ignorant need to learn a lesson."

Kyubei summoned two teenage apprentices who ran all kinds of errands. Both boys instantly froze when they entered their boss's room. Kyubei greeted them with a shrill voice, like a wounded bird, and curtly gestured for them to sit down. But, the two *zabutons* that lay stacked right next to them remained neglected.

The merchant opened his both arms theatrically. "So," he began, "I often hear you two are obedient and quite dedicated to your duties. That's wonderful, because it's crucial for young fellas like yourselves to listen carefully to your superiors and follow their instructions. That's the key to becoming a successful merchant. Isn't it?"

The fledgling workers shifted simultaneously on a hard tatami but remained mute, unsure of how to respond.

"ISN'T IT?" demanded Kyubei.

"Y-yes, sir, I think so, sir," the taller boy replied.

"You *think*, huh? What's your name, boy?"

"It's Rikiya, sir." His voice grew fainter, sounding almost guilty. He bent half, his forehead touching the tatami.

"And I'm Sota, sir," added the other boy, his voice trembling like a death rattle.

"Speak only when spoken to," commanded Kyubei, his pitch cold and inhuman.

"I'm so sorry, sir," Sota instantly shrank up.

As he meticulously smoothed his side hair with saliva, Kyubei let out a snort. "Pay attention, *Roki* and *Sata*. Now, I'll tell you a little story."

On his way home after the successful public stunt at the manor site, Kyubei had been formulating a despicable scheme. It was sheer luck that he had overheard Kento and Yuri. He cared little for their relationship with the individual in question; he merely wanted to confirm that they acknowledged the young man with supernatural powers. Their eagerness to protect their friend excited him even more, because then harsher consequences would most likely await them once the truth about the man's identity emerged.

And more importantly, if his ploy unfolded as intended, the outcome could lead to unprecedented wealth and status for Kyubei, beyond what a mere merchant could possibly achieve. This was the opportunity he had been craving all his life. A natural megalomaniac, he quivered with anticipation at the prospect. *That witch is going to make me richer and the most powerful man in this province. Whoever or whatever you are, Ryu, I'll get you, you son of a bitch.*

When Kyubei's speech ended, his apprentices had nearly become hypnotized. He had, of course, omitted the most bizarre part of his story, the true identity of Ryu. Yet, they remained numbed, all the same, visibly hesitant to accept the tasks Kyubei pressed upon them. He grew impatient. "Well? Will you do what I've just said?"

"Umm, but, sir —" Sota fidgeted with his shabby kimono.

"Do I need to remind you two of how grateful you should be for all I've done for you? Hmm?" asked Kyubei softly.

"No, sir. And thank you so much for taking us on as your apprentices, sir," answered Rikiya, straightening his posture.

"I know you do." Kyubei leaned forward, nearly sniffing the odor of the two boys' unwashed bodies. He let out a grunt. "So don't make me regret hiring you in the first place. Now, I'll ask you again. Will you help me? Will you do it for me?"

The adolescent employees turned into two frightened puppies, involuntarily leaning back.

"Think about the terms I've outlined, the reward you'll get. No one your age will get such a sum." Kyubei's tone became softer once again as he recognized the effectiveness of a carrot-and-stick approach.

Rikiya and Sota stopped shaking as they pondered the potential fortune. The reward money could buy anything they wanted, and they knew it. They exchanged glances, silently discussing the matter with nods and shakes of their heads.

"Sir, umm...I...we'd like to know if our tasks are considered...umm...legal, so to speak?" asked Rikiya tentatively.

Recognizing Rikiya as the leader of two, Kyubei grandiosely shifted his body toward him and said slowly, "Is that what you worry about, boy? Huh?"

Rikiya felt suffocated under his boss's intimidation. "Well, sir...yes, kind of. We...I don't want to be imprisoned. I've heard rumors about prisoners being tortured to death," he said, grabbing Sota's sleeve hard. Sota, in return, cooed like a baby.

"Who do you think I am, huh? I'm the richest man in this valley. And an honorable member of the Guild. No one can possibly touch me. Do you morons understand?" Kyubei shoved his skinny fist in front of his employees.

Kyubei took out a wooden case and an iron kettle from the drawer behind him, completely ignoring his frightened apprentices. He put the kettle on a *hibachi* sitting next to a low table. As he solemnly laid out each item that the case held, he began to hum again. A dark ceramic bowl larger than his fist, a bamboo whisk, a long bamboo spoon, and a black lacquered cylinder adorned his table. "These are fantastic!" he said aloud to himself, content. He resumed his ceremonious steps, opening the cylinder's lid and using the spoon to scoop green powder into the bowl. "You two have no idea what this is, don't you?"

His employees whispered something to each other's ear.

After quickly dipping his index finger into the kettle and pulling it out, he retrieved a bamboo scoop from beside the hibachi and poured the hot water into his bowl. Immediately, he began whisking in fluid motions. An aromatic steam, earthy and bitter, slowly permeated the damp room.

"You see, boys, I can afford luxuries like this as easily as I drink water from a clean well. That's the extent of my wealth. I can buy anything and ANYONE." He sipped his drink, his upper lip coated with green foam.

The two young servants kept whispering, pointing at the master's emerald liquid.

Kyubei placed the ceramic bowl down with solemnity and indulgently patted his thin lips dry with a hemp cloth as if tending to his vanity. "In any case, don't fret. It'll be all arranged before you begin. Wise young fellas like yourselves, unless you want to stay dumb, should understand what that means, shouldn't they?"

"Yes, sir!" they chorused.

Kyubei nodded approvingly. "Five percent of my potential reward should certainly be more than generous for young boys like you."

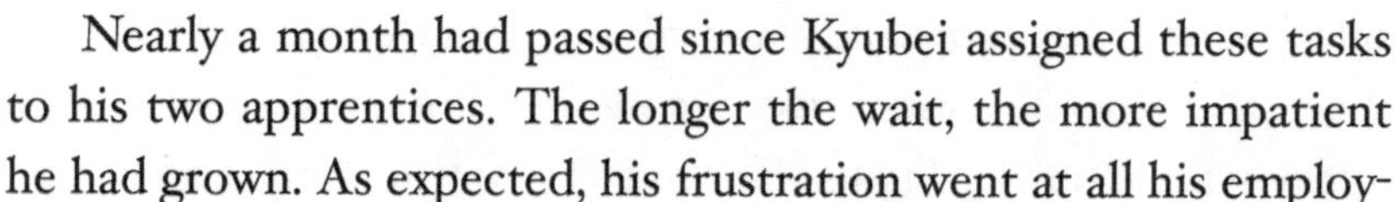

Nearly a month had passed since Kyubei assigned these tasks to his two apprentices. The longer the wait, the more impatient he had grown. As expected, his frustration went at all his employees. Then, Rikiya and Sota ended up in the Kyubei's den, once again.

"So, my loyal lads, haven't I heard that you two have made remarkable progress on the matters on hand?" asked Kyubei in an overly amiable tone. He took a deliberate sip of his hot green drink and flicked his hand at his pupils.

The two of them instantly froze and turned into trembling small animals, acutely aware of their owner's displeasure. The room seemed to freeze as well, the silence slashing the space.

"Damn it!" spat Kyubei, "spit it out, now! And don't even think about euphemizing."

"Umm...so sorry sir... 'euphe..'?" asked Rikiya, his words trailing off.

"Ah! Yes, I thought so, too. Who am I kidding?" Kyubei muttered to himself. "Needless to say, it means watering down the truth, you hopeless morons! I already know you both have failed miserably. So, don't dilute your incompetence and stupidity." He rearranged the tea set on his table.

"Sir, I've been tailing Kento and Yuri for a month," said Rikiya, "but I haven't caught them conspiring or making contact with your fugitive. The pair meet every four days or so and their usual meeting spot is the shrine. I have yet to find out their secret, sir, but soon... " He pressed his shaking knees down. "So, in that sense, sir, I have't actually failed you... have I? Not so sure about HIM, though." He leaned back, isolating Sota.

"You're a smart aleck, aren't you?" said Kyubei as he prepared the second drink. "And you, the other one. Tell me how pathetically useless you have been."

Sota jumped. "I...sir... I haven't had a chance to break into their houses because someone was always in — "

The next moment, Sota let out a loud cry as Kyubei's tea splashed over his face. The boy collapsed, writhing in agony from the scald. Rikiya instinctively recoiled in horror. Kyubei calmly put down his bowl. "That's the price for your incompetence, boy.

I asked for one thing, one simple thing, and you can't even act on it."

Sota began to wail on all fours, trembling in pain and shame.

"Life is always tough for people like you, and now you've made yours even more miserable because...what? If you can't follow a simple order, you can't complain about consequences."

"Yes...I mean, no sir..." said Sota weakly as he wiped his face with the back of his hand.

"No." Kyubei irritatingly whisked the green mixture, forcing out coarse sounds and splashing the liquid across the table.

"I'm so sorry that I haven't been able to comply with your order. But please, sir, if you give me another chance, I'll get it done. Please." Sota pled, enduring the burn.

"Alright, I'll give you one more chance because I'm merciful. One last chance, boy."

A month later, Kyubei sent Rikiya and Sota back empty-handed to their respective regions.

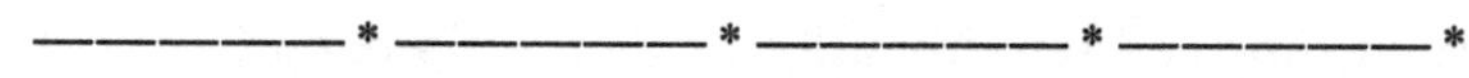

The autumn breeze carried the faint scent of damp earth as Kyubei sat at his desk, surrounded by a scattered array of intercepted messages and maps. His chambers were dim, lit only by the warm glow of a candle. He toyed with the corner of a parchment, his thoughts preoccupied. *Still no word of him...* He clenched his fist, crumpling the note that confirmed what he already knew. A knock at the door disrupted his brooding silence. "Enter," he barked.

A young informant stepped in, bowing low before approaching. "Sir, I bring news from Kyo."

Kyubei raised an eyebrow, waving for the boy to continue.

"The Imperial Palace grows restless," whispered the informant, casting a wary glance around the room. "Rumors suggest Emperor Godaigo is stirring. They say he's plotting to overthrow the Kamakura bakufu, yet again."

Kyubei leaned forward, thrusting his chin. "And the bakufu? Do they suspect?"

"Not yet, sir. But tensions are high. It seems the emperor's ambitions were not quelled after his failure six years ago."

Kyubei's lips curled into a calculating smile. He rose, pacing the room as his mind churned. "The emperor, still scheming in his gilded cage. And the bakufu, blissfully unaware..." He chuckled to himself. "It seems the winds of change are blowing, after all."

The informant hesitated, unsure if his presence was still required. "Is there anything else, sir?"

"No, that will be all. Leave me." Kyubei dismissed him with a wave, already lost in thought.

When the door closed, Kyubei stared at the flickering candle, poking his temple with the tip of *sensu*. The search of Ryu had proven futile. Every lead turned into dust, every effort a waste of time and resources. Kento and Yuri's relentless determination to find their friend had only highlighted the futility of his own approach. He needed a new strategy, something bold and ingenious. Not seeing the witch but forcing the witch to come to him.

A thought crept into his mind — a dangerous, exhilarating possibility. *Yuri. The witch had twice saved the girl. Once from the ocean and again at the River Hasu. Her life had always been his tether. Could it work? Could endangering that girl draw him out of hiding?*

"No," muttered Kyubei to himself. "There's a better way." He returned to his desk, clearing away the clutter to unroll a fresh scroll. He dipped his brush into the ink, letting it hover above the parchment as a new plan began to take shape in his mind: not one born of reckless desperation but of calculated precision. He smiled as the idea crystallized, with each piece of the puzzle falling into place. "If the emperor's plotting rebellion, there will be chaos. And in chaos, opportunities arise."

He began writing, his strokes confident and deliberate. The parchment bore no signature, only the seal of an anonymous benefactor. As he sealed the message and set it aside, he leaned back on his zabuton, chuckling triumphantly. "Let's see how long the witch can stay hidden when the world starts burning," he said, his voice tinged with satisfaction.

The plan was underway.

Part Five

HELLFIRE OF VENDETTA, 1332-1333

21

HEIAN-KYO

As Kento and Yuri stepped through the city gates of Heian-Kyo, an overwhelming din greeted them. They instinctively clapped their hands over their ears as their rural upbringing was unprepared for the sheer chaos of the *miyako* — a capital. Over the past three days, they had passed though several large towns, each busier than the last, but nothing compared to this.

The streets were alive with activity. Merchants barked their wares from wooden stalls, their voices competing with the clatter of oxcarts and rhythmic shuffle of sandaled feet. Mothers clutched their children close, weaving deftly though the throng, while vendors called out prices and hawked brightly colored silks and baskets of dried fish. Even the dogs, lean and quick, darted through the crowds and barked at one another as they scavenged for scrapes.

"This is unbelievable," muttered Yuri, her voice barely audible over the commotion. She clutched Kento's sleeve, her eyes darting from the towering rows of uniform wooden buildings to the neatly paved streets marked by deep cuts. "I've never seen so many people in one place."

"It's like a maze," replied Kento, his own voice tinged with awe. "But...meticulously organized." He pointed to the streets stretching out in straight lines, crisscrossing the city like a *go* board. "It's nothing like Kasuga."

The pair moved cautiously, their steps hesitant as they dodged traders balancing loads of pottery on their heads and shoppers carrying bundles of fabric. Unlike in their village, there was not a single hen in sight — only the polished efficiency of a city where every resident seemed to have a role.

Their awe soon gave way to curiosity. "How come there're no farms here?" Yuri wondered aloud.

"Farming isn't allowed inside Kyo," explained Kento, repeating what he had overheard from a traveler. "The city's for trade and culture. It's been like this since it was built, modeled after some place in China called Chang'an."

They continued to meander from one street and the next. The towering silhouette of the Imperial Palace loomed in the distance, its once-pristine walls now bearing the weight of whispered conspiracies. Kento and Yuri had heard the rumors during their journey — that the emperor himself had led a failed revolt against the Kamakura bakufu and was now imprisoned. Yet, the bustling city seemed oblivious to the unrest brewing within the palace walls. While courtiers schemed and solders prepared for what might come next, the people of Heian-Kyo carried on. To them, the emperor's rebellion was just another tail from behind the palace gates — one that mattered little to those concerned with daily survival.

"I do like this place, Yuri," said Kento, "unbelievably different from our village. It's not only about the clamor but also the pace. And I can feel a strong civilian spirit, too. What about you? What's your take on this place?" He read store signs and poked and prodded at all kinds of goods as they strolled down the street.

Yuri shooed a burking dog away. "Well...as long as they stay out of my way, it's an attractive place for a change of pace, for sure."

"Yeah, okay...but?" Kento shook a daikon stem in front of Yuri's face.

"This is not the place I would choose to live in, thanks for asking." Yuri took the stem and tossed it away. "But, Kento, this could be your place. That's another reason we came here. To search for your art apprenticeship."

"I do hope so." Kento stepped on the stem.

Before leaving the village, Yuri had told her parents she needed to search for Ryu, while Kento had set out on his first extended trip without sharing his intentions with his family. Yet, Kento's pursuit of his dream to become an artist did not overshadow his desire to reconnect with Ryu. He firmly believed that true friends played as important a role as his passion.

Over the past nine months, they had searched every place they knew to find Ryu or information leading to him. In desperation, they even ventured to the region where Yuri's divorced family lived. However, the same response disheartened them: no such young man existed. Even so, they clung to hope. Eventually, they both agreed that if someone sought to vanish from a small society, a large city could easily hide them.

"He could be here, right? I can picture him in one of those stores." Kento placed his hand over his eyebrows.

"Yup, this is the perfect place for a jack-of-all-trades," said Yuri. "All kinds of businesses thrive here."

"And that's what Ryu claimed to be. If he was telling me the truth, though." He resumed his stroll.

"What do you mean by that, Kento? Are you saying he lied to you? For what reason?" Yuri quickly caught up with him.

"You know...some people want to present themselves bigger than they really are."

"Wait...what's your point?" She clung to Kento's arm.

He gently removed her hand. "My point is, he might've wanted to impress me with an array of experiences."

"That's just ridiculous, Kento." Yuri countered. "Why would he do that?"

"I don't know, Yuri, I don't know," responded Kento and stopped again. "But, don't you find it weird that some of the things he mentioned completely contradicted what he had said earlier? I know you do. I watched you become puzzled when it happened."

Yuri kicked a pebble toward an empty cart. "Well...I can't deny that he actually looked more like frightened than embarrassed when you confronted him with those contradictions. But... hmm."

After that, the pair fell silent. Their breath formed white vapor in the chilly air.

Although a flat, immaculately organized urban area, Kyo still lay in a valley, just like Kasuga. Evidently, its climate mirrored that of any other valley region in the country, with all four seasons exhibiting distinct characteristics.

"I've never expected Kyo to get this cold at this time of year," remarked Kento finally. "Just like Kasuga. Another month, and the sakura will bloom."

"Yeah, I know. But enough of being sentimental for now. We'll need to find a place to spend the night. I don't want to freeze to death." Yuri shivered, wrapping her arms around herself.

"Don't you worry about that, Yuri. One great thing about this place is, there're plenty of temples and shrines that accommodate us for free!"

They laughed together.

The next morning, Kento and Yuri woke beside a snow-draped garden in Shoko-ji temple. The low, steady chants of sutras seeped though the thin walls, wrapping the frigid air in a somber rhythm. Kento lit a candle and glanced at Yuri, who was still shivering as they dragged their half-asleep bodies out of the austere room.

The sky remained an ink-black canvas, with dawn yet to break. Outside, the snow glowed faintly in the flickering candle-light, casting an ethereal light over the temple grounds. Kento's gaze wandered to the garden beyond the wooden walkway — a simple arrangement of rocks and raked gravel, now softened by a delicate blanket of snow. He knew gardens like this were meant to evoke stillness, but the sight only reminded him of how quiet and lonely the place felt.

"Shoko-ji is even smaller than I imagined," murmured Yuri, her breath misting in the cold. She wrapped her arms around herself as they made their way to the main hall.

"It's not about size," replied Kento. "Most Zen temples are like this. Simple and focused. It's all about discipline. Monks do all the cleaning, meditating, and begging for food themselves."

Yuri nodded but remained silent, squinting in the dark to see the distant glow of lanterns as the monks prepared for the day's rituals. The temple grounds were a stark contrast to the bustling streets of Heian-Kyo they had wandered though yesterday. Shoko-ji, nestled in the city's southwestern corner, seemed worlds away from the clamor and commerce.

As they passed the main hall, the muffled sounds of sweeping brooms reached their ears. The monks were already hard at work, not paying slightest attention to the two strangers walking past them. Yuri paused and glanced again at the garden. "I've never seen one like this before," she said softly. "Just rocks, gravel, and...nothing else. It's so different from the gardens back home."

"It's called *Karesansui,*" explained Kento. "It's meant to make you think. No flowers, no clutter, just...simplicity."

Yuri tilted her head. "It feels...peaceful," she said. "Even under the snow."

Suddenly, an elderly monk around in his late sixties dressed in black and white glided toward them soundlessly. "Good morning," he announced politely. "My name is Sojin, the chef priest of this temple. One of my monks informed me of your visit. You must be starving. Come join us for breakfast." The ancient, beautiful sound embraced the two unexpected visitors. Deep wrinkles ran across his face as he greeted them, revealing his toothless gum lines.

Caught off guard by the warm greeting, the pair stood in uncertainty as they wiggled their semi-numbed toes. "Umm... thank you so much for your hospitality, sir," responded Kento. Then, they followed Sojin into the dining-cum-reading area, awkwardly mimicking his gait.

Upon entering, they found seven food trays arranged on the wooden floor. Four subordinate monks, clad in traditional dark grey *samue*, sat on thin zabutons behind their respective trays, facing each other in pairs. The young monks, seemingly as young as Kento, remained emotionless as the two newcomers took their seats opposite Sojin. Then, all the monks, including Sojin, joined their hands in payer for over twenty seconds in unison. Just like it began abruptly, the prayer ended all at once. Yet, none of them moved, nor did they open their mouth, as each man kept his solitary moment. Feeling almost intimidated by the solemnity of their ritual, Kento and Yuri remained silent. After offering a deep bow to the simple meal devoid of any living creatures, the monks finally began to eat in silence. The petrified pair followed suit.

Once the quiet breakfast finished, the young monks rose in unison, trays in hand, and glided solemnly out of the room. The space continued to exude an air of tranquility. A moment later, two of them quietly came back in, nimbly whisked their mentor' and guests' trays away, and left the room. All the while, Sojin meditated as he remained in a *seiza* position. "So, would you mind sharing what has brought young people like you to this humble temple?" he asked, showing his gums again.

Kento and Yuri exchanged non-verbal words. "Well...it's a long story, sir. And somewhat embarrassing as well," replied Yuri and corrected her posture.

Even though Sojin had mildly been surprised by the young woman speaking up before her male companion, he never showed it. "Ah, I see. However, time is something we monks cannot possibly exhaust. So, unless you have pressing matters elsewhere, please indulge this nosy old monk with your story." His wrinkles etched even deeper into his face. "And how may I call you?"

"Oh, I am so sorry, sir. My name is Yuri," replied Yuri, mortified.

"And my name is Kento, sir." He slightly brushed.

"It's a pleasure to get acquainted with you both, Miss Yuri and Mr. Kento. Please, make yourself comfortable while filling me in on what's bothering you."

Yuri and Kento told Sojin their story, including all the trivial details that might have nothing to do with the experiences they had with Ryu. They became so engrossed with their own talk that they lost track of time. Sojin hardly interrupted them with questions, his eyes remaining closed for most of the time. By the time their story finally concluded, the contours of the garden had traced intricate lines in the morning sun.

The chief priest slapped his thigh. "Hmm...fascinating. Yes, indeed. And this man does sound mysterious. And Elusive as well."

"Yes, he is. That's why some people say he's done something wrong that made him a fugitive." Yuri clutched the hems of her kimono.

"And you never believe such an accusation."

"Of course, I don't, sir."

"But, sir," Kento chipped in. "If you were in that situation, would you meet others in public, let alone perform a heroic act like carrying a well-known girl on your back across the village?"

Sojin uncrossed his arms and stroked his chin. "Not unless I had a special interest in this young woman."

Yuri leaned forward. "Sir, are you saying he...likes me?"

"Not necessarily, or at least not romantically. He may have some other feelings toward you. But then, we have another concern here. How come he just left you despite knowing you were still in recovery?"

"That's right, sir. It doesn't make any sense..." said Kento.

"Well, one thing I know about hiding is," Sojin added, "it's extremely difficult to find someone who doesn't want to be found. Not all the young monks here had willingly come to this temple. Some came here because they needed to disappear from the society they belonged to."

"Sir, you don't think we can find him?" Yuri asked.

Sojin slowly shook his head. "Have you considered giving him as much time as he needs until he's ready to come forward on his own? There must be a reason why he doesn't want to be found. But whatever that is, it's his issue, not yours."

"But, we can't give up now, sir." Yuri slumped.

A long silence fell in the room.

The gentle chirps of a *uguisu* — a Japanese nightingale — pleasantly filled the cold air. It perched on a branch of a pine in the Zen garden. The bird kept singing.

Kento's index finger moved fluidly on his thigh. "This garden must be magnificent with that pine. It's a shame it's all covered in snow."

"Yes, it is. I'd very much like you to see how stunning it is. In fact, our temple is known for this garden." Sojin stood up. "I'll show you something instead. Excuse me." He opened a small sliding door on the wall behind him and took out a scroll. "Just because monks don't adorn our humble abode doesn't mean we don't appreciate beauty," he chuckled and handed it to Kento.

Kento gasped as he unfurled the scroll. A skillfully drawn *karesansui* instantly captivated him. Every single motif and brushwork in the monochrome art transcended his understanding of drawing. The tree, with its graceful curves of branches, particularly appealed to him. His index finger delicately traced the brushstrokes. Then, he detected the undeniable resemblance between the tree on the scroll and the pine in the garden. "It's the same garden right here!" exclaimed Kento.

"That's correct," said Sojin.

"Did you draw this, sir?" Kento passed it to Yuri.

"I wouldn't have been a monk if I were such a gifted artist," Sojin chuckled. "Years ago, a gentle man came here for this garden and drew it. And he generously donated his art to us."

"Such a revered artist..." Kento muttered.

"Indeed. And a honorable man as well."

"Do you remember his name and where he lives, sir?" Kento's eagerness burst.

"Well, it's on the back of the drawing. I heard that he lives on *Kujo-oji* street in the Sakyo district."

Kento snatched the drawing from Yuri. The impressive calligraphy on the back read: '*Hosei Ichimura, 1324*.' "Do you think he's open to taking on an apprentice?"

"That, I have no idea. You'll have to ask for yourself. One of my trainee monks takes that particular route for his mendicancy every morning. He'll take you two there."

"Thank you so much, sir, for your hospitality and kindness. I can hardly express my gratitude." Kento bowed deep.

"And thank you for your insight into our search, sir," said Yuri and bowed.

Sojin reciprocated their bows. "The pleasure is all mine, Mr. Kento and Miss Yuri. Please, feel free to come back anytime. Our gate is always open for those who need us. And good luck with your search for your friend."

Soon afterward, with the morning sun warming their

backs, Kento and Yuri headed toward the Sakyo district, accompanied by a young monk.

When Kento turned around to catch one last glimpse of temple, the chief priest was still standing at the gate.

22

TSUBAKI-YA THE TEASER

"So, Chuji, you can take this home for your wife. It's on me," said Kyubei, picking up a bamboo basket from a shelf and tossing it to his messenger.

"Oh wow, thank you so much, sir!" exclaimed Chuji, fumbling to catch the basket. "I never knew you're such a generous man."

"Ha! What're you talking about? I'm the most generous man in this valley!" Kyubei laughed, his mood unusually buoyant all morning. For a man known to keep his emotions tightly leashed, this display of exhilaration was almost unsettling.

Chuji watched his employer with a curious tilt on his head. "You've been in a good mood all day, sir. Got something exciting cooking?"

Kyubei merely smirked, leaning back against the counter. His sharp eyes swept the room, landing briefly on the scroll Chuji had delivered earlier that morning. The message contained exactly what he had been waiting for: the mediator he had dispatched to Kamakura had finally succeeded in securing a lucrative agreement with a bakufu official. Kyubei would soon join the elite ranks of retailers granted exclusive business dealings with the bakufu once the emperor's insurrection was suppressed.

For months, Kyubei had played a delicate game of persistence and cunning. His visits to Kamakura had been grueling, each round trip spanning 20 days and laden with costs — a palanquin, his bearers, lodgings for himself and them. The expenses were substantial, even for a man of his wealth, but Kyubei regarded them as investments. "Carelessness is your greatest enemy," he often reminded his employees, and he held himself to that standard with ruthless discipline.

"Yeah, I get that, Tsubaki-Ya san," Chuji interrupted Kyubei's reverie. "But what I really want to know is your terms. What is it that you promised them?" His voice rose with excitement.

"You'll see." Kyubei waved him off with a flick of a wrist.

"Agh, you're such a tease!" muttered Chuji, shaking his head as he retreated.

Kyubei chuckled softly, but his thoughts turned inward, savoring the memory of his negotiations. The first two meetings with the shogunate official had gone as expected — dismissive scoffs and condescending remarks about "peasant money-grubbers." But Kyubei, ever the strategist, had allowed the disdain to wash over him, knowing he would savor his eventual triumph all the more.

His offer had been simple, yet irresistible: Ryu. Kyubei had withheld the truth about the young man's identity as a wizard, presenting him instead as a psychic with extraordinary abilities. The official had been skeptical, of course, but Kyubei had anticipated that too. By their fourth meeting, he sweetened the deal with a generous bribe, sliding a parcel wrapped neatly in a purple furoshiki into the official's chest. "Sir," Kyubei had said, his tone low and conspiratorial, "you need not report this meeting to your superior. At least not until you've seen the psychic for yourself."

The official, burdened with debts to gambling houses, had

eventually relented, his resistance crumbling under the weight of his desperation. Kyubei's thorough research had paid off, as it always did.

Now, holding the scroll that marked the next step in his plan, Kyubei allowed himself a rare moment of satisfaction. One piece of the game lay firmly in place, and the rest of the board awaited his next move. "So far, so good," he muttered under his breath, a sly smile creeping across his face. "Hopefully, I won't have to deal with that hypocrite ever again."

23

THE CRUCIAL INFORMATION

After parting ways with the young monk, Kento and Yuri lingered on Kujo Street. The crisp morning air had given way to a warm spring breeze, and the snow blanketing the street quickly melt. Unlike the bustling downtown they had experienced the day before, this area near the city limit saw no human activity. The vibrancy of urban life clearly bypassed the neighborhood. The pair soon realized that they stood in a residential district with no stores and shoppers in sight. Every gate and door stood tightly closed as if the residents sought isolation. Uncertain of their next move, Kento and Yuri wandered amidst the eerie quietude of what felt like a ghost town.

Their reverie ended when a woman and a little girl came out of a nearby gate. The girl's tiny hand firmly clung to her mother's. Their impeccable attire amazed Kento, and he wondered whether everybody in Kyo was rich. "Let me talk to them," he whispered to Yuri, then slowly and politely approached them. "Good morning, ma'am. I'm terribly sorry to bother you. My friend and I are visiting from a distant region to look for an artist named Mr. Hosei Ichimura. The chief priest of Shoko-ji told us this gentleman's residence is on this street. Would you be able to tell us which one?"

The girl innocently waved at Kento and Yuri while the mother cast her eye over their rural clothes and snorted. "I know of no such man on this street," she replied curtly and pulled the girl closer. Then, the mother and daughter briskly walked away before Kento said his thank you.

Yuri stuck her tongue out at the unfriendly woman. "What a rude, snobbish woman!" she exclaimed after the mother and daughter turned a corner. "See, Kento? People like her are why I do NOT care much for this city. Who does she think she is, huh? No one is superior or inferior to anyone else, in my opinion."

"I know what you mean, Yuri," responded Kento, putting a hand on her shoulder. "Well, let's hope she's not the only representative of Kyo."

Much to their relief, a gentleman appeared from the corner. Yuri immediately approached him and repeated Kento's question. "Yes, I know the house. I can take you there. Follow me," he told them and set off eastward along the street. The pair followed him from behind.

After passing roughly ten houses, the man stopped abruptly in front of a mildew-infested sliding door. "Here we are," he said. "But I must warn you, he's quite a character. So, good luck getting him to see you."

"Umm, sir...what do you mean by —" Before Kento could finish his question, the man had already walked away. "Thank you so much!" Kento said aloud.

The pair stood perplexed in front of the door as if waiting for something to appear from the other side. "Well, I hope Mr. Ichimura isn't as strange as the man just described," said Yuri.

"There's only one way to find out." With a deep breath, Kento tentatively knocked on the door twice. They waited for a while but received no response. He tried again and again. Still, the door remained shut. He gave Yuri a worried look.

Just before Kento's fist struck it yet again, the door slowly slid open, revealing an elderly woman's face. She immediately withdrew. "Excuse me, but we're not expecting any visitors today," she murmured behind the door. As if trying to avoid unnecessary communication, she did not even stepped out of the entrance. Instead, she offered a slight bow, politely signaling a farewell, and began to close the door.

"Please, wait, ma'am," plead Kento. "We're not beggars or anything as such. We came here to see Mr. Ichimura. Sojin-osho of Shoko-ji told us Hosei-sensei resides here. He showed us the stunning karesansui that the sensei had drawn years ago, which led us here."

"I'm sorry, but I'm afraid you've got a wrong address. There is no man named Hosei living here." The woman withdrew even further as she spoke.

Yuri sensed that the woman was lying. "Ma'am, please. We've traveled for three days to get here. From a distant valley by Wakasa Bay called Kasuga. My friend Kento here hopes if..."

A white-haired elderly gentleman, seemingly in his sixties, suddenly stood behind the woman. He was short and supported his left leg with his hand. And yet, his distinct aura, particularly his dignified features, clearly indicated that he was no ordinary elderly man.

The woman immediately sensed his presence, straightening her posture, and bowed to him. Noticing him massaging his leg, she gently pulled his hand, then whispered something to his ear. He waved her off and said to Yuri, "What did you say you're from, miss?"

"We're from Kasuga Village of Wakasa Province," responded Yuri confidently as she took a step toward Hosei.

Kento elbowed Yuri lightly. "Sir, are you Mr. Hosei Ichimura?"

"I am, young man," responded Hosei indifferently. "Miss, you don't need to bolster your identity. Not to me."

Yuri's nose bulged out with mortification for a split second, but quickly regained her composure. "I'm not doing any such thing, sir. I just wanted — " stopped herself, not wanting to behave like a child or jeopardize Kento's chance to become an apprentice. "If anything, I'm proud of being a peasant woman," she declared. It was an exaggeration, she instantly admitted, regretting her words.

"Yes, you are, young lady. Just like Saki."

"Who is Saki, sir?" Kento said.

"You're a nosy lad, aren't you?" chuckled Hosei, pointing a finger at him.

"I... didn't mean to —"

"So, you two are from Kasuga. Did I hear that right?"

"Y-Yes, we are, sir." Kento tugged Yuri's sleeve. "And the reason I'm here is to ask whether —"

"Has the shrine been repaired?" Hosei stuck his hand in his garment and started scratching his chest.

"I'm sorry?" responded Kento and Yuri at the same time, confused. They began to understand what the pedestrian had mentioned about the master artist, not having a smooth conversation with him.

"Kasuga Shrine. Has the roof been replaced? And the door of the Nishiya?"

Kento scratched his head. "I... don't understand. Have you been to our village, Sir Hosei?"

The elderly woman cleared her throat nervously, a signal implying that she had had enough. Then, she turned around and whispered something in Hosei's ear again, to which he responded by placing the index finger to his lips. The woman bowed deeply in apology.

Inside the entrance, darkness blanketed everything except for the uneven earthen floor, visible only a few steps ahead. No sound came from beyond the dim hollow. Despite the spring sun on their backs, Kento and Yuri felt a chill. Standing for quite some time, they began to shift on the gravel.

"Hmm, let's see," said Hosei at last. "It was more than thirty years ago. Is that right? Osen?" Before the woman answered, he continued, "I visited the half-dilapidated shrine on top of the hill. The sight still saddens me."

Kento suddenly felt a connection with Hosei, sensing a shared experience with his potential mentor. "Umm, no, sir. The roofs' repairs are long overdue," he said, "the spring storms had made them worse. As for the door of the Nishiya, it's been in good shape."

"I'm glad they at least fixed the door."

"I just can't believe you've been there, sir. You visited our village for your drawing, I assume?"

The woman leaned toward Kento and Yuri, this time to cut off the conversation, her nose right in front of them. "I'm sorry, but he really needs to rest now. So please, excuse us."

"Osen, show some manners," said Hosei, his voice soft yet controlling. "Go ahead and straighten up the studio so we can sit down and talk."

"Yes, very well, sir," said Osen sharply, her clenched fist lined with veins. Then, she asked the young visitors to wait until the room was ready and disappeared into the dark.

"Ha, where are my manners? I'm Hosei. And that woman is my younger sister, Osen. Did I catch your names?"

When Kento and Yuri entered the studio, Osen was lighting up several candles despite the daytime. "Thank you for your —" Before Kento finished his words, she nearly trotted out of the room. The flickering flames only emphasize the gloom of the space. Sunlight would hit the room late afternoon, Kento assumed. Connected to the engawa, the wood-floored room could warm up quickly as daylight flooded in until sunset.

However, at the moment, Kento and Yuri could not shake

off the chill. The thick zabutons they sat on provided little warmth to their legs, and their breaths lingered in the air before dissipating into the dimness.

Kento curiously observed the studio from his seat. The room, unlike the familiar layout of residential spaces in Kasuga Village, lay entirely isolated, with the shoji screens as one of the walls, akin to a hidden sanctuary accessible only from the engawa. No ostentatious furniture disgraced the room; only a modest *kiri* cube chest with four hinged doors and a matching tall cabinet adorned the space. Though not an expert on carpentry, he could easily acknowledge the refined woodworking of a skilled artisan, a clear testament to Mr. Hosei's discerning taste.

A glistening, hollowed rock sitting on the graveled garden seduced his senses. Droplets from a skillfully pruned pine danced on the rock with each impact. The whiteness of the gravel purified the melting snow as they merged, while the thin shades of the pine weaved into the white whirlpool. The aesthetic of the scene sang poetry for Kento.

An enormous sumi-e drawing eerily loomed on the wall opposite the garden as Kento' eyesight became accustomed to the dimness of room. "What on earth...?" he muttered involuntarily. Though barely discernible in the candlelight, the exquisite brushstrokes unmistakably bore Hosei-sensei's signature style. As Kento stepped back to get a better view of the art drawn directly on the wall, Kasuga Village against the rugged backdrop of Mt. Toki gradually took shape before his eyes.

Yuri, too, recognized the subject of the drawing. Standing next to Kento, she absorbed the details. "Kasuga is stunningly beautiful..." she marveled.

While the pair stood numb, the creator of the art came into the studio. "I apologize for the wait," said Hosei indifferently, out of courtesy. "Sometimes, it takes an outsider to truly appreciate the beauty of one's home." He dramatically swept the air in front of the drawing, then took a seat behind a small table. Kento and Yuri promptly resumed theirs opposite him.

Osen came back, holding a tray with both hands. Setting the tray down on the table to Hosei's left, she apologetically said, "I hope this meets your preference...sir," and sat beside him. He tapped her hand twice. As if on cue, she left the room just as apologetically.

I would never call Amuro 'sir' even if we were their age, Yuri thought sympathetically.

Hosei placed a ceramic bowl in front of Kento and Yuri, and set the last one before himself. "It's cold in here, isn't it? I know. Hope this will warm you up." Steam from each bowl lingered through the candlelit space. "One of the benefits of being commissioned by the Imperial Palace. Normally, I don't care for exotic things, but this..." He paused, took a sip of matcha from his bowl, and licked his upper lip. "Hmm, this is something. Why don't you give it a try and judge for yourself?"

Kento and Yuri tentatively sipped their beverages. "Ugh!" Yuri said involuntarily. Kento, on the other hand, managed to stop himself spewing it out.

"Not for you?" Hosei feigned surprise.

"I'm so sorry, sir. It's just so..." Yuri could not finish her sentence, embarrassed.

"Disgusting? I know. That was my initial reaction too. Yes, it's an acquired taste and certainly not for everyone." Hosei chuckled.

Recovering from the unexpected experience, Kento pulled himself together. "Hosei-sensei, thank you for inviting us in. I don't wish to interrupt your important work, so let me get straight to —"

"Tell me more about the village if you don't mind?"

"I'm sorry? The village?"

"Yes, your village, Kasuga. You two noticed the drawing,

didn't you?" Hosei pointed at the wall. "Please, indulge me with its bucolic charms, first. Then, ask what you came for."

Kento and Yuri proceeded to paint a vivid picture of their village for Hosei; they spoke of the current state of the shrine, the Guild, Mt. Toki, and the River Hasu, detailing the perpetual rivalry between Kasuga and Inaki, recounting the tragic famine and Amuro's sacrifice, and sharing the latest phenomena that had staved off potential disasters. They, of course, mentioned Ryu, who had mysteriously appeared to them but was now missing and might have been linked to the inexplicable occurrences.

When their narratives came to an end, Hosei stood in front of the drawing if seeing it for the first time. Kento wondered if the artist had even listened. "Umm...Hosei-sensei? Are you alright, sir?" he asked.

"Fascinating," Hosei murmured to himself. "Although your village has certainly gone through a lot, especially the unspeakable tragedy as you vividly described, it still fascinates me. There's something about that land that speaks to me." He stretched his arms to the drawing. "Just like it did the last time I was there. I didn't plan to draw this one. But my instinct compelled me to do it anyway."

"And that was thirty-something years ago, sir?" asked Yuri.

"And yet, sometimes it feels like yesterday," said Hosei, his back still to his guests. "When I look at this drawing, it evokes bittersweet memories. After coming back from the trip, I regretted having painted it for a while."

"But, your work is breathtaking, sir," chipped in Kento. "As stunning as the one you did on the Shoko-ji's karesansui. And that's why I came to you." He made a desperate effort to steer the conversation back to his intended course.

"The more beautiful your work is, the more cruelly your memories haunt you," Hosei observed cryptically.

Kento and Yuri had no idea what Hosei was referring to, but decided not to pursue the topic further.

A hush fell over the studio. As Hosei floated in his own world, the pair could not tell whether he was reminiscing about his past or lamenting it.

After a while, Hosei put his bowl back on the tray, waiting as the green foam slowly disappearing at the bottom. "By the way, does the name Kyubei sound familiar? He owns a store called Tsubaki-Ya or something like that, in the valley or the village?"

"How do you know about the obnoxious man, sir??" asked Kento, stunned.

"I don't. But gossip always follows wherever people congregate."

Then, Hosei shared what he had heard about Kyubei with his visitors: a peasant merchant from a valley near Wakasa Bay aggressively pitching his business vision to an imperial official; his most valuable "product" being a singular psychic who could help the emperor achieve an unprecedented legacy that none of his predecessors had dreamed of; in return, once the emperor's insurrection succeeded, Tsubaki-Ya would become the leading imperial merchandiser; and Kyubei had already bribed some of the key players in the Imperial Palace to expedite the deal.

Kento and Yuri fell into a somber silence, processing the crucial information they had just received. They had heard rumors that Kyubei continued looking for "a strange young fella" who would bring him "an unbounded fortune." It was hard to comprehend that Ryu had been a subject of Kyubei's shady scheme. Even more ludicrous, Kyubei genuinely belied that Ryu possessed psychic powers. They knew that some of the villagers in Kasuga insinuated Ryu's involvement in the inexplicable incidents, but labeling him some kind of a mastermind surpassed the definition of insanity.

But, does it really? Yuri's mind lingered back again to Ryu's past and questionable identity. *He changed his stories when he was questioned. And what about his birthplace? My Inaki cousin said she had never heard of him. So, why the lie? How come he had to make up the story? Is Ryu really who he said he was? If not, what on earth does he gain from all those lies?*

"Yuri?" muttered Kento, pulling her sleeve. "Yuri? What's wrong?"

Yuri's eyes were twitching, wide and wild. "Huh?" she replied vacantly.

"You look so out of it."

"I'm sorry, Kento. I just got carried away."

"Kyubei? Yeah, I understand, Yuri. Same here." Kento shook his head. "Unbelievable...that son of a bitch."

Yuri grimaced embarrassingly but said nothing.

"But I think we've made a progress," whispered Kento, glancing at Hosei, who sat opposite them with his eyes closed.

"How??" Yuri almost hissed.

Kento recoiled, rubbing his ear. "We have, Yuri. We may not be able to find Ryu, as Sojin-osho said. But now we have the upper hand in the situation. Don't you see?"

"Enlighten me."

"All we have to do is stop Kyubei. To keep Ryu safe. Then, we'll look for him again or wait until he shows up on his terms."

After contemplating, Yuri took a sip of her green tea and instantly spat it out into her bowl. "Ugh!"

Hosei opened his eyes and tittered.

"Anyway, you're absolutely right, Kento. His safety comes first." Yuri gripped Kento's hand.

Hosei stood next to Kento. "Before you leave, show me your drawing if you have it on you."

"How did you know my intention, sir?" asked Kento as he handed the artist a piece of paper. "If you ever find —"

After a quick critique of the artwork, Hosei folded the paper neatly and gave it back to Kento. "Come back to me, when the issue with this merchant is resolved."

"Sir?"

"You'll be my apprentice whenever you're ready."

24

FROM KAMAKURA TO SEKIGAHARA

In early spring, as plum blossoms began to dot the barren branches, Kyubei received an urgent summons to Kamakura from his bakufu liaison. He read the message twice, his sharp eyes narrowing at the cryptic wording. The civil war, it seemed, had reached a critical juncture, though the specifics eluded him.

Kyubei prided himself on his ability to navigate the shifting tides of power, but even he felt the murkiness of the current political waters. News of the war trickled in sporadically, whispered in tea houses or carried by traveling merchants. Most of the common folk remained blissfully unaware of the struggle unfolding many mountains away. For them, war was an abstract affair — something fought by lords and warriors in distant lands, far removed from the mundane routines of planting rice and raising families.

To Kyubei, however, ignorance was not an option. Wars of the past had always followed a familiar pattern: two factions clashing for dominance, the weaker inevitably conceding. The time would be no different, or so he believed. Still, the liaison's message unsettled him, its tone suggesting something more than the usual posturing of rival powers.

The scent of damp earth filled the air as Kyubei prepared for his journey. "God…I'm so over with the rural shit," he grunted. He tightened his haori and stepped into his palanquin, wondering what awaited him in Kamakura and how he might use it to his advantage.

Eight days later, despite his uncertainty, Kyubei arrived in Kamakura with cautious optimistic. Wandering through the bustling city, he could not stop daydreaming about his future Tsubaki-Ya that graced the illustrious Wakamiya-oji street leading to the majestic Shinto shrine, Tsuruoka Hachimangu. Such thoughts left him exhilarated.

The scene lay against a backdrop of vermillion shrine architecture and an azure sky, overlooking the verdant mountains in the distance. The dynamic panorama prompted pedestrians to pause in wonder. The bustling street boasted an array of businesses: inns, clothing stores, food markets, rice merchants, ceramic and artifact shops, and even moneylenders, all thriving with customers. The common thread among them was prosperity. Kyubei fell into a reverie, further envisioning his business thriving in this city as he made his way to his contact's residence.

Upon arriving at Shizuma Muramoto's opulent abode, Kyubei noted its grandeur with a tinge of envy. Though acquainted with Muramoto for some time, he had never before been invited to his home. "You were certainly not exaggerating about your house, Mr. Muramoto," muttered Kyubei to himself as he prowled around the message premises. The imposing wooden gate barred entry with a sense of defiance. Kyubei stood on tiptoes, trying to peek over it, and grunted as the tip of a pine tree sneered down at him. "What secrets are you harboring there? A Golden Buddha?" He laughed at his own jest.

He banged the thick gate three times.

After about twenty seconds, the gate swung open inward

and a young woman of barely 20 years old greeted Kyubei. "Please, follow me, Mr. Tsubaki-Ya," she said after a deep bow.

He wondered how she recognized him, but said nothing. As he followed her, Kyubei further marveled at the property. The meticulously tended garden not only lent aesthetic charm but also provided a buffer against the clamor of the street. At the rear stood the stately single-story residence armored in thick cedar walls. Kyubei could almost smell Muramoto's wealth.

Kyubei expected Muramoto at the entrance, but instead another young female maid guided into the house. He followed the housemaid down a lengthly hallway to what seemed to be Muramoto's study, and yet the man himself was not present. She politely instructed Kyubei to wait, indifferent to his uncertainty.

Despite Muramoto's wealth, the room hardly boasted anything, except for a small low table that sat on the center. The walls lacked adornments, as if imprisoning Kyubei in a sense of desolation. He could not find a zabuton, so sat directly on the hard floor. As the quiet wait dragged on, he became increasingly nervous while the bustling sounds of Wakamiya-oji he had heard earlier echoed in his mind.

With no sign of Muramoto after what felt like hours, Kyubei's apprehension mounted. He could not shake the feeling of impending unpleasantness, pondering over potential grievances that had summoned him here. *Have I inadvertently offended Muramoto? Will he demand more bribes, or worse, cancel the carefully crafted deal?* The more Kyubei dwelled on these thoughts, the more intensely his unease grew.

Just as Kyubei's nerves reached their breaking point, Muramoto finally swaggered into the room, clearly indulging in the merchant's discomfort. The oppressive weight of Muramoto's presence seemed to constrict the air. Standing over his guest, Muramoto wasted no time. "Don't bother," he snapped, waving away Kyubei's attempt to stand. "I'll be brief, Tsubaki-Ya. You're to bring your young psychic to Kamakura immediately."

Kyubei blinked, his mind scrambling for footing against the abrupt command. "Ah...I...umm..." he faltered, swallowing the slimy saliva of his fear. Sweat seeped from his pores, soaking through his fine robes as Muramoto's chilling aura loomed over him. *Think!* Kyubei's thoughts scrambled uncontrollably. *I need leverage...something to keep me afloat.*

Images of Kasuga's villagers flickered in his head — faces hardened by years of heavy tax burdens. The cruel consistency of the taxes, unchanged even during the hardest times, had driven some families to unthinkable measures. Kyubei had heard whispers of parents parting their children to scrape together enough to appease the previous lord. And he knew the accounts — stories of those who had resorted to deceit to survive. Some were caught, enduring public beatings before grudgingly repaying their debts. But one man still eluded capture.

Kyubei clenched his fists under the table to stop them from shaking. The retired lord's wrath against this elusive debtor had been legendary, his proclamation of eternal unforgiveness echoing through the village. Rumors claimed that the debt, compounded by exorbitant late fees, had grown to four times its original size — virtually a death sentence as the villagers whispered about.

A scapegoat. Kyubei thought grimly. He needed one to snare Ryu. He had initially considered Gensuke or Heijiro. Their bonds with Ryu through their children, Yuri and Kento, had seemed like ideal bait. But, the new lord's affable report with the two men complicated things. Takeru might show them mercy, and Kyubei could not risk the plan unraveling. "There must be someone else in the village," he muttered under his breath. A man cleaver enough to evade taxes while keeping a steady income. Someone articulate and respectable.

"Did you hear what I just said, Tsubaki-Ya?" Muramoto's voice cut through Kyubei's haze of scheming. "My superior needs to determine if this individual truly holds any value to our Lord, as you claim. Time is no longer on our side. Do you fully grasp the gravity of the situation?"

"Who is this Lord? Is it Sir Takatoki Hojo?" asked Kyubei.

"How dare you say his name so brazenly! You peasant parvenu!" retorted Muramoto.

Kyubei clasped the hem of his silk kimono, shaking in anger. "Mr. Muramoto," said Kyubei as he slowly rose, "in case you forgot, I've handsomely paid you to iron out any obstacles I may face. So, it's safe to say I, *peasant parvenu*, hold every right to ask you anything and demand anything from you." The tip of his head barely reached Muramoto's broad shoulders.

"I don't give a damn about your right. You have the audacity to approach a man so out of your league. But, a peasant is after all a peasant." The bakufu official sneered down at the sly hillbilly.

"YOU —" Kyubei clenched his fists.

"In case you forgot, I'm also a samurai," declared Muramoto and took out a *kaiken*, a dagger, from under his impeccable kimono. "Now, listen Tsubaki-Ya, you must understand what you've gotten yourself into, because there will be no turning back for you. The bakufu demands your loyalty now." He played with his weapon. "Did I make myself understood?"

Kyubei staggered backward until his back bumped against the wall, and began to shiver violently. He tried to speak, but no coherent words came out of his dry mouth. "I- ahh- agh...."

"Now, get the hell out of my house!" shouted Muramoto. "And come back with your man by the next full moon. I don't need to remind you what's going to happen if you don't. Do I?"

As if on cue, Kyubei sprinted down the long hallway and out of the residence.

As the bustling street with a large crowd offered a sense of safety, Kyubei slowed down. Glancing back to make sure Muramoto was not following him, he collapsed on all fours in the street. The deliberate intimidation in the silent house stated a stark warning. He now realized why Muramoto had invited him to his grand residence and made to wait for so long; it was all part of the intimidation tactics. Psychologically and physically threatened, Kyubei regretted underestimating Muramoto and the gravity of his plight. From the official's extreme reaction, Kyubei came to realize that the bakufu stood on the verge of a humiliating defeat.

All the way home, the alternative scenario nauseated him. Raw images of him being hanged repeatedly played in his head. Feeling so sick, he had to stop his palanquin several times and throw up. *I gotta catch that little shit. I don't care how.* He no longer cared about his future business and prosperity at all as his life was at stake. "I'd happily come forward as a tax evader if it helped me escape the bakufu!" he shouted unconsciously.

"What's wrong with this man?" said one of the porters to his partner.

"Greed, my friend. That's something we ain't gotta no worry about!" He laughed out loud.

Two days later, an urgent letter arrived at Muramoto's residence, sealed with the distinctive emblem of the bakufu. Muramoto tore it open with impatient fingers and scanned the contents as his face twisted in disbelief.

The letter detailed a scandalous revelation: one of Muramoto's secret agents he had planted deep within the Imperial Palace had overheard a conversation between two courtiers. They spoke of an "obnoxious peasant retailer" who had brazenly bribed his way into their good graces in pursuit of a business contract. The audacity did not end there. According to the eavesdropping agent, the retailer had sweetened the deal with the promise of a mysterious incentive — a man with extraordinary abilities. Though the couriers seemed clueless about the man's exact powers, one phrase had stood out: *psychic*.

Muramoto's hands trembled as he read and reread the

damning account. His expression darkened, his face contorted into a mask of unrestrained fury. "That disgusting primitive reptile!"he roared, tearing the letter to shreds. "You double-crossed me? The bakufu? You're a dead man, Tsubaki-Ya! I'll kill you, and I'll do it brutally!" His rage consumed him, surging through his veins like wildfire. He screamed incoherently, kicking and smashing his writing box. His maids stood aghast, trembling.

Snapping back into action, Muramoto barked orders, his voice a whip of raw anger. A messenger was dispatched to his fellow general, Watabe, to inform him of the abrupt change in plans. With his blood boiling and vengeance driving his every step, Muramoto set out for the west, flanked by two of his most trusted subordinates.

The road ahead promised no peace — only reckoning.

——————— * ——————— * ——————— * ——————— *

The purple light of dawn gradually bathed Mt. Ibuki, the highest peak of the border of Oumi and Mino Provinces. Revered as a domain of a god, the mountain exuded an aura of spirituality throughout history. The promise of a bright day embraced the vast plain known as Sekigahara. Spring's verdant hues and wild-flowers burst forth across the fields, the air redolent with the scent of fresh vegetation after months of snow.

In an unnamed rural community, the tranquil morning lost its mystical quality as the thunderous rattle of hooves approached from the west of Sekigahara. Half-asleep peasants jumped out of their shacks and peered in the direction of the commotion through the dense morning fog veiling the gently sloping foothills. All of a sudden, a cavalry of around 50 samurais emerged through the mist. As they shifted their pace from a furious gallop to a casual trot, clouds of dirt diminished around them. Clad in colorful armors of iron and lacquered leather — dark vermillion, black, and brown — they resembled human-sized horseshoe crabs. The heavy coverings made dry crackles as the horses trotted. The samurais carried longbows and blood-imbrued arrows on their backs, their gazes fixed ahead as if disregarding near-derelict houses and dirty-faced peasants around them.

Now, the entire village stood in awe as no one had never seen a samurai or a horse before. They pointed at the grotesquely dressed men on horseback from a safe distance, intrigued yet mostly frightened. Some of the elderly women knelt and prayed for their dear lives, while other began to sob. Soon, all the peasants fell to their knees, placed their hands on the ground, and bowed deeply while chanting a mantra.

Out of nowhere, a little boy, evidently unable to resist his curiosity, ran toward one of the samurais, giggling. Just as he reached his small arm to touch a front leg of the horse, the stern-faced warrior horsewhipped the boy's cheek. "Get your dirty peasant hands off my horse, you disgusting little shit!" he bellowed and then swung his whip at the stunned crowd. The boy squealed like a wounded animal, covering his reddened face with his trembling hands. His wail echoed through the misty village as his mother instantly rushed to his aid and whisked him away.

With uncertainty hanging in the air, the villagers remained motionless, afraid of similar treatment. While they remained on their knees and hands, a few senior-ranked samurais exchanged quick words. Then, the one who had reprimanded the boy approached the crowd. "We must stay here for a while," he announced. "In the meantime, we request your hospitality and sustenance. Is that clear?" The villagers whispered to each other and resumed their bows. The samurai soon realized that they could not understand his Kamakura dialect, so he switched to a local tongue, repeating his demand. This time, all quickly stood up and ran back to their respective homes.

One of the villagers obediently came up to the samurai. "Sir, we'll do as you wish."

The senior samurai waved the peasant off and returned to his cavalry, gesturing for them to dismount from their houses and set up tents nearby.

After a frugal porridge at their tent site on the field, the cavalry finally relaxed. They had traveled for two days from Settsu Province without food or rest until they reached this rendezvous point. They could have returned their home in Kamakura, instead of making a detour. Yet, not a single man complained, displaying their loyalty to their general, Katsuhide Watabe. And he was grateful.

One of the seniors glided soundlessly beside General Watabe, who sat cross-legged on a traditional low stool, idly poking his temple with a sensu. Bowing low, the man got down on one knee. "Sir, some of the young ones wish to... pursue the peasant girls," he said, clearing his throat. "Should I tell them not to —"

Watabe smirked. "Let them, Sasaki," he replied with a dismissive hand. "They deserve it, and it's natural for young men to satisfy their desires. Let's not be needlessly rigid."

"Yes, sir. I'll inform them right away" Sasaki bowed and rose to leave.

"Wait." Watabe's voice cut through the air, stopping Sasaki. "Has he shown up yet?"

"No, sir. General Muramoto hasn't arrived yet. But, I'll inform you as soon as he does."

Watabe grunted in acknowledgment. "Very well. I'm going to rest for a while." With that, Watabe lay down on the grass, one arm tucked behind his head, the other draped across his chest.

As the pleasant afternoon breeze rustled the grass, Watabe's mind wandered to Muramoto. Foe, comrade, rival — their paths had always intertwined. They had risen through the bakufu ranks together — but with different perspectives. Watabe had never forgiven Muramoto's tendency to bend Bushido to suit his own ambitions, his penchant for prioritizing personal gains over the samurai code.

That elongated, preposterously thin mustache of his... Watabe almost sneered at the thought. Everything about Muramoto grated on him — his ostentatious air, his overly polished tone, even the garish silk robes he insisted on wearing.

And yet, Watabe knew that Muramoto likely viewed him with equal disdain. A loyal servant to Takatoki Hojo, Watabe has sacrificed his own comfort time and again for the ruler's sake — a principle Muramoto had scoffed at repeatedly. No doubt the man considered him obstinate and boring — a samurai too bound by tradition to see the border picture. So be it, Watabe thought. *Some lines must never be crossed.* The rhythmic sway of the grass lured Watabe into a light doze, but his mind remained alert. *Muramoto would arrive soon enough. He always does when it serves him...*

"Sir, General Muramoto has just arrived," Sasaki whispered to his dozing superior's ear. "Sir?"

Watabe instinctively reached for his kaiken, then set it aside and put his eyepatch over his scarred right eye. Sasaki stepped back to give himself space and bowed. "Shall I escort him over here, sir?"

"Don't bother. I'm right here, General Watabe," declared Muramoto as he swaggered into the partially-enclosed space.

"You're lucky, General Muramoto, that I'm only half asleep," responded Watabe, his indignation oozing out. "Otherwise, I'd draw my sword in a heartbeat on whoever comes close to me unannounced." He dismissed Sasaki with a backhand swipe. Sasaki slipped out noiselessly like a ninja.

"And you're lucky as well," replied Muramoto coolly, "because I don't usually hesitate to slit a man's throat when he flashes his kaiken at me."

Watabe scoffed. "Oh, by the way, allow me to stress the

importance of punctuality. We generals should be paragons of Bushido. Don't you agree, *General* Muramoto?"

Muramoto smirked. "Hmm...funny, because I don't recall reading about the regulation of itineraries in my Bushido handbook. Would you mind telling me which page?"

The two samurai generals approached each other, nose to nose, and held their poise before breaking away.

Watabe decided to cut to the chase. He did not want to waste any more time with this despicable man than he had already done. "So, enlighten me, Mr. Muramoto. Why do you require my men?"

Muramoto briefed Watabe on the situation: the darling bargain of a peasant merchant, the elusive psychic with rare abilities, the merchant's brazen betrayal, and Muramoto's imminent retaliation against the traitor.

"So, let me get this straight," said Watabe, "you intend to attack a civilian, a PEASANT no less, with MY calvary. Did I hear right?"

"Yes, because, in fact, I plan to ravage the village where this traitor lives."

"And why is that?"

"Because that was what my ancestor tried to do in his time with the bakufu about 60 years ago," Muramoto confided. "He was severely punished for his action. But this one is a completely different situation."

"So, it's personal," scoffed Watabe, remaining seated with his elbow resting on his thigh. He drew the sensu from his chest and tapped his other thigh with it.

"No, not entirely so." Muramoto immediately countered. "Our Lord will appreciate and value this action as a warning to anyone foolish enough to deceive him."

Watabe laughed derisively. "Again, Mr. Muramoto, why does it sound like a personal agenda?"

"Who doesn't have it? You, Mr. Watabe, certainly have got one, too, haven't you?"

"Yes. Mine is to eradicate those who don't honor the code of ethics."

Muramoto laughed exaggeratedly. "That's a good one! Anyway, my action will reflect positively on you as well, since I'll use your cavalry. I'd use my own if it were all about my gain. And I'll personally reward your men handsomely for their commitment. In the end, you won't even have to lift a finger to add another glory to your legacy."

Though the mention of credit insulted Watabe, he found some relief knowing his men would benefit financially from Muramoto's little campaign. The balance between servicing the bakufu and living one's own life had often troubled Watabe, given the meager pay lower-ranked samurais received for their sacrifices. Indeed, every once in a while he personally gave each one of his subordinates small allowances, but it was still not enough. *This selfish gokenin is clearly a lot more well-off than I estimated*, he admitted. Watabe's tone slightly shifted as he mulled over the proposition. "What about risks? And the psychic? Could he pose a threat?" he asked. "I won't allow anyone to put my men in unnecessary risks."

"What risks? It's a peasant village, for heaven's sake," retorted Muramoto confidently, his eyes flashing. "I don't need the entire cavalry. Four or five men should suffice."

25

THE CURIOUS CASE OF A MADMAN

When Gensuke was hammering away at a lump of iron with a blazing mallet, he heard something behind him. But, deafening clanks made it almost impossible to discern what had caused it. With the job already behind schedule, he continued to beat the sizzling red mass in front of him. Then, a hand pushed him hard on the back, causing him to nearly hit his hand with the mallet. Enraged, he turned around to confront who had done it. In front of him, Kyubei was barely holding himself together, violently shaking, his bloodshot eyes twitching uncontrollably. Gensuke recoiled. *Does he have a nasty hangover, sleep problems or what?* A trickle of drool also leaked from the corner of his mouth, dampening his unshaven chin. Sweat spots and dirt smudges spread all over his expensive kimono. With a pallid complexion and unkempt hair, the wealthy merchant had turned into a madman, breathing noisily through his nose.

"Umm...Kyubei-san?" asked Gensuke hesitantly, as if waiting for confirmation from the man in front of him.

"W-where is your daughter!?" shrieked Kyubei, his

clenched fists shot out. “I need to see her now!” His screeches resembled those of piglets.

Gensuke gulped tensely as he witnessed the deranged behavior of someone he knew, especially someone like Kyubei, who was known for his shrewdness. And yet, at the same time, he became alert, for Yuri had kept telling him about the merchant’s guile and clandestine scheme to capture Ryu. “Umm... are you alright? You seem very ill. Let me get you some water.”

“Don’t you move, Gensuke! I need your daughter!” screamed Kyubei. “Tell me where she is! Is she home?” He took a few steps toward Gensuke.

“Please, calm down, Kyubei-san,” said Gensuke. He put his tool down on a workbench and began to step back from the madman, with his hands in the air.

Kyubei threw his right hand behind his back and pulled out a rusty sickle from under his sash. As he waved his weapon frantically, he advanced unsteadily toward Gensuke. “I’ll hurt you unless you tell me where I can find her. I will....I swear,” His breathing deepened, with each step he took. His shadow invaded further across the earthen floor toward Gensuke, whose back nearly touched the wall.

“Hey, Gen, time to go — What the hell?!” shouted Heijiro, upon setting foot in the workshop. Although he only saw the back of a man, he instantly identified who it was. “Kyubei-san, what are you doing with that thing in your hand? Put that down, please!”

Kyubei turned his head, still holding his weapon above his head. But, he became slightly calmer. “Heijiro.... I want you to help me find your son.... and Gensuke’s daughter,” he said and walked toward Heijiro, who stood still by the door.

Heijiro mouthed “What the hell” to his friend over Kyubei’s shoulder. Gensuke, in response, shook his head frantically. “Look, Kyubei-san. I have no idea what you want from my son, but I don't know where he is," said Heijiro calmly. "He and I've not got along well lately. So, I can't help you."

As if collapsing from inside, Kyubei's shoulders suddenly slumped heavily, the sickle hitting the dirt floor with a faint thud. He let out faint falsetto sounds like an eerie, pitiful birdsong. Heijiro quickly approached Gensuke and patted his back. "Gen, what's this all about?"

"No idea, Jiro. He just barged in and threatened me like a lunatic. And now, this." Gensuke pointed at Kyubei kneeling on the ground.

"Well...at least he won't do no harm now."

Kyubei suddenly staggered to his feet, a sinister mask taking over his face. "You pieces of shits!" hissed the madman, pointing his trembling index finger at both of them. "You'll see what I'm capable of. Very soon." Gensuke and Heijiro shivered. With that, Kyubei nonchalantly walked out of the workshop, his devilish laughter sending a chill down their spines.

"He WHAT??" shouted Shodai, nearly spatting.

"Snuck up on me at work and threatened me with a sickle. It was a total shit show," explained Gensuke with animated gestures.

"You're making that up!"

"Wish I were, sir." Gensuke rubbed his hands together and blew into them.

"My god... But...what did he want from you??" Shodai started a hibachi. The charcoal immediately turned red, sending a stream of smoke into the cold air.

"He demanded to see my daughter." Gensuke warmed his hands over the fire.

"And my son," Heijiro chipped in, joying Gensuke.

"Why?? It doesn't make any sense at all..." Shodai positioned himself opposite his younger colleagues.

Shodai, Gensuke, and Heijiro sat by a wall in the Higashiya

discussing the earlier incident from that afternoon. The trio remained in the building after the Guild meeting, where the procedure for an annual *hanami* — cherry blossom viewing — festival had been discussed. The meeting had ended with a spontaneous clap from all the Guild members, absent Kyubei. They showed their enthusiasm for the upcoming festival, especially since it had been called off the previous year due to the heavy storms. They left the building in high spirits.

As Gensuke and Heijiro shared the details of Kyubei's deranged behaviors, Shodai could hardly contain himself. He interrupted their narratives a few times as if seeking the confirmation of the story. "God...no wonder he didn't show up today," concluded the headman.

"Was he acting normal the last time you saw him? When did you see him last, sir?" asked Gensuke.

Shodai stroked his long white goatee as he pondered. "Hmm...let me see," he said, "I don't really remember how long ago, but I do know it was the day before he set off to Kamakura, because he was so unusually cheerful that day. It was as if something joyful was about to happen to him."

"What does Kamakura have anything to do with him?" Heijiro added more charcoal.

Switching to a whisper, Shodai leaned toward them. "Yeah, that's the thing about Kyubei," he confided, "most of us don't know, but he's been so keen to relocate Tsubaki-Ya to Kamakura."

"Why, sir? His business is irritatingly good here." Gensuke placed an iron kettle over the hibachi.

"Well, obviously he has a different agenda, though," explained Shodai, "he told me before that he has grand ambitions and Kasuga is just too small to satisfy them."

"Yup, that sounds like him pretending to be larger than life," scoffed Heijiro.

Shodai leaned even closer to them, avoiding smoke and steam from below. "I believe there is more to the story." He paused, creating a moment of suspense, then continued, "I know he bribed someone in the bakufu to smooth out some bureaucratic difficulties for his plan to relocate smoothly."

"But it's hardly a surprise to us, sir. Kyubei-san is Kyubei-san, after all," said Heijiro, shrugging his shoulders.

"Yeah, but what's bothering me is, on top of the bribe, it seems that he also tried to 'sell a man' to the bakufu. Someone very valuable to them would be my guess."

Heijiro poured hot water into three little cups and passed the two of them to Gensuke and Shoda. "Umm... this is getting outrageous. No disrespect, sir, but how did you come by all this information?"

"I'm the headman of the Guild. Don't underestimate my network," replied Shodai as he sipped his hot water.

Gensuke sat in silence, his thoughts spiraling as Yuri's words echoed in his mind: Ryu might fall victim to Kyubei's schemes. At first, he had dismissed it as youthful paranoia as she must have been overthinking the merchant's eccentricities. But the pieces no longer aligned.

Kyubei's recent behavior — his veiled threats, his aggressive dealings in Kamakura — had painted a darker picture. Gensuke's gut twisted as he recalled his own tense encounter with the man earlier that afternoon. Yuri had warned him, and now, the chilling thoughts crept in. *What if she was right? What if she had unwittingly become entangled in Kyubei's conspiracy?*

A surge of dread gripped Gensuke. The image of his daughter caught in the web of Kyubei's desperation was unbearable. "We must keep Yuri safe from that lunatic!" he blurted out. Shodai and Gensuke were jolted, staring at him. He rose from his seat and began to pace. "He's dangerous and reckless now. Something must've happened in Kamakura. Whatever it is, it's driven him to madness. This isn't the same Kyubei-san we used to know."

Dusk had begun to fall. "Gensuke, where is your daughter

now?" asked Shodai as he peered outside through the door. "Kyubei might be still roaming somewhere in the village."

The cup dropped from Gensuke's hand. "Oh god, I have no idea where she is, sir."

Tranquility shrouded the riverbank. The gentle murmur of the River Hasu added a sense of serenity. Moonlight danced gracefully on the water's surface, casting sporadic gleams that harmonized with each ripple. Even Mt. Toki, in the distance, stood peacefully. The twilight air hung perfectly still, inviting a leisurely stroll.

Yuri's footsteps harmonized with the scene, emphasizing the hush. With no one else around, the stillness complemented her state of mind. However, despite the lovely setting, her thoughts wandered elsewhere as she strolled along the bank. In fact, her heart quickened, not due to the walk, but because of the memories flooding back. Every time she came to this spot, her thoughts invariably drifted back to the flash flood from two years ago and Ryu, who had bravely saved her from drowning. She could almost hear her heartbeat quicken as she envisioned his strong shoulders carrying her through the rice paddies. *How come I passed out... so stupid!* She cursed silently. *I could've touched him, could've smelled his hair...*

Two years had passed, yet Yuri still had no idea where Ryu had gone — or if she would ever see him again. Despite her effort to remain hopeful, doubt often crept in, threatening to shatter her resolve. *Will I ever find him?* The question lingered like an ache in her chest.

Her concerns extended far beyond her fondness for Ryu. Kyubei's shadow loomed large, his malicious presence a constant source of unease. Yuri could not shake the memory of her time in Kyo, where she had stumbled upon fragments of his scheming. Since her return, she had quietly kept an eye on him, following his movements. So far, there had been no signs of trouble. No secret meetings, no underhand dealings — nothing to suggest that Kyubei's plans had come to fruition. It brought Yuri a measure of relief, though not enough to dispel her vigilance. *For now, at least, the village is safe*, she thought, gripping the fabric of her sleeve as she stared out into the horizon over the River Haus.

She stood on the wooden platform lining the riverbank. It lay as sturdy as ever. Every now and then, she still caught the locals gossiping about Ryu's involvement in this creation and witchcraft. *Typical rural folk...*, Yuri thought as she plucked a dandelion sticking out between the logs and smelled its scent as if trying to evoke a memory.

"Are you going to wear it in your hair?" A high-pitched voice startled her from behind. "I bet you'd look even prettier."

Yuri was petrified. The last person she wanted in this world was approaching her. As Kyubei drew closer, he laughed derisively, with his arms stretched. Repulsed, she instinctively backed away, measuring the distance between herself and the edge of the platform. To her horror, Kyubei continued to advance. Before long, her foot touched the edge. She was cornered.

Devouring her desperation, Kyubei taunted her further. "Aww, you poor thing," he teased, mimicking Kento's voice. "You think I'm going to hurt you? Why? I'm not a bad man. Just looking to make friends with you. Is that too much to ask? Huh?" With each word, he inched closer.

"Don't get any closer, you creep!" hissed Yuri, taking another step back. Her right foot stepped out of the edge, but she managed to balance herself. "I mean it!"

"Or what? What are you gonna do? Huh?" Kyubei sneered, reverting to his usual malicious self. "Stop acting like a little girl. I'm not gonna hurt you. As I said, I just want to talk to you, sweetheart."

"You heard her. Leave her alone." A man's frosty voice sliced through the tension, freezing Kyubei. He frantically moved his head around. From behind a large oak tree near the bank, a tall figure emerged. "I'll give you a few more seconds to leave." As he got closer to the platform, Kyubei snatched Yuri's arm. "Let her go, or this isn't gonna end well for you," the man warned. He stopped a few meters away, standing face-to-face with them.

"Ryu!" exclaimed Yuri.

"Hands up, you bastard, and walk away from her! Now!"

Kyubei clapped his hands theatrically. "My, oh, my," he marveled. "I was right after all. I knew you'd show up like this! I really appreciate your participation in this lovely evening." He sniggered.

"Just get the hell out," commanded Ryu.

"Oh, no, no, no. You and I are gonna have a little talk tonight. I'll take you to my place. How does that sound?" Kyubei pulled out his sickle and waved it in front of him.

"Don't get any funny ideas. You'll get hurt." Ryu took a few steps closer.

Kyubei burst into hysterical laughter. "'Don't get any funny ideas. You'll get hurt.' Yeah, that's really funny!"

In a split second, Yuri swiftly dodged her attacker and moved to Ryu's side. Unconsciously, Ryu took her hand and gave it an assuring shake. Yuri instantly felt safe.

"Aww...what a sweet reunion," said Kyubei. "Unfortunately, however, your time is up. Come on, chop-chop, let go of his hand, sweetheart. He's mine now." He swung the blade frantically over his head, hissing and laughing.

Just as Ryu was about to make a quick move, a hand stuck out from under the edge of the platform, grabbed Kyubei's right ankle, and yanked it forcefully. The next moment, with a loud thud, Kyubei's face hit hard on the wooden floor. His weapon flew across the platform and landed on the grassy bank. Gensuke climbed up breathlessly from below the wooden structure. After nudging the still body of the madman with his toes, he embraced Yuri in his arms. "I was worried sick about you," he said, nearly on the verge of tears. "I'm so glad you're okay."

Seeing him like this emotional for the first time since Amuro's final day, Yuri felt awkward rather than grateful to be cared for. "Thank you, Father. I'm okay, really," she said embarrassedly and freed herself from his embrace.

"Ryu, you showed up, finally!" said Gensuke out aloud. "We've almost lost —"

"Why... I mean, where have you been for the last two years?" interjected Yuri, "What's happened to you? Why didn't you come back to the village sooner? We've been looking for you everywhere! Me and Kento. We even went to Kyo!"

Hearing her speak earnestly and freely, he felt a profound sense of guilt for having had to slip away the way he had. *But it was necessary*, he reasoned, *because if I had stayed longer, even one more day, I might have put everybody in danger, just as Sir Shinzan said.*

Ever since crawling back to the cave from the flooding River Hasu two springs ago, Shinzan had dissuaded Ryu from returning to the village, fearing dire consequences if his powers, let alone his true identity, were ever exposed. "Just let them worry about you for a while," Shinzan had said, "they are safe, at least for the time being. You'll go save them again eventually, anyway, won't you?"

However, the status quo could face unimaginable danger because of Kyubei. That prospect had compelled Ryu to come back unexpectedly. "I know, Yuri. I'm so sorry for having made you worry about me," admitted Ryu. "I could apologize as much as you let me, but not for now. Time is running out for us."

"What do you mean?"

"It's imperative that you two trust me with what I'm about to tell you." Ryu placed his hand firmly on Yuri and Gensuke's shoulders.

If only everyone were as steadfast as these two, Ryu thought as he glanced at Gensuke and Yuri. Their quiet determination gave him hope, but also sharpened the weight of the deception he was weaving. *If they could just stay focused, eluding the raid might still be possible.*

Walking along the riverbank, Ryu spun a tale, carefully crafting each word. He claimed to have stumbled upon a cavalry mobilizing for a raid on the village. Over the past two years, he told the father and daughter, that he had been in Kamakura, where he had uncovered a military plan to eliminate Kyubei, who had betrayed the bakufu. The lies tasted bitter on his tongue. Each detail he fabricated left a knot of discomfort in his chest, but he pressed on.

As he finished, Ryu caught himself holding his breath, waiting for questions, and accusations that might pierce through the fragile veil of his story. Yet, to his surprise, neither Gensuke nor Yuri probed further. They seemed preoccupied, their expressions clouded with lingering unease. Perhaps, Ryu thought, they were still reeling from the chaos by the river not long ago.

A sign of relief escaped him, though it brought little comfort. He hated lying to them, especially Yuri. But for now, the truth felt like a luxury they could not afford.

The trio eventually arrived at the central part of the village, where many reputable and influential families resided. Candlelight flickered through cracks in doors and walls, casting warm glows all around the neighborhood. Faint laughter of children echoed from some homes, while the occasional hoots of owls pierced the night air. The lull before the storm, Ryu noted anxiously. Clouds covered most of the moon, and Gensuke's lone lantern barely illuminated the vast promenade leading to the lord's grand manor.

"So, Ryu, this general Muramoto is a grandson of the ringleader of the unfinished invasion sixty years ago?" asked Gensuke incredulously.

"That's correct, sir," answered Ryu. "It's just pure coincidence. History is a collection of random happenstances."

"And now this'll be his redemption. He wants to finish off

what his ancestors failed to accomplish. Once and for all. And Tsubaki-Ya?"

"Exactly, sir. And we'll stop —" Ryu tripped on a bump, nearly dropping Kyubei, who slung over his back.

Gensuke's expression betrayed hesitation instead of determination. "I'm supposed to convince the lord that a new invasion will come by tomorrow afternoon at the latest?" he asked rhetorically. "He's fond of me, but I'm not so sure if I can do this."

"Yes, sir, you can," Ryu assured Gensuke. "And you have to. I believe you and trust you. This village relies on you and the lord."

"What about him?" Yuri chipped in, pointing at the unconscious Kyubei. "What're you gonna do with him? This is all his fault, after all."

"Yes, I'm aware of that. And he'll pay for his arrogance one way or another." Ryu gave Kyubei a playful shake.

"Very well, then, I'd better get going," said Gensuke, "and please, make sure she's safe with the rest of the village." With that, he set off on the promenade.

Ryu suddenly felt nervous being alone with her, while Yuri became eager to take advantage of the situation. "I like you, Ryu," confessed Yuri, her heartbeat quickening. "So, I don't need your apology. I'd like you to stay in the village this time, or at least somewhere close by. I want to know more about you. A lot more." She got closer to Ryu, her middle finger caressing his sleeve.

Ryu backed off. *Oh no, Yuri, please...* A mixed feeling of mortification and sympathy rushed over him, a complex yet raw turbulence he had never experienced before. He became mute.

"Well...I see. Being non-responsive sucks," said Yuri, "but, tell you what, Ryu, I won't take a no for an answer so easily. Hope it's okay with you." With that, she twirled around, turning her back to him, and hummed softly.

Ryu hesitantly tapped Yuri on the back, but she kept humming, toying with his discomfort. *Oh, this is beyond embar-*

rassing. He hated himself for it. "So, Yuri, how's Kent been doing? Where is he at?

Yuri turned around. "Oh, wow...thanks for saving us from a coma with the thought-provoking questions!" She immediately regretted her sour retort. "I'm sorry, Ryu. Anyway, lately, he's been spending time with this artistic type in Inaki, someone as passionate about drawing as himself, you know..." she explained, "I'm quite sure that's where he is now."

"Oh, okay, great. He's safe, then." Ryu grunted, shifting Kyubei on his back.

"Why don't you dump him on the ground? He doesn't deserve royal treatment." Yuri yanked Kyubei's kimono down.

"I'm good. I don't want this man to run before he faces his fate."

Just as the weight overwhelmed Ryu, Kyubei stirred at last, drooling. "Ow! My head...," he moaned weakly. Then all of a sudden, remembering his predicament, he started to writhe violently on Ryu's back. "Goddamnit! Let go of me, you son of a bitch!" he spat and flailed his arms and legs like a petulant child while continuing to yell and curse. Having taken enough, Ryu released his hold and dropped Kyubei to the ground. "OUCH!! Damn you, asshole!" Kyubei rubbed his hip.

"You asked me to let you go. So I did, you pathetic prick," retorted Ryu. "And if I were you, I'd go back home, take everything I could, and flee the village tonight."

"Shut your mouth!" snapped back Kyubei. "What I'll do is..." He tried to grab Yuri's arm.

"It's a little too late for that," said Ryu, twisting Kyubei's hand. "We know about your schemes in Kamakura and Kyo. And so does Muramoto. He knows you double-crossed him. In fact, he's on his way here to deal with you."

Kyubei recoiled at the revelation but managed to remain belligerent. "Ha! That's the most fascinating story I've ever heard!

I don't believe a word of it. Don't try to be smart with me, you piece of shit!" He spat at Ryu.

"Alright, suit yourself, because we will evacuate the village. And you're the primary target anyway," said Ryu calmly. "We could've left you by the river for Muramoto to find, but we brought you here out of mercy."

Kyubei's bravado disappeared instantly. He started shaking, his hands clutching at the air, as illegible words escaped his throat. Then, with a final shrill cry, he wetted himself. The warm sensation of his own urine brought him back to reality. No sooner had Ryu said 'run!' than he broke into a sprint to the direction of his store.

"He won't cause any more trouble for sure," said Yuri, after the cries of a wounded animal dissipated into a shroud of night. "Well, we should get moving and let everybody know about the evacuation."

"Actually, Yuri," said Ryu, "I want you to stick to my plan. I'll go check to see how much time we have until the cavalry reaches here."

"What?? No way, Ryu!" protested Yuri. "You're not leaving me now. I won't allow it!"

"Hey, hey...don't worry. I'll come back and join you as quickly as I can. I promise. Trust me, this is as important as your part."

"But, how will you—"

Ryu was already on the move.

26

THE BLAZING BONFIRES

Ryu's lungs burned for more oxygen as he climbed up Mt. Yashiro at full speed. It offered an ideal vantage point to watch over the entire land, sitting near the north end of the village where the River Hasu flowed down into Wakasa Bay in the far distance.

As he sprinted, Ryu's thoughts raced to Yuri and Gensuke and their task of evacuating the whole village within a narrow window of time. Evacuation might be unnecessary as Ryu determined to stop the impending invasion before the attack of the samurais. However, he grappled with uncertainty regarding the miracle he needed to conjure and the necessity of concealing his actions from the public eye. For these reasons, sending the villagers away from their homes was a wise precaution in case unforeseen circumstances arose.

He groaned, knowing that ibises could not fly after dark. Although he had enough time before dawn, his apprehension mounted as the forest echoed with the haunting cries of nocturnal creatures. *Have I truly been ready for what lies ahead?* An overwhelming doubt gnawed at him as the lingering premonition weighed heavily on his mind.

The sequence of fragmented images had repeatedly played in his thoughts for the past three days: samurais on horseback wearing war masks, their colors vivid in red and black, screaming defiantly at the sky; burning objects flying over the river, illuminating its surface as they landed on thatched roofs, grain sheds, and livestock shelters; terrified villagers and screeching animals darting aimlessly across the fields under the sea of leaping sparks in the semi-dark sky.

Suddenly, despite the mild temperature and occasional breezes, acute thirst seized Ryu. He wondered if it had anything to do with the haunting images of the burning village. While he had faced disastrous incidents in the past, confronting an actual enemy capable of inflicting such devastation terrified him. As apprehension surged, so did his thirst.

The faint murmur of a creek came from the distance. Relieved, Ryu instinctively entered into the pitch-black forest. Before long, animal smells filled his nostrils, and the backs of his feet felt soft dirt instead of vegetation. *A game trail!* He tensed up. After a cautious trek along the trail, a damp smell permeated his surroundings, quickening his pace. As he trod on, his feet finally touched cold water. He waded into the creek and bent over, touching the water.

The next moment, a menacing growl lacerated the tranquility. Ryu slowly turned. A large wolf with bristling dark fur crouched low in the shrub merely five meters away. His instinct told him to remain still while the wolf continued to snuffle at him. With cautious deliberation, he began to wade through the water backward. The beast circled around as if waiting for the perfect moment to strike. Ryu stopped when the water reached chest height and slowly submerged himself. He remained underwater until his lungs screamed for air. When he emerged, the creature was still circling at the water's edge. As Ryu's body lost sensation, he fell into a trance and began an incantation. Right on cue, the wolf stopped its march, scratched the muddy ground, and let out a prolonged whimper. Still unconscious, Ryu continued his mantra until the wolf turned into a cooing dog. Then, with a mournful howl, it disappeared into the depths of the forest.

As his body regained feeling, so did his cognition. *What's just possessed me? I can communicate with animals.* Remembering how thirsty he had been a moment earlier, Ryu cupped his hands, scooped water from the stream, and swallowed it in one gulp. He continued until he could not drink anymore. With his adrenaline drained after the tense encounter with the wolf, acute fatigue overwhelmed him. Stillness usually made him focus on his tasks, but now all he wanted to do was close his eyes and rest, though he knew he could not afford to fall asleep.

Shivering in his soaked clothes, he made a fire in a makeshift pit by the water and sat on the damp grass. The murmur of the creek seduced him into a hypnotized state. He longed for the safety and sanctuary of Shinzan'z cave and a conversation to stave off sleep.

The drawing room of the lord's residence represented ultimate wealth without ostentation. The entirety of the space, including the ceiling, was crafted mostly from hinoki cypress and varnished with pine resin. At the center of the floor lay a large square cutout filled with fresh green tatamis. Devoid of large furniture, the room felt even more spacious. Candlelight shone on every surface, radiating a rich glow of deep amber. The lord's motto, 'Moderation will go a long way toward building a successful life,' without a doubt, reflected his temperate nature.

"Is this young fella, Ryu, trustworthy?" asked Takeru, the lord, to Gensuke. He politely reminded his visitor to drink green tea on the table. "I just need to make certain he isn't making everything up."

"No, sir, he isn't," answered Gensuke firmly. "And I believe what he told us. Ryu may be as young as my late son, but he has a certain aura just like you do. People would listen to a man with such charisma." He sipped his tea.

"Hmm, I wonder what kind of life he has lived so far," said Takeru thoughtfully. "Anyway, Gensuke, let's get to work, shall we? We've got lots to do before dawn."

"Yes, my lord."

Gensuke and Takeru set off immediately after the meeting. While they were walking down the hill with lanterns in their hands, Takeru said, "Although his actions so far are unforgivable, I feel sorry for Kyubei."

Gensuke stopped, taken aback by Takeru's remark. "Why, sir? He caused this," he asserted.

"Oh yes, I know, no doubt about it. And we both know he isn't an honest man. But we don't really know what he went through after he lost his fertility before being blessed with a single heir."

"With all due respect, sir, my daughter lost hers, too," responded Gensuke. "But she's trying to come to terms with her nightmare. So, there is no excuse for him to be a greed-driven selfish prick." He trembled with emotions.

"You're absolutely right, Gensuke," Takeru quickly conceded and placed his hand on Gensuke's shoulder. "But he is a man from a wealthy business family. He must've had a dream to leave his fortune to his son, an heir. And without such an objective, his life must be a lonely voyage devoid of a beacon.'

"But, sir, still —" Gensuke nearly spat.

"I understand, Gensuke, understand." They reached a fork. Clearing his throat, Takeru added, "I'll go to Sir Jintoku's."

"Yes, sir. And I'll stop by the Headman's first. Hope to rendezvous with the rest of the village in Mt. Yashiro by midnight." Gensuke took the left fork.

The night was still young, but the fields stayed as quiet as midnight. Smoke and steam from cooking dinner wafted through many homes. When Gensuke approached Shodai's house,

Tokuko, his wife, was picking up a few pieces of firewood stacked against the outside wall.

"Let me help you, ma'am," said Gensuke as he took them from her.

Tokuko stretched her back. "Phew...thank you, Gen-san. I hate being old. Everything's getting so difficult for me," she said, wiping off the dirt from her garment. "Enough about me. So, you came for my husband, I assume?"

The door slid open, and Shodai came out. "Oh, Gensuke. I've been worried about your daughter. You found her? Is she okay?"

"Yes, she's alright, sir. But a more urgent issue has come up. It's a long, complex story..."

As soon as Gensuke finished his explanation, Shodai fetched a lantern from his shed. "We'd better hurry. Fetch all the Guild members. Then, the rest of the village."

"I'm on it, sir," said Gensuke, "and I'll meet you at the shrine by midnight." With that, he sprinted off into the night.

It took no time for Yuri to convince her mother of what had just happened at the riverbank. However, Katsue grew increasingly skeptical, interrupting the narrative with constant exclamations as Yuri's explanation reached the most outrageous details of the imminent threats Ryu had unfolded. "Oh, Mother, please," Yuri groaned, "let me finish. Will you?" Katsue raised both her hands apologetically. Yuri admitted inside that persuading someone like Katsue proved almost impossible. *She's so fragile and stubbornly refuses to face the ugliness in this world. Am I going to be like her when I get old?*

The sliding door opened, and Kairi's head poked out. He had been overhearing the exchange between his sister and mother. "Hey, sis, is Ryu your boyfriend or what?" he teased.

"None of your damn business!"

"Please, Yuri, no cursing in this house," interjected Katsue.

"Anyway, I find it extremely hard to believe what you're telling me. But I didn't find Ryu dishonest when I met him."

Yuri grew irritated. "Mother, he saved my life not once but twice! Twice!" She held up her index, then her middle one. "You really think he's making this up? For what??"

"You're right, I'm sorry," conceded Katsue. "He must know something that no one else does. And he's only trying to help us."

"Yes, mother. Whatever it is, I trust him, and so should everyone else. He said this was only a precaution and nothing too difficult. We just get together with the rest of the village at the shrine and later head up to Yashiro. That's it."

Kairi slapped his thigh. "Great, I'm definitely going with you, Sis. Yoriki and Haruki, too," he chimed in playfully. "And I wanna see your *boyfriend* there." He laughed at his own joke. "Mom, are you coming with us or not?"

On their way to the shrine, the Karubes made a stop at Heijiro's house. Tami, Heijiro's wife, greeted them during dinner. "What's up? You wanna join us? It's just me and Chisa tonight," she said, wiping her hands with her apron. Chisa, her daughter, cheerfully waved at the Karubes' three boys, her mouth full. "Oh, by the way, Gen-san had come to fetch Jiro right before you folks arrived," Tami added. "He told me to go to the shrine right away but didn't tell me why. I was in the middle of making dinner, and my girl was having a tantrum, you know?" She slid the door open wider. "Anyway, come in."

"Actually, Mrs. Tami, we came to pick you two up. We're all gonna join the rest of the village at the shrine," said Yuri quickly.

Tami stepped out and closed the door behind her. "What's going on, Yuri? Does it have anything to do with Kyubei-san?" she whispered. "Jiro told me everything." She softly stroked Yuri's arm.

Yuri shushed Yoriki and Haruki, then responded to Tami, "I'll fill you in on the way."

"Umm...okay, sure. But what about Kento?"

"I believe he's with his friend in Inaki."

Before long, the Karubes, along with Tami and Chisa, set out.

They soon joined other villagers, who were just as puzzled as Tami. Some of them speculated about their unexpected march, exchanging their own versions of fables and fantasies about the legendary monster of Mt.Toki. "The red one will come get another young flesh," joked one of them, laughing. His companion elbowed him, sensing a change of mood around them.

"Shame on you!" hissed Tami, pointing an angry finger at them. "I cannot believe this. What disgraceful people! I'm so sorry, Katsue. You shouldn't have had to listen to that crap."

Katsue took a side step, avoiding the unwanted attention. "It's okay. I'm fine, Tami. It's a long time ago."

Tami tenderly stroked Katsue's arm, then turned to Yuri. "So, Yuri, why don't you tell me why we're doing this."

She did.

By the time Yuri finished the story, excluding the intense encounter with Kyubei, the two families, together with more than fifty villagers, stood on the grounds of the shrine. Seven blazing torches stood on the ground, yet they barely provided enough light in the dark. All the same, the crowd huddled around the fire, coughing with tears in their eyes, and exchanged information. Katsue and Tami joined in. Kairi, Yoriki, and Haruki got together with other boys, showing off their spinning top tricks, while Chisa engaged in giggling chats with her friends. Yuri navigated through the sea of people in the hope of finding Kento. After a while, she rejoined Katsue and Tami by the fire.

"Oh, there you are, Yuri," said Tami. "No offense, but I've never heard of anything like what you've just told me." She scratched her watery eyes with the back of her hand.

Yuri leaned to Tami. "Mrs. Tami, I know exactly what

you're thinking right now. 'What on earth is this girl talking about? I wasn't born yesterday.' Right?"

"Well..." Tami winced.

"No, I completely get it, and I don't blame you. Most people here would probably feel the same as you do." Yuri stretched her arm toward the people across the fire. "But I'm neither crazy nor making it all up. So, bear with me a little longer, please. My father and the lord will be here at any moment to confirm the situation."

"Alright, dear, we'll stay. Besides, I'm supposed to meet Heijiro right here," said Tami, glancing around the group. "But I'm a little worried about Kento."

"He's not here. I checked. That means he's still at his friend's place. The samurais won't attack there."

"I do hope so."

The night deepened, and the earlier warm air had created a fine mist that gradually blanketed the shrine precincts. As small children began to whine about the cold, the Guild members built a couple of large bonfires that instantly drew two shivering crowds. The dark smoke mingled with the mist, creating an eerie atmosphere. The shadows of the holy buildings swayed as the flames danced. The people constantly coughed, yet they welcomed the temporary diversion from the uncertainty that hung in the air. What had started as a contingency plan now felt more like a social gathering. Soon, they began to feel relaxed.

"Sir Jintoku, you experienced the samurai raid some 60 years ago, didn't you?" asked Shodai.

The eldest of the village immediately stiffened. "Damn right, I did. Those merciless animals!" he snorted indignantly. "One of my cousins was assaulted repeatedly! By more than one savage! She was only fourteen! It was a miracle she didn't get pregnant!"

"That's pure evil. Evil." Shodai cleared his throat. "By the way, I have no idea what's gotten into Tsubaki-ya. Would you believe that?"

"Ha! That slimy money-grubber!" spat Jintoku, "I never liked the son of a bitch. Never!"

"I guess he's learned a lesson this time."

"A lesson, my ass! My guess is he's fled the village already."

Shodai wiped Jintoku's spit off his face, grimacing. "Right, that makes sense, given what he's done to the samurai. Well... if all this was true."

"Oh yeah, it's all true, I'm positive. But there is more to his secret," Jintoku whispered suddenly.

"Oh? What is it, sir?" whispered Shodai, too, leaning forward.

"He owes the old lord a lot!" hissed Jintoku. "The bustard is the biggest tax evader and an abhorrently clever one! The lord's sure of it, but has yet to find clear evidence to incriminate him."

"So, he fled before he could be caught! He must've known he was getting cornered."

"Precisely!" Jintoku thrust out his index finger.

"But, how did you know all this?"

"Because I've lived long enough," said Jintoku, patting his left chest.

The crowd began to murmur and quickly moved toward the landing. There, Gensuke, Heijiro, and Takeru were panting hard. hands on their knees after running up the steep steps. A few people in the crowd approached them and asked about the unusual situation. Gensuke raised a hand to signal them to wait. While the trio coughed and gasped for breath, Katsue, Tami, and the lord's wife, Kiyo came next to their respective husbands and gently stroked their backs.

"The lord... the lord has a word with you all now," announced Gensuke. "Please, listen quietly." He turned to signal Takeru to step forward. "Sir."

Complete silence fell on the area. The spectators held their breaths.

After adjusting his clothes, Takeru acknowledged his audience, standing ceremoniously as if nothing had happened to hinder his breathing a few moments earlier. "Everyone, thank you for your patience," he began. "This village is facing its first threat in twelve years. We're in grave danger as of now." He paused, spreading his arm toward Jintoku, who bowed humbly and continued, "Only a few of you have lived long enough to endure the unimaginable atrocity committed by a group of barbarians over sixty years ago. And yet, after all those years, they're about to come back and..."

By the time Takeru finished his statement, his people remained silent, but this time with horror. Only the occasional crackles of the blazing bonfires broke the silence.

27

THE DEATH OF SEVEN SAMURAIS

By midnight, the mist had thickened, an opaque screen unfurled across the fields.

As over 300 people traversed the idyllic field, the visibility quickly diminished. Through the flickering lantern lights and the glow of burning torches, only the vast expanse of white lay ahead, blotting out the blackness of the night beyond. Silence prevailed, broken only by the steady rhythm of footsteps, enclosing the refugees in a trance-like state. Bereft of equilibrium, several of them stumbled over nothing but their own feet, some even tumbling to the ground. However, except for their muttered oaths, silence ruled as their desolate march continued.

Meanwhile, Yuri's thoughts drifted back and forth. *How come Ryu is always with me every time I face danger? In the ocean seven years ago, on the bridge two years ago, and tonight at the riverbank? Coincidences never repeat three times. So, what is this? Did he know beforehand? How? And what about all the details of the samurai raid and Kyubei' scheme?* These mysteries lacked crucial pieces, and the harder she tried to solve them, the more elusive they became. Yet, at the same time, she hesitated to uncover the truth about him. *Is his background that important? Would I like him much less if he turned out to be someone I didn't expect? Shouldn't my feelings toward him matter most regardless of who he is?* Yuri had always rejected blind conformity, challenging prevailing beliefs. Yet now, she clung to her idealized image of Ryu. She unconsciously clenched her fists hard, leaving nail marks on her palms.

Katsue noticed her daughter's change of mood. "What's wrong, Yuri?" she asked. "You've been awfully quiet for a while, and that's not like you."

"Mother, do you think I'm selfish?" asked Yuri bluntly.

Katsue stopped short. "What??"

"Am I selfish?" Yuri repeated and pulled her mother aside from the line of the evacuees.

"Define 'selfish.'"

Yuri shared her observation about Ryu, the enigma of his true identity, and the inner conflict that stirred within her.

As Katsue listened, she wondered where Yuri had inherited such divergent perspectives. In a way, she found similarities between Amuro and Yuri, although they did not share the same blood. *They are brother and sister after all.* "Well, Yuri, all I can say is you're different from me and other women," said Katsue eventually.

"What do you mean?" Yuri stepped back.

"For one thing, we women never question what is widely believed," Katsue began. "We're taught that way from the moment we're born. If you start questioning, society will pick on you, and eventually, you may end up ostracized. For us, conforming comes natural, whether you like it or not, and it secures our roles as dutiful wives."

"That's not me, Mother."

"Yes, Yuri, I know that." Katsue took Yuri's hands in hers.

"Are you disappointed that I'm so unconventional?"

"No, I'm jealous."

"Jealous? Of what?" Yuri recoiled.

"Yes. Because I might've had a different life if I were like you. But here I am, and I'm still happy to have lived a simple, conventional life."

Yuri withdrew her hands. "So, I'm still selfish?" she asked again tentatively.

"No, Yuri, I've never thought you're selfish. For what it's worth, you're simply you."

A man walking at the end of the march signaled them to hurry up. They quickly rejoined the group.

The midnight procession eventually reached its destination — the no-man's land between two villages, Kasuga and Inaki, at the foot of Mt. Yashiro. Many evacuees lay on the ground, breathing shallowly, some cradling their children and babies while others attended to their aging parents and relatives. The small children stopped kidding around and whispered to their parents and siblings. They all waited for the leaders to decide what to do next.

Takeru, Shodai, Gensuke, and Heijiro held a deep discussion. Entering Mt. Yashiro, Inaki's territory, required prior permission, a formality impossible to fulfill at this late hour.

"Our request will be denied even if we miraculously get hold of the Inaki headman," Takeru admitted. The rest of the men agreed.

"He wouldn't believe us anyway," Gensuke added, spitting.

Heijiro yanked a twig apart and threw it away. "What do you suggest we do, Sir Shodai?"

"I don't think we've got many choices," Shodai answered instantly. "We have only one choice: enter."

After relaying this to the exhausted crowd, the four men set forth into the mountain, the villagers following suit, with the rest of the Guild members acting as rear guards.

The faint glow of the lanterns and torches proceeded at a snail's pace and eventually merged into the hushed darkness of the mountain.

"Sir, I have something to tell you," said Amuro hesitantly.

Shinzan set his blind eyes on his young pupil, letting a moment linger before he ceremoniously cleared his throat. "Go on."

Despite the encouragement, Amuro's usually composed demeanor faltered, his fingers nervously toying with the grass he sat on. "Umm, this might be quite difficult to process..."

"Get to the point, son! Time is of the essence, and you know it."

"You're my ancestor, sir!" Amuro blurted out, then slumped. "I discovered it two years ago, but I wasn't sure if I wanted to share it with you, because —"

"Take it easy. No need to be dramatic, son. I knew it the moment you first contacted me. I've known all along." Shinzan chuckled mischievously.

"B-but....how?"

"I, too, have my own resources, just like your grandmother."

"My gran... How did you...?"

Shinzan got up, waving off the question. "Oh, I don't need to bore you with the uninteresting details."

Amuro rose to his feet. "Okay, I see. You find this conversation amusing? Fine. But, you should've told me, sir. I would've appreciated your candor."

"Well...it is what it is." Shinzan began to walk away.

As Amuro caught up with him, with his arms crossed on his chest, he noticed the sennin without his cane. With each stride, Shinzan's footsteps grew louder ...

Ryu awoke instantly, feeling dampness seeping into his clothes from the moist grass. The scent of smoldering cedar from the fire pit permeated in the air. The glowing embers cast an orange circle around it. He remained on the grass, laying on his side, still dizzy from the sleep.

Soon, he heard incessant thuds coming from behind his head, while the dense fog enveloped him like a veil. With nearly zero visibility despite the faint illumination from the ember, Ryu just lay still and listened to the mysterious sounds. As his vision adjusted to the darkness, to his horror, the wolf, the same one he had encountered earlier, loomed right before him. The beast snorted softly, tilting its head like an innocent puppy. The tip of the wolf's nose nearly touched his. With a surge of instinctive fear, Ryu held his breath, feigning death not to provoke the creature.

When he squeezed his eyes shut, irregular hums echoed in his mind. *A message!* He instantly recognized. As he deciphered the urgent communication, an image of the calvary advancing right outside the valley flashed in his head. Ryu leaped to his feet and sprinted to a nearby clearing, where he glimpsed seven faint orange glows in a far distance passing through Inaki. He threw his hand over his mouth. *God, they'll cross the river any moment!*

A doleful howl made Ryu's head turn. The wolf cocked its head toward the direction of the game trail and howled again. Instantly, Ryu headed to the trail that led back to the River Hasu.

When he turned his head around while running, the wolf had already vanished.

Yuri heard Heijiro's excited hiss from up ahead: "Right here! Come quickly!" She quickened her pace. However, the majority of the evacuees, worn out from the long journey, did not respond to his enthusiasm. "Come on, folks!" urged Heijiro again.

"Calm down, Jiro. What's the rush?" responded Shodai, pushing aside branches and swatting insects in front of him.

There, Heijiro was prodding a fire pit with a twig. A burnt smell lingered in the area, blocking the narrow path along the creek. Gensuke, Jintoku, and the lord joined the headman and

Heijiro. With nowhere else to go, the rest of the group scattered around the clearing near the water and collapsed on the grass. Some of them fell asleep immediately, while others just sat with vacant stares.

"What do you think, gentlemen? The samurais?" asked Heijiro as he pointed at the pit.

"No, it's too small, Jiro. I don't think it was them," responded Shodai. "This was for only one person or two."

Jintoku stroked his white goatee, grunting exaggeratedly. "Well, we cannot be so sure, though."

"They would've attacked the village by now if they were this close." added Lord Takeru.

"No, it had to be Ryu," interjected Yuri from behind them. "My sincere apologies for my intervention."

Everybody turned their heads at once. Gensuke became mortified, pulling Yuri aside from the group. Shodai, Juntoku, and Heijiro continued their debate, with their backs to her.

The lord opened his arms. "No, please, young lady, join us," he said and gestured for Yuri to come close.

Yuri bowed to the men. "Right before Ryu and I parted," she began, "he said we were all gonna meet here in Mt. Yashiro. He was certain this would be the nearest and safest place for us to hide out, because they don't know we know they're coming. Even though they crossed the river, they would end up attacking an empty village." She paused to see if they were taking her seriously. "Our land may be ruined, but not our lives. We can rebuild it many times over as long as our spirit remains unbroken, just like we did twelve years ago. I know that much."

"Well said, young lady, well said." Shodai praised Yuri. "That being said, did this Ryu say anything more about the situation we are in? And more importantly, where is he now?"

All eyes turned to Yuri.

"I'm sorry, sir, that I cannot answer your questions. But if he's not here, then there must be a reason. He doesn't leave us like this. I trust him —"

"Look over there! Look!" a male voice shouted in the clearing. The evacuees gasped all at once, their trembling fingers stretching toward the River Hasu.

In the distance, right across the river, a group of shadowy figures vaguely projected by torches was circling around.

Dawn gradually neared in the valley.

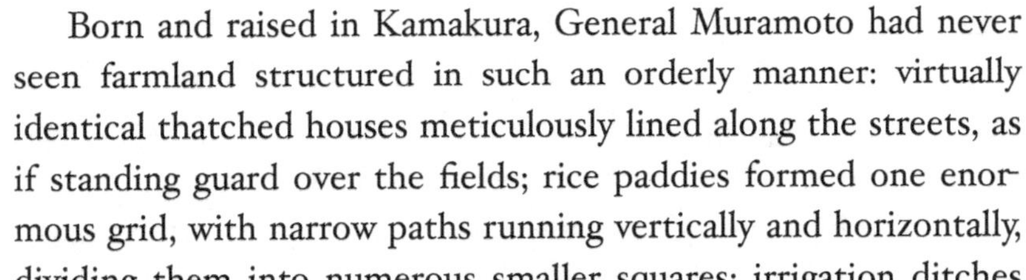

Born and raised in Kamakura, General Muramoto had never seen farmland structured in such an orderly manner: virtually identical thatched houses meticulously lined along the streets, as if standing guard over the fields; rice paddies formed one enormous grid, with narrow paths running vertically and horizontally, dividing them into numerous smaller squares; irrigation ditches enclosed the entire grid into which water from the river systematically flowed. While the rest of the village resembled those found in any rural region, this almost-clinical precision impressed Muramoto. *No wonder that son of a bitch has money.*

His troop, exhausted from a three-day cavalcade through mountainous regions, lay on the damp grass at a riverbank. The mist began to thin out, and the temperature slightly rose. Muramoto's two subordinates, who had accompanied him since Kamakura, sat cross-legged away from the rest of the cavalry, polishing their bows and arrows. Two of Watabe's men dozed off fitfully, while the other two devoured their hardened rice balls, cursing their plight and aching teeth. "Hey, Sakuma, look at those two," said one of them, jerking his chin toward Muramoto's men. "What're they thinking, polishing their weapons? For what? We're attacking a peasant village, for heaven's sake!"

"Whatever, Tachibana. I just want to get this over with. Right now," spat Sakuma. "We've got nothing to do with this. General Muramoto is not our general."

"You can say that again." Tachibana angrily uprooted a handful of grass and threw it away. "Tell you what. If something goes wrong, I mean really wrong, I'll slit Muramoto open. Misfortune always happens on battlefields, you know?"

"Save his head for me!" Sakuma chuckled.

Muramoto, still astride his horse, repeatedly cursed the river in front of him. "The village is right there, and I can't cross this stupid river! It's damn deep!" The irritating laughter of Watabe's men further aggravated his dilemma. *That lowlife merchant is one lucky bastard.* Images of Kyubei's store being looted, him being stripped naked in public, tormented in various ways, and crying for mercy continuously played in Muramoto's head as he pulled the reigns hard. His horse neighed, kicking on the ground. He spat indignantly and eventually dismounted.

As Muramoto walked toward the resting warriors, they all jolted upright. Two of them, who had just taken a nap, yawned involuntarily, failing to cover their mouths. The general's whip slashed the grass beside them, galvanizing them into action. "Alright, everyone, listen," he said, rhythmically tapping his palm with the whip. Immediately, all the men knelt on one knee. "A change of plan is required. We'll attack our target from here."

"General, so we will not cross the river?" asked one of the samurais.

"No, we won't, Kijima. Not until after we make sure enough damage is done. Then we'll enter the village from the upstream route where the water is shallow."

"Yes, sir." Kijima bowed.

Sakuma got to his feet, leaning forward.

Muramoto raised his right hand to silence him. "What did I just say? *Listen,*" he said forcefully. "As you can see, the river is too deep for the horses to wade through. We'll shoot those houses from here and set them on fire." He pointed at the misty village across the water. "You can, of course, shoot at anything and anyone you like. Remember, they're not ordinary civilians. They're all traitors to the bakufu."

Sakuma cleared his throat loudly. Irritation flashed across Muramoto's face. "What is it, Sakuma? Is that it? Your name?"

"Yes, it is, Sir Muramoto. So, General Watabe mentioned our special reward, and —"

"There's a prosperous store called Tsubaki-Ya in this village. Loot it all you want."

On his way to the River Hasu, Ryu made a brief stop at a communal livestock shed to free the animals. When he unbolted the doors, much to his surprise, none of them moved. *They've grown so accustomed to confinement that they've forgotten what freedom feels like.* He opened the gate and shooed them out of their cages. At first, they huddled together for a while, circling around by the gate, but eventually formed a line and disappeared into the darkness beyond the rice fields.

Ryu was promptly back on track. All the houses he passed by appeared deserted, with no candlelight filtering through the doors. As he made out the contour of the river at last, seven flaming torches loomed on the other side of the bank. He also heard the faint blows of horses. His pace spontaneously quickened, his heart beating fast.

With his lungs screaming for more oxygen, he finally made it to a large pine tree by the riverbank and crouched behind it. From there, he could barely make out the shapes of heavily armored warriors and their horses across the water. The murmurs of the samurais traveled through the air, but they were too faint and patchy for Ryu to decipher as sentences. Despite his growing nerves, he fought to catch the elusive communication over his own blasting heartbeat. He soon detected fragments of words *'arrows'* and *'trajectory.'* On impulse, he got to his feet, looking up at the purple sky over the river.

"FIRE!" Muramoto's commanding voice cut through the stillness of dawn.

In the next moment, Ryu watched as six flaming arrows, with chilling swishes, penetrated the fog far above his head. Within seconds, they landed in a rice paddy and extinguished upon hitting the water. "Fire!" commanded the general again, even louder. Five seconds later, four arrows missed their marks, but two struck a shed's roof. His heart skipped a beat. He suddenly stood upright beside the tree with his arms raised, his eyes possessed, glaring at the sky.

A few seconds later, seven fireballs erupted into the air. Ryu then let out a loud screech as he rotated his arms overhead, his eyes tinged with dark amber, locked on the flames. In a split second, the blazing arrows stopped in midair, rearranged their positions, and together formed a gigantic ring. As his arms continued to rotate, the fiery wheel began to spin and then gradually transformed into a sphere.

Across the river, General Muramoto and his warriors staggered backward, their bows dropping, as the unearthly spectacle unfolded in midair. The horses hissed, moving back and forth. Kijima, Muramoto's right-hand man, dropped to his knees and began to pray, while the rest simply stood there in silent awe, staring up at the hellfire, mouths agape, lost for words. "W-what the hell is happening..." muttered Muramoto coarsely, his knees shaking.

The colossal ball of fire cast an ominous light on the seven tormented faces and the river's surface as it began to spin like a top. The air around it compressed rather than expanded as the rotation continued to gain speed by the second. Despite the massive fire above their heads, the samurais breathed out white vapor, their eyes glaring in red horror.

Ryu closed his eyes and began to chant:

'Your sins are the mirror of the malevolence you cannot resist/now it's too late to pretend you were born good/let yourself burn with remorse/and prepare yourself for Hell.'

He opened his eyes and gazed across the river. On the opposite bank stood Muramoto, clad in deep vermillion armor, his trembling hands slowly removing his war mask. Their eyes briefly locked on each other, mutual recognition passing between them — Muramoto aghast, Ryu composed. Instinctively, General Muramoto staggered to his feet, recoiling in horror, while Ryu stretched out his right arm and defiantly pointed his index finger at his foe.

As if on cue, the general turned to his men. "R-retreat! Now!"

The six samurais instantly panicked, scrambling to ride their mounts, but the animals shook their heads, neighing, and soon began to bounce alarmingly. Although the samurais desperately pulled the reins and patted them on the necks, their horses, possessed by some mysterious force, turned violent toward their owners, kicking and squealing at them, and then broke into a raging gallop across the grass field. The riverbank became a war zone.

Amid the chaos, everyone milled around the riverbank, their arms stretched out, hands grasping at the empty air as they screamed incoherently. "For heaven's sake, run! Just run!" shrieked Kijima at the top of his lungs, pushing and shoving his fellow men out of the way. In the next moment, he stumbled over a dead torch on the ground and fell flat on his face. Before he could rise, a frantic horse— 500 kilograms of solid muscles— stomped on the back of his head with a sickening thud. A muffled yet grisly bellow did not last even a second. His body spasmed violently for a brief moment before a crimson pool covered the grass beneath his fractured head. His pupils remained dilated but mirrored only the blackness of death.

The hovering hellfire seemed to possess a malevolent will.

As the six samurais fled northward, toward the waterfall, it followed them tauntingly. Some cried, and others shouted, as they kept running in the predawn light. Glancing back at the sky, Muramoto ran zigzag across the field, but the fiery orb chased him in every direction. "Get away from me! Ge the hell away!" he screamed. The five men suddenly stopped and followed the general's gaze. "Don't just stand there like a bunch of morons! Move!" He moved his arm erratically, urging his men forward.

Despite their efforts, the samurais made little progress, stumbling and falling in their terror. "H-hey Sakuma, stab Muramoto! K-kill him!" yelled Tachibana over his shoulder while running. "That thing's following him, not us!"

"To hell with Muramoto!" Sakuma yanked Tachibana's sleeve and ran past him.

Eventually, the six frantic men reached the river's end, a dead end. Ahead lay only the waterfall that dropped thirty meters down into Wakasa Bay. The incessant roar of water thundered through the area, a reminder of an impending finale to the samurais' journey. The enormous flame remained in midair as if teasing the vulnerable targets below. With roaring booms, it suddenly split into six smaller balls and aligned in a menacing formation. The deranged samurais screamed even louder, paralyzed, their faces twisted like the *Nio.* After a tense pause, the six balls launched toward their respective targets.

The six men scattered across the area, crying out for help. But the fireballs cut off every escape route, tauntingly forcing their prey back toward the deathly cliff. The samurais found themselves cornered as they backed up until their feet touched the edge. With nowhere to go, they froze as the flames flew directly at them. In the next moment, their bodies were airborne, upside down.

The last thing Muramoto saw before colliding with the rocky shore was the ferocious dark waves below. At least he was spared the ignominy of witnessing the fall of the Kamakura bakufu in a month's time.

From afar at Mt. Yashiro, at first, the Kasuga evacuees could barely make out the seven panicked samurais scuttling across the riverbank. However, as the dawn gradually broke, the occult phenomenon frightened the onlookers. Some cried and howled like animals, while others prayed to the gods on their knees. One elderly woman even wetted herself, mumbling incoherently.

Shodai, after helping the woman to her feet, staggered to his colleagues, who were standing agape. "I...uh...What's happening there? What're we watching?" Nobody uttered a word for a while, their shoulders slumping.

"A... psychic? B-but —" stuttered Gensuke to a halt.

"A what?" said Shodai and Jintoku in unison.

Gensuke shook his head like an insane person. "It can't be possible...It just can't."

"Gen, what can't be possible?" Heijiro yanked his friend's arm.

"Umm...Yuri said before that Kyubei-san was pushing his secret bargain to... Never mind."

The four men went quiet again as they watched the samurais vanish under the sea cliff. A collective gasp erupted from the distraught spectators standing on the grassy field. A middle-aged woman approached the Guild members, still shaking. "I don't understand any of this, Sir Shodai. Can you tell me what we saw?"

"I'm sorry, no one can," said Shodai, and walked away.

Jintoku briskly slapped his knee. "Well...whatever that was, I can proudly say we finally put an end to our 60-year-old grudge, can't I? This is our vendetta."

Yuri, meanwhile, was just as stunned while her mother spoke to her fearfully. "What caused this?" Yuri muttered to herself, completely immersed in her thoughts.

Much like after he had performed the miracles two years ago, Ryu fell on all fours, his back heaving. He stayed on the ground as guilt engulfed him. *What have I done??* Soon, he began to shake violently. The grotesque bloodshed replayed in his head, though part of him accepted a sense of relief. *What have I become?* Torn between his guilty conscience and self-righteousness that he threw up. Painfully aware of the risk of being seen, he tried to crawl to the safety of the nearby bush. Yet, his numbed limbs abandoned him.

Suddenly, footsteps approached from behind. He froze momentarily. Before he turned his head, a young man's voice called out, "Ryu... is that you?"

With a lantern in his hand, Kento leaned toward Ryu.

*—————— * —————— * —————— * —————— *

The day after the samurai threats, Yuri, Kento, and Ryu met at Kasuga Shrine, where the lingering fumes of bonfires still faintly hung in the air. It was a secret meeting because Ryu had become 'the person in question' overnight, the latest gossip in the village. Because of her ambiguous relationship with Ryu, Yuri constantly had to answer her neighbors' questions about him on her way to the shrine. "I was about to ask you the same thing," she had told them.

The meeting proceeded like a Q and A session rather than a sentimental reunion. Yuri's hows, whys, and whats monopolized the conversation. The stronger her tension grew, the louder her voice became. "What?? It makes absolutely no sense at all," she nearly yelled. "Why, Ryu? Why?"

"Shh! Keep it down, Yuri," hissed Kento involuntarily. "We're gonna be overheard!"

She swung her head around exaggeratedly. "I see no one. Just us, Kento. Relax, okay?"

"I meant it figuratively, but... whatever. Just stay calm, please," whispered Kento.

"Anyway, Ryu, please go on," said Yuri, "and define 'after a while.'" She stuck her chin out.

He had already explained to Yuri and Kento that he decided to leave the village and return in the winter at the latest, though he kept the real reason for his departure from them. He concluded that facing a barrage of questions over his decision should be more tolerable than discussing the inexplicable incident he had conjured the day before. In fact, Yuri's shift in focus to interrogating him unburdened Ryu.

"*After a while* means exactly what it means, Yuri." He sighed heavily. "Did I say I'd never come back? No. I just need to take care of my ailing aunt, who lives in Bingo Province. She's been suffering severely, and she has no one but me to turn to. You satisfied?"

Yuri repeatedly lashed her palm with her *kanazashi*. "You told me and Kento that all your family were gone."

"Yeah, that's right, I remember that," interjected Kento, snatching the hair ornament from her hand.

"You two are right about it. I have no family left back in my village. Aunt Sechi is my last remaining relative, who lives far away."

"How can you be so sure you'll be back by winter?" demanded Yuri.

"Because she only has about six months left. Her lung disease is terminal."

"She could be contagious!" Yuri almost jumped up.

Ryu pushed Yuri back down gently. "So I'll be extra cautious, especially because I'll come back to the village. Right?"

Kento shrugged. Yuri took her kanazashi back from Kento

and roughly pushed it into her hair, her defiant eyes locked on Ryu.

Part Six

HEALER AND BELIEVER, 1333-1334

28

NOVEMBER FAREWELL

The newborn baby's healthy cries dispelled the miasma of fear and uncertainty that hung in a shabby house since midnight. With fluid movements, the midwife cut the umbilical cord and nestled the baby boy in his mother's arms. She immediately shed tears, her forehead glistening with sweat. As she stroked the baby's back, Shinzan came to her side, tears running down on his cheeks, and wiped her forehead with a damp cloth. "It's a boy," she said to Shinzan. The morning light filtering through a crack in the door shone on her exhausted yet beautiful face.

"Good, good..." Shinzan trailed off.

She rested her hand on his shoulder. "Yes, yes...he's going to stay healthy and live long."

Shinzan lifted his head. "Did you just —"

"What can I say? it's my habit." She giggled weakly. "Anyway, what name are we going to give him?"

"He's just entered our world. I'm soaking up this moment right now." Shinzan gently patted his son on the back. "Okay, what do you have in mind?"

"I'm leaning toward AMURO. It's unique but sounds strong for a boy. What do you think?"

"Amuro?? What on hearth does that —"

Shinzan bolted up on the cold floor, disoriented and drenched in sweat. *Again...the same dream.* He staggered across the cave to a wooden barrel sitting on the ground. When he brought a water-filled dipper to his mouth, Amuro's word 'Sir' pounded inside his head. He recoiled, splashing the water over himself. With his face soaked, he groaned.

"I'm sorry, sir. I didn't mean to startle you.

Shinzan wiped his face with the back of his hand. "What brings you back so soon, son? I specifically told you to say away for a while, didn't you?"

"Yes, you did, sir, but I couldn't wait any longer."

"What is it?"

"Sir, I don't want to lie about my identity anymore. It feels like a betrayal to the people I care about and to my family."

Shinzan slowly scooped water again and swallowed it. "We still have one more thing to do, don't we? You cannot afford to jeopardize your plan now."

"No, sir. But, if I come clean to them about who I really am, I won't have to resort to actions like what I just did, ever again. I still can't believe I killed those samurais. It harrows me."

"Because it's war, son. They had their cause just as you had yours. And regardless of the cause, war is war, no less. But after all, in this world you live, war is an inevitable part of life, no matter how cruel and senseless it may seem."

"I don't think I can condone any violence."

"No, you may not want to, but sometimes you have to. Look at the system people face now. You think it's fair? The poor are exploited by a privileged few. And when this system exceeds beyond the limits, some may fight back for a better life. Then, it becomes a war that's called an insurgency, whether you admit it or not."

"But..."

Shinzan gently shook his head. "That's the life you aim to protect. Is it worth it to you?"

———— * ———— * ———— * ———— *

The aftermath of the supernatural event of the spring grabbed the village by the throat throughout the summer. So profound was its impact that the mundane aspects of rural life had become too trivial for the locals to care. Children and teenagers reenacted the spectacle by throwing straw fireballs into the air. Meanwhile, adults indulged in guessing games, conveniently neglecting their tedious work. A handful of the religious even convened nocturnal meetings in the Higashiya and delved into the significance of what they had witnessed. On occasion, the sessions spiraled into cult-like rituals that went on well after dawn. Despite their varying manners of communication, the general consensus among locals was that Kasuga exuded an aura of mystery that defied conventional understanding.

For Yuri, the scorching summer felt interminable, as if testing her patience. Sleepless nights and an unrelenting wave of numbness had been dominating her days since Ryu's departure, which had little to do with the oppressive heat. As her behaviors grew increasingly erratic, her mother, Katsue, become concerned for her well-being. However, Yuri withdrew further despite her mother's apprehension. "Mother, I'm perfectly capable of handling myself," she insisted.

Her agitation stemmed not only from her separation from Ryu, but also from his unexplained absence that fateful night. She had demanded an explanation the day after, and yet Ryu's vague excuse — "I was so exhausted that I fell asleep by the river" — left her suspicious. *Did he have anything to do with that eerie event, directly or indirectly? Did he make up the convenient excuse to leave the village? And how come his presence is always short and spotty? Have I been fooled all along, after all? Who on earth is he, really? Is all his captivating charm a charade? Is his name even real? Probably not.* The more desperately she tried to shake her doubts off, the more complex they grew. Katsue often caught Yuri mumbling to herself during her chores. One day, Gensuke asked her to deliver arrowheads to Shodai's, but she ended up standing on the wooden platform by the River Hasu that Ryu had created two years ago, juggling them absentmindedly.

At the shine and the riverbank, Yuri often caught a group of teenage girls giggling as they whispered the names of the boys they adored. Annoyed, she quickly walked past them without even nodding. Yet at the same time, a pang of jealousy simmered inside her. *How come I can't have the innocence those girls have, though I do miss him so much?*

"Hey, Sis, when can I see your boyfriend Ryu?" Kairi tauntingly asked Yuri one night during dinner. She poured water over his head and stormed out of the house without saying a word, her fists tightly clenched. The summer night humidity further aggravated her, making her sweat with emotion. *What am I doing, losing control? Who do I blame but myself?*

The door slid open. Katsue came out and stood beside her daughter, putting a gentle hand on Yuri's shoulder. "I know, Mother, I know. That was very mature of me," said Yuri, staring at the countless dots of soft light dancing above the shrub by Gensuke's workshop. "I hate to admit this, but it's gonna be a long summer."

———————— * ———————— * ———————— * ———————— *

By the time the relentless summer finally loosened its grip on the valley, the villagers turned their focus to the pressing tasks of the season. The rice fields stool tall and golden, ready for the harvest that would begin today. Less than a month away, the barley sowing followed close on its heels — a reminder of how crucial this stretch of autumn was for their livelihood.

Heijiro stood at the edge of the early morning fields with his new sickle in hand and another hanging from the rope tied around his waist. He swung them with a bit of swagger as he glanced across the paddies. The village had thrived under Lord Takeru's progressive policies, especially the 'operational autonomy' he had granted them. It was a bold departure from the rigid feudal norms, allowing the Guild to decide how best to meet the yield targets.

"Morning, Bunji!" called out Heijiro, waving to a man knee-deep in a paddy. "What a great first day, eh? Looks like you're ready to go!"

Bunji laughed, tipping his straw hat back to wipe his brow. "If this sun doesn't kill me first!"

"Nah, the sun's friend today," retorted Heijiro, grinning. He crouched to examine a sheaf of rice, running his calloused fingers along the grain. "You've done good work here. This will be a fine harvest."

The villagers had chosen well when they appointed Heijiro as head worker, a decision that had been unanimous and immediate. Since taking on the role, he had proven himself indispensable, balancing the demands of his own crops and the responsibility of overseeing others'. It was not just his skill with the sickle or his knack of planning; it was the way people naturally sought his advice as they trusted his steady hand and clear judgement.

"Oi, Heijiro!" called out another voice from the neighboring paddy. "How about a suggestion for these water channels? They're running a bit low!"

Heijiro straightened, brushing dirt from his knee. "I'll be there right away!" he shouted back, already scanning the horizon for the source of the problem.

The air buzzed with activity, the rhythmic rustle of blades slicing through rice stalks. Heijiro relished the energy of the day, a reminder of what they had built together. Under Takeru's leadership, the village had transformed, and Heijiro had become more than just a farmer; he was a guide, a steward of this shared prosperity.

As he strode across the fields, offering a word of encouragement here and a tip there, Heijiro felt a swell of pride. Today marked the beginning of another season of hard work, but it also stood as a statement of what they could achieve when trusted to forge their own path.

"Oi, Jiro, wait a second," shouted Bunji, hurrying toward Heijiro while swinging his tool. "This is kinda dull. It sucks. Any chance I can borrow one of yours?"

Heijiro unhooked the one on his waist and handed it to Bunji.

"Wonderful, Jiro! Really appreciate it!" Bunji bear-hugged Heijiro.

"Don't mention it." A proud grin spread across Heijiro's face.

"By the way, are you by yourself? I got my boys helping me today." Bunji pointed at two young boys who sat cross-legged devouring rice balls in the paddy.

"Nope, I got mine —" Heijiro stopped, turning his head. His clenched fists began to shake.

"Uh...well, Jiro...see you later, huh?" With that, Bunji hurried back to his work.

"BOY!! Move your damn feet!" bellowed Heijiro, pointing his tool at Kento shambling lazily along a path far back. With his hands on either side of his waist, he impatiently waited until Kento caught up with him. "Even a toddler can crawl faster —"

Kento walked past his father, ignoring him as if no one was there.

"Oi! I'm talking to you, ungrateful brat!" Heijiro yanked down the back collar of Kento's kimono violently. Kento fell backward, landing hard on his buttocks. Embarrassed, Heijiro swung his head around. "Get up already, boy!" Then, he headed to his paddy, leaving Kento on the ground.

Kento endured the degradation, his shoulders slumping forward, trembling. Silent tears slowly streamed into his mouth. He spat them out. The children's innocent laughter further humiliated him, and when he raised his head toward the sounds, his eyes met Bunji's. The peasant awkwardly looked away and shooed his sons. Kento remained there until the trembling stopped. Wiping his cheeks, he got up and staggered off.

As Kento dragged his numbed body across the fields, his fellow farmers threw him fist pumps and let out celebratory roars. He didn't even wave, walking past them. One of the men snorted at Kento's back. "I guess we're too crass for the famous artist!" The rest burst into laughter.

When Kento reached a fork in the path, he turned right. Immediately, Heijiro's voice called out from a golden paddy at the left fork. "Oi! Where the hell do you think you're going!?" Kento did not even flinch. "Get your ass over here, you little shit!" shouted Heijiro louder as he ran across his field. Kento dropped his tool and kept walking away from his enraged father. "That's it. No dinner for you tonight! And don't even come back!"

Kento finally arrived at the riverbank. The riverscape somehow drew him whenever the nightmare of life became too relentless for him to swallow. He took a deep breath and drew it out, smelling bittersweet reminiscences. As usual, the sight of the new bridge made his breathing shallow, and flashbacks of his encounter with Ryu two years ago took control of his emotions.

Kento teetered toward the bridge and slumped on the timber floor as soon as he reached the exact spot where the two of them had met for the first time. He sneered at his helplessness, and once again, tears ran down his cheeks. *What on earth am I? How come I'm not like other men? What am I doing here? I can't even pity myself. Damn Ryu, it's all your fault!* Kento unconsciously banged the deck.

Two women rinsing vegetables under the bridge jumped, almost dropping them. "Is anyone up there?" shouted one of them, annoyed.

He carried on until exhaustion smothered his agony, then eventually stumbled out of the riverbank.

————— * ————— * ————— * ————— *

"Mother, Father, um...I'm going to Sakuko's, okay?" said Chisa after dinner, and quickly left the house.

"Look what we did, Tami, huh?" Heijiro yelled at her back. "Chisa didn't want to see us argue.

Tami made no response, doing her needlework with her back to her husband.

"Oh, you still ignoring me? That's great. Just great!"

Tami sighed, still facing away from Heijiro. "She wanted to get away from you, Jiro."

"What??"

Tami turned around. "You just went on talking shit about Kento in front of her all day."

"Because he deserves it! It's great that he's not home tonight! Otherwise —"

"Enough, Jiro. Just cut it out, okay?" Tami turned her back to him again.

"Why would I do that, Tami? He's a disgrace to my family!" Heijiro forcefully threw a piece of cloth into the wall in front of Tami.

Tami slammed her clothes against the floor and turned to face Heijiro once again. "You think you're the only one who's struggling to accept our son's behaviors??"

"ACCEPT?? What the hell are you talking about? What he's doing is wrong, Tami! It's a sin!"

"But Kento is our son! And he's hurting. How come you can't see that?" Tami's voice quivered with emotions.

"To hell with that! It's his punishment. He deserves to suffer!"

"How dare you say something like that? I know it's so damn hard for us to see him like this. But I still want to understand the way he is —"

"Understand WHAT??"

"God damn it, Jiro! Stop it! Just stop!" she stormed, tears welled up in her eyes. "Unlike you, I'll refuse to give up on my son, no matter what. And I'll always see him for who he is."

"You do know what they call someone like him, don't you? A *chigo*! It's laughable, because he's not a child anymore!"

"Don't you dare insult our son!"

"Oh, yes, Tami. I'll call him however I want." Heijiro paused, crossing his arms on his chest, and added, "until he becomes a real man and has a family of his own."

Since the spring spectacle, Kento's eccentric behaviors had become an open secret drawing whispers among the villagers. Heijiro often met the uncomfortable stares of his fellow workers in the fields. They awkwardly looked away as soon as he approached them. A wide-spread innuendo taunted him further, hinting that he forever owed Kento's life to Amuro and the Karube family. As he overheard the insults, feelings of shame and betrayal crushed his fatherly love for Kento.

"Gensuke's boy Amuro was the son I should've had... " muttered Heijiro to himself.

"Good grief..." gasped Tami, covering her mouth. "What on earth has gotten into you?? Where has your love for our son gone, Jiro!? You used to be such a great father until that summer twelve years ago."

"Kento was supposed to succeed me. But he's turned into someone I can hardly approve of." He paused, shooting a pleading glance at his wife. "Maybe... it's still not too late for us to have another son."

Tami stared at her husband in disbelief. "Do you even hear yourself?"

"My son, my only son, broke my heart..." he whimpered.

"No, he didn't. You did it to yourself," countered Tami. "And you know it."

Heijiro clenched his knees, head down. "Bullshit..."

Tami resumed her needlework without another word.

Kento sat in the corner of Higashiya's engawa, grasping his knees with his chin resting on them. An evening breeze and the chirps of *suzumushis* from a nearby shrub calmed him. His eyesight slowly adjusted to the deepening dusk, with a lantern sitting by his side. He held his breath while a tall figure bowed and prayed silently. After the brisk bell sounds, the silhouette left the shrine. Silence hung in the compound.

Kento's mind began to wander, and he shook his head irritably as Ryu penetrated his repose. As always, Ryu smiled at him mischievously, with his head tilted to one side, running his fingers through his wavy hair. Kento became slightly annoyed as Ryu spoke muted words. *I can't hear you. What are you saying to me?* Suddenly, Ryu took Kento's hand and strolled along the riverbank, continuing to sing silent lyrics. His grip was strong and gentle, making Kento's heart race.

The next moment, they lay side by side on the sunny grass field. Kento cocked his head toward Ryu, swallowing thickly. Ryu blew dandelion fluff into Kento's face and laughed like a little boy. His warm breath caressed Kento's nose. He sneezed and put his fingers into his mouth, spitting out the white fluffs. Then, he tentatively slid his damp fingers along the grass toward Ryu's vulnerable hand. Kento's heart burst, and he almost choked. Just as his fingers found their home, his heartthrob stood up and broke into a sprint, leaving him flustered and regretful.

Kento let out a heavy sigh as Ryu's back evaporated into the darkness. He lay down on the hard floor and closed his eyes.

———————— * ———————— * ———————— * ———————— *

The once-golden rice fields had now transformed into lush carpets of young barley. Meticulously planted rows of green grass showcased the diligent work of the peasants. Against the backdrop of the azure sky stretching over the verdant horizon, a striking contrast unfolded.

Although the vibrant scenery was a reminiscent of a warm spring day, bitter northerly winds whispered a different story on this frosty November morning as Yuri briskly traversed a narrow path cutting through the verdant fields. The faint sound of ice-cracking footsteps echoed around her, intensifying the chill of the sunny day. Her teeth chattered as the biting gusts battered her. Her nose and ears reddened, throbbing, and her fingers, despite being tucked under her armpits, remained nearly numb. By the time she passed Heijiro's paddy, the short-lived sun had already begun to decline toward the western horizon.

Yuri and Kento typically rendezvoused at places like Kasuga Shrine and the River Hasu. However, today, he had invited her to his home. It had been over two years since Yuri last visited, a time when they had desperately been searching for Ryu. She was curious to see how the place had changed. Also, Yuri looked forward to seeing Tami as she admired her outgoing and candid nature. Among the neighbors, Tami stood as an exception, never engaging in whispered gossip about Yuri's heartbroken marriage or uncertain future.

Yuri quickly picked up her pace when Kento's house finally came into view.

Upon settling in the house, Yuri immediately sensed the palpable tension hanging between the mother and son. Kento began to aimlessly poke at the ash in the irori with a stick, while Tami picked up a pea pod from a basket on her lap, only to put it down again as she cast furtive glances at her son, who sat opposite her. When her eyes met Yuri's instead, she winced weakly. As Yuri opened her mouth, Tami quickly shook her head. Chie, the family's youngest member, was settled behind Tami, engrossed in her dolls. The house felt chilly, despite the smoldering ash emitting heat from the irori, slightly dampened by the steam rising from a kettle perched over the ashes.

After exchanging a few caring words with Tami, Yuri leaned toward Kento, who slightly recoiled while continuing to play with the ashes. "Alright, Kento, stop procrastinating. What is it that you want to tell me?" demanded Yuri. "Whatever it is, considering what we've been through only six months ago, I won't be shocked."

"Yuri, I'm leaving the village," said Kento determinedly, "tomorrow, at first light."

Yuri had vaguely anticipated this announcement for quite some time, ever since they had visited the master artist Hosei in Kyo a few years ago. "Kyo, right?"

He nodded. "I'm sorry. I should've told you earlier."

"It's alright," Yuri replied with a dismissive shrug. "I knew you haven't been happy here for a while. But why tomorrow? Can't you wait until Ryu comes back?"

"No, I'm afraid I can't. It's now or never." Kento finally put down the stick.

Tami nearly jumped up, scattering the peas all over the floor. "Yuri, Kento is —"

"Mother, please! Let me finish this with my own words." He chocked up. "Yuri, I can't see Ryu anymore..."

Kento carefully unfolded his long-kept secrets that he had determined not to share with anyone: his atypical sexuality, naive infatuation with Amuro, identity crisis, perpetual conflicts with Heijiro, hidden love for Ryu, and a pang of jealousy toward Yuri.

Yuri had heard rumors about young male servants catering to prominent samurai lords in every way, especially their physical needs while on battlefields. She assumed that these young men were molded into such roles to perform their duties. However, she had never imagined encountering a man born with such specific orientation, let lone befriending one.

When Kento's narrative got to the part about his agonies of utter rejection by Heijiro, he began to weep silently like a little boy. Tami stepped out the house, with one hand over her mouth and the other clutching her chest. Kento's shaking shoulders squeezed Yuri's heart. Yet, despite her sibling-like affection, she simply gave Kento some time to let his pent-up emotions go. After a while, Kento finally calmed down and finished up his story.

"Pathetic, huh?" said Kento to Yuri, forcing a sarcastic smile. His eyes were red and swollen from crying. "Hope I didn't bore you with my sob story."

Yuri fought back her own tears, pinching her thigh hard. "Actually, it was much better than I thought," she said cheerfully. "I was afraid you were gonna propose to me!"

Checking out each other's wet cheeks, they burst into laughter.

The dawn arrived earlier than Kento had expected. He had slept little. Between the drowses, his mind wandered through visions of a potential future in Kyo, rather than dwelling on his desolate days in this remote valley. Every agonizing scene he had experienced thus far raced through the back of his head, already becoming history. His chest swelled with a sense of pride in embarking on this new chapter of his life, instead of running away from his demons.

Tami, too, had been awake for most of the night, weeping with her hand over her mouth as memories of the young Kento incessantly toyed with her. At one point, Heijiro's snores got on her nerves. She got out of the futon and sat by the irori shivering, her eyes swollen, until Kento eventually joined her.

Tami handed Kento a small parcel that contained four rice balls and some pickled vegetables. He wrapped it with a large furoshiki and carried the bundle on his shoulder, securing it tightly with a knot across his chest. Then, she slipped a thin envelope into his hand. Kento opened it and immediately handed it back to her.

"Mother, I won't be needing it," he said, "I'm an apprentice now. I'll be living in my mentor's house, and he'll give me a small allowance." He put his warajis on in silence. Tami gently placed her hands on his shoulders from behind, sobbing inside. He turned around and took her hands in his.

The mother and the son stood in silence for a while. Heijiro's irregular snores ruined their final moment together, reminding them of the very reason why Kento had to sneak out so early.

"Kento..." whispered Tami, biting her lips.

"Say nothing, Mother." Kento released her hands and handed Tami a piece of paper. "It's for Father." He cocked his head toward Heijiro, who was fast asleep, and opened the door. "So long, Mother." Before Tami could react, he disappeared into the semi-darkness of the field.

Tami stood still, her hand clutching the note tightly.

Heijiro woke long after sunrise, unaware of Kento's absence. Two rice balls and a bowl of miso soup sat on the table beside the irori. Casually, he called out Tami's name, but when no answer came, he snorted. As he picked up his chopsticks, a folded paper with '*To Father*' written on the front caught his eye. He unfolded the letter and began to read.

'*When you read this, I'll already be gone.*

I'm writing this while wondering how you'll take my decision. A misfortune? A shock? A betrayal? I think not. I see fear in your eyes, not disgust. Admit that you feel relieved. That you feel lighter. You rejoice because you'll no longer need to gloss over the inconvenient truth that your fellow workers superficially sympathize with. Don't worry. They know as much as you do and as little as you do.

No matter how grotesque my existence is to you, I am what I am. I can't change that, and no one can, not even the great Inari-no-Kami. I may see things differently from others because of who I am. I embrace this beautiful, suffocating world called Kasuga, even when others lament its unfair system. And I abhor the righteous indignation and exclusivism it harbors that, in fact, demand only skin-deep harmony in society. I've had trouble breathing for quite a long time, screaming for salvation. Have you noticed? Have you heard my cries?

But don't blame yourself. You're a proud peasant, born to embrace the starkness of rural ugliness. You breathe in the familiarity of black and white, just like your hardworking neighbors. Yet, you're relentless in disgracing other colors, barely acknowledging their existence. Conceit is a powerful sword, isn't it?

There are horizons you'll never be able to cultivate, within your reach yet unattainable. Inconveniently, I'm one of them — your disgraced son. So close and so distant. Admit it, then you'll feel spared. You'll struggle no more.

Father, take my departure as your salvation and redeem yourself.

Kento'

. . .

As Heijiro traced Kento's fluid handwriting, his hands trembled uncontrollably, faint sobs escaping from his tightly pressed lips. He tilted his head back, staring at the ceiling as he sniffled. Then abruptly, he tore the letter in half, flung the pieces on the floor, and stormed out.

29

BEHIND THE FACADE OF KINDNESS

The winter had finally arrived in the valley.

On the first morning of *Shiwasu*, December, every surface of hills, mountains, and residential areas lay dressed in a delicate sheet of snow, glistening in the sunlight. Spared from the snow's threat, the River Hasu etched a dark, winding sash into the endless stretch of pristine field. The thatched houses pierced through the snow-covered landscape, while wisps of steam and smoke from their lattice vents lent a lively flavor to the expanse of whiteness. The waterwheels attached to some of the buildings turned calmly, putting the finishing touch to the rustic landscape painting.

In front of each house, the residents, both young and old, diligently cleared the snow, some wielding bamboo rakes while others brandished brooms. Laughter of the children constantly blasted as they played spirited snowball fights. The adults fretted over the potential impact on their crops.

Amid the activity, one of them threw his rake, massaging his lower back. "Can we still rely on Heijiro to take charge of the situation?" he whispered. "I mean, he's been a wreck ever since his son left!"

"You can say that again. I thought he'd find some peace, now that Kento's gone," chimed in another. "Hey, speaking of the disgraceful son, did you know...."

Overhearing the gossip, Gensuke, who tackled on a pile of snow in front of his workshop, clenched his fists. "Assholes," he spat under his breath.

Ever since Yuri's unfortunate return home from her marriage over two years ago, the Karube family had fallen victim to backbiting. Rumors and whispers followed them wherever they went, stirring up shame and indignation. Once, in frustration, Gensuke had yanked a gossipmonger's clothes down and nearly thrown him to the ground. While Gensuke had steadfast faith in the village, the meddlesome nature of the residents who could not resist prying into other people's lives always sickened him.

Gensuke continued to curse under his breath, violently throwing masses of snow over his shoulders.

Katsue brushed the snow off her head "I'd rather worry about Tami. She has to put up with her neighbors...and her husband," she said, dying her hair with a tenugui.

"Huh?" said Gensuke, slowly turning around with his nose swelling up. "What are you insinuating, Katsue?"

"Nothing. It's just that men sometimes forget about their wives, but not the other way around."

"I don't know what you're talking about." Gensuke dismissively shock his head.

"I personally know such man," muttered Katsue, looking away.

"What? What's that supposed to mean?" Gensuke slummed the rake on the ground.

"It means, you don't get to think you're the only one who suffers a traumatic event, Gen."

"Oh, this is about ME now, huh? Where did this come from? And you're angry with me over...WHAT?"

"You never asked me how I was coping with Amuro's death. Never once!" Katsue squeezed her tenugui hard. "As if you assumed I was incapable of feeling anything. And all the while, I kept asking you about your pain and grief. You have no idea how devastated I was, how lonely I was."

"Why didn't you tell me before??"

"'Why didn't I tell you?" Katsue's voice cracked with emotions. "Is that all you can say after all these years? Like it was my fault you didn't notice my bereavement? Have I always been that invisible to you?"

"I have no idea what the hell you're talking about!" retorted Gensuke. "Clearly, you're so upset about something I've done. What is it?" He raised both hands, his eyes bulging out.

"Oh, Gen...you don't want to admit it, do you? Fine, I'll say it aloud for you. You did absolutely nothing for me. You abandoned me when I needed you most. It would've been better to be nagged to move on than being left in the dark all alone..." Her chest heaved violently. Then, she started to sob.

Gensuke fidgeted, scratching his head. Nodding toward Gensuke and Katsue, the two rumormongers whispered to each other, with their physical work completely neglected.

Yuri came out of the house, clearly noticing the commotion outside. The sight of her mother in tears stopped her heart. "Mother!" she exclaimed, rushing to her side. "What happened? Are you alright? Did you hurt yourself?" She shot an accusing stare at Gensuke, who stood aimlessly. "Father, why're you not helping her? She's freezing!" Shaking her head, Yuri gently held Katsue's trembling shoulders and guided her back into the warmth of the house.

Gensuke heard the excited murmurs from behind. "What're you two looking at, huh?" he blurted out, his face turning red. "The show is over!"

The two gossipers hurried back into their respective homes.

As soon as he closed his workshop door behind him, Gensuke threw his mino furiously against the wall. "Aggghhhh!" he screamed, breathing erratically. Then, he set up his workstation and got the kiln started.

Soon, the defining clangs pierced through the cold afternoon air.

"I'm sorry about yesterday, Yuri," said Katsue softly, her voice barely audible over the crackling of the irori fire. She stared into the embers as if searching for the words she could not quite find. "I have no idea what came over me."

"It's okay, Mother. I understand," Yuri replied, though in truth, she did not.

They sat side by side in the dim morning light, sipping hot water in silence that felt too fragile to break. Katsue spoke in fits and starts, her words halting, while Yuri only nodded along or murmured responses. The air inside the house was damp from the stream rising off freshly washed clothes, clinging to the cold walls and their unease.

Outside, the frosty day was alive with the sound of the three boys — Kairi, Yoriki, and Haruki — laughing as they rolled snowballs for a snowman. Their playful shouts occasionally punctuated the stillness within, reminders of a world unburdened by the weight of grown-up strife.

Gensuke, meanwhile, had retreated to his workshop as soon as breakfast ended. The tension with Katsue remained raw, and he had chosen to keep his distance, hoping time and space would ease the sting of yesterday's argument. He had spent the previous night at Heijiro's, returning just before the mean, but his heart had not fully returned home. Grappling with Katsue's emotional outburst had drained him, and avoidance felt like the kindest option for everyone, including himself.

Katsue glanced at her daughter, a faint, sorrowful smile flickering across her lips. "No, you possibly can't understand, Yuri," she said finally. "And you shouldn't have to. You're too young foo fully grasp the fear and pain of losing trust in someone you've shared your life with."

Yuri shifted uncomfortably. "What does that mean, Mother? Father and you are the perfect married couple I've known. Always kind to each other."

"Your father and I are good at wearing that mask in front of the children, aren't we?"

"Wait...what??" Yuri bolted up, knocking over her cup. "That...that's a horrible thing to say. What's happened to you two?"

With a resigned sigh, Katsue shook her head dismissively.

"Mother, please!" Yuri's voice trembled. "I'm not a little girl anymore. I can handle things that are hard to hear. Or, at least I can try."

The boys' shrieks of laughter outside pierced the tense silence inside the house. Taking it as a cue, Katsue sipped her hot water and winced.

"Oh no, Mother...please, don't tell me...has he been unfaithful to you?" Yuri's face tightened with fear rather than pity.

Katsue flinched. "Oh, no. He's not. That's one thing he doesn't do."

However, images flashed through Yuri's mind: the scandalous stories whispered over market stalls — tales of ruined reputations and brutal punishments. In the valley, adultery was not just a betrayal; it was a crime. Once exposed, the unfaithful faced public disgrace and exile at best, or physical punishment at worst. Whips, stones, and even the cruel water cure were not uncommon. Yuri had once seen the aftermath of such justice: a neighbor hobbling out of the village, their face a grim testament to the community's wrath.

But, what terrified her most was not the punishment; it was the ripple effect. Families shattered. Children ostracized. The stigma lingered long after the wounds healed. In Kasuga, where there were no brothels to urban distractions to temper desires, such betrayals often began close to home, infecting the community like a disease.

Yuri shuddered, her hand tightening around her cup. "You're sure?" she asked tentatively, needing to hear it again.

"Yes," assured Katsue firmly.

"Then, what's he done to you?"

"On the contrary, he's done nothing for me. Absolutely nothing. And that's the worst thing he's done to me."

Yuri shook her head. "I don't understand, Mother."

Katsue confided in Yuri the grief, suffering, and depression Amuro's tragic death had triggered. She also admitted that thoughts of suicide had crossed her mind more than once. As she recounted her pain, her eyes eventually brimmed with tears. She turned her head away from Yuri and wiped her cheeks.

"Oh, mother...I feel so awful," Yuri said. "I had no idea you'd been tormented by such horrible thoughts. I was so ignorant..." Tears wetted her cheeks too.

"You were just a little girl. How could you have possibly known?" Katsue gently dabbed her daughter's cheeks with a tenugui.

"But, why didn't you tell Father about it? He would've helped you heal, so you two could've cared for each other and shared the grief."

"Your father's a wonderful man, a hard worker who provides for his family more than most men in the village ever could," said Katsue firmly. "And I'm so grateful for that. But he's not flawless. No one is. And, sadly, he failed to see how much I was hurting, because he was overwhelmed by his own pain. He couldn't even look after his children as he should've for a while after that day twelve years ago. So I let him grieve as much as he needed. And all the while, I made sure you and the boys were well taken care of. I simply didn't have time to properly grieve, not that I pitied myself for it, though. I just wished he could've recognized my pain as his."

"I'm so sorry," mouthed Yuri, choking up. An acute pang of guilt stabbed her as streams of tears dripped on her lap. *Mother's suffered all this time and even now, probably. And what about me?*

Gensuke and Katsue had initially convinced Yuri to believe that Amuro was sent to a distant relative's. A few years later, they finally shared the truth about his death with her — their parental discretion to protect her from the unspeakable reality. Yuri cried so much after the revelation, but her actual bereavement did not last long. Within months, she felt only a tinge of emptiness.

"It's okay, Yuri," said Katsue, "it's been twelve years, and I've learned to cope with my sadness. It won't disappear completely, but it's diminished to the point where I can share it with you. And I'm glad you didn't succumb to misery as I did."

"Mother —"

"I'll be okay. So will your father. And he and I will together find a way to reconcile with each other." Katsue held Yuri's hand and gave it a firm shake.

The sliding door burst open, and Kairi, the eldest of the three boys, stuck his head in. "Mother, the twins and I are going to Hayato's. Hope you don't mind!" he blurted out and shut the door before Katsue could respond. The vigorous footsteps quickly faded, and the outside fell silent.

Nostalgia swept over Yuri. "Was Amuro about the same age as Kairi when he...you know?"

"Yes, close enough. He was nine," said Katsue.

"How on earth did Amuro come up with such an intricate plan? You know?" Yuri shook her head. "Most little kids that age can't even tie their obis right. I couldn't. He must've been born with something I wasn't."

Katsue fell silent as she pondered Yuri's implication.

She and Gensuke, along with Ine, had never before revealed the secret of Amuro's birth to anyone, including his siblings. The only other person in the village who knew was Jintoku, who had still firmly kept it to himself. Despite their fear that Yuri might stumble on the truth someday, twelve years after Amuro's heroic death, the secret remained buried with him.

"Mother, is something wrong?" asked Yuri.

"Yuri, I have something else to share with you," said Katsue in a determined tone. "It's about Amuro."

That night, Yuri had a dream about Amuro for the first time in years.

He sat opposite her by the irori, holding both her hands. His face was blurred by thick steam, and he spoke to her in choppy gibberish. Yuri remained clueless about his intentions and became impatient. All the while, Amuro kept talking, as if toying with her annoyance. When she heard his laughter, irritation boiled up inside her, and she roughly shook off his firm hands. She tried to ask him to stop, but no words came out, despite her mouth forming the words. *I don't know what you're saying! What's so funny?* She opened her mouth again to get these words out, only to hear her own heavy breathing. *Hey, Amuro, now you're dead, I don't care about your true identity and how you came into my family. But it's your fault they have to wear a gentle mask for us kids*. Soon, she found herself crying as she breathed harder, her mind becoming irrational. Her head started to spin from hyperventilation. All of a sudden, the steam over his face thinned out. The man in front of her looked nothing like Amuro or any version of him she had envisioned all these years, except for his thick, wavy hair. *Am I hallucinating? Or...*

The young man stood up and showed a broad smile that

somehow reminded her of Ryu. "Alright then, we'll catch up again sometime soon. Like I just said, believe in yourself, Yuri." His voice was strong and calm.

"Who the hell are you?!" screamed Yuri.

With that scream, she woke up with a jolt, just as the man in the dream vanished into thin air.

30

WRATH OF GOD

It began with perplexity.

One morning at a communal well, a villager spat out water after filling her mouth, grimacing in disgust. "What is this? It tastes foul!" she exclaimed. Her neighbor, skeptical, took sips and immediately recoiled.

When an elder drank it, however, he smacked his thigh and declared, "Sulfurous water! It's good for your health." Yet, even he could not explain how the well water had suddenly turned sulfurous.

Later that day, a farmer was feeding his bull when the animal shoved him aside, cracking one of his ribs. A few days later, a horse lashed out, kicking its owner in the face and knocking out his front teeth. Then, a boy was attacked by another horse as it burst free from its shed.

At first, these incidents were dismissed as routine misfortunes — common hazards of rural life. But, when identical accidents recurred for five days straight, each more severe than the last, the villagers grew uneasy. Whispers of bad omens spread quickly, and some began refusing to work, fearing for their safety.

By the time the eleventh mishap was reported — a male dear thrusting a farmer's thigh with its horn — the mood in Kasuga had shifted from annoyance to dread.

Fearing unrest, Shodai called for an emergency meeting.

The Guild convened the following afternoon at the Higashiya. An improvised irori in the center did little to dispel the biting cold as the members huddled together, their breath misting the air. One by one, Shodai questioned them, hoping someone could explain the pattern of strange events. Each answer was the same: "I have no idea."

Tension mounted as the discussion stretched into all afternoon. Frustration grew, and some members began to pace, their teeth chattering despite the warmth of the fire. Just as Shodai was about to call it a day, one member leaped to his feet, his face pale. "My cousin told me a story once," he began, his voice growing tense. "Years ago, in a distant region, strange things started happening, just like here. Animals behaving violently, the water turning foul. No one could explain it. And then..." He paused, looking around the room. "The ground shook. Violently. Hundreds of homes collapsed. Many died."

Silence fell over the room, broken only by the crackle of the fire.

"What the hell??" exclaimed Heijiro. "I don't understand, Sakichi. What was that, exactly?"

"Wish I knew, Jiro." answered Sakichi with a shrug.

"It's an earthquake," interjected Jintoku.

"A what, sir??" asked another man.

"Earthquake!" the eldest of the village shouted. "Who cares? It's just a damn name. All I know is, every once in a while, the ground we stand shakes powerfully for no obvious reasons and out of the blue. Usually, it's just like a small jolt, but sometimes the ground cracks and trees fall. Shits like that. Deadly serious!"

Although Mother Nature posed calamitous events like floods and droughts to the valley in history, earthquakes had somehow spared the region for centuries. For a while, everyone fell silent, some resting their chins on their fists while others shook their heads. Sakichi whispered to the men around him, then put the index finger on his lips.

"But, Sir Jintoku, how do you know all this?" asked Shodai. "Because I don't." His tone conveyed a doubt rather than innocent curiosity.

"My grandmother lived in the region east of Kamakura before marrying my grandfather," said Jintoku reminiscently. "Anyway, she told me when I was little that all the eastern Provinces were notorious for earthquakes. She experienced lots of them, including a huge one that shocked her to the core. Scared shit out of the entire village. 'The wrath of our god' is what she called."

"Well, Sir, that's an illuminating account of your grandmother," said Gensuke, clearing his throat. "But setting that aside, how seriously do we have to take into account the possibility of a disaster?" He scanned his fellow mens' faces. "Anyone care to shed some light on this matter?"

Many of the members either scratched their heads or simply lowered their eyes while elbowing each other. A middle-aged man scoffed, saying, "No disrespect, Sir Jintoku, but I find it damn hard to believe what you've described." A few others nodded in agreement.

Heijiro jolted up. "Hey, shut your —"

"Suit yourself, Sabu," responded Jintoku coolly. "I don't intend to impose my story on anyone."

Shodai scanned the room. "He's quite right. Our agenda today is not to persuade others. We're here to share the information and thoughts."

Gensuke smacked his thigh. "Well, folks," he began, "here are my thoughts and what I'll do first thing tomorrow. I'm concerned about this, so I'll reinforce my house, just in case ground shaking happens. With a couple of simple props against each of the outside walls, before it 'scares shit out of me.'"

The room immediately erupted into a cacophony of voices. "Alright folks...folks, please quiet down," ordered Shodai and waited until the room hushed. "Some of you may think it's nonsense to fear the unknown. But I feel the opposite. I'm scared because it's unknown."

By the following evening, improvised beams braced the walls of many homes. Sabu's was one of them.

———————— * ———————— * ———————— * ———————— *

The fateful days dawned in an eerie, perfect silence. Snow blanketed the valley in thick, sound-muffling layers, deadening even the gusts of the north wind, the cheerful chirps of winter birds, and the faint murmurs of the River Hasu. The waterwheels, which usually hummed a soothing rhythm through the day, stood still, their spokes frozen and buried under the weight of ice and snow. Human activity, too, had ground to a halt. Even the village's early risers, who typically broke the morning calm with clattering tools and lively calls, remained cocooned indoors, unwilling to venture into the bitter, endless white.

Whiteout conditions consumed the landscape, leaving the village adrift in a silvery haze. Only the dark, angular patches of house walls beneath their steep roofs and the dull sheen of the frozen creeks broke the monotonous expanse. Beneath the overcast sky, even the usual blue undertone was absent, replaced by a pale, oppressive gray.

But, as the morning wore on, life stirred within the village. Chimney smoke curled into the frozen air, and muffled voices emerged from behind snow-dusted doors. Gensuke, bundled tightly in layers, was among the first to step out. He hurried across the snow toward his workshop, his straw boots crunching faintly against the icy ground. Just as he closed the door behind him, movement in the sky caught his eye.

A large flock of crows flew into view, their black silhouettes stark against the pale horizon. Their cries shattered the morning calm, a raucous cacophony that made Gensuke wince. The birds moved erratically, flapping their wings as though in a frenzied chase. They flew southwest, their dark forms growing smaller until they vanished behind the jagged outline of a distant mountain.

"What do you think that was, Gen-san?" called out Roku, the young peasant who lived next door, his breath fogging in the icy air as he gestured toward the mountain.

"Birds being birds, I suppose. Who cares?" replied Gensuke with a laugh, though the unease in his voice betrayed him. He glanced at the fading horizon one last time before stepping inside his workshop and shutting the door firmly behind him.

Later on during the work, Gensuke felt multiple dull thuds beneath the earthen floor. In a few seconds, with a loud bang, a powerful upward jolt came. Just as he steadied himself, an even mightier force slammed him against a wall. Immediately, the ground began to shake. His instinct forced him to lie flat on the stomach. Though panicked, he moved his head around, taking in his surroundings while stretching his hands to hold on to something. It seemed as if everything in the room rocked in unison. Even amidst the chaos, he made out the contours of each of his tools clearly. He could also differentiate between various sounds: creaking walls, roof, and door, and clanking hammers and tongs. All the while, the ground continued to rage. The rumbling sounds intensified as heavy objects on the workbench flew over and landed all around him. He desperately crawled away from the bench, veering toward the door. *Sir Jintoku was right!* His straw boot flew toward him, and before he could dodged, it hit his forehead. The bamboo baskets hanging from the ceiling fell around him and on his back. Despite his desperate effort, he bellied across the floor at a snail's pace. *When will this stop? The roof may fall on me any moment!* At last, his right hand touched the bottom of the sliding door. As he crawled out into the open air, the quake stopped as abruptly as it had started. It had lasted merely fifteen seconds or so.

Gensuke gradually regained his composure as the initial shock ebbed away. The first thing he noticed was a wall of snow that completely blocked the view outside; the quake had caused a pile of snow to cascade down. The snow barrier stood as high as his eye level. Above it, another layer of white obscured the dark summit of Mt.Toki. He picked up a large mallet lying on the floor and began to break through the snow wall. Before long, the entrance became leveled, revealing the full view of the snow-covered village spread out in front of him. He gasped in disbelief. Some of his neighbors' houses had been reduced to piles of rubble buried in snow. He staggered out to the white fields, lost for words.

The residents stood by the ruins, some with their heads in their hands while others muttered incoherently to themselves. A man and a woman screamed, "Baa-chan!" as they frantically dug through the white rubbles with their bare hands. The snow mercilessly muffled their desperate cries for help. And yet, their misery, against the backdrop of white, somehow seemed surreal and almost theatrical to Gensuke. Soon, more villagers emerged, many barefoot, oblivious to the frigid ground, their faces etched with shock. They began to speak all at once with frantic gestures, paying no attention to the miserable couple tackling the rubble.

Roku and his wife, who was holding a baby, saw Gensuke and approached him. "What...what just happened??" shouted Roku, wide-eyed with astonishment. "We barely got out of our house right before the ceiling gave way!" As if echoing the chaos, the baby burst out crying.

Instinctively, Gensuke slammed his house's door open. Four pairs of frightened eyes immediately fixed on him. Katsue and the three boys were huddling together at a corner of the dirt floor, still trembling with fear. "Did any of you get hurt? Are you all okay?" he asked, stepping inside. They nodded their heads in unison. Yoriki, one of the twins, rushed into Gensuke's arms, tears in his eyes. Gensuke gently stroked the boy's head.

The house was filled with smoky fume, with the kettle buried in the smoldering ash of the irori. Suddenly, Gensuke noticed the absence of his daughter. "Katsue, where's Yuri?" he asked in a demanding tone.

"I...don't know," she answered, trembling. "She went out after the meal but didn't tell me where she was going."

"In this snow?? And you didn't ask her why or where?" Gensuke released Yoriki and stepped over to his wife.

Katsue's face twisted with guilt. "I-I thought she'd be back soon. I would've stopped her if I had known —"

A loud knock on the door made everyone jump and then fall silent, the family drama suspended. With another bang, the twins ran back into Gensuke's strong embrace.

"Sir Gensuke, are you folks alright in there?" A vaguely familiar voice called from the outside.

Gensuke swung the door open. Standing there, breathless and clad in thin garments despite the freezing temperature, was Ryu. Gensuke's eyeballs nearly fell off. "Oh, thank god, it's you!" he exclaimed, clinging to Ryu's shoulders. "Please, Ryu, could you help me find Yuri? She's missing, and I have no idea where she is or... if she's safe."

"Oh no... Yes, of course, sir. I'll do anything in my power to help you and your family," affirmed Ryu earnestly.

"Oh, thank you, thank you!" Gensuke tightened his grip on Ryu's shoulders.

Ryu quickly scanned the interior of his old home. "Is everyone okay? No injuries?"

"Thank you, Ryu," said Katsue, "we're all fine, still a bit shaken though, especially the boys. They've never been this terrified before." She held them close.

Ryu's heart burst, his arm involuntarily stretching toward the vulnerable boys, Kairi, Yoriki, and Haruki, whom he met for the first time.

"Anyway, Yuri should be somewhere in the village, I believe. It's my fault she's not here with us..." said Katsue, her voice trailing off.

"No, ma'am, this is no one's fault," Ryu reassured her. "Nobody could've anticipated what's just happened. No one has an ability to foresee it."

Katsue, listening to Ryu's reassuring voice, broke down on the floor, her hand covering her mouth. While Gensuke hesitated, fiddling with his snow hat, Ryu stepped inside and placed a gentle hand on her shoulder. Instantly, her body jolted with an emotion she could not define. *What did Yuri say about him more than 10 years ago?*

"Ma'am," Ryu said, interrupting her thoughts. "I'll find your daughter and bring her back here. You have my word." He gave Katsue a firm nod.

"Yes, please."

"I'm gonna check the river," Gensuke told Ryu. "There's a spot she often goes to. What about you, Ryu?"

"I'll try the shrine first," Ryu responded. "And sir, on your way to the river, could you tell as many people as possible to head to the bamboo forest by Mt. Toki? I know it sounds strange, but that's our best bet for safety."

"Why? We all need time to recover now, after this horrific nightmare." Gensuke gestured toward the mess the earthquake had caused.

"This must sound insane, but there's going to be another one hitting soon, and it may be even worse. More buildings could be destroyed. It's not safe to stay inside. The forest will provide solid shelter, because bamboo trees are flexible and can withstand strong vibrations that other species can't. People will feel and be safer out there."

"B-but how the heck do you know it's gonna happen again?? You just said no one can predict it. And yet, you can?"

Ryu bit his lip. "Look, sir. We don't really have much time. I know it's difficult, but please trust my instinct, just as you did before. And if it turns out to be a false alarm, then all the better. So please." With that, he sprinted off toward the shrine.

Gensuke scratched his head, his gaze following Ryu's back. Kairi, the oldest boy, tugged on Gensuke's sleeve. "Father, was that...Ryu? Sis's —"

"You'd better get going, Gen," urged Katsue.

"Yeah, right..." Gensuke dashed off in the opposite direction.

As Katsue picked up bowls and cups scattered on the floor, she suddenly gasped. *Is Ryu...?* A cup slipped from her hand. "What the devil has just gotten into me?" she mumbled to herself.

31

FORCE OF NATURE

A crested ibis landed in the woods behind Kasuga Shrine, and a moment later, Ryu emerged breathlessly.

The damage to Kasuga Shine disheartened him, though he had foreseen the ferocity of the earthquake. Both the Nishiya and the main sanctuary lay in ruins, reduced to rubble. The Higashiya, the last structure still standing, had its roof toppled by a nearby cedar. Large holes, as wide as the wheels of an ox cart, left the holy compound nearly unwalkable. And yet, amidst this desolation, the snowy landscape created an eerie illusion, much like it did across the village fields.

Standing in front of the wreckage, Ryu heard only the deadly silence. *Could Yuri be buried under the ruins or trapped in one of those holes?* A muffled thud echoed, and then a chunk of snow slipped down from the remaining part of Higashiya's roof. "Yuri!" he shouted at the top of his lungs. "It's me, it's Ryu! Come on, Yuri, call out if you're here!" The snow toyed with his desperation, mercilessly swallowing his cries. No response came back. He helplessly repeated the call until his head spun from hyperventilation. Though Ryu heard nothing back, his instinct told him she lay somewhere in this mayhem. He slumped to the icy ground.

It was pitch black and cold. With no sounds or lights, Yuri had no idea where she was. She did not know how long she had been there as she had passed out briefly. Yet, she knew she was trapped in a cramped space similar to a cabinet. Her limbs struck the panels as she moved her body. When she touched her numbed bottom, she felt icy wetness, and her hand jerked back reflexly. Desperate to escape, she pushed against the locked door with all her might, but it would not budge. Something heavy seemed to be weighing it down from the other side.

She tried again and again until she panted and her shoulders ached. As time passed, panic set in, her pulse quickening with every second. She rubbed her hands together intensely while blowing warm breaths on them. Soon, her breaths grew shallow, and she teetered on the brink of blacking out once again.

Then, a voice called her name. The door slid open, and a man's face poked in. The same young man she had seen in her recent dream crouched in front of her, running his fingers through his wavy hair. He smiled mischievously. "Boo! Got you!"

"It's you again! Who are you?" Yuri yelled at the man.

"Yup, it's me again, Amuro. Your adopted brother." He exaggeratedly straightened his posture.

"What? Why are you saying that? It's not funny. Tell me who you are!" Yuri gripped the edge of the door hard.

"Already told you, Yuri. I'm Amuro."

"Stop it!"

"Why? You expected me to stay a 9-year-old forever? After all these years?" He held up his hands.

"But...I don't understand..."

"Relax, Yuri. This is just a dream. And look at yourself. You're no longer a 6-year-old girl, either."

Yuri instinctively touched herself, feeling the two soft

mounds on her chest, and gasped in shock. Amuro handed her a bucket of water and gestured for her to look at her reflection. A beautiful young woman stared back at Yuri, her delicate features glowing on her face.

Amuro laughed fondly. "Yes, Yuri. You've blossomed like a real *yuri*." With that, he vanished from her view.

"Wait!" cried out Yuri. "I need to —"

Suddenly, her surroundings became lighter and clearer...

A muffled clank of metal echoed under the rubble of what had once been the main sanctuary. It sounded as if someone had struck a bell. On impulse, Ryu zigzagged fast around the holes to a heap of ruins. "Yuri! Is that you?" Just as another clank sounded, he raised his right arm over his head and waved vertically, with his eyes closed. At the same time, he intoned an unintelligible mantra repeatedly. Soon, one by one, broken timbers rose into the air, as if being hoisted, and landed on the snow-covered ground with a hushed thuds. His performance continued with a rhythmic movement. Gradually, a new mass of debris piled up next to the original one. When both mounds became nearly the same height, a wooden offertory box emerged, miraculously unscathed despite being buried under the heavy rubble. Ryu stopped his mantra and opened his eyes. On top of it sat a large *suzu*, a Shinto bell, still connected to a thick woven rope. His heart raced as he anticipated finding a person — most likely Yuri — who must have sent him the signal. He unconsciously held his breath.

"Help..." a weak yet familiar voice called out finally. "Please, pull me out of here." It came from a partially enclosed triangular space, with the three sides coincidentally formed by the ground, a large plank, and the offertory box.

"Yuri!" shouted Ryu, "hang on, I'll get you out now." He yanked out a broken lattice once mounted over the ceiling. The tip of the lattice struck the bell, and a shrill sound momentarily broke the silence.

Yuri lay on her side, half of the body buried in snow, shivering violently. "I'm so cold...so cold," she murmured, seemingly semiconscious. And yet, both her hands clung to the rope, the lifeline she had indeed used by jiggling to ring the suzu while trapped under the rubble.

Immediately, Ryu lifted her up onto his shoulder and sprinted down the long stone stairs, heading back toward her home. Vivid flashbacks from three years ago flooded his mind — a potent feeling of deja vu as he remembered carrying the half-wet, semiconscious Yuri home. This time, however, no one paid the slightest attention to him, desperately moving and digging through the ruins in front of them. He passed ten or so houses crushed and buried deep in the snow.

The earlier winter breeze quickly picked up. As Ryu ran across the frozen field, he felt a tinge of numbness on his nose and ears. Yuri's body grew rigid on his back, her temperature dropping alarmingly. *Oh, no! Not Again! How come her plight always worsens when she's with me?* He quickened his pace.

Ahead, a woman was raking a pile of snow that blocked the entrance of a house. He approached her from behind. "Excuse me, ma'am."

The woman jerked upright and turned around.

"I'm sorry for startling you, ma'am." said Ryu.

She snorted.

"This may sound rude, but would you mind lending your *mino* to this young woman?" He released the unconscious Yuri from his back, letting her lean against his chest.

The woman flinched. "Is she the Karube's —"

"Yes, ma'am, she is. She's freezing and needs your mino. I'll bring it back as soon as I get her home." Ryu rubbed Yuri's shoulder. "Please?"

The woman peered at Yuri's face and mumbled something under her breath, then took off her straw coat and handed it to Ryu.

"Oh, thank you so much for your kindness, ma'am!" Ryu threw the coat on Yuri's shoulders. "Thank you."

The woman pointed in the direction of Yuri's home. "Aren't you going?"

"Right." Ryu sprinted off, Yuri on his back once again.

As he continued on, the dark gray sky finally gave to a cascade of white. With the temperature plummeting even further, every muscle in his body grew rigid despite his strenuous run. Just as he reached down to his numbed thigh, the root of a fallen tree sticking out from the snow caught his foot. He lost his balance, staggered for a second, and fell flat on his stomach, with Yuri still on his back.

"Amuro..." she mumbled inaudibly.

"Yuri? Are you alright?" whispered Ryu, turning his head. But she did not respond, slipping back into unconsciousness. *Maybe I'm the problem causing her problems. I have to stop showing up like this, or I'll end up ruining her life.* He quickly got up and resumed his run.

When the house finally came into sight, Ryu bumped into a large group of people marching toward the bamboo forest. All of them looked tired and despondent, their gait sluggish. As he and the crowd passed each other, he caught a random exchange.

"I've no idea why we do this," one of them complained. A murmur of discontent sympathized with him.

"Because whatever the Guild decides is a message from God!" exclaimed Ren sarcastically. A piteous laughter erupted from the crowd. Jintoku cleared his throat exaggeratedly. "So, sorry, Sir Jintoku. No offense, though." Ren quickly ducked behind the man in front of him.

"Yeah, yeah... whatever you say, Ren. Whatever you say," grunted Jintoku. As he quickened his pace, a tall young man piggybacking a woman passed by him. *Isn't that girl...?* Jintoku stopped instantly and turned around, but the young pair had already faded into whiteness.

As soon as Ryu slid the house's door open, the warm, smoky air hit his face, the *kamado* on and glowing. Much to his surprise, Katsue rushed toward him. "I thought you've gone with your family, ma'am," he said, brushing the snow off his head and shoulders.

"Yuri!" gasped Katsue, stroking her daughter's head with a trembling hand.

Ryu moved to the center of the room and gently laid Yuri down by the irori. "I found her at the shrine. She's been groggy, but she'll be alright."

"Oh, thank God..." sighed Katsue, removing the snow-covered mino from Yuri, who slightly shivered. She then put a quilt over her. "I can't possibly thank you enough, Ryu."

Ryu shook his head, holding his hands over the smoldering irori.

"Oh, almost forgot I've got *kamado* going," said Katsue, putting an iron pot on it.

With sudden fatigue setting in, Ryu lay down on his side opposite the sleeping Yuri. Her earlier pale complexion gradually returned to its normal color. Watching her chest rise and fall rhythmically, he let out a deep sigh and reached out his hand toward her face. But he reluctantly pulled it back. *I shouldn't...*

A pungent smell of ginger and fermented rice slowly permeated the air. Ryu's mind responsively drifted back to the time when he was a little boy. Katsue would make him *amazake* every time he had a cold — wistful memories he had forgotten until now. Bittersweet feelings tugged at his heart.

Ryu's reminiscences came to a halt as Katsue returned to his side with a tray balanced on her palm. "Here you go, Ryu," she said, handing him a steaming cup filled with a thick white liquid. "Amazake. This will warm you up." She smiled fondly.

"It's so nice of you, Mrs. Karube." Ryu sipped the sweet, tangy drink. Nostalgia almost overwhelmed him, but he held back his emotions. "This is lovely, ma'am. Thank you."

"You're very welcome," said Katsue, setting the tray down, "and this is for Yuri." She picked up the other cup.

"Let me help you," said Ryu, as he gently sat Yuri up, supporting her from behind.

Katsue brought the cup to Yuri's lips and spoke softly. "Yuri, wake up and drink this. It'll warm you up."

Yuri's eyes partially opened and fixed on the steamy white liquid. She took two slow sips of the amazake as if testing it out, then grabbed the cup with both hands and swallowed the rest in three gulps. The strong, fermented flavor instantly filled her nostrils as the hot drink seeped into her body. She moaned with satisfaction, her eyes finally fully open.

"How're you feeling now, Yuri?" asked Ryu gently, "you've been trapped under the rubble of the shrine. Laying on the snow. Glad you're safe now."

Yuri turned her head to see the man holding her, but the kind face staring back at her did not register. *Who is this man? He's not the man from the dream.* "Umm... Mother, how did I ...?" she asked, rubbing her temple.

"Ryu brought you back home," replied Katsue. "I was worried sick. If it wasn't for him, you might've frozen to death." She adjusted the blanket over Yuri's body. "So, how're you feeling?"

"Better than when I was out in the cold, I guess," answered Yuri, her voice frail but steady. "The back of my head hurts a little, though." She touched the spot and grimaced involuntarily. "Ouch! I've got a bump."

"The lattice must've hit your head when it fell," said Ryu, tentatively touching the swelling. "You poor thing."

Yuri jerked herself away from Ryu and said to him, "So... who are you, anyway?"

Ryu and Katsue exchanged a startled look. "Don't be silly, Yuri," she said.

"No, I'm not. I don't know who this man is. Never seen him in my life."

Ryu recalled an intriguing conversation with one of the residents in heaven. This woman had told him that she did not remember her own name, age, or where she had come from, though she did know she was dead and how she had died. She had fallen off a cliff while foraging wild mushrooms and hit her head on a rock. The head trauma had caused partial amnesia, another dweller — an imperial physician — explained to them. According to the doctor, it was not unusual to suffer amnesia after a traumatic event, particularly a head injury. He assured that the injury should most likely be temporary and would heal itself over time, whether within a few days, months, or five years. "No one could tell when, but only the god does," he had said matter-of-factly.

"Yuri, you're scaring me," said Katsue, confused.

"Mrs. Karube, I think she's experiencing temporary memory loss because of the head injury, I assume," said Ryu.

"What?? I don't understand."

"A friend of mine back in my village had the same symptoms. It'll pass eventually, or at least that was the case for him."

Listening with only half an ear, Katsue squeezed Yuri's hand. "Do you know who you are, who I am, where you are?"

"Yes, yes, and yes, Mother," responded Yuri in a slightly annoyed tone. "And I got my head hit and passed out. This young man pulled me out, and I'm so grateful to him. I just don't know who he is, but clearly you do." She gave Ryu an apologetic smile. "Thank you for saving my life, umm..."

"Ryu."

"Yes, Ryu. But I'm so sorry I don't recognize you." Yuri uncomfortably shifted on the futon and faced him.

"Don't worry, that's not the end of the world," said Ryu, wincing. Yet, he felt relieved that Yuri's affection toward him had vanished along with her memories of him. *What's happened to her may be a blessing in disguise.* "You'll be just fine, I promise you."

Yuri cocked her head like a little girl.

"Ryu, you said another tremor would hit soon, didn't you?" asked Katsue. "How sure are you?"

"I'm very sure, ma'am. It'll come, unfortunately. The reason I came back was to give Yuri enough time to recover and warm up. But now, we all have to go. Swift evacuation is imperative."

As Katsue listened to Ryu, her suspicion grew. His eloquence, his tone, and his choice of words were all so peculiar. *Swift evacuation? Imperative? No ordinary rural young man uses such words unless he was....*

"Mrs. Karube? Yuri?"

"Yes, right away," said Katsue and put her arm under Yuri's armpit to help her up.

"I'm okay, Mother, don't worry. I'm perfectly capable of taking care of myself." She got up.

"I can carry you to the forest, Yuri, in case you're still dizzy," suggested Ryu.

"Thank you, Ryu, but no. I feel completely fine."

"Alright, then," he said, "I'll meet you two there. I need to check around the neighborhood one more time to see if there are people who need help."

Once outside, Katsue looked hesitant for a second. "Umm, Ryu. Will you come back to Yuri and to us all, please?"

Ryu gave her the familiar smile, then darted into the field.

Katsue and Yuri stood there until his back became a dark dot, then set off for the bamboo forest.

After covering enough distance from the neighborhood, Ryu slowed his pace. With the adrenaline now wearing off, his entire body twinged in the frosty air, particularly his feet. He had been caught off guard, unable to predict the exact moment the earthquake hit, and barely making it to the village barefoot for Yuri's rescue.

Another two kilometers lay ahead until his final destination. The backs of his feet began to bleed, and his toes were nearly frostbitten. Hastily scanning the area, he spotted what appeared to be a shrub by the river. The snow-covered mound looked like a small ridge, perfect for concealing oneself behind it. Upon approaching the ridge, he checked his surroundings to ensure no one was nearby, then slipped to the other side.

Five seconds later, a majestic crested ibis sprung out of the snow-covered ridge and instantly soared high into the sky.

"Thank god, Yuri!" exclaimed Gensuke, relief rushing over him as he spotted his wife and daughter making their way up a gentle slope in the bamboo forest.

The forest, nestled to the east of Mt. Toki, stretched high with towering bamboo that pointed skyward like sentinels. The slightly elevated ground resembled a colossal *kenzan* — a "sward mountain." Since Lord Takeru's reign began, access to these lands has improved drastically. By lifting the burdensome taxes his father had imposed. Takeru allowed the locals to gather bamboo freely. These tall stems were vital to daily life, shaping furniture and tools, while their shoots provided sustenance. Now, the forest offered more than utility; it promised refuge.

Gensuke had brought twenty villagers with him, including Heijiro and his family, though many others had refused to leave their homes. Fear and the bitter cold had paralyzed them as they were still reeling from the horrors earlier that day. On the way, Gensuke had stopped at Shodai's home to enlist help in persuading more to evacuate. He also sought out Lord Takeru, explaining the dire situation and requesting permission to use the bamboo grove as a temporary shelter. Takeru, ever gracious, granted his request. Though unwilling to leave his manor due to his bedridden father, he gave his blessing for the evacuees to burn the bamboo if needed.

As Yuri and Katsue drew closer, their worried expression gave way to faint smiles. The sight of Yuri was a balm for

Gensuke's frayed nerves. He hugged his daughter tightly, oblivious to her weary state from the arduous walk. "I was worried sick about you!" he said, his voice almost cracking with emotion. "Ryu found you, didn't he?"

"Uh-huh," replied Yuri and awkwardly backed away from him.

"I haven't been myself since your mother, and I had... well, you know the rest," said Gensuke, fiddling with a bamboo twig. "I've noticed you've been avoiding me as much as you could, and I don't blame you for that."

"Father..."

"No, no. You don't need to explain yourself, Yuri. Anyway, I'm so relieved that you're safe. And so grateful for Ryu's help and courage."

"Gen, about Ryu..." interjected Katsue hesitantly. "I want to talk about him with you. Alone."

"Where is he?" Gensuke turned his head all around.

"He took off," said Yuri. "He wanted to help more people evacuate. But he said he'd join us here as soon as possible."

"He took off, huh..." Gensuke narrowed his eyes and fell silent, crossing his arms over his chest. His mind flashed back to the occult event in the spring. *Ryu promised to join us at Mt. Yashiro before taking off, but he never came back that night. What was his excuse for his absence? Slept in the field! Something was off, and so is it right now...*

"But Yuri, you still believe him after what he did in the spring?" he asked.

"Well, can't say I do, because I don't remember him or what happened in the spring, Father," answered Yuri with a shrug. "It seems like I've lost a large portion of my memories when the shrine collapsed on me."

"You what??"

Katsue quickly filled her husband in on what had happened

to Yuri, including the strange condition Ryu had expertly laid out for her.

"Typical of him," grunted Gensuke, "Somehow, he always has the right answer at the right moment! What's with the coincidence?"

Yuri began to shiver, feeling her temperature dropping again. "I need to warm up, so you two should catch up," she said, then joined her brothers and the rest of the group by a bonfire.

Once Yuri was out of earshot, Katsue shared her nagging thoughts about Ryu with Gensuke: his uncanny similarities to Amuro, his inexplicable behaviors, and his knowledge of peculiar subjects. As she went on, her own doubts began to terrify her more than when she had kept them to herself. By the time she finished, she regretted confiding in Gensuke, despite having expected to feel better afterward. "Tell me I'm insane, Gen."

Gensuke swallowed hard. "Well, obviously, no one saw his body. Not even Sir Shodai," he whispered, his voice hoarse. "And we didn't bury him, either. That's for sure."

A chill ran down Katsue's spine, and her eyes widened. "You don't think —"

"Have you heard of a spiritual concept called *Rinne Tensho*?" Gensuke's tone shifted.

"Uh-uh. What is it?"

"It's a Buddhist idea that after you die, your soul will transmigrate into another being or something else, depending on what you've done in this life. The cycle of rebirth."

Katsue's eyes suddenly flashed as if she had been struck by enlightenment. "I remember your mother saying something like that before she passed away."

"Yeah, Sir Jintoku must've introduced the idea to her, just like he did at the Guild."

Katsue leaned toward Gensuke, her face nearly touching his. "So?? What now, Gen? Where does that leave us?"

"Hey, hey, don't get too carried away. It's just a concept, alright?" Gensuke casually patted her shoulder.

"Then, why did you even bring it up?"

"Yes, I know. Maybe I shouldn't have. Look...religion and faith are always with us. But sometimes they can be manipulative, depending on a situation we're in. And this is exactly—"

"What situation?" A voice from behind made the married couple jump. "Sorry, I didn't mean to s-scare you. But you two are too...too loud...even to my old ears," panted Jintoku, putting his hands on his knees. Behind him, Shodai was climbing up the slope with a large group of people.

"Oh, great, sir! I'm so glad you and Sir Shodai brought more people. I didn't expect it, because most folks I talked to on the way were still recovering from the shock, and they simply wouldn't listen to me. But anyway..."

Shodai finally completed his climb and joined the couple and Jintoku. He, too, was out of breath.

"So, Gensuke, what kind of situation were you two talking about?" asked Jintoku innocently.

Gensuke and Katsue exchanged a hesitant glance and shook their heads.

"Well?"

"Umm...it's about...Yuri," replied Gensuke. "She seems to be having some trouble with her head, because, I guess, she passed out for a while under the rubble."

"Oh, that's terrible!" exclaimed Shodai. "Poor girl. Hope it's not too serious."

"I'm gonna see her, then," said Jintoku, and he left the trio.

By the bonfire, Heijiro and Tami looked up in the sky, their fingers pointing at a flock of birds that were uttering frantic squeals while flying agitatedly. "What on earth?" he shouted. Every eye in the forest instantly fixed on the birds as they flew south, away from the coast. Then, a lone ibis emerged out of nowhere, flying fast toward the coast, and eventually melted into the pale white sky. The evacuees remained bemused, gazing up at the spot where the ibis disappeared.

The conversation with Yuri from seven years ago suddenly struck Katsue. *A white bird...* "Gen, do you remember Yuri's story about when she almost drowned in the ocean?" she asked, shaking his shoulder.

"Huh? Yeah...vaguely. Remind me," said Gensuke, looking away from the sky.

"She told me she saw a large white bird right before she sank in the water. Then Ryu showed up right after. Remember now?" She paused, checking Gensuke's reaction, and continued, "is it just sheer coincidence that he just left us at the house and then the ibis showed up?" Katsue saw Gensuke's eyes glint with anticipation. "Are you thinking what I'm thinking?"

"What are you two talking about?" asked Shodai, throwing up his hands.

Gensuke and Katsue tugged at each other's hands. "We need to follow that bird," they said in unison, ignoring Shodai. Abruptly, they broke into a sprint, leaving Shodai scratching his head.

——————— * ——————— * ——————— * ——————— *

Takamine Bay, a sub-bay cradled within the vast expanse of Wakasa Bay, shimmered under the pale winter sky. Its calm waters, enriched by minerals, sustained a thriving aquatic habitat. For generations, the locals had depended on the bay's bounty, their livelihoods intertwined with its rhythms. Along the ria coast, the jagged interplay of headlands and inlets created natural sanctuaries where the sea reminded tranquil year-round, even when storms raged further offshore.

From the nearby hills, the view was nothing short of breathtaking — an endless stretch of glistening water cradled by the curving coastline. On this day, the seascape unfolded in serene stillness, its beauty untouched by the season's chill. Snow blanketed the ground, muffling the sounds of the world, as if nature itself were holding its breath.

High above the hills, the crested ibis hovered, its outstretched wings catching the cold breeze. The bird's sharp eyes scanned the coastline below, tracing the snow-covered cliffs and frosty vegetation. With a sudden shift, it angled downward, diving toward a flat clearing that overlooked the bay. Five seconds later, it landed on the pristine snow, its slender legs sinking slightly into the surface. The air remained still, unbroken by the delicate arrival, as if the ibis had become one with the hushed landscape.

However, the impact inflicted an acute pain on the backs of Ryu's feet. He rubbed them vigorously, trying to warm them. But soon, a far greater apprehension gripped him. *Here it comes!*

An ominous rumble crept in from beneath Ryu's feet, and the snowy earth instantly began to shake violently. The ferocious tremor knocked him off balance and sent him crashing onto his back. As the earth's rage intensified, he lay there in horror, the cold and his numbed feet forgotten. The ominous rumbles from the ground continued to roar, much like thunder threatening mortals from above. He remained flat, helpless, as nearby trees succumbed to the force and slid down the slope.

When the tremor finally subsided, Ryu found himself trapped between two vertical cracks in the ground. To his horror, the gaps grew wider, and the earth beneath him began to sink. Before he could even sit up, the entire clearing started to slide downhill, taking with him. The furious mud dragged him downward, mercilessly toying with his helpless body. He tried to breathe in as he tumbled down, but every time he opened his mouth, dirt stuffed it and clogged his nostrils.

After what felt like an eternity, the mudslide finally came

to a halt at the base of the slope. Ryu had vanished off the face of the earth.

Meanwhile, Gensuke and Katsue continued to run after the white bird. It kept flying at a relatively low altitude, likely to avoid strong gusts. As the pair crossed the snowy fields of the village, many people left stranded after the quake asked for help. But, they had no time to stop and lend a hand, despite feeling sympathetic. Their determination to chase the bird drove them forward.

As they pressed on, the landscape quickly shifted from residential areas to wilderness. Along the way, some hills revealed rugged surfaces, scarred by the quake. Fallen trees forced them to zigzag on their path, and fissures and holes caused unexpected detours, slowing them down.

Gensuke and Katsue kept running north, with the wind against them. As they climbed a small elevation, a salty smell hit their noses. At the hilltop, the distinctive view of the bay greeted them. They found the ibis hovering high above a hill along the curved shore. The white bird let out a piercing shriek and, a moment later, plunged into the snow-covered ground. A moment later, a figure emerged from under the thick snow. They gasped.

"Was the man hiding under the snow?" whispered Katsue.

"I've no idea..." Gensuke took a few steps forward, trying to get a better look. "And where did the bird go?"

Ryu slowly got up, his hair covered with snow.

"Is that —" Katsue's words were cut short as a menacing rumble echoed from under her feet.

The earth once again began to shake violently, instantly slamming Gensuke and Katsue on the snow. He got on his knees immediately and helped his trembling wife up as the quake intensified. Before they could even stand, the tremendous force knocked them back down, the two helpless bodies rolling down the slope. The powerful tremor lasted for a while before its intensity dwindled down to faint vibrations. When it finally stopped, they found themselves separated, half-buried in the snow. "Thank heavens..." gasped Gensuke. "Katsue, are you alright?" He crawled over to her side. "You okay?"

Katsue, on all fours, breathed laboriously, merely nodding.

"Oh, god...that was...hellish!" said Gensuke, still catching his breath. "Oh my... Look!" He pointed toward the hill where Ryu had emerged.

It had disappeared, and so had Ryu.

It did not take long for Yuri to regain her composure after the quake. The second tremor, which Ryu had mentioned earlier, lasted much longer, but the intensity was not as severe as the first. All the evacuees huddled together in the flat expanse of the bamboo forest the moment the earthquake hit, and the ground held up firmly, just as Ryu had assured, leaving no visible damage. Some people screamed and cried all over again, but most managed to remain calm under the circumstances. Still, commotions erupted here and there.

Her family's absence suddenly struck Yuri, and she pushed through the sea of stunned people in the clearing, searching for them. "Father, Mother, Kairi? Where are you?" she shouted at the top of her lungs.

"Sis!" Kairi cried out by the bonfire to Yuri's left.

"Oh, Kairi!" She ran to him and saw Yoriki and Haruki huddling together on the ground behind Kairi. "Are you all alright?" she asked.

The three boys nodded in unison.

"Sis, where are Dad and Mom?" whimpered Haruki.

Yuri stroked his cheek tenderly. "I'm gonna fetch them. You three hang in here until then, alright?" With that, she left them.

As she circled around the bonfire, a man's voice called her

name. "Yuri, over here!" Shodai waved at her from the middle of the commotion.

"Ah, Sir Shodai, do you know where my parents are?" asked Yuri urgently. "They were with you right before the tremor. Where did they go?" Unconsciously, she grabbed his shoulder.

"Yes, yes... I was about to tell you that. Your parents seemed to have gone after... umm... the ibis."

"What...the ibis?? The one we just saw? Why on earth??"

"That, I don't know, young lady," he replied sympathetically.

What were they thinking? Leaving us children behind without telling anything? What are they up to? Yuri staggered back toward her brothers.

With an animalistic roar, Ryu burst out of a mound of snow-mixed soil. Immediately, he gasped for air and spat out dirt several times until his panic subsided. As his breathing returned to normal, the full extent of the damage around him sunk in. The mound he had landed on earlier had vanished. Instead, he found himself sitting on the damp soil and decayed leaves. A sharp, earthy, moldy smell filled his nostrils.

Another, much smaller jolt startled Ryu, though it had lasted only a few seconds. On impulse, he turned his gaze toward the sea. The surface remained as peaceful and quiet as ever. "The calm before the storm," he mumbled to himself.

The semi-circular shoreline stretched east to west, untouched by buildings. Several groups of fishing boats were moored to the piers jutting into the sea. Ryu noticed the water level slightly rising with each gentle wave that struck the pier poles. Before he knew it, the water surface swelled, each tide advancing farther onto the shore. Then, he spotted what could only be described as 'a dark ridge' forming on the open water, far away from the shore. To his horror, it steadily grew taller and closer, gaining momentum as it moved, driven by the bay's funnel-like geography. Soon, a fully formed tsunami loomed at the mouth of the bay, poised to swallow the inlet. *Once it passed the beach, nothing could stop its advance on the land!*

Ryu sprinted to the shore as fast as he could. The smell of the ocean overwhelmed him as the rocky beach drew closer. The tsunami, dark and furious, had nearly reached the height of a 100-year-old cedar and stretched across the entire shoreline. He recoiled involuntarily at the sheer enormity of nature. And yet, the wave's unified force reflected a sheer wonder to behold. Every droplet of water possessed a collective will, transforming together into a hungry menace, ready to devour anything in its path. All the while, the immense wave continued to gain velocity and grow in size until its shadow engulfed the shore entirely.

Dusk slowly approached, and the temperature had already dropped, with strong gusts blowing down from the mountains. Ryu repeatedly opened and closed his palms, warming them with his breath, and positioned himself at the edge of the water. Listening to the baleful roars of the waves,

he closed his eyes and raised both arms over his head. The tsunami loomed over him. After reciting a short, incoherent verse three times, he forcibly swung his arms downward.

The massive wall of water stopped its advance abruptly and turned into a soaring vertical barrier. Then, with a series of dry crackling sounds, it began to freeze from the bottom up. The frozen surface rapidly expanded upward, growing thicker as the waves crashed within. Ryu's breathing grew shallow, pumping out thick vapor in the frigid air. Before long, the dark ocean beyond had transformed into an enormous block of ice, encased and trapped. Ominous rumbles echoed from within, but they quickly diminished. An eerie stillness eventually enveloped the coast as the sounds faded.

Ryu opened his eyes and reeled backward involuntarily. The dark, colossal structure stood only a few steps away.

Although he had envisioned this miracle in his trance before, its physical manifestation stunned him all the same. He tentatively reached out and touched the frozen wall. Its chill reminded him of the ice on a canal in the village. Despite the lingering effects of the prolonged earthquake, this ethereal scene poignantly spoke to him — a testament to the force of nature with a purpose cut short. Suddenly, a chill ran down his spine as he imagined potential havoc and loss of life in the village. He swallowed heavily, shivering.

"Ryu..." a familiar voice called out from behind him.

Startled, then resigned, he hesitantly turned around. "Mrs. Karube, Sir Gensuke, I guess you can't erase what you've just witnessed."

Katsue and Gensuke stood a few meters away, as if struck by lightening, their eyes filled with a mix of fear and sorrow. "W-what is all this? What just happened? And why you?" asked Gensuke, his cheeks twitching. Katsue, with her gaze fixed to the threatening frozen hill, staggered back, speechless.

"I believe It's best not to tell," replied Ryu firmly.

"It's a little too late for that, Ryu," lamented Gensuke. "When I was a boy, my grandfather often amused me with the legend of a sennin. This sennin lives in Mt. Toki, possesses extraordinary abilities, can change his appearance at will and so on, so on. It was supposed to be a teaching, but mostly just folklore and stories to sleep to. At least I thought so...until now."

"Sir —"

"Or, perhaps you're...umm...someone my family have been missing for over ten years?"

"Sir, please, don't say a name." said Ryu, shaking his head. "Otherwise... No, I just wanted to save the village and..." He cautiously stepped away from his parents.

"Yuri? And us?" pleaded Katsue. "Please, tell us who you are!"

"If I told you the truth, it'd be over. For me, and for your family. There's a reason I can never do that. Please, understand. Please."

"What's over, Ryu? What is it?" demanded Gensuke, extending his arm toward Ryu.

"You and Yuri believed in me before. I ask you to believe in me one more time. Please, promise me you will before I go."

"No, Ryu, you can't leave us now!" cried Katsue. "We need you, Yuri needs you. You have to help her get her memories of you back. And heal her pain."

Listening to her emotional plea, Ryu felt his chest churn. "I wish I could stay, Mrs. Karube. I really do, but I can't."

"Why not??" Gensuke stamped his feet, his fists clenched.

"Because my presence could do more harm than good for your family, sir."

"I don't understand..."

Ryu took Katsue's hand in both of his own. "If you trust me and keep the faith, I promise we'll meet again someday." Then, he gave Gensuke a determined nod. "Until then, please stay positive, and give my best to Yuri." With that, as if escaping his dilemma, he turned his back on them and broke into a sprint along the shore.

Gensuke and Katsue's gazes followed Ryu's back until it faded into the landscape.

Before long, a large ibis sprang up into the semi-twilight sky.

32

A DENOUEMENT

The Archive sat well beyond the wall of dense clouds in heaven, hidden from random passersby.

Amuro, the only visitor, drew a deep breath upon stepping inside, as he did on every visit. He had repeatedly asked Ine about the enigmas of this magnificent edifice, but her answers were always elusive. "Oh well...but that's another story," she had said with a giggle, "Only those who care about history, myth, and literature can appreciate the existence of the Archive. So, embrace your privilege." Yet, despite the vagueness of her responses, he found himself somehow indulging in these conversations, convinced that he and his grandmother shared something most spirits in heaven did not even bother to explore.

He probed — or more like scavenged — one shelf after another, searching for a vital piece of information. However, Amuro's efforts had so far proved fruitless. Each day ended up a disappointment, with documents and scrolls scattered across the floor. With over a hundred shelves to search, the daunting task of navigating the vast expanse of the Archive left him dispirited.

Today marked the fourth consecutive day without a single

hint of success, the hours slipping by aimlessly. As Amuro immersed himself in his quest, doubts began to creep in. *Am I only fooling myself? Am I clinging to wishful thinking?*

Just as he decided to call it a day, Tsugumi, the curator of the Archive, noiselessly glided across the quartz floor. He was crawling on his hands and knees, cleaning up the mess he had created, when she appeared beside him. Their eyes met in an odd angle. He wondered whether she had shrunk since he last saw her up close. Yet, her presence exuded reassurance, and for a moment he forgot about his frustration.

"You're right, boy," said Tsugumi flatly. "There's no such document in this building, nor has it ever existed."

A pile of documents, precariously balanced between Amuro's palms and chin, fell to the floor as his jaw dropped. "H-how??" he stammered, eyes wide. "I mean...how on earth did you know what I'm looking for?"

"You've been quite vocal," she replied.

"Oh...I didn't know I was talking to myself," he said, then remembered her hearing impairment. "But wait...I thought you have trouble hearing." His shout echoed through the deserted space.

"I do," she said, "but no need to scream. I'm standing right besides you." She covered her ears. "Anyway, who said I 'heard' you?"

"I don't understand... You heard me talking to myself, didn't you?"

"Hmm...let me put this way. I can and did *read* your thoughts," she explained triumphantly.

Amuro's jaw dropped once again.

He had heard that a handful of highly-trained spiritual beings possessed the ability to read minds. According to arcane narratives, no females had ever achieved such a level. This clearly reflected the society's view of women as innately inferior. However, despite the prejudice, he had encountered a female medium before he died. And having an astute grandmother like Ine had led him to question the veracity of these legends. All the same, he had never met anyone who claimed to be a mind reader — until now.

"Oh, but I have," said Tsugumi, raising her chin.

Amuro let out a shriek. "Stop it! You're frightening me, ma'am!" he shouted. "So, you do have the ability. Were you trained?"

"I'm gifted, just like my husband. But, he excels on so many different levels."

"I hope to get to know him someday."

"You already have."

"But I haven't gotten acquainted with a gentleman here who fits that description," he said, scratching his head.

Tsugumi chuckled. "I didn't say 'my *late* husband.'"

Silence spread across the space. Then, Amuro suddenly jerked upright. "B-but...it's impossible, isn't it? He's... Wait, then you too are... my..."

"Aah, heaven never disappoints, does it?" she said, clapping her hands. "Anyway, ask him about the procedure. He'll help you through it. And please, do not tell him about me."

"Why?"

"He'll be better off that way."

On his way back, Amuro wondered how many more surprises like Tsugumi awaited him on his journey through the afterlife.

Ine's humble abode in the north wing of the sleeping quarters was warm despite the early spring morning. A gentle light streamed in through the small vents on the wall, casting a soft glow. Beyond the door, in the botanical garden shrouded in misty clouds, a group of elderly residents of heaven took a brisk stroll.

Her futon was already neatly made, and the floor gleamed proudly. Ine had been a meticulous woman throughout her life, and that attention to detail remained unchanged even in heaven. A pungent scent of incense tinged the air. A ceramic vase with a single plum twig from the garden sat on a modest reading table next to the futon. The delicate pink blossoms exuded an organic essence in the otherwise monotone room. Also on the table sat a copy of *The Sarashina Diary*, a memoir written by the daughter of Sugawara Takasue.

"This is a unique work of literature," began Ine as she picked up the copy. "I say 'literature' because it doesn't quite strike me as a diary. It has a theme, though very much subtle, and diaries in general don't have themes as they are supposed to be daily records of the writers themselves. A good read, nevertheless. I wish I had the keen perspective this author did. A remarkable woman, and equally an excellent writer of her time, Lady Sarashina or whatever her real name was." She put down the copy. "Anyway, enough of my literary gibberish. Shall we talk about you? Tell me what's on your mind."

Amuro fidgeted with the plum twig, avoiding eye contact with Ine.

"Or perhaps, tell me what you don't want to talk about." She beamed at Amuro.

"Alright, alright, Grandma. You're quite a negotiator," he said resignedly, then let out a heavy sigh. "Well...I've been thinking since I came back after the tsunami. Ultimately, what I want to do will probably hinder...."

His monologue stretched on, but all the while, Ine listened patiently with her head down, never once interrupting him. At some point, she remained so quiet that Amuro thought she had fallen asleep. When he finished, the sun had already passed the north wing. The room felt cooler. Amuro lowered his head to level with hers. "Grandma, are you —"

When Ine finally looked up, her eyes were moist. Amuro had never seen her cry, not even when he was a little boy. Leaning forward, he opened his arms toward her, but she raised her hand to keep him from getting any closer. She shifted herself on her zabuton and dabbed her eyes with a tenugui. Then, she straightened up. "I agree, Amuro, you don't belong here," she said. "And in life, we all must confront and embrace what it brings us, both the good and the bad. Just because life is not always what you wish it to be doesn't mean it's daunting. People are capable of finding a small joy every day, even in their darkest times, just as a long night eventually gives way to dawn. What leads us to misery is ultimately our inability to accept life as it is and to believe in our own resilience."

"You're so positive, Grandma. Then why the tears?" asked Amuro softly.

"Because I've already missed my boy..." Ine's voice trailed off.

With that, they embraced each other one last time.

———— * ———— * ———— * ———— *

"Do you truly mean it, son?" Shinzan asked Amuro. "There's no turning back once it's done. And you'll no longer be able to protect and heal those you so care about."

Shinzan had listened to Amuro's emotional request, just like Ine had, yet with a different demeanor. The relationship between Shinzan and Amuro had evolved over the years. It was not because of the shocking revelation about their shared bloodline, but rather due to the bond that had naturally formed between them. Initially, driven by irresistible curiosity and fascination, Shinzan had involved himself with the young spirit despite his role as an observer of the natural order. But now, genuine compassion for Amuro had unexpectedly blossomed in him. *It's all about human nature. After all these years, I'm still controlled by it...after all these centuries.*

"Yes, I'm fully aware of that, sir," replied Amuro firmly. *"But I just thought..."*

"But what?"

"I thought you'd let me go without such a warning."

"I need to make sure you won't regret your decision. That's all. Don't get any ideas, son." Shinzan nervously cleared his throat.

"Sir...you care about me, don't you??"

"Don't talk nonsense!"

"Yes, you do, sir! You care about me and worry about me. I truly appreciate your sympathy, and it touches me...."

Shinzan let Amuro continue with his monologue. While only half listening, he reminisced about the extraordinary seven-year journey they had undertaken together. It felt like yesterday when the young boy's voice first resonated in his head. Stunned as he was, he felt a sense of thrill. Yet, he was torn between instinct and conscience. Ultimately, he let his curiosity guide him and helped Amuro achieve his miracles over the years. However, he could not shake the feeling that he had gotten himself misled into participating in what he considered unethical. *No, it was always myself willingly and eagerly crossing the line.*

Shinzan noticed the silence. "Have you finished your harangue?"

"Actually, I've been searching for an answer." replied Amuro hesitantly.

"What answer?"

"For those innocent boys before me."

"What about them?"

"Can't we bring them back to life?"

"And then what, son?" said Shinzan. "They have no one to take care of them back in the village anymore. Centuries have passed, if you haven't noticed. Besides, they're more content in heaven with their parents now than they ever were in their lifetimes, because the entire village, including themselves, was doomed to be annihilated."

"Such a cruel fate..."

"No one can elude or alter their fate, however unfortunate it may be. But you did, and you've decided to do that again. Is it worth that much to you?"

"Yes, I want to choose my course of action, sir, to live life to the fullest."

———— * ———— * ———— * ———— *

The next morning, Mt. Toki woke up in the dense fog. The rugged landscape loomed through the blue light of dawn. As the nocturnal creatures retreated to their lairs, complete stillness fell over the forest.

Shinzan stood still at the edge of the Pond, clad in white as usual, his blind eyes firmly fixing on the surface. The water, darker than ever, reflected nothing, stagnant and unearthly. The reeds encircling the Pond stood erect, not swaying in the slightest. Together, all the immobile elements emanated an air of serenity, involuntarily participating in the scenery.

Shinzan began his mantra, his palms pressed together in front of his chest. Though hardly audible and intelligible, the chant continued for a while before he separated his hands. He stopped suddenly. Ever so gently, a breeze caressed the tips of the reeds. Before long, the entire green blanket created rhythmic waves that circled the Pond. The winds picked up, causing the water's surface to dance in response. Soon, rain began to fall.

As the winds and gusts howled louder, Shinzan, his garments and long white hair desperately clinging to him, let out a strong grunt and pointed his cane at the center of the Pond. The water surface stopped moving instantly, and a small whirlpool appeared where his cane aimed. The circular motion grew faster as its size swelled. The eye of the whirlpool widened and got sucked deep toward the bottom, creating a large hollow in the depths of the water.

With a sharp swing of his cane upward, Shinzan commanded the forces at play. The next moment, what looked like an enormous serpent surged up out of the depths of the whirlpool. The mythical creature *ryu* — the Japanese dragon known as a water deity — wore brownish scales on its back and blue-greenish skin on its stomach. Its calloused face bore a large protruding mouth with serrated teeth, a needle-like mane, two thick whiskers, and two bulging eyes, all of which made the dragon look even more otherworldly and menacing. It soared into the rainy sky, swirling and sculling with four three-clawed feet. Prolonged swooshes echoed through the air as it ascended.

Upon reaching above the clouds, the ryu circled around dynamically over and over, writhing with increasing speed. After twelve laps, the vigorous dance stopped abruptly. The serpentine creature, still coiled in midair, shrieked once, and then plunged into a nosedive. The rain storm intensified over the valley, but the ryu's bloodshot eyes fiercely fixed on a target below. The next moment, with thunderous splashes, the water deity returned to its sacred home.

As soon as the pandemonium subsided, a misty fog veiled over the Pond, restoring the usual stillness. Shinzan, who had become entranced during the spectacle, collapsed onto the muddy ground. On all fours and soaked, he breathed laboriously, his shoulders heaving erratically. Though blind, he had perceived every detail of the event through his third eye, which had communicated with the monstrous deity throughout. Everything had unfolded exactly as he had anticipated.

Soft splashes from the Pond rippled through the stillness of the air. Shinzan raised his head and immediately sensed the presence of another person ahead. He already knew who it was.

A tall young man waded through the murky Pond,

approaching Shinzan. Water continued to drip from the man's white gown and unkept wavy hair. He got out of the water and immediately helped Shinzan to his feet. They stood in silent for a while, oblivious to their soaked bodies.

Amuro opened his mouth to speak but stopped himself before the first word could escape. Instead, he beamed at Shinzan, knowing well that the blind sennin could not return the favor. He took Shinzan's hand. Shinzan, stone-faced as usual, cupped Amuro's hand, squeezing it as hard as he could. The two men shared a moment of mutual appreciation in silence.

Amuro broke the handshake gently. Then, without a word, he turned around and briskly walked off into the dense fog. Shinzan remained there long after, as if making sure that Amuro would not come back.

His mind unexpectedly conjured a scene of a young man of keen countenance and a pretty woman holding a baby. Their conversation was muted, but Shinzan unconsciously recited the exchange word for word.

Much to his surprise, he felt a string of tears trickling down his cheeks for the first time since his wife, Tsugumi, had passed away centuries ago. But, as the first daylight broke through, it quickly dried them.

———————* ———————* ———————* ———————*

Kasuga Valley awakened to the vibrant embrace of spring, shaking off the remnants of its harsh, months-long winter. A myriad of colors painted the landscape — green, white, yellow, and pale pink — creating a spectacle as elegant as a Nishijin-ori kimono gracing a noblewoman. Sakura petals floated gently on the shimmering waters, while wildflowers dotted the lush hills and fields, turning the valley into a living canvas of seasonal splendor.

The breathtaking panorama stood as a testament to the village's resilience. Four months has passed since the earthquakes scarred the land, claiming lives and leaving devastation in their wake. Yet, the villagers has rallied together, treating the restoration of their home as a sacred mission. Almost every damaged or fallen structure now stood strong again, thanks to their relentless labor. Only Kasuga Shrine remained under reconstruction — a project long overdue but now fully funded by Lord Takeru, its progress symbolizing the community's rebirth.

Even the land itself bore nob trace of the disaster. Fissures and gaps in the roads, paddies, and gardens had been meticulously filled and smoothed. The landscapes sprang back to their picturesque selves sooner than anyone had anticipated. As the villagers walked among the blooming flowers and newly restored paths, a sense of pride and relief swept through the air, their spirits reaching an all-time high. It was not just the beauty of spring the celebrated, but their own strength and unity in the face of adversity.

Rumors of Ryu's involvement in the successful evacuation had lingered briefly among the villagers, fueled by Jintoku's accounts of seeing Yuri on Ryu's back during the chaos. Yet, as no one could uncover his identity or explain his sudden appearance, interest waned. Daily survival and rebuilding soon replaced speculation, and Ryu faded into the margins of memory, mentioned only in passing, if at all.

But, for Gensuke and Katsue, forgetting him was not as simple. They often spoke of the mysterious man who had saved them, their conversations filled with admiration and unease. Over time, though, the topic became a silent wedge, threatening to unearth fears they could not face. Reluctantly, they stopped discussing him aloud, but each harbored a private hope that Ryu might one day return. This unspoken yearning, oddly enough, brought them closer — a fragile bond they had not shared in years.

Yuri, however, found no solace in silence. The gaps in her memory gnawed at her, refusing to be ignored. For months, she pressed her parents for answers, but their vague responses only deepened her frustration. "What aren't you telling me?" she would demand, met only by sidelong glances and half-hearted reassurances. Desperation drove her to question others in the village, but their indifference stung. *How could they forget so easily? Didn't they owe their lives to him?* With every shrug and dismissive response, her determination grew. *Who was Ryu? Why did he haunt my mind as if he were more than just a fleeting hero?*

By winter's end, her quest for the truth had consumed her, an obsession that defied the frost and silence of the season.

One warm spring day, Yuri had a surprise visit from Kento, who had come home for the first time since last autumn. Though his stay would be brief, he seemed determined to make the most of it, especially with her.

From the moment they met, Yuri noticed something different about him. He carried himself with a quiet confidence, his once restless energy tempered. Listening to his animated stories, she felt a swell of pride for her friend. Kento had found the life he deserved, even if his absence had left a small void in hers.

They wandered toward the River Hasu, the air filled with the hum of insects and distant chatter of villagers. "So, Kento, tell me about your new life in Kyo," said Yuri, her smile warm and curious.

"It's been wonderful. Better than I could've imagined," replied Kento, plucking a horsetail from the ground. "My apprenticeship is everything I hoped for. Hosei-sensei is not just a brilliant artist but also a truly kind person. There's always something happening there, too. Festivals, performances, new faces every day. It's exciting!" He paused, twirling the horsetail between his fingers. "But most of all, I love the freedom. I never realized how much I'd been craving it."

"Yeah, but....don't you miss this?" teased Yuri, snatching the plant from his hand with a playful grin.

"As mush as the slurry pit by my father's paddy?"

They burst into laughter.

"That's just great, Kento!" said Yuri, though, her fingers toying absentmindedly with the horsetail. "So, nobody bothers you there as much?"

"Not like here, that's for sure. Kyo is full of people like me. Outcasts, expats, dreamers. Everyone had their own business to mind. It's refreshing, really. I like being left alone, and I think...I like being an outsider." His voice softened as if confessing. "It suits me. But I don't feel lonely. I have my passion to keep me company."

Yuri's smile faltered, though she quickly looked away. *He's outgrown me...* "I'm so proud of you for being honest with yourself," she said quietly, her words genuine but tinged with an unspoken sadness. Seeking to shift the mood, she asked, "By the way, how are things with your parents? Especially with your father?"

Kento stopped abruptly, turning away from her. For a moment, he crouched by the path, plucking fresh blades of grass and pressing them against his nose as if searching for something he could not find. "Sorry," he muttered at last.

Yuri stepped closer, placing a gentle hand on his arm. "He'll come around."

Kento gave a faint shrug. "Maybe. Maybe not. It is what it is."

They resumed their walk as awkward silence enveloped them. Each carried their own unspoken thoughts, swallowing their pity they felt for themselves — and perhaps, a little for each other.

"Anyway, enough about me," said Kento eventually, "fill me in on your days. I know you've lost all your memories of Ryu. I'm sorry, Yuri. I can't imagine what you're going through."

"Agh...," exclaimed Yuri, rolling her eyes. "Your mom told you, didn't she?"

"Yes, she confirmed it. But I actually dreamed about it first, believe it or not."

"What?"

"Yup. One night, Ryu popped up in my dream and told me about the disasters in the village and your mysterious symptoms."

"No way! That's impossible! You're making it up!"

"No, I'm not. I ignored the dream for a while, but then Hosei-sensei said he heard about unprecedented incidents. So, here I am."

As they neared the river, Yuri slowed her pace. The fragrant smell of cherry blossoms temporarily distracted the pair from their insecurities. They sat on the elevated platform Ryu had created three years ago.

"Well, take pity on me," confessed Yuri with a wince. "Nothing's changed on my side, and it's driving me crazy. Asked everyone in the village about him, literally everyone, but no luck whatsoever. My parents seem to know something, I can tell. But they wouldn't tell me, and I don't know why."

"Ahh, I see. But no surprise."

"Oh yeah? Then, can you tell me about him?" Her eyes widened.

Carefully and sincerely, Kento shared the memories of their dear friend with Yuri: their suspicions about his questionable identity, his possible involvement in the miracles, and her feelings for him as well as his own for him. When the long, detailed narrative finished, Yuri's mouth was wide open.

"Some story, huh?" said Kento.

"Wow, yes. I mean...how on earth could anyone forget anything like that?"

"I know, Yuri. I know."

"This is too much to take in, though, Kento. He and I? Really? And do you think he is —"

"I can tell you who he is!" a male voice suddenly interrupted from behind, making Yuri and Kento jerk backward. They turned, shielding their eyes from the glaring sunlight. The stranger sat down in front of them. "But please, try to be nice and open-minded."

Yuri stammered, with her trembling finger pointing at him. "You! I...I've seen you...in my dreams!"

Kento switched his gaze to her. "What are you talking about? How??"

"Bizarre, I know. But it was this man, I'm positive."

"Oh heck, come on!" shouted Kento, then moved away from the man. "Will you tell me who the hell you are?"

"Hey, Yuri, Kento, it's been quite a long time," said the man, clearing his throat theatrically. "It's Amuro. I'm back! I guess we've got a lot to catch up!"

Yuri and Kento's jaws dropped.

Amuro beamed at his beloved sister and friend, his thick, wavy hair dancing in the warm spring breeze. "It's a perfect day to start over! Don't you agree?" He grinned, gesturing toward the sky.

Above Mt. Toki, a rainbow arched majestically, casting its vibrant colors across the blue sky.

EPILOGUE

Yuta sat in the studio Airbnb in Shinsaibashi, Osaka, incessantly fidgeting with a pen. The room was chilly and slightly steamy, filled with a lingering aromatic scent. His coffee — the second dose of caffeine — had gone cold, forgotten on the desk. He checked the time displayed on his laptop computer.

'6:03 AM.'

He had woken up an hour earlier to the sounds of a garbage truck idling near the building's dumpsters. Since then, adrenaline had kicked in, forcing his blood to run faster. He always had this feeling of impatience in him, an anticipation that something could finally break the monotony of his life. And today should mark the day that would either bring happiness or misery. Of course, he grew tense, and rightfully so.

The thick curtains stubbornly blocked out the early morning lights, sparing Yuta a brief moment of Zen. His mind ran deeper, muting all the mundane sounds, including his own heart-beat. Though having completed all the necessary preparations, he still needed to focus on what awaited him in just three hours. He read and revised his resume three times in the dim light, checked his gray suit for lint and wrinkles, polished his shiny new shoes, obsessively combed his wavy hair, even trimmed his eyebrows straight, and, of course, shaved until his chin reddened. "It's just another job interview, not a life-and-death verdict," he murmured, trying to convince himself. But so far, he had failed miserably.

At 23, Yuta had graduated from Kyoto University only two months ago. His mother had always expected him to continue on to grad school. However, he had chosen a different path, eager to face the challenges of the real world. With this mindset, even before graduation, he had sent out his resume and reference letters to prospective companies. To his great surprise, he received job offers from two of Japan's leading brokerage firms. But, today's interview was the one he had dreamed of: an up-and-coming enterprise that specialized in global trade. Born and raised in a small community, he had yearned for the prospect of traveling around the world ever since his adolescence. He had spent the last four years intensively honing his English skills for an opportunity like this, and today, it was time to prove himself. And yet, no amount of preparation or confidence seemed sufficient.

When the clock on his computer screen hit 7:30, he jumped upright.

He decided to head out, even though it would be another hour and a half until the interview. After one last check on his resume, he put his suit and shoes on, only to strip them off again, jumping into the bathroom. Then he slapped his forehead, scoffing at himself. *I just took a shower 30 minutes ago! Boy, I sure am pathetic!*

Yuta quickly tidied himself up once again and hit the street to catch a subway. However, upon reaching Shinsaibashi Station, he changed his mind and stayed on Midosuji Street, hoping that the crisp spring air would calm his nerves. His Apple Watch indicated that the destination lay 30 minutes away. He continued strolling north.

By the time he reached Yodoyabashi, it was only 7:58, but the area was already bustling with activity. The foot traffic grew heavier by the minute, with hundreds of commuters pouring out of the subway station. Across the Yodoya Bridge, on the 2-mile-long urbanized strip known as Nakanoshima, the headquarters of Tokiya Trade Co. stood elegantly. On impulse, Yuta's heartbeat quickened. *Don't fuck this one up...*

Ten minutes later, he found himself settled on one of the benches on Nakanoshima, facing east. The newly paved promenade was teeming with early joggers sweating through their pre-work runs. A group of female workers in uniform, undisturbed by the chaos around them, enjoyed breakfast at a picnic table along the promenade. From there, Osaka City Hall, watchful and grand, stood only 100 meters away. In the distance, the famous sakura trees at the Japan Mint emanated an organic aura amidst the rather inorganic settings. On a normal day, the historic Neo-Renaissance edifice of Osaka City Central Public Hall could awe him, just as it had every time he visited. He still remembered the summer blast when he first visited during Tenjin Matsuri four years ago.

However, despite having visited Nakanoshima so many times before, today Yuta found it distant and even intimidating. None of those familiar landmarks and fond memories could ease his tension. The people around him faded away, leaving him to drift in his thoughts. Time slipped away aimlessly.

The timer Yuta had set on his watch earlier went off, and he got startled by the beeps.

'*8:30 AM.*'

As if on cue, his smartphone vibrated. He checked the caller's name on the screen.

'*MOTHER.*'

"Hey, Mom," he answered.

"Hi, Yuta. Your interview starts in 30 minutes, right? How're you holding up? I know you're tense now."

"Could be worse. Nah, I don't even know anymore, to be honest. I just have to deal with it."

"Listen. Whatever happens, it's not the end of the world."

"It's not? You sure about that, Mom?"

"I'll tell you what I'm sure of. You'll be fine, or better yet, you'll be awesome regardless."

"How so, Mom? I feel like a scared little kid not knowing how to contain myself, because this job may hold my future."

"No, Yuta, it won't. You hold your future, however it may unfold."

Hearing her speak in the local dialect he had tried to hide for the past four years, Yuta felt his demons gradually diminish. "Thanks, Mom. I feel much better now,' he said in the same vernacular.

"Good, good. I'll talk to you later, then."

Twenty units later — after stepping out of the elevator on the wrong floor and entering a conference room full of senior executives — Yuta finally sat in a leather armchair in the reception room of Tokiya Trade Co., waiting for his name to be called. A female receptionist sat opposite him, merely five meters away. With his earlier nervousness gone, he felt relaxed, if not confident. The antique furniture, sculptures, and the rows of cyclopedias on international laws lining the bookshelf no longer intimidated him.

The intercom on the receptionist's desk rang once. She picked up the receiver, pressed it to her ear, and with a quick '*Right away, sir,*' she hung up. Then, she gave Yuta a polite nod. "Thank you for waiting. The assistant manager will see you now. The second door on your left."

The eyes of a crested ibis stenciled in gold on the door seemed to gaze curiously at him. For a split second, he thought he heard it whisper, "Good luck," as he raised his hand to knock. Adjusting his tie, he knocked.

As soon as Yuta took a seat, the assistant manager closed

his MacBook and wiped his gold-framed glasses with a dark plaid handkerchief. "So, Mr. Karube, tell me about yourself."

www.ingramcontent.com/pod-product-compliance
Lightning Source LLC
LaVergne TN
LVHW091253150826
845673LV00006B/1398

9798896910930